★ HANOI 1954

Ho Tay

Trucbach

BOTANIC
GARDEN

THE
CITADEL

DOUMER
BRIDGE

RIVER

Little
Lake

HANOI
STATION

Thien
Quang

Bay
Mau

LANESSAN
HOSPITAL

```
0          .5          1
|----|----|----|----|
        MILES
```

THE

BLUE

DEEP

Previous novel by Layne Heath

CW2

THE
BLUE
DEEP

LAYNE HEATH

WILLIAM MORROW AND COMPANY, INC.
New York

Copyright © 1993 by Layne Heath

It is the policy of William Morrow and Company, Inc., and its imprints and
affiliates, recognizing the importance of preserving what has been written, to print
the books we publish on acid-free paper, and we exert our best efforts to that end.

Library of Congress Cataloging-in-Publication Data

Heath, Layne.
    The blue deep / Layne Heath.
      p.   cm.
    ISBN 0-688-10313-8
    I. Title.
    PS3558.E263B57   1993
    813'.54—dc20   92-27418
                                                                         CIP

Printed in the United States of America

First Edition

1 2 3 4 5 6 7 8 9 10

BOOK DESIGN AND ENDPAPER MAPS BY JEFFREY L. WARD

for Robert Gottlieb

AUTHOR'S NOTE

I would like to acknowledge the assistance of Michael Buscher and Patrick Girault, the friendship of Lucio Garcia, and the expertise of Adrian Zackheim, none of whom is responsible for points of view or errors contained in this story.

Though we disagree on matters of U.S. involvement in the Indochina War, I have relied on the work of the late Bernard Fall for detail and the general progression of the battle of Dien Bien Phu.

Much of the locale, most of the events, and all of the characters in this story are fictional.

THE

BLUE

DEEP

Chapter One

THE OLD COLONEL sat on the edge of his bed, waiting for a French lieutenant who might be the answer to everything. He checked his watch, then stood to examine himself before a mirror. Though there had been no sleep at all, the pajamas were suitably rumpled, the snowy hair raked, the eyes equipped with an all-purpose glaze efficient at blending with any environment. Another time those eyes might have revealed the wisdom of an old warrior, the polished savvy of a senior official, even the denied desperation of a submerged alcoholic, but in the company of pajamas they were eyes that merely looked old, presently deprived of sleep.

When the strumming bell announced the guest precisely on the hour, the colonel reached for his treasured robe. He secured the sash, adjusted the lapels, and beamed at himself. Suddenly he was something more than just an old man gotten out of bed. There was in the mirror the power of his position, a face that could make things wrong or right. The eyes instantly completed the transformation.

The robe was an outrageously expensive gift from a friend in Hong Kong. Rich navy with wide lapels, it glistened in the lamplight. Across the body were countless thumbnail dragons embroidered in red silk, each twinkling an eye of pure gold. The colonel found his derringer among the bedclothes, wrapped it in a red silk handkerchief, and dropped it into a pocket with a tip of cloth protruding.

When the bell rang several times in quick succession, the colonel remembered he had failed to inform Fatima. Fatima was an old Vietnamese woman, a grandmother whose name was Xuan or Chuan—Ezra was never sure—so he had given her the name of a maid in Georgetown. She had a one-room house, a converted toolshed behind the garage where her one-eyed husband, the gardener, slept. Except for weekends when she had guests, Fatima slept in a storage room down from the kitchen. Smith could hear her now, muttering bitterly in Vietnamese as she went to the door. Fatima was a good cook and a thorough housekeeper who performed every duty well so long as no verbal response was required. She took orders willingly, acknowledged with an abrupt nod, but spoke only when she was angry. Sometimes Ezra would hear her ancient screech, the broken brakes of a locomotive, emitting with piercing force from the shadowed shed. The old gardener would suddenly appear in a crippled rush, bare feet and dust and loose trousers, stabbing along on his hoe to a place beyond the last screech before pausing to scratch at the earth.

Fatima liked schedules and silence, and this person at the door represented neither. She damned him in her quick language.

The center of the house was open to the second floor, served by a wide staircase and an ornate brass-and-crystal chandelier. Besides making a grand presentation of a rather small house, the arrangement made every word uttered between the front foyer and the dining table at the back windows exceptionally clear to a listener upstairs. Smith cracked his door to be sure, then closed it and waited. Soon Fatima knocked, then grumbled in her high Asian whine, "You have guest."

"Who is it?" he said, but she was already gone. He lit a cigarette and sat again on the bed, watching the colorless swirls cross over to blue in the splay of light. It was essential to allow this thing to develop its natural speed. Although everything had checked out, there still was the possibility that this Frenchman was not what he purported to be. The sneaky bastards were always up to something, some contrived nonsense that did more to satisfy an innate need to play at life than to cause real damage. But they always gave the game away. Nonetheless, Ezra Smith had gone to embarrassing lengths to keep them unaware that they were dealing with an old master, whatever the game.

If the lieutenant was not a plant, he was assuming considerable risk. That much was perfect; he would be hamstrung by a need for secrecy. Discovery by French authorities would be most physically unpleasant, perhaps affecting the remainder of his life. Smith had learned that the lieutenant was, at least, who he claimed to be—an administrative assistant in the Hanoi office of French Internal Security, ostensibly in Saigon on a recreational pass. Contact had been made openly on the patio of the Continental, a walk-up self-introduction with some prattle about his father having known him from the war days in France—all while a note was passed, insisting on a private meeting the following night to discuss a matter most urgent. The lieutenant handled himself well, departing with such casual indifference that the watchers from the Sûreté and the CIA were fooled. Whatever else the man might be, Smith noted, Solo Jacobé was cool under fire. He also had done his homework: His comments about Europe, the dates and places, were as accurate as the bit about his father was a lie.

Smith had considered dismissing the man, to instruct the guard to turn him away or to arrest him for the French. There was a distinct possibility he was a decoy. But the colonel could not refuse to hear what the Frenchman had to say. It was a slim chance, but Solo Jacobé might possibly be the fruit of seeds planted long ago.

The colonel twisted the spark from his cigarette, then field-stripped the butt into an ashtray. When he stood, the mirrored movement startled him, and the face he found there was a stranger. The winding path toward the future had seen the evolution of a vague young man into an adult and ultimately a decaying old man so foreign as to have been impossible to predict. Looking back, the path was precise, but the young man in the distance—what he was, what he stood for—could no longer be recalled. With a grunt of satisfaction at the attractive lie, Ezra Smith placed his cigarettes in the pocket beside the derringer, dropped the lighter on the opposite side, then began the descent to meet his guest.

The colonel's residence was at once modest and sumptuous, a narrow two-story villa just outside the U.S. Mission, surrounded by a wall and tall trees, a guardhouse at the street. It was a stucco affair of French design, its cream walls tastefully trimmed in forest green.

To one side stood a one-car garage, while in back near a colonnaded porch was a patio surrounded by gardens. The grounds and the home were not large, but from all appearances Colonel Ezra Smith might have been an important diplomat.

As he descended the stairs he was reminded of all he would soon be giving up. But it was time, and he was almost prepared. He allowed himself a benign smile as the next thought came, divergent but equally entertaining. Such mental side trips had grown more frequent of late, but he made no effort to resist. What came this time was the specter of the waiting nemesis of men his age—that of reaching retirement only to be rewarded by falling dead within a few weeks, a heart attack puttering around the house, bored absolutely to death. Such was not the way he would go, that much was assured. The old pump might well give out one day, but it was not likely to happen in some goddamned tomato patch. He openly grinned as he perceived that final scene: groaning, lunging, roaring toward oblivion when the knowledge was nigh, draining down from a frosted bruise between a lovely woman's legs, leaving her crushed with his dead weight and dead smile, white buildings in the distance, Mediterranean sky.

He found his visitor perched on the edge of a red leather chair in the study. The lieutenant was a sturdy man of about twenty-five, reddish hair, glasses that made him look scholarly. He was gazing up at the walls, staring at rows of books embedded in wood. He jerked when he saw the colonel standing between the doors, then quickly stood and came to rigid attention. The colonel smiled. "For heaven's sake, young man," he said in his most fatherly tone, "relax." He extended a warm hand, and got a brief smile and a brisk, hurried handshake.

"Lieutenant Solo Jacobé," the man announced, looking the colonel straight in the eye. "I apologize for disturbing you at this unreasonable hour, sir, but it concerns a matter of great importance."

Smith was watching every detail, ready for any slip while covering himself with a gentlemanly manner. "Let's hope so," he said with a frown that he followed with a smile. "I trust that your judgment as an officer would not have permitted you to come here otherwise. Have a seat. Care for some coffee?"

"Only if it is already made, sir."

Smith stepped toward the door and almost collided with stony ferred to send somebody else, but there was not another man he personally knew who possessed the same combination of soldierly skill, discipline, and—despite the recent experience of Korea—an enduring sense of duty and honor. Marsh McCall was the only man for the job, he decided. He might not survive the experience, but he almost certainly would not fail.

Fatima. She was barefoot, dressed in a black shift, white-streaked hair pulled and hastily pinned. She held a silver tray bearing white china, which she placed on a mahogany sideboard, then served the men without a glance. When Solo Jacobé thanked her in her language, her nod was imperceptible, lips stitched and drawn. She made a fractured bow, and the colonel watched her leave the room. Petite Fatima, who had not always been a grandmother; her old butt was almost gone.

"I forget to tell her you were coming," he said.

"This is a wonderful room," said Solo Jacobé, turning with admiration. "I could live in such a room."

The colonel smiled and glanced around. "My sanctuary," he said. He enjoyed showing it off to one so young. The room, with its twelve-foot ceiling and tall arched windows, had been a useless parlor until he recognized the potential. The government had footed the expense of remodeling, but the books were his own, shipped from the States. He now spent all his spare time within its walls, relishing the deep red comfort of the chairs, the moving odors of tobacco, leather, and wood, the satisfying feel of life's accumulation. It could perhaps be reassembled in another place, but he was unsure if it would ever feel the same. He squelched the thought, leveling imperious eyes on the daring young Frenchman. "Now tell me, Lieutenant, why are you here?"

If Solo Jacobé was surprised at the tone, or by the change in the eyes, he did not show it. He lowered his cup, thrust his chin forward, and said with convincing sincerity, "I am here, sir, because you are the only man in Indochina capable of helping me, and who I know with absolute certainty I can trust."

"We have never met."

"Our interests are the same."

"Your father and I never met."

"My father and *I* never met," Jacobé said with a smile.

Ezra Smith formed a look of mild irritation. "It's very late," he said, "and I am tired. Could we get to the heart of the matter? — And let me say right now that I am not in the business of handling personal problems."

"This is anything but personal, sir. I am a junior officer in the Hanoi office of Sécurité Intérieure, the group that was formed after the humiliation of the Affair of Generals. Our job is to investigate the military—that is, to investigate ourselves." When the colonel made an impatient gesture, Jacobé hurried ahead. "I am here because the corruption has not subsided as many believe. Rather, it has increased in proportion to U.S. aid, touching every level of every organization in Indochina. Not everyone is corrupt, of course—the large majority are not—but most choose to do nothing because they fear for themselves, they realize the hopelessness, or they benefit indirectly from the system. The black market is so ingrained that it has come to be regarded as essential to the economy. The mere suggestion that a problem exists can get a man shipped off to a remote island in the Pacific, or to permanent assignment in one of the mobile combat units where death is assured. The power of the organization is so complete that even men who would like to see it destroyed are willing to work on its behalf."

Ezra Smith slumped in the chair, pinched the bridge of his nose, and dug for a cigarette. The derringer was still in place, but he knew now he would not be needing the weapon. There was, however, still the possibility that this was a ruse, a deceit by the French or even some wayward element of Central Intelligence, groping around to see what might be flushed. He extended the pack, but the Frenchman declined.

"Lieutenant Jacobé," he said, "you are not the first to tell me such things. The market system is an evil which accompanies all wars. We can fight it, but we can't stop it, not completely. I am aware of the situation perhaps better than you. Volumes of U.S. equipment, guns and ammunition, are finding their way into enemy hands. Part of the problem is such places as Formosa and the Philippines. We have equipped their armies, but as soon as our backs are turned, their generals sell what we have given them, then claim it was lost to guerrillas. The generals retire rich, and the weapons find their way, presently, to Ho Chi Minh. And some of the material right here is being lost. I have even heard reports of French soldiers forced to buy on the black market the very weapons that were intended for them in the first place. I could go on. I know all about the problem. What I don't know is the solution. I don't wish to be rude, but it is the middle of the night." With effort, he rose from the chair.

"You have not allowed me to finish," Jacobé said, no longer so respectful. "I am not here to tell you what you know, and I did not assume this risk for nothing. Forgive my abruptness, sir, but if I may continue..." Ezra Smith poured them both coffee, then sank silently into his chair. "I am here to ask for help," the lieutenant said. "I realized long ago that in my position only a fool would open his mouth. But I cannot sit and watch this happen. My country is losing its war, and the black market is partly to blame. I asked to come to Vietnam to serve France, but then I received this dead-end assignment where nothing is expected from me except to keep my mouth shut while my friends are slaughtered. I tried for a transfer, but it was always denied. They keep our group small and stable. Our sole function, I finally realized, is to satisfy appearances. When I accepted the fact that I could never escape, I decided to at least fulfill my personal obligation—to put my life on the line for France. Since that day I have been working without the knowledge of my superiors."

Smith stubbed his cigarette and hunched forward, thinking maybe, just maybe. "And what have you learned?"

"Not as much as I hoped," Jacobé said. "But I have irrefutable evidence of who the first man is in the northern link, and I know who he sells to. There are others involved, but the double secrecy of my work is a severe handicap. I cannot be certain of learning more, so I have come to you."

"To do what?"

"To help!" Jacobé shouted. "Send somebody, find an excuse, find some way to help me break this thing!" He lowered his voice, embarrassed by his outburst. "Sir, there are stories about how much you accomplished against the black market in Korea," he said. "You are the only hope I have. I am trapped."

The colonel stood and paced the room. Despite his precautions to let nothing show, his opinion of Solo Jacobé was cemented. The hasty investigation of the lieutenant had revealed much more than the Frenchman had let on. The boy was an orphan. He had thus missed the leg up that a father in the military might have meant. Or—who could say?—he might merely have avoided being the son of a Vichyite, having then to fight his way through months of grueling combat, making recompense for being in the wrong place when the lines were drawn. At any rate, he graduated number two in his class at Saint-Cyr. He had then passed up a rare opportunity to serve in Paris, turning his back on the political advantages, the rapid advancement, the wives of other soldiers that such an assignment

17

could mean, electing instead to go to Indochina.

Now that Jacobé was before him, no longer a thin dossier, the colonel could glimpse the future. There was much to admire in this young man. The risk he was taking was substantial: Besides those directly involved, there were numerous people with enough at stake that having a lieutenant murdered would not require a second thought. Even to the best of men Jacobé would be practically a traitor for endangering the system, and especially for going to an American with his problem.

"You say that you have been working alone?"

"Yes, sir, but I have confided in a friend who I would trust with my life."

"That may be precisely what you have done."

The colonel circled the desk, took his place in a tall swivel chair, and pulled a leather cord suspended from the wall. Soon Fatima appeared, stone-faced as always. "Could we have a fresh pot of coffee, Fatima?" he said. "It appears the lieutenant and I have much to discuss."

Smith crossed his arms and stared at his desk in meditation, hiding the excitement that a rush of thoughts unleashed. This was even better than he hoped—good enough to avoid the mistakes of an earlier, stumbling attempt. Solo Jacobé was indeed the real thing, the possible key to the perfect culmination of a long career. The black market system had operated successfully for an awfully long time. Now the moment and method may have arrived for shutting it down.

The timing could not have been better. The French were presently baiting Ho Chi Minh into a confrontation at a place called Dien Bien Phu. It was too soon to say what might develop, or who the winner would be, but if the approaching battle fulfilled its potential it could mean the conclusion of the Indochina War. In spite of that—or because of it—a U.S. training outfit was soon to be deployed up north, presenting the perfect vehicle to send someone to poke around. All Smith would have to do was find the right commanding officer, someone who could handle the extra demands of the assignment. Somebody like Marsh McCall.

The name popped up spontaneously, and though he realized what it might mean, he understood at once the correctness of the choice, and the necessity. He admired McCall and would have preferred to send somebody else, but there was not another man he personally knew who possessed the same combination of soldierly skill, discipline, and—despite the recent experience of Korea—an enduring sense of duty and honor. Marsh McCall was the only man for the job, he decided. He might not survive the experience, but he almost certainly would not fail.

Chapter Two

IT STARTED WITH BRANTLEY, one of the warrant officers, spouting from the moment they left Inchon about all the wonderful snatch waiting ahead in Haiphong. No one had ever seen the place, but a couple of sailors had heard stories in Manila. That was enough. By the time they arrived, the lies and mysteries and six days at sea had it all sounding pretty fantastic. But, of course, Winslow knew better. All that lay ahead was another Asian armpit—or crotch—the only difference being that this one smelled of France. He did, however, concede the innate obligation, the farming urge to plant foreign furrows. Nothing wrong with that. Korea might be hard to beat in that regard, but maybe in a month or so when things had settled down he could find himself one of those happy little China dolls to walk naked up and down his back, twittering like a little bird. The idea brought the first sergeant as close to a smile as he had been in weeks, but before it could form he remembered Atherton.

From a point near the bow he swung his eyes around the river bay. Beyond the far shore where abandoned vessels of every size lined slick mud flats, paper-blue mountains stood on edge beneath a milky sky. Framed against the backdrop of those mountains and limestone monuments, a fleet of native fishing boats was crossing the estuary, brown sails of battened reeds aloft like fins of exotic lizards. From a jetty beyond the docks came a porpoising launch, a tricolor flag cracking in the breeze. The craft drew a wide arc before crossing the dark water beneath freighters at dockside. Winslow dropped his gaze to the water below, where bamboo boats were milling about, peasants staring blankly up toward deck. He worked his cheeks, spat and watched a dark torpedo fall. A weathered man with encrusted teeth smiled up and jabbered.

The USS *Saraffin* lay anchored in the dredged inner bend downstream from Haiphong, waiting its turn at the docks. With the long-expected battle at Dien Bien Phu a week under way, the French needs of war matériel exceeded the capabilities of the port. A thousand feet astern lay another U.S. ship, one on permanent loan to France and manned by French sailors, loaded like the *Saraffin* with munitions and war supplies.

Winslow had an almost end-on view of the nearest ships at dockside, a pair of Algerians with black, rust-streaked hulls and white, rust-streaked cranes and cabins. The near ship still had gangplanks in place, and the work continued, but aboard the second craft the cranes had been stowed. The sergeant's skin was burned, his arches ached, and his bowels had not budged for three days, but he was suddenly hopeful. A move dockside now would mean a chance of off-loading before dark. With the officers gone it would be a rough job, and even if they showed up ashore, there would likely follow a miserable night. Nonetheless, Winslow was ready. Nothing could be worse than spending another day on this sonofabitching boat.

That morning after mess a curly-headed French captain had come aboard from the same shore boat now making the rounds. After paying his respects to the executive officer of the *Saraffin*, he parleyed with Atherton at the port rail, smiling like a teenager on tit. Soon Atherton was wearing the same grin. Winslow could smell it like the rotten soup the ocean shoved to shore. The bamboo boats that paddled out each day had hardly arrived when the lieutenant came strolling along in his sidling way, perpetually aimed in any direction but the one he was traveling.

Since arriving at Haiphong four days ago, the ship's captain had been giving shore leave to his sailors by rotation, sending another group into town aboard a launch every six hours. It had been understood from the first that the tiny Army contingent, ten men, would remain aboard to help with the aircraft in case the *Saraffin* moved unexpectedly dockside. It was a minor torment for the enlisted men, especially after the stories of the first returning sailors. There was no guarantee they could make up for the lost time later—that would be strictly up to the new major—but with the sole exception of Private Tooler, no one had complained.

Three of the four officers were going ashore, Atherton said—he and Cowan and Brantley—to make preparations for tomorrow. The French captain had brought word that it would be at least noon the following day before they could move dockside. In the meantime, there were arrangements to be made ashore, preparations for convoy, and so forth. Dukemire would stay behind as the officer in charge.

Winslow accepted the news with a practiced absence of expression, thinking only that the job of a noncommissioned officer lay somewhere between that of a mail-order bride and an indentured whore, condemned to serve whatever prick came through the door. He stared toward the swarming humanity on the distant dock, hoping the new major was there.

The officers were gone no more than an hour before Kinney and Acres came with the latest scuttlebutt—a big bash was planned by the French that evening at a Cam Street teahouse named Luan's.

Winslow stared down at the water as if seeing the peasants there for the first time. The men were weathered as old wood, but the women had wrapped their necks and faces with gauzy rags against the salt and wind and sun, leaving only almond eyes exposed, surprisingly deep and expressive. The men shouted up and worked the slender oars while women held aloft fresh shrimp and fish and limp white squid, green vegetables, brown eggs in nests of straw, and startled ducks. Sailors lined the rail, and when a deal was struck they lowered money in a pail, then hoisted the merchandise aboard.

Winslow turned abruptly, intending to go aft, and almost crashed headlong into Dukemire, bumbling along in a trance. The kid was like a day-old calf, eyes big and blank. He stumbled and almost fell.

Winslow had already decided that Dukemire had been brought up without a father. Blond becoming brown, he had the makings of a manly face if only the eyes could develop more steel. His most irritating attribute was his flawless manners. It made Winslow want to shake him. Whenever Dukemire was around, the professional lines of the first sergeant's face and the gruffness of his tone both softened as if he were dealing with a mental case. It began to happen now, and it made him furious. He set his big jaw, flared his nostrils, and pulled down his graying brush-pile brows. His lips drew back in a spontaneous snarl.

"What do you want?" he yelled. "Uh, I mean, *sir.* Uh, what do you want, sir?" Still not right. "What was it that you needed? *Sir.*" Now he sounded like an idiot. He thanked God that nobody was in earshot.

Dukemire recovered from his cringe, pulled himself almost to attention, and said quitely, "Lieutenant Atherton wanted me to tell you he will try to be back before nightfall. He's got to make arrangements ashore so things go smoothly."

Winslow was momentarily lost, thinking about what would surely be arranged ashore and how smooth it was likely to be. Dukemire's face began to twitch from holding the smile. "Yes, sir," Winslow said. "Thanks for coming out to tell me. Now that you're in charge, sir, you got any command decisions you'd like to make? This is your opportunity."

Dukemire looked pained, then saw the joke and smiled. "No, First Sergeant," he said, "no decisions. I'll leave everything up to you."

"Very good, sir," Winslow replied. "You're not in charge of much anyway. Just me and five men. Maybe you could order us all to get haircuts." He waited for the warrant officer to laugh, but the kid was gazing toward shore. Winslow knew it was hopeless. The 22d Training Detachment was supposed to have been volunteer duty, but Dukemire was not the type; nobody ever volunteered for someplace else when he had no idea where he was to begin with. When the call went out for anyone wanting to go to Vietnam, Dukemire got volunteered. Not that he was alone. Private Tooler, a twice-busted, do-nothing ex–staff sergeant, had arrived the same way, the only difference being that the aging flatdick knew it and bragged.

"Have you ever been here before, Sergeant?"

"No, sir," Winslow said. "No one's ever been here." Now it was his turn to be absent. A splash of color upriver had caught his attention, and he stared a moment before turning to Dukemire. "That's really not true," he said. "We even had a handful of men here during World War II. Until recently, most of the U.S. advisers and such were down south, but now there's some Air Force people here, mechanics and whatnot, along with that aviation outfit that works for the CIA. Other than that there's probably a couple of liaisons, a few diplomatic types, plus the usual crazies we keep back in the hills in places like this."

"Before we left Korea, I'd never heard of the place."

"Neither had too many others."

Sailors were gathering along the rail where a few more boats had just arrived from the city. A sampan was loaded with young pigs in bamboo cages, and a tattooed sailor immediately began shouting for one. A deal was made, and the bucket lowered. The boatman selected a pig, looked up for approval, then tied its legs with strips of cane and sent it up. The novelty of a pig on deck drew a larger crowd. The men grinned and watched for officers, expecting the sailor to turn the animal loose. But when he had untied the creature's legs he merely held it aloft in his tattooed hooks and tossed it over the side. The pig squealed all the way down and made a loud whack and thud as the cavity of water collapsed. When the confused boatman retrieved the animal, the sailor shouted that he wanted to buy it again. The man was unsure, but when his wife spoke behind her cloth he tied the legs and sold the pig once more. The scene was repeated, and a husky shout went up as the creature smacked into the water. A few peasants were smiling, but the man was now angry. He fished the pig from the river, and did not look again at the ship. The sailor yelled and lowered his pail, and the woman hissed at her husband and held her coins. Stiffly the man tied the legs a third time. He gave no notice when the pig tried to bite or when it vomited green foam on his feet. The exchange was made, a coin delivered to the woman's hand. A single laughing sailor sputtered silent as the pig lurched upward, its empty belly heaving. When it came down again there was not a sound, not even from the pig, just an isolated thud and splash. The strangling animal came up retching, nothing for eyes but marble. The boatman looked at his wife, then paddled over, leaned, and slipped a short blade beneath the water. The pig gave a grunt of relief, its eyes came around, then it disappeared in a bubbling swirl of red. The man bent to his oars and the boat moved away while the woman sat beneath her hat, a tight brown fist clenched hard around some coins.

Dukemire hurried to the opposite rail to vomit. Winslow gave him only the briefest glance before turning his attention upriver.

Five tugboats had materialized, drifting slowly—squat, ugly craft with crude steel cabins, loud with color. They emerged from a scene of mud and haze and dull structure like colorful life bent on escape from an old photograph. Rows of trucks tires draped their bows. Winslow marched aft to locate Sergeant Whitney and to alert his men, leaving Dukemire leaning over the side. The bamboo boats moved away toward another ship while lacy pink foam dissolved downstream.

The driver was a thick-eared old man with a slick mustard scar like something left by lightning. It climbed from his collar past the hollow of his throat, slashing the ravines of his face before disappearing into his scalp. He sawed the wheel as the traffic thinned and the street grew wide. Huge trees formed a graceful canopy between facing villas. A feeling of space developed, then the villas gave way on one side to a park with pools of green water and on the other to a blankness of distance across a polished lake as white as the sky. The driver turned twice, guiding the Citroën up a curving brick drive, begrudgingly mumbling, *"Le Café Ho Tay."*

The restaurant was cream stucco, blistered white, with a flat roof above wide arched windows that caught the lake and toneless sky. Tremendous trees protected gardens all around. Beyond a canopied porte cochere were open doors where a lovely French-Vietnamese woman stood. She eyed their uniforms and greeted the officers in European English. "Welcome to Hanoi, gentlemen." She was dressed in an elegant silk *ao dai* of brilliant blue over red slacks, an embroidered pattern of fiery tendrils rising from her breasts. Her hair was long and silky black with combs of carved ivory, and she needed no makeup beyond a touch of red lipstick. On the wall behind her was a wooden sign which read in French, "No Legionnaires."

"Thank you for honoring my place of business," she said, nodding as if with a bow. "My name is Su Letei. Please, leave your things." Her accent was an appealing blend of French, British, and Vietnamese influence. A wooden old man in gray tunic appeared and carried their bags into an alcove.

"Good afternoon," the major said. Madame Letei was every bit as handsome as he had heard. "I'm Marsh McCall." He glanced at the others. "Mr. West, Mr. Rankin."

26

Cody West was gazing around the restaurant like something flushed from a patch of mesquite, tall and lean with sun-pinched eyes, a permanent morning look. He turned and gave a polite smile. Burd Rankin, several years older, lined and dry and with the beginnings of gray sideburns, gave the woman an appraising glance and looked away.

"May I show you men to a table?" said Madame Letei. "But I must apologize—it is the lazy part of the afternoon, and my cook is taking his sleep. If you will settle for soup or something simple, I am sure we can satisfy your appetites."

"Anything at all will do," McCall said. "It's been a long time since morning chow." Cody West expressed agreement, but Rankin merely continued to survey the surroundings with the same appraising look he had given Letei. He was a chief warrant officer, a CW3, wiry but not tall, with gray-brown hair and guarded gray eyes.

She led them to the rear of the restaurant where large windows wrapped a corner table. The dining area was L-shaped and open, while in a darker, elevated part adjacent to the kitchen stood a bar with stools and several tables. Lazy afternoon or not, the place was half filled with men, many in French uniforms. Most noticed the newcomers.

When they were seated, Su Letei disappeared toward the kitchen. Cody West watched her go, the sleek column of hair swaying just short of her shining hips. Soon a Vietnamese waiter brought coffee and chilled mineral water, butter in a bowl of chipped ice, three small dishes of dark pineapple preserves, and a basket of _petit pain_, small golden footballs of bread.

"Is beer okay, sir?" Rankin said, his voice scratchy as he dug for a cigarette.

"Sure." McCall turned to the waiter. "_Une bière Hanoi, s'il vous plaît_," he said. The waiter nodded, returning almost immediately with the drink and a glass. With an automatic motion, Rankin wiped the neck in a palm, then drank from the brown bottle. West was busy with the bread and preserves. McCall sipped the dense coffee and glanced around, noting that their arrival had been expected.

For years he had heard of the Café Ho Tay. It enjoyed something of a reputation as an international crossroads, a bit off the beaten path, but the natural place to stop in northern French Indochina. Nonetheless, there was nothing impressive about the Café Ho Tay.

Even with the odors of French and Vietnamese food still hanging about and the rich scent of coffee competing with that of baking loaves outside, there was little to set it apart. Yet it had survived the invasion of the Japanese, the brief reign of the Viet Minh, the subsequent and terrible occupation of the Chinese, and the eventual return of the French Army—all without contamination by any faction, all without closing its doors. The Café Ho Tay had an indefinable charm, a feel to its placement at the limit of the city near the water's edge that made it seem that here, among all restaurants of the world, was one in precisely the right place. A shift of only a few feet might have spoiled it. Through the grace and diplomacy of its lovely owner, the Café Ho Tay was acknowledged as neutral ground where blood enemies might meet, sharing drinks at forty feet as they contemplated one another across the room.

Today's clientele was a mixed bunch. At the far end of the room, hunched around a table of worn wood, sat three older colonials embedded in wordless assertion that this was where they always sat. Each was dressed in loose khaki trousers and baggy white shirt with long sleeves rolled to the elbow. The French *colons* looked exactly like their counterparts down south, wore the same weary arrogance, an unquestioned superiority polished by years of telling other people what to do. They bent close with forearms on the table, speaking quietly and glancing toward the Americans. Near a front window were two men who seemed to be cops or agents disguised as civilians, not quite bored enough to carry it off. Scattered about were a few officers in uniform, a businessman in polished shoes and wilted shirt, and a couple of Chinese in tan slacks and tan canvas shoes who might have been tea buyers or money changers or smugglers of opium. In the bar, speaking now to Su Letei, was a very old man in baggy sailor's whites, his face prickly with a white ten-day beard. A few tables away from McCall sat a man in unmarked fatigues who wore the wasted look of one who had lingered too long in the tropics—jet-black hair, unwashed and swept back, a salted mustache bristling beneath a bony beak. His eyes were fierce and dark and deeply set, piercingly focused on Marsh McCall.

The waiter arrived with plates of prawns, bowls of snake bean soup with bits of green onion and pork, and a saucer stacked with flatbread wafers still steaming from the oven. The younger pilot immediately helped himself to the food. Rankin quickly downed his

28

tremely unpleasant surprises for those unprepared. I am sometimes compelled to assume a small risk."

During this time Cody West was busy processing groceries. He pulled the antennaed heads from the prawns, then peeled and quickly consumed the tails. When the soup was gone he inhaled the flatbread, then stuffed down the last of the loaves before using his napkin. He never paused or showed concern that McCall might not be getting his share; the major was enjoying the woman. When he was done, Cody leaned back and gazed about, noting each man within view before pivoting toward the windows. A flagstone veranda and terrace wrapped the room, but the tables outside were empty. The day had been warm, but there was a coolness in the shade beneath the trees. Beyond the terrace on two sides were tall walls smothered in vines. To the right behind the kitchen, separated by a breezeway and a masonry fence, stood a two-story cottage that matched the restaurant, its windows arched and protected by screens that opened like doors. Peach shutters were latched open for light, and beyond were lace curtains. Leaning in his chair, West could see a second-story porch beyond a balustrade, commanding the terrace and gardens, likely yielding a view of the lake beyond the treetops. Sunlight and shadow patterned the wall. He was studying this terrain, wondering who lived there, when a young woman emerged with a bamboo basket, dressed in a white sleeveless blouse and thin patterned skirt. He could not see her face clearly, but she had nice legs. A smoothness in the way she moved said she was barefoot. She began to hang a few damp articles on a line: two panties, two bras. It was then that Su Letei noticed his stare, and bent forward until she was able to see.

"She would die of humiliation," she said softly. West immediately flushed scarlet, glanced at the woman, then looked away, anywhere but in the direction of Su Letei or the girl on the balcony. "She may not turn quite the color you are now, but she would not forgive you. Her name is Moni', my niece. She lives with her father outside the city, but visits on weekends."

West was unable to make any intelligent sound. He nodded solemnly and formed a twisted expression that he meant for a smile. He could feel the heat on his cheeks. Across the table, he noted, the major sat smug with age and impending impotence, amused by his misfortune. Cody focused his anger to help him recover, but lost it

31

to an image of the girl, her arms above her head, a breeze fluttering the skirt against her legs. He realized then that he had hardly seen her face. He dared not chance another look.

Su Letei turned to McCall, who was carefully studying his coffee. "As for you, Major," she said, "perhaps I can later be of assistance by making a few introductions. Do not hesitate to ask. For now"— she glanced quickly around—"besides the Sûreté men, there are of course the *colons*. The one with thinning white hair is Paul Gereau—once a powerful colonel, the son of an early settler, he is now retired but does not seem to enjoy it. He continues to fight wars in his head. Notice he still wears his pants bloused into his boots."

As she spoke, a barrel-chested Frenchman of about sixty entered the restaurant. His hair was thick, evenly peppered gray, and he looked fit in his uniform. When the doorman tried to greet him, he made a backward sweep of his hand as if driving away an annoying insect, then walked majestically toward the long table, where he joined the others. Su Letei motioned to a waiter. "Colonel Maurice de Matrin," she said to McCall. "Once prominent in the Resistance, he has settled down now to a secure job as the head of Northern Vietnam Matériel Command. Said to be contemplating retirement, apparently awaiting the outcome of this war."

She turned toward the bar. "The old sailor is American, named Larkin. He took his retirement here more than thirty years ago. Married a Vietnamese woman, now dead. He has no money. Before you leave he may ask you to buy him a beer. In return he will try to tell you a story."

The man in fatigues had still not taken his fierce eyes from McCall, staring with the mad intensity of a spider. When at last he stood and walked toward the table, Su Letei made a look of displeasure. "I was going to tell you about this one," she said, "but it seems that will not be necessary. Please excuse me, I am neglecting my guests. I hope that during your stay you will consider my place your second headquarters. The surroundings are humble, but there is much here to be learned." The gaunt stranger, smelling of unhealthy sweat, stood now at the edge of the table. On one side of his throat was a goiter the size of a small fist. McCall kept his eyes on the woman, but was plainly prepared. "How long do you plan to be in Hanoi, Major?" said Su Letei.

"I don't yet know that," he replied. The statement was only partly untrue. "Perhaps you can tell me."

"Frankly, I am surprised that I cannot," she said with a smile. "I said there were few secrets here, but there are at least some. I can tell you, however, that they do have extremely short lives. In any case, I hope you will be here long enough for us to become better acquainted."

McCall nodded and stood as she turned and said, "Mr. West."

Cody, who had been gazing again out the window, looked around guiltily. The woman suppressed a smile. When she walked away, he fastened his eyes on her hips. She was in awfully good shape for a lady nearly old enough to be his mother. The major observed his interest, and took a quick look himself.

Marsh McCall had two very different eyes: one that was bright and lively, the one people talked to; but the other was practically dead, a turtle's eye, glazed and yellowed and old, that stared out in silence. It was the eye that people avoided, the one that sometimes turned and came suddenly to life like an awakened god, able to see so much. He had never learned to control it, but he was aware of its nature and often sat on one side of a person or the other, according to the way he wanted to be known. Now he turned that bad eye on the repellent reptile who had driven the woman away.

"Anything in particular I can do for you, mister?" he growled.

"You can begin by changing your attitude, Marshy," the man rasped in a voice less substance than air. His teeth were long and mossy gold. Without looking in their direction, Cody West moved his chair from the table, got his feet under him, and began checking faces. A few men were watching, but the stranger was on his own. He glanced toward the bar. Burd Rankin was seated at a table with two civilians, his back partly turned, talking with his hands. Cody lowered his eyes, then swept them just above table level. The man was unarmed, his hands trembling. Black veins wormed across bones.

Marsh McCall had missed the man's words. He had long been aware that the ridges and wrinkles that women bewilderingly found attractive could have a completely different effect on some men— an equally mysterious fact that more than once had proved damned inconvenient. But surely this scrawny weasel has something else in mind. Then he heard what the man had said, and he stared into terrible eyes. "Jack?" he said. *"Jack?"*

"None other."

"Sperek?" McCall searched, but could find little familiar. Slowly he held out a hand, and the old friend he was still not sure he recognized filled it with one that felt like a glove full of bones. "Sit down, fella," McCall said. He was shocked by Sperek's condition, but was less surprised to find him in Hanoi than to find him alive at all. Men like Jack Sperek did not live to be old. He looked him up and down. "What's happened, Jack?" he said. "Have you been to a doctor?"

"I'm okay," he said, settling into a chair. "Can't seem to keep any weight on. Dropped forty pounds in the past four months. Some kind of fever, allergic to city life. But I still have my strength."

That was clearly untrue. The man's collarbones showed sharply white, his throat was chicken skin beneath the goiter. "So what are you doing, Jack?"

"Same thing, just different. Till recently."

"You working for the French?"

"I did for a few years, but now I'm working for Harman."

McCall knew the name. Roach Harman had been in command of all OSS operations in the Asian theater in World War II and now held the same position with the CIA. He ran shop from Hong Kong and had built an empire to proportions of legend. There was not a man in Washington, including the president, who had the courage to try to unseat him. As Harman's power increased, so had his desire for secrecy, exemplified when *Time* planned a cover story on the CIA's role in the McCarthy investigations. Roach Harman's photograph—one from the OSS days—was to have graced the cover, accompanied inside by a sidebar concerning his influence on the agency's development. But Harman succeeded in having the entire feature pulled within hours of publication. In mute response, *Time* produced an issue with an all-white cover outlined in red, splashed with the stenciled word CENSORED. No explanation appeared inside the slim issue, and none of the thousands of questioning letters were ever published. It was left to other publications to speculate in print, and eventually to reveal the story in open rebellion. McCall was aware that few men could claim having seen Harman in recent years, but the casual way that Sperek used his name suggested they were personally acquainted.

"What brings you to Hanoi, Marsh?" Sperek said, his voice flat, the answer known.

"Oh, a temporary job for Ezra Smith," McCall said. He watched as Sperek eyed him in open warning. Much had changed since they last had met, but the brutal honesty was still intact.

Cody West was staring toward the bar where the sailor still sat, looking as sad as an old man in a cemetery. When Cody pushed away from the table he caught the major's attention. "Sir, all right if I go talk to Grandpa?"

"You'd better be prepared to buy the beer."

"Yes, sir."

"Do more listening than talking."

Sperek flicked his eyes between them, then watched with McCall as the pilot climbed the two steps. The old sailor turned and stared at the kid in astonishment, then his entire face became a rubber smile. His four front teeth were gone.

In the foyer a skinny Chinese in a black suit was attempting to enter with a yellow bull terrier on a leash. Su Letei was adamant. She made no gesture, but her back was as stiff as steel. Finally, the man left with his dog, haranguing back over his shoulder. When Su Letei turned, her eyes were blazing pure lightning.

"She belongs to the Chinaman Chang Wu," Sperek said.

McCall watched as she regained control. From what he had seen, Su Letei did not seem the kind to belong to anyone unless she decided. He wondered about the man named Chang Wu.

"So where are you staying?" Sperek asked.

"I don't know yet. We weren't due here till tomorrow. I wanted time to get dug in. In the morning I'll make my arrival official, then get to work. The rest of the outfit's coming in by boat."

"Outfit?" This time the question was genuine.

"Just a handful of men, a few helicopters to train some French pilots."

Sperek managed a smile. "An aviator," he said.

"No, I'm a ground-pounder. Once this assignment is done, that's what I'm going back to."

"Birds with broken wings."

"What's that?"

"What the mountain tribes, the T'ais, call helicopters."

McCall chuckled. "Good description," he said, thinking of a similar line from an old nursery rhyme.

"You'll probably be quartered at Lam Du," Sperek said. "Tell you what, you and your men may as well stay at my place tonight. I've got a run-down villa all to myself. Technically, I share it, but things in the bush are busy. There's never anybody there but me. You and I have a few years of catching up to do."

McCall wondered how long that would take. It was plain enough that Jack Sperek was not the same man he'd once known. Sperek had said as much himself by dropping Roach Harman's name. "Sounds good enough," he said. "Tonight you can fill me in on the situation here, what the prospects are."

"I can tell you right now it's not good. Nobody's going to be here long. It's almost time to bring in the bodies."

"If things are so hopeless, why are you here?"

"Everybody's got to be someplace."

The remark was the Jack Sperek that McCall remembered. The man had been charred to the core long ago, but no other work suited his character so well.

A jeep turned into the curved drive, screeched to a halt just long enough to discharge a passenger, then pulled ahead to wait beneath the trees. A man in uniform came up the steps, where he was greeted by Su Letei. His red beret was tucked neatly beneath an arm, and he wore an expression of concern. They exchanged a few words and looked toward McCall's table.

"Your escort," Sperek said. "The gambler."

The French major was handsome, well-built, and had curly brown hair. He was outfitted in khakis and boots, his tunic cinched by a gleaming belt which held an automatic—a U.S. Colt .45. He strode briskly toward the table, his face softening until he arrived relaxed. His pants were tailored, bloused into paratroop boots. Jump wings adorned his chest. "Major McCall?" he said. McCall got to his feet. "Welcome to French Indochina," he continued, stressing the adjective. "I am Major René Legère of Logistics North. I have been assigned to assist you during the few weeks you will be here. I wish to apologize for failing to meet your flight, but you were not expected until tomorrow."

"That's my fault," McCall said. "I was anxious to see this part of the country. From the air, it's a lot more interesting than down south."

"Yes, but we pay for that difference with more miserable weather. Today was unusual. You may have been wise to arrive early—twice in the past week flights have been diverted by fog. But soon that will change."

"Will you join us?" McCall said. "Do you know Jack Sperek?" Sperek was still seated, not looking at Legère.

"We are acquainted," Legère said. "Since you were not expected, Major McCall, I have made arrangements for you here in a hotel in town. Tomorrow you will be lodged in something less comfortable but perhaps more appropriate to your assignment."

McCall glanced at Sperek, lighting a cigarette with nicotined nails. "Tell you what," he said. "I appreciate the hospitality, but I've already made plans to stay with Jack tonight."

Legère frowned, then tried to smile. "That's really not necessary," he said. "I am sure you will find my arrangements considerably more comfortable."

"There's nothing more comfortable than swapping lies with an old friend," McCall said. "Thanks again, but Jack's the reason I came early."

"I really must insist," Legère said. "You are our guest."

McCall was suddenly tired. He watched as a balding man in a gray suit took a seat in the bar, then let his eyes fall to the floor. The gray-green stone was hazed with the scratch of a million boots. Maybe it was their country, maybe not, but the French were only there because of the United States and Great Britain. Just as France had surrendered to Germany early in the war, French Indochina had bowed to Japan without a fight.

"How tactful do I have to be?" he said, turning his evil eye. His lips formed a flattened smile.

Legère was jarred, but instantly recovered. "My apologies, sir," he said more amiably than McCall could have managed. "I do not blame you for wanting to visit an old comrade. Tomorrow we shall get to work. May I pick you up at oh nine hundred?"

"Perfect. But I don't know the place."

"I do," Legère said. He drew himself to attention and made a slight bow. "Tomorrow," he said, then turned and marched out of the restaurant. When he passed the long table that served the *colons* he gave a half-salute to the man with gray hair. The only response was a thoughtful stare.

McCall raised a brow as he eased into his chair. "They don't want us here," Sperek said. "You'll get the royal treatment until you become a nuisance. They haven't forgotten that we helped train Ho Chi Minh's army and supplied them with guns. They tolerate us only because they're desperate."

McCall listened to the jeep leaving the drive. "Did Harman move you to town when you got sick?" he asked.

Sperek's eyes shifted with disgust and shame. "No, it's the other way around," he said. "I started out fighting Japs with the Viet Minh. Later, it was Lao rebels with the Limeys, then northern Laos to fight *against* the Minh for the French. Last, I was two years with the T'ais near Suvui up on the Black River, Trinquier supplying us by air. When I first came in from the mountains I was doing little jobs close in for Harman, short-term stuff, dropping in at night. But this is no place for that kind of work, not for a white man. No place to hide. I wanted to go back to the mountains, but then I was losing weight. I'm a city rat now. Not so different from the jungle. I spent my first few months going over it, getting it mapped out in my head. Just like in the bush. Now Harman just has me hanging around, waiting for a job." Sperek's voice was a rattle in an empty shell. He pulled at his cigarette, signaling the waiter for two beers.

The man in the suit used the break in the conversation to approach the table. He was wide around the middle. Beneath long, untrimmed brows were the eyes of a man growing rapidly tired of the game. McCall pegged him as a diplomat.

"Major McCall," he said, "if I may have a minute of your time, I'd like to introduce myself. My name is Walter J. Pearbone, the American vice-consul." McCall stood, and the two shook hands. "I wanted to welcome you to the area, and to invite you to stop by at your earliest convenience for coffee and a short briefing."

"Briefing?"

"As close as I can come in a word. Just an informal discussion to familiarize you with a few of the area's eccentricities. I am sure you will find it enlightening, and it should help you avoid a few mistakes. Now, I shan't disturb you any longer. Here is my card. My office and the compound are a few blocks beyond Little Lake, but I maintain a private residence not far from here which might be more appropriate. Feel free to call any day after three, or anytime on the weekend. Good day."

McCall pocketed the card, and watched Pearbone make his exit. He was slightly intrigued, but not sure he wanted to hear what the man had to say.

There was a sudden but subtle change as the lake and descending sun threw a filtered glow beneath the trees, coloring the air, demolishing shadows. More vehicles began to arrive. A pair of *colons*, both with gray weathered hats with wide brims, joined the others at their table. Then came several younger French officers, laughing with Su Letei as she led them through the restaurant. McCall wondered about the genteel atmosphere and how desperate the French really were. From what he could see, not only was the war somewhere beyond Hanoi, Hanoi was well beyond the war.

"Do you remember a kid named Solo Jacobé?"

McCall frowned. "I don't think so. Where from?"

"He said you knew him as Lapeste."

"Lapeste! Sure I remember him." Lapeste was a name that had been hung on a teenager his maquis had found one morning in the forest northwest of Grenoble. When brought into camp, the boy said he had come to join. He was held at first as a potential spy, then was kept on as mascot with the promise that he would be handed over to authorities at the first opportunity. But no one seemed in a hurry to get rid of him. The weeks went by, and always Lapeste was there, watching and whispering questions. When it was finally decided to take him to town, the move was further delayed by Germans sweeping the hills. Then one morning the group became trapped, pinned against cliffs. It was the fourteen-year-old Lapeste, left behind in a cave to nurse a sick man, who crawled five hundred yards with a heavy machine gun and ammo to gun down twenty-six Germans and save them all.

"He's here," Sperek said. "All grown up, a lieutenant now. Right over there." He nodded toward the officers.

McCall followed his gaze but could find no familiar face. When one of the men looked in their direction, Sperek crooked a knotty finger. The Frenchman seemed to hesitate, but said something to his companions and approached the table.

"*Bonsoir*, Monsieur Sperek," he said formally. He wore gold-rimmed glasses, had dark cinnamon hair and freckles. His features were youthful, but he carried himself with the confidence of one much older. His friends and the *colons* were watching. He nodded at McCall, then turned to Sperek. "Was there something..." He looked back at McCall, a smile beginning to spread. "Monsieur Marsh!" he said. McCall stood and extended a hand, which Lapeste took before grabbing McCall in a sudden embrace, kissing him on both cheeks. *"Fantastique!"* he said. Then he remembered his surroundings and assumed a beaming semblance of formality. "This man is the only reason I am alive today," he said. Sperek was grinning like a hungry wolf.

McCall stepped back to look him up and down. The man was moderately muscled, just under six feet, a filled-out version of the kid McCall had known. On his shoulders were the gold bands of a lieutenant. "Good to see you, Lapeste," he said.

The lieutenant colored. "My name is Solo Jacobé," he said, wagging a finger. "No longer may you call me Lapeste. So what brings you to Hanoi, Monsieur Marsh?"

"He was sent here by Ezra Smith," Sperek said without looking up.

Jacobé's smile began to collapse like warm wax, changing and blanching as if he were ill. "You will command the American detachment waiting now in Haiphong," he said.

"The lieutenant is with military intelligence," said Sperek.

"Internal Security," Jacobé said absently, his thoughts clearly ahead of his words.

"That's correct," McCall said with a puzzled frown.

The lieutenant's face assumed its original stiffness. He glanced quickly toward the *colons*, then the table of officers, all staring. When he turned again to McCall there was pain in his eyes, replaced immediately with the sterile defense of a stranger. "I am sorry," he said huskily. "I have made an unfortunate mistake. It is very good to see you, Monsieur Marsh, but it will not be possible for us to be friends just now. Perhaps we shall later be acquainted. I sincerely hope so." With that he turned abruptly and walked away. Solo Jacobé sat at the table with his back to the Americans, nodding stiffly to questions. Soon he excused himself and departed the restaurant.

★

He chose a spot at the foot of the dockmaster's tower where he could use the ladder for a view and give the men a visible anchor in the crawling chaos of the dock. There was still no sign of Atherton—or of the major who was to have met them—but Winslow was not surprised. He was accustomed to shorthanded work, and had quickly devised a plan and issued orders to his men. He watched the faceless workers between the tower and the gray flat sides of the *Saraffin*. There was not a thing to suggest that only minutes ago they had watched a man die. The blood of the coolie was already tracked away.

He stepped up to the first rung to look. Everything seemed under control. The six helicopters were lined up in pairs against a rusty warehouse wall, guarded now by Kinney and Billy Mano. The two had found rough boards, and were holding them like pugil sticks, striding about and warning people away. Jim Kinney caught sight of Winslow, glanced down the dock to where Two Acres guarded the steel equipment containers, then gave a thumbs-up. Beyond view, but somewhere in the crowd between Winslow and the *Saraffin*, was Sergeant Whitney, waiting for the first jeep to emerge. Private Tooler was still aboard, overseeing the rigging. A few feet behind Winslow stood Dukemire, frowning and looking useless, glancing at coolies and gripping a leg of the tower.

It had been madness at first, getting the birds unloaded. Winslow had anticipated the confusion. He had made his plans from the deck of the *Saraffin* with a methodical and sincere Sergeant Whitney. From the vantage of elevation they had been able to study the layout of the docks. Everywhere were Chinese coolies, jogging along in lines or waiting in groups for a net to descend or a piece of equipment to pass. Through the melee moved heavy fork trucks driven by Frenchmen. While they watched a lumpy net emerge from a hold like a dirty gemstone brought up from the depths, there arose a punctuated scream that pierced the common roar. A circle of silence moved out from the scream, causing work to stop and men to stare even far beyond view. Winslow and Whitney moved aft and saw a fork truck on top of a man. Only the head and shoulders and one extended arm were in view, a couple of fingers tapping. The driver looked down, pounding the wheel and shouting. Three coolies peered beneath the vehicle and tugged at the arm. The driver yelled again, still in his seat, then slipped into a snarling curse as if the crushed coolie were to blame. Then the dockmaster appeared. A squinting man with a pleated face, he descended his ladder, took one look, and spoke to the driver. Winslow was no more than a hundred feet away, and plainly saw the wordless, fluttering lips, the waxy pallor of the driver's face. The man stared ahead, then the engine revved, the tires spun, and the vehicle lurched over the body. The dockmaster moved his hands, and four coolies picked up the pieces and hurried off. The visceral smear was avoided until the place was gradually lost, then barefoot men tracked it around until the crud of blood and dirt and grease was everywhere the same.

It was only a sudden change in light that made Winslow remember the time. All day a white haze had lent the sky a glaring fluorescence, weakly penetrated by an anemic eye. But suddenly the sun was safely beyond the mountain teeth, able to send its rays beneath the dome, claiming water and land in a yolkish light. Winslow had always been a sucker for a sunset, and he paused to watch. For a little while the world was all aglow, a golden hell reflected off the heavens. The coolies were cast in black and gold; their hair disappeared, and in their eyes were tiny sparks. Then the angle passed and the vision vanished. Dusk settled over the land.

The first jeep cleared the deck, swung high across the dock, then descended into a circle of coolies. The men poured over it like ants. Winslow held his position, expecting to see the vehicle roll by with Whitney at the wheel. But nothing happened. He climbed another rung, and could just make out the jeep. Whitney was yelling, waving his arms. The second jeep was overhead, beginning to descend, before he prevailed and took the wheel. With several coolies pushing, the first jeep came past, leaving the second unattended. Winslow stepped down from the ladder. "Sir, could you get the second jeep?" he yelled.

Dukemire looked surprised, glad to have something to do. "Sure, Sergeant!"

"Just get in it and steer. We'll park them just to the left of the choppers."

Dukemire waded into the coolies and disappeared. A couple of minutes went by, but no jeep appeared. The third was already emerging from the hold as Whitney hurried past to help. Winslow stepped again on the ladder, and saw Dukemire arguing with someone already in the seat. In the opposite direction, Kinney and Mano were still guarding the aircraft and the first jeep. When Mano looked,

Winslow pointed at himself, then in the direction of the jeeps. He stepped off the ladder just as a whistle blew, a deep wailing tone that rose strangely at the end. The docks were already crowded, but were now overwhelmed as waves of fresh coolies poured out from the streets, colliding with an equally mindless wall moving the other way. While Winslow was trapped at the base of the tower he became aware of the men.

He had seen them earlier, drifting about, tough-looking Frenchmen in blue fatigues and T-shirts, like soldiers out of uniform. Now he saw that they were spaced around the dock in pairs, against the warehouse walls, along the stacks of containers and crates. Winslow suddenly saw it all. He took a quick step up the ladder and found Kinney in agitation, waving his board and pointing in the direction of Two Acres. Winslow made a sign to stay put, but Kinney said something to Mano, then dived into the crowd, disappearing beyond a wall of crates. Within seconds a shout went up; the battle for the containers had begun.

Winslow jumped from the step and came face to face with two muscular men. "It's going to take more than two of you fucks," he said. One of the Frenchmen smiled, and the sergeant saw that he was surrounded. "Okay, you side-switching bastards, let's see if you've got more balls than your big brothers had." He brought the toe of his boot up between the legs of the nearest man, spun and crushed a jaw, then kicked another in the chest before the attack was unified. When it came there was no pain beyond a soggy, bruised sensation, a dull electric numbness. For several seconds he held his smile, yelling to the crunch of opposing teeth. He dimly saw two jeeps roll past with Frenchmen at the wheels. Then came a blur of brown, a crunching thud and shock as his brain bounced off his skull. He saw Dukemire stumbling past, blood streaming from his face, then his knees were gone. Calvin Winslow kissed the concrete.

Chapter Three

WHENEVER SOLO JACOBÉ began to feel doubt, whenever the survival caution of fear gnawed the belly of his thoughts, he would recite a pledge. When it was very bad and the rage and vow of retribution were not enough, he would review it all from beginning to hoped-for end. This did nothing to remove his fear, but it renewed his strength and held him to a relentless course.

I will not fail, I will not give up, not even at the cost of my life.

He removed his glasses, put them in their case, and left them beside his bed. He had once worn the neutral lenses to make himself seem older, but now they were employed for other effect, a reflective shield between anyone and what might be revealed in his eyes.

"I do not think you should go," said Antoine.

"I have no choice. He is an old and true friend. I cannot take the chance."

"Chance? The chance you are taking is practically suicide." Antoine held his hands to his head. "God, I'll be glad when this is all over."

"It has only begun."

"If you had told me your plans in the beginning, I could have shot you then and saved you the trouble. It is moments like this which make me glad I do not know more."

Solo Jacobé managed a smile, reassured that he had decided correctly. He trusted his roommate completely, but there was no need for him to know more. Besides avoiding the physical danger, he did not want his friend to be able to argue successfully. "I will be back before daylight," he said. "If not, you know where to look."

Antoine made an angry grimace. "Let me drop you off," he said. "I could not sleep anyway. I will go drink coffee with the gendarmes, see what is coming in on the radios."

"You will not try to interfere?"

"No, damn it. I will come back after an hour, then every thirty minutes after that. If you are not at the levee by oh four hundred, I'm coming down there with an army."

"Make it oh four thirty. We can take my jeep."

Antoine reached beneath his bunk, then followed Jacobé outside. He dropped some items between the seats.

"What are those?"

Antoine held up a foot-long tube. "Hand flares," he said. "You can take a couple with you to signal in case there is trouble."

Solo Jacobé smiled. "They would be useless," he said. "They have guards. I will be searched."

"Maybe you could hide them somewhere."

"Just drive."

They left the north gate of the Citadel, ignoring the sleepy salute of the guard. Their positions with Sécurité Intérieure lent them a certain mobility, an expensive freedom when measured against what a misstep could mean. Because their stated assignment was to prevent anyone from meddling in matters which *they* were supposed to investigate but never did, there was always a valid reason for creeping around in the night. That they were sometimes watched by the Sûreté was balanced by the fact that they often were watching the watchers.

They proceeded west and north past the Café Ho Tay along the causeway road to the levee, then northward toward the edge of town. Antoine drove without speaking, paying no attention to drowsy gendarmes on patrol.

This was only the first emergency, Jacobé told himself. There would be more, and he would handle each as it came, one at a time, one day at a time, until time ran out.

I will not fail....

He wondered how things had ever come to such a stage. He knew the story, all the windings of the past, but he would never understand. For more than half of his twenty-five years, France had been at war with *someone*. Even his childhood had been spent in an atmosphere of impending war. The world war was barely ended when another fight began. France bombarded Haiphong with tanks and artillery because the Vietnamese made the outrageous claim that Vietnam belonged to no one but themselves. It was the shameful beginning of a shameful war, a humiliated France in search of old prestige, believing it might be retrieved by pounding an enemy it perceived to be small. Ho Chi Minh retreated to the caves of Thai Nguyen north of Hanoi, where he recruited men with the promise of returning Vietnam to its people.

The rise of someone like Ho Chi Minh had been inevitable, easily traced to the early colonization. Those who were willing to leave France to face tropical hardships and disease were not normally among the cultural cream. Some came with honest intentions, but an equal number were drawn by greed, the availability of near-slave labor, and the governing tenet that even the sorriest white man stood somewhere above the most distinguished Vietnamese.

Since the Haiphong attack the war had dragged endlessly on, consuming again the young men of France, bringing at last into question whether what they were fighting for was of any value, and if so to whom. The answers did not bear close inspection. After watching the war for more than two years, his disillusionment complete, Solo Jacobé began to see things in a different light. Indochina was not France's land, it had never been, and the only people who gained anything by its occupation were the investors and bankers of France. For that, ninety thousand French Union soldiers—twenty thousand of them French—and upward of half a million Vietnamese had died. But it could not last forever. Suddenly everyone could see that the opportunities of greed were about to be permanently lost. Corruption erupted everywhere as the maggots of war made feast upon the withering corpse.

Solo Jacobé had read of this very thing on editorial pages in Paris, but never had he believed that it was anything more than desk-bound drivel. But *now* he believed, now that 60 percent of the men in his officer class were dead, now that he had seen with his own eyes how the system worked, now that he had been locked in a position where he was forced to watch while his fellow soldiers were sold for slaughter. The shame and bitterness were impossible to bear.

Finally, in November, the load had become too much. Dien Bien Phu was reoccupied by French forces, promising plainly that thousands would soon die there even as French High Command blithely announced that the major campaigns of the season would occur farther south in the Central Highlands.

Solo Jacobé could no longer accept being helpless. He began to develop a plan. It would involve great risk, and possibly terrible consequences whether he was successful or not. But whatever it took, he decided, whatever momentary torture or agony of years, whatever death he might have to endure, he would do his part to bring the slaughter to an end and to send those responsible to a just and burning hell.

I will not give up. . . .

When they came to a dusty turnoff, a side road pounded to powder, Antoine turned the vehicle about. "I could go as far as the edge of the village," he said.

"No." Solo Jacobé checked his pistol, a wasted gesture, then stepped into the dust. "One hour," he said, holding a finger before him. "No sooner. And do not come into the village."

"I think you should take the signal flares. Perhaps you will not be searched."

Solo Jacobé shook his head. He watched the jeep pull away, and when the sound was gone, followed the weaving roadway down into the hamlet. There was no light where he walked, only the dim fluttering glow of a wick lamp low through a window, only tired hazy stars overhead. He walked slowly, trying to stay on the powdery path between ruts and old mud holes. On either side were sleepless sounds—a quiet footstep, the chuckle of a hen, a patter of urination, a frightened growl advancing on rigid legs. He held to the center of the road.

Not even at the cost of my life. . . .

For a time he was afraid he had waited too late, but when he reached the far side of the village he could see two sets of headlights across a field, and beyond them a section of wall and one yawning door of a large building. A truck with sideboards was backing into position beside the door, assuring Solo Jacobé that his timing was right. He stepped into the open, and had walked only a short distance when a Chinese voice said in French, "Give me your weapon."

He halted and handed over his .45 to a thin black shadow, and with the man at his back, moved carefully forward on uneven ground. Soon he was able to see his feet in the spray of light. Men were speaking Chinese, silhouettes struggling with objects moving out through the door. Then came a quiet voice ahead, the sweep of a hand as a massive figure gave casual commands.

"Wait," said the man at Solo Jacobé's back. The lieutenant stopped and lifted his arms as the thin man patted him down for weapons. "Continue."

When Solo Jacobé stepped forward, he was faintly trembling, more from rage and revulsion than from any danger. He wanted to run and be away from there, and he wanted to kill everyone in sight.

I will not fail. . . .

Between the rear of the truck and the bright doorway where the fat man stood was a pile of dead dogs. Two men emerged with another, and with a common grunt, threw the body onto the stack. They stood smiling at the fat Chinese, catching their breath and wiping their hands on their pants.

"Hello, Lieutenant," the fat man said. Beside him on a leash stood a gray dog, leaning to sniff the bodies. "I did not expect you down here again. I assume there has been a new development." The two workers and another on the bed of the truck turned to stare, faces hidden in darkness.

Solo Jacobé glanced at the bodies, perversely glad they were there. The light was on his face, and the gruesome sight would compensate for his not bringing his glasses. "They sent someone I did not expect," he said.

"Someone you know?"

"A friend from years ago." As the odors of blood and dead flesh moved through his head, Solo Jacobé controlled a shudder, sickened by the man and the place and all they represented.

When the fat man observed that the work had stopped, he waved a small hand. The men reached down, then heaved a stiffening corpse to the truck. The man on the bed kicked it into position, then dragged it forward.

"And you want reassurance."

"Even were he a stranger, it would be equally important that nothing occur." Another body slammed onto the steel bed with a meaty thud and a crunch of bone.

"I am surprised at you, Lieutenant. Your youth is showing. This visit was unnecessary, and can only jeopardize your position. We have an agreement. As long as it is to my advantage that this man remain alive, no harm will befall him at my hands. I may even take measures to protect him. But you know I cannot speak for all of Hanoi, and I cannot say with any certainty that my own position will not change."

When the next animal was loaded, there came a soft whimper from the pile, prompting a growl and a sudden bristling from the gray dog. The fat Chinaman made a look of distaste. "Now, if you will excuse me, I must go inside. Do not come down here again for any reason, Lieutenant."

As Solo Jacobé watched him walk heavily away, the dog glancing over his shoulder, there came a sickening sound of impact. One of the loaders was straddling a body, smashing a small head with a hammer. Solo Jacobé whirled in rage and self-hate. He held out his hand for his weapon, then stumbled away into darkness.

I will not give up. . . .

He was still so upset when he reached the levee that he thought someone had stolen his jeep. Then he saw approaching headlights and remembered Antoine. His roommate pulled up beside him, his voice urgent. "There has been trouble in Haiphong," he said. "Somebody arranged a reception for the Americans."

Life came to the city like a factory left vacant all night. Throughout the morning, people funneled toward town along the levee road above the floodland hovels, but it was the old women who awakened the roosters. With a handful of cold rice in their bodies and a lump rolled tight in banana leaf, they stood beneath their poles and set off along the paths before anything happened to the sky. Carefully at first, then with confidence as the joints warmed, they hustled along in a rhythmic gait timed to the spring of the pole, heads down, huffing softly, free arms pumping like pistons.

They carried the goods of the earth and skilled hands: yellow and green papayas, blushing mangos, manioc and sweet potatoes; onions and garlic and greens, oranges, grapefruit, and litchi; chicken and duck eggs in hairlike beds of shaved bamboo, fuzzy yellow chicks and dumb little ducklings stacked in woven cells; gigantic piles of baskets, golden and fresh with new bamboo fragrance, bundles of short green bamboo for tearing into strips to fashion all manner of things; bundles of reddish wood, thinly split for tiny cooking fires; bundles of unruly white cane ribbon for lashings and chairs; tiered flats of sprouts, jute bags of medicinal barks, live eels and damp brown snails in beds of wet weeds; joss sticks and candles, wood carvings and charcoal, colored weavings from far in the highlands; and rice: tons upon tons of rice, one peasant at a time, one back-aching, pole-bouncing, arm-swinging trip into town at a time, forever and always, rice.

Heavier items such as brick and tile and thick bamboo poles for construction and rocks from the quarries and sand and gravel from the river all would come later by ox-drawn cart. These things could not be hurried, and so were not sold at market.

By six the street below the levee was crowded, the better spaces filled, vendors still getting arranged. By seven business was brisk among dealers, stragglers filling the gaps. By eight the street was swarming with people and bicycles, cyclos and cars. Then a rippling shock as the first convoy came through, choking black smoke and blaring horns, shouting, belligerent drivers. The crowd flowed aside and back like water splashed from the street.

Live cargo arrived throughout the morning to be sold directly from vehicles: bicycles with bamboo racks immense with dozens of chickens hung by their feet, turning pink faces in red-eyed terror; alert white geese, upright and dignity intact, beaks deep orange in morning light, giving speculative honks, rich, sonorous, and improbable. In the beds of weathered carts were bamboo cages stuffed with pigs or chickens or ducks or dogs, each frantic and filthy, each defecating on those below while waiting its turn at the stile.

Every morning of every day it was the same, and in the afternoon the roads were lined with peasants.

★

He awoke before the automobiles began to bleat along the levee, but lay a long time with the growing colors. The room was on the second story, looking down through tall windows on a narrow street, letting onto a covered porch in back. Inside were blue louvered doors matching solid ones of wood, and across the windows were cracked and dusty shutters. He had slept with the doors and windows wide, shutters drawn, permitting a cooling breeze to clean the room. Against one wall stood a wooden wardrobe that held some stranger's things, but in the dim early dawn it was easy to imagine that the place was his. On this particular morning, at least, half of it was. Burd Rankin had made a deal with the major, spending the night somewhere else. It was the age-old conspiracy of gray hair, old farts covering for one another, but Cody did not mind. He was glad to have the upper floor to himself.

Sperek's "villa" was a run-down, dirt-toned stucco job in a rotting portion of town a few blocks from the levee. It needed paint, the plaster repaired, an iron gate rehung on its post, new plumbing and roof tiles, a lot of caulk, and several panes of glass. But despite its condition, the house had a homey appeal, a curious essence few places possess, stirring the need to paint and repair and plant gardens. He was surprised by the thought, but the house merely needed some work. The private shuttered light and cool morning air made him think of the girl at the Café Ho Tay. He saw the flutter of cloth against her legs and remembered her name was Moni'.

He raised the bleached netting and cracked open the shutters to peek out at a cantaloupe sky, stabbing pink shafts over vanishing darkness. Silhouettes moved along the levee. The rooftops blushed beneath layers of soot, and suspended above were strands of breakfast smoke as fine as blue hair. A stooped woman came down the street with a cloth-covered basket, turned in at the broken gate, then soon emerged to return the way she came. Cody pulled on fatigue pants, found his towel and soap, and went downstairs.

The house formed a square U around a covered stairwell that opened to the rear. Below was the bath with a corroded toilet, its water tank up high, that flushed with the pull of a chain, and next to that was the only bidet Cody West had ever seen. He was puzzled by the broken contraption, suspecting it had something grotesque to do with French women. There was only cold water, so he showered, lathered, and rinsed in two minutes flat. He heard McCall's deep voice through the wall and went quietly upstairs, not wanting to give up the morning.

He dressed quickly, then took a chair from the room, propped his feet on a blackened rail, and watched the developing day. The enclosed yard was small and neglected, a tight grove of bamboo trees trembling in one corner. In every direction were rooftops and gables, shutters and ironwork, aged in a smoky-hazed scene that might have been morning in Europe. A rooster crowed, and beyond the wall were the chirping sounds of children.

For the first time since arriving in this strange land Cody West had a sense of place, a feeling that this would later be the day he would trust his memory. The week had been an onslaught of things he did not understand. The flight up from Saigon had been mainly over water, paralleling a spectacular coast and blue-green mountains. They passed patches of weather where jungle turned blue, and paddies gray, and damp charcoal clouds clung to the soggy heights, everything mirrored in marshes and paddies and inlets below. Approaching the north they came inland again where the land was flat and overdyed green, studded with abrupt stone mountains like bad teeth. He could hardly wait to be down there among them in a chopper. As he surveyed the land, a thought came which he tried to suppress: He wished that his old man could have been there to see it, especially the mountains. He guessed that was not too much to allow for the one who had taught him to fly.

He scanned the rooftops, thinking how different it was from what he had expected. Everyone in flight school had talked of Korea with a mixture of dread and desire, straining and sliding toward whatever their future would be. Then something terrible occurred: The armistice was signed. Rumors quickly spread that new pilots like Cody were to be jettisoned from the Army. He was utterly ill, so envious of those only a few years older. The world war had presented such opportunities, so many great lives to live. Men were killed, of course, but that was merely the pilot's price for refusing a place on the ground. When his name appeared on a list of those bound for Korea he was totally thrilled. But en route he was pulled from a flight in Tokyo, held overnight with no explanation except that his orders were changed, then put on a plane to a place called Saigon. It was not until he met Rankin and Major McCall that it began to make sense, and not until the flight up the beautiful coast that he stopped being angry about missing Korea.

From below came the rumble and rasp of morning-thick voices, prompting a shake of his head. Sperek and McCall had still been going strong beyond midnight when Cody had left them, sick of the stories of war, sick of the strangeness of Sperek. The wizened little man, spooky enough at the Café Ho Tay, was doubly so in the confines of the house. Sperek had done most of the talking until McCall's memory was loosened by beer. The stories were as different as the men. McCall was a big guy, thick arms and big shoulders, and looked like what he was. Sperek required more time to assess. His hands were large, and the arms, though shrunken, were stringy and hard. The major told of people he knew, brave or foolish things they had done, time he had spent in the hospital, and amusing anecdotes. Sperek spoke of personal war, and not somebody else's: gutted men, macheted heads, bloody, terrible, simply told, stories spanning eleven years of war, five nations, too much to expect anyone to survive. Cody had been raised among famous liars and knew all the signs, but with Sperek's unnerving darkness it was impossible to say. But whenever the man was silent his eyes became calm, completely apart from the desperate face, causing Cody to wonder if the darkness was no more than a leftover visage, the ribboned reward of a lifetime war.

The stories revealed a common beginning—a group called the Jeds that dropped in by threes behind German lines to organize and supply maquis in work begun by the British. When the Seventh Army finally came through and put them out of a job, McCall returned to a line outfit. But Sperek was too much the guerrilla to quit. He hardly noticed when the war ended, still doing the same work in different places, always paid—directly or otherwise—by the United States.

Feeling out of place with the two old paladins, Cody listened without interrupting, having long ago learned that old men did not want to hear from the young. They sat on the dining-room floor, legs outstreched on an oxblood rug, threadbare around a missing table. Fancy moldings, decorative plaster, an old cracked mirror built into the wall; decaying trappings of a better past. Sperek kept offering a basket of the old woman's bread, little loaves like those at the Café Ho Tay. "Want some?" he said. Cody always declined, refusing to eat anything that the man might have touched, trying to avoid staring at the swollen goiter. He stopped listening to the talk, and soon began to nod, dimly embarrassed that the need to sleep was simply one more difference between the men and the man-not-yet. He wondered how old he would be when life grew so dull that he no longer needed to sleep.

Shaking cobwebs, he went out through the kitchen to stand on the porch and stare at the black empty night. The sky was low with reflected light, but beyond the shape of Sperek's beat-up jeep the night was impenetrable darkness. He could just make out the pale letters painted the length of the vehicle in crude yellow strokes. Sperek had bought the jeep in Chiang Mai, and said that it came with its own story: twice captured by the Japs in the Philippines, twice recaptured, abandoned because of its battered condition, finally sold as surplus. Somehow it arrived on the mainland, where it acquired several Chinese characters inked along its dash. How it had arrived in Thailand nobody knew, but the yellow message along its flank, a tag apparently acquired in the Philippines, was well worn when Sperek bought the vehicle from a Japanese expatriate who owned a bar. The jeep badly needed painting, but nobody ever had the heart to obliterate the message: *"Help me, Maria, please help me."* Whatever it meant, the plea sounded sincere. Much of Hanoi had seen it and wondered.

He started to step out into the dark yard, but was suddenly racked with unexplained fear. He stood his ground to prove that nothing was wrong, but when he went inside he was fighting an urge to run. Afraid that his fear might be recognized by the old warriors, he wandered the house. It was the kind of place where you would expect to find Jack Sperek, a house where no one lived but someone sometimes stayed. The kitchen was a kerosene stove with two crusty burners, a rusty sink tilting from a filthy wall, a vacant pantry, a chipped steel table with a leg too short. The rest of the house was no better. Down a hall behind a blocked front door, a spider moved in quick electric jerks. A back room was empty, but the one in front was occupied by a couple of cots, a wooden trunk, and a locker. The shutters and windows were closed, and the air smelled of ashtrays, caked socks, and a sickly, unwashed man. Cody backed away as if someone were there. When he rejoined the others the talk had changed.

"Have you been there?" McCall was saying. He held a fresh beer toward Cody and said, "It'll keep you awake." Cody took the brown bottle, sat, and dutifully began to drink. He was wide awake from the trip outside, and he listened now with interest. The men were finally speaking of important things.

"Not for two years," Sperek said. "It's undefendable, a paddied valley, the only rice-growing region in a wide land of mountains. Important as a crossroads in the opium trade from Laos, the main commodity of the Viet Minh for buying weapons. Dien Bien Phu is eight miles from Laos, two hundred from here by air. A stream, airstrip, and village. Enough hills to make the French scatter their forces among several positions, all overlooked by mountains owned by the Viet Minh. The best road from here to there is so bad the Viets have a joke about it: From here to Na San the potholes are called chicken holes, but from Na San onward, another good hundred miles of mountains and jungle, they call them elephant holes. I've driven it, and that's right; you build road as you go."

"Do you think Navarre can make a difference?"

"Maybe he could, but he won't."

"Why's that?"

"Maybe he wants to lose." McCall just stared at him. "It's been a long war," Sperek continued. "Impossible to win. Could be that Navarre has acknowledged the obvious. And who knows, maybe that's why they sent him here. Anybody can see he's arranged a battle that can't be won. And Navarre knows that the United States will not save them because that might mean war with China. China can only be beaten with hydrogen bombs. Which brings in Russia. They have the same bomb, and it becomes a question of whether or not they would allow the buffer of China to fall. Old enemies or not, I expect they would come to China's aid. If nothing else, they would use it as a pretense to take the rest of Germany. Which brings in Great Britain. All it would take to remove them from the great nations is the delivery of just one Russian bomb. Plus they've got Hong Kong to think about. That's money, and money controls war. That means the Brits have a considerable stake in keeping U.S. participation nonnuclear. That can only be done by avoiding war with China, meaning that France will fall. The U.S. will make a big show of helping, and we'll spend a lot of money, but we won't make any real attempt to save them. But maybe that's not so bad. There's a lingering idea that we've done too much for too many years already."

"What do you think of our chances if we do come in?"

"All things equal, I'd rather be on the other side. If we come atomic like they're saying, sure we can do it, provided we don't start a world war. Otherwise, we don't have a hope in hell. The only chance would be to kill Ho Chi Minh *and* General Giap, and that's not likely to happen. And we won't be using the bomb. Besides the threat of Russia, every square inch of Tonkin except one tiny corner at Cao Bang drains right into the paddies of this delta. They may as well go ahead and bomb the entire country; everybody would be dead from radiation in a few months anyway. If we come conventional, it's a huge mistake. Guerrillas against conventional? I'll take the guerrillas. And now they've got good supplies. On top of that, there's no way a GI is going to want this place as much as he's got to want it to win. France can't do it, and they think it belongs to them. We've got nothing, just Korea to open some eyes."

"Is Ho's army in that good a shape?"

"They've got the French on the run. People who weren't taking sides are taking sides now."

"What about arms?"

"China's providing maybe half of what they need. With Korea ended, the gates are wide open. Same war, different land, different people dying. They want the white man off the continent. There's tons of stuff coming down from Kunming and Liuchou. Russia is getting increasingly in on the act, despite their problems with China. This has stopped being strictly a guerrilla war. The French themselves are the source of another quarter—stuff they leave on the battlefield—thirteen hundred tons at Lang Son alone. The only thing ever holding Ho back was a lack of equipment. He's got the method and the men, and now he's getting the gear."

"Some of the stuff at Lang Son was artillery, wasn't it?"

"Only about a dozen howitzers, but also four hundred fifty trucks, twelve hundred machine guns, eight thousand rifles, tons and tons of ammunition. The bitch of it is, it wasn't taken—the French simply walked off and left it. They *gave* it to the enemy, ignoring direct orders to destroy it."

"That's the exact opposite side of the country from Dien Bien Phu," McCall said. Sperek made no response. "What about the rest of their stuff, the other quarter, where're they coming by that?"

"Various places."

"The black market?" Again, Sperek did not reply. "I keep hearing that a lot of the weapons and ammo the Viet Minh use are of U.S. manufacture," McCall said.

"Captured here from the French, some of it captured in Korea and sent down from China."

"That's not the part I'm talking about."

Sperek was silent a moment, not looking at McCall. Then he shrugged. "People do whatever it takes to get by."

"Get by?"

Now Sperek met the major's eyes. "Just a little advice, Marsh— be careful about what questions you ask around here, and especially *who* you ask. People might get the wrong idea about why you're here."

McCall studied him a moment, then moved to safer ground. "So you think they're about to bite the dust."

Sperek was slow responding. "Real soon," he finally said.

"Think they'll fight to the end?"

"Sure do. This is the last hurrah, and they know it. You won't find an army with a greater fixation on dying with honor. These men, a lot of them just kids in those days, are paying the debts of Pétain in blood."

Cody had completely lost the thread. The major was wrong about the beer; it was all he could do to keep his eyes open. When he stood to make his excuses and head upstairs, he wobbled and reached for the wall. In the cracked mirror he saw Jack Sperek, no longer talking, just staring ahead with that same easy look that he noticed before. But now it was different, a reversal of vision, the way Sperek could see himself. Cody instantly knew that he had it all backward, that the reflection was real, and anything peaceful about Jack Sperek was mere illusion. Here was a man who could smile so softly as to cause you to question his leanings, and that was the way he would look one day when he came with an unseen knife and shoved it up under your ribs.

Sperek sensed the assessment, and his eyes found Cody's in the glass, yielding confirmation with a trace of a smile. "Here you go, kid," he said. "Take some bread with you—you're going to need it."

When he reached the top of the stairs Cody threw the two loaves spiraling far into the night. He crouched as the kitchen door came open and Sperek emerged to piss from the edge of the porch. "God help us if we ever run out of enemies," Sperek said to his jeep. Cody remained concealed, wondering how long it had been since Marsh McCall had really known the man Jack Sperek.

Major René Legère arrived in a new American jeep, its canvas top in place. The morning cool had become a moist heat like warm breath, an unpredictable haze which might have been clouds suspended above. The French major looked brisk in fresh khakis, a crimson beret set squarely on his head. He gave two quick taps on the horn, and was smiling when the men rounded the side of Sperek's house. "Good morning," he said. Whatever troubles he might have had yesterday seemed gone.

The Americans responded with only a mumble, Cody West feeling reserved in the company of majors, but McCall simply sick. He had begun the morning by vomiting in the sink. When Sperek called it a virus, or something from the Café Ho Tay, West had said without thinking, "Maybe it was the bread."

He climbed into the backseat with their bags while McCall sat in front, as green as the jeep. Legère was wearing a perfumed aftershave, and his hair gleamed with rose-scented oil. "Morning," McCall managed more firmly. The street was crowded with peasants, half riding bikes. Legère weaved a course, tapping at the horn. "Any word about the *Saraffin?*" McCall asked. Sweat beaded his face.

"Not much you will like," Legère said. "I received word just an hour ago they are still waiting for a slot. There was a delay, a labor dispute. We should know something by noon. In the meantime, we will go to Lam Du. I will introduce you to Captain Sarot. He will be your liaison with the French Air Force, help you coordinate the flying end of things."

"That'll be fine," McCall said, "but after that I need to go to Haiphong. I want to meet my men, make sure everything is ready when they get off that ship."

Legère smiled. "I understand your concern, but everything has been arranged. It would be a wasted trip. We will go tomorrow, and will arrive in plenty of time. Convoy space has already been allotted."

McCall was uncomfortable, having so little control. He was puzzled that René Legère, who ran the largest depot in Tonkin, had been assigned to nursemaid his outfit. But he conceded that it made as much sense as placing a major of paratroops in charge of a supply point in the first place. Or, for that matter, putting a worn-out foot soldier in charge of an aviation outfit.

"One thing I would like to mention," Legère said as they turned along the levee. "The French are a suspicious people. In Indochina they are paranoid as well. You might be treated rudely. For that, I apologize. We owe much to the United States. We need help but do not want it, and in truth we do not need too much. Others have a different opinion. Captain Sarot is one. He may later ask you to do more than just the training, to put your aircraft to maximum use. He is a good officer, but overly energetic. We are perfectly capable of fighting our own war, and I would hate for any of your men to be harmed. So, please, simply ignore his requests. No one will be offended."

They took a spiraling approach to a bridge which crossed the Red River. "Paul Doumer Bridge," Legère said proudly. "One thousand seven hundred sixty-one meters." Black beams angled overhead and hissed past the door. The men stared in silence. Erected near the turn of the century, the bridge was a feat of engineering, spanning a river that many said could not be spanned. When completed, detractors then said it would fall. Even as late as 1930, the renowned engineer Jean Roux de Flave published a piece from retirement proving with mathematical precision why the bridge must surely collapse. But to the consternation of only a few, Doumer Bridge endured while Jean Roux gave out and died. The roadway's only concession to years was a slight warpage between beams, giving a wavelike motion to the jeep. Instead of remarking on the structure's grandiosity, McCall hung his head out the side and heaved, then stared bleakly at the narrow channel. A bridge support was anchored on a long teardrop of sand between two streams, and alongside the city several barges were discharging gravel and sand. The river was deceptively placid. It was more than a mile between levees, and when the monsoon rains flowed down from China and most of the mountains of Tonkin to crest in late August, all the space would be filled by a flow even greater than the Nile in flood. The streets of Hanoi would then lie twenty feet below that crest, and people would stand along the rim and stare.

As the jeep left the basin, the land took on a recumbent mood as if every hill had eroded away and all the flowing streams were gone and nothing remained of earth but utter flatness. Diminishing lines of slender eucalyptus defined the miles. At the turnoff to Gia Lam Field they pulled over and stopped as a convoy emerged. "They are going to Ben Tai," Legère said, his face shadowed with sudden fatigue. He checked his watch as the trucks rolled past, belching black smoke, sending a shudder through the jeep. A half-track brought up the rear, and when it had clattered past, a veil of new dust lay over the jeep. Legère made the turn, crossed the railroad tracks, passed an African guard, then veered sharply right to a gravel road curving west and south of the field.

Gia Lam was Hanoi's civilian airport as well as a French airbase. With the recent escalation of the war the military aspect had gained dominance. The runway ran southeast into the prevailing winds, and on the northern side sat a civilian terminal, the hangars and quarters of the 5th French Air Force, and facilities employed by the CIA's proprietary airline, Civil Air Transport. Opposite lay a compound of French Army units—rear elements of artillery and mobile groups, a reserve paratroop battalion, two transportation outfits, and several support units—collectively named after the area's dominant feature, the supply depot commonly known as Lam Du. The vast yard of Logistics North lay at the end of Depot Road, served by a railway spur and by wide steel aprons and taxiways connecting to Gia Lam Field.

As the jeep drew parallel with the field, they were met by a pair of C-119s wobbling along the uneven taxiway, sides as broad and flat as the Flying Boxcar name suggested. The odor of burned fuel washed over them. The first aircraft paused at the end of the runway, then the gasping engine sounds rolled suddenly smooth, climbing to a rich melodic roar. The plane shuddered and began to move, and soon was hurtling along with a husky timbre. When the pilot finally raised the nose, the crates and webbing in the doorless hold tilted earthward, the vision trembling in the trailing fumes. Soon the next plane followed. The twin-tailed birds assembled, then turned westward on a course toward Laos.

"We've really got the Viet Minh on the run out west," Legère said. "It won't be much longer until we have Ho's head on a stick." The lips were smiling, but the eyes were increasingly frantic.

As they weaved around chuckholes on Depot Road, McCall's sickness was suddenly past. Gazing upon rows of paratroops' tents, the clutter of military junk, even the common stacks of bleached sandbags, his discomfort dissolved. This was the place he belonged. It had cost a marriage and maybe the life of his son, banishing delusion, leaving only a muscular dumbness where all things were felt and nothing was known—nothing except that this was where he belonged.

Legère's frown had deepened. Suddenly the tents and quarters were past, replaced on the left by a wide pierced-steel ramp where aircraft were parked, and on the right by a narrow field leading to the patterned berms of an ammo dump.

They slowed for a convoy unloading directly from the road to the ramp. Legère scowled terribly as he guided the jeep toward the gates of Lam Du while McCall stared ahead, amazed. Row upon row of equipment and crates lined a vast macadam field, lending a new perspective to Major Legère. The entire war in Tonkin, all but what went directly from Haiphong to Cat Bi Field, came through these gates—every bomb, bullet, truck, and tent stake. It was a lot of weight for one man, and more than justified the way Legère now looked.

"I'm curious," McCall said. "How does someone who wears the beret of a parachutist come to have a job such as yours?"

Legère smiled unhappily. "I had the misfortune to be assigned as temporary assistant, then the man in charge was killed." He stopped just short of the gates. "This will be your new home," he said, gazing ahead.

"Beg your pardon?"

Legère seemed to awaken. He looked beyond McCall. "There," he said, indicating the vacant field.

McCall could only stare. Colonel Smith had not said how his men would be housed, but he had hoped for the use of the empty tents of a unit now in the field or at Dien Bien Phu. His men would arrive with all equipment required, but setting up camp would cost them at least a week. "That'll be fine," he said. The field was a corner formed by Depot Road and another which led along the fence toward the ammo dump. On one side lay the tent city of the paratroop battalion, and on the other was Lam Du. The detachment would at all times be in view of Major Legère.

At a plywood building beyond the gates, Burd Rankin sat on a porch. He had gotten a haircut, and the clipped gray of his sideburns gleamed silver. He stood and saluted. "Good morning, sir," he said, then stepped down to help with the bags.

"You may leave your belongings here as long as you wish," said Legère. "They will not be disturbed." He opened the door of the office and looked inside. "I had hoped that Captain Sarot might have arrived. Perhaps he is taking a late breakfast." He paused at the top of the steps. "I am sorry, Major McCall, but I have a bit of business I must attend, after which I am yours for the morning. But let's make a quick attempt to locate Sarot."

McCall signaled the pilots to hold tight, but the men had not moved twenty paces when they heard an urgent vehicle honking for passage. Jack Sperek and his beat-up jeep burst from beyond the convoy, trailing dust and angry shouts. When he skidded to a halt he gave Legère a jubilant glance, then said to McCall, "Your boys are locked up in Haiphong jail."

The gendarmerie and jail commanded a wide meeting of streets at the head of the Boulevard of the Republic, a mass of square-cut stone oblivious to the mile of gray silt beneath its foundation. When they were parked, McCall jumped out, then waited for Sperek. The drive from Hanoi at the tail of a returning convoy had seemed endless, continually halting for passage on one-lane bridges over streams and canals. The trip had taken three hours, and McCall had smoked a pack of cigarettes. His tongue was burned, and he could smell the damp ashtray odor of his breath.

Sperek led the way through a side door, up a half flight of stairs, and down a hall to a room that connected the front offices with the cell row. The place smelled vaguely of ammonia. Guarding the administrative corridor was a heavy wooden door equipped with a gated port and a blue-clad gendarme with a black submachine gun. Opposite was another door with a barred window, and beyond that a hinged barrier of woven steel. Through the glass the men could see a long aisle of facing cells, a sunless place of flat bars and rivets, yellowed paint and rust. Beneath the door oozed odors of piss and vomit and mildew.

Behind a counter was a police sergeant with pendulous ears, sagging eyes sentenced to life. McCall addressed him in French. "My name is Major McCall of the 22d Training Detachment. I am here to pick up my men."

The sergeant glanced at Sperek, studying a wall map on the far side of the room, then turned to a lieutenant at a desk. When the officer approached the counter looking annoyed, the sergeant stepped aside and stared dully ahead. The lieutenant was a skinny little prick with purple lips and a penciled mustache. He composed his face. "I am afraid that will be impossible," he said. "Innocent people were injured by your crew. One lost some teeth, another's jaw is broken, one has a fractured skull. There will be considerable damages assessed and paid, but that process has not yet begun. I suggest you come back in two days."

"Your thugs are fortunate to be alive," McCall said. "There will be no money for damages, or for you. I am their commanding officer, and I accept responsibility for my men. We won't be hard to find." When the lieutenant seemed obstinate, McCall turned his dangerous eye and added, "I'm not leaving without them."

The sergeant's eyes grew wide, and he glanced at the gendarme at the door. The policeman spread his feet and flexed his hands upon his weapon, blinking alertly between McCall and Sperek, who chose that moment to turn and smile at the lieutenant. The lips went pale.

"Monsieur Sperek," he said, then looked apologetically at McCall. "But you are together. . . . " Without waiting for a response, he turned to the sergeant. "Release them immediately," he said, then he spun about and departed through the guarded door.

The sergeant gave McCall a weird, gleeful look, then stepped to the windowed door and swung it wide, drawing a cancerous belch into the room. McCall winced and caught his breath as the man lifted his keys. There was a metallic scrape and bump, then the flat bars groaned, brittle ricochets on concrete walls. Sudden fingers gripped the front of cells like mated leeches.

"Hold it," McCall said. The police sergeant raised his brows as the major motioned him back into the office and closed the wooden door. "Who do I have in there?" he asked.

"Two men. A master sergeant named Winslow, a corporal named Acres."

"Tell them I'll be outside."

"You find the odor offensive?"

"To the contrary. It brings back memories of Paris." The man's eyes bulged, his flabby jowls shuddered. "Do you have some soap?" McCall said. The brows came down and the eyes turned stubborn. Then Jack Sperek scratched an ear. The sergeant found a crude brown cake in a cabinet.

When they were again outside, the cell odors still wafting off McCall, Sperek said, "Get to you?"

McCall shook his head. "I've had better days, but I'd like to save what pride those men have left. Let's wait at the jeep." He lit a cigarette, and frowned at the burn.

Soon the men emerged, squinting and unsteady. When they spotted the jeep, McCall stepped forward, threw the soap, and pointed. A Vietnamese man with an untreated harelip was watering flowers near the front of the building. The two hurried over, took the hose from his hands, and turned it on one another. They scrubbed themselves from top to bottom, including their boots, to the considerable amusement of the gardener. When they were done, the men slung away the water, slicked down their hair, and straightened their sad fatigues to meet their commanding officer. The sergeant bent to tie a boot and to screen a whisper to the corporal. When they made their approach, McCall stepped out to meet them.

"First Sergeant Winslow and Corporal Acres reporting, *sir!*" the man growled, throwing a beefy salute. Winslow's upper lip was hugely swollen, one tooth broken off at an angle. An earlobe was ripped, and a trickle of fresh blood ran down his neck in a stream of water. One cheek was an ugly lump.

"At ease," McCall said, returning their salutes. Both shifted to parade rest. He had been watching them closely, particularly the first sergeant. If the man knew his business they would have a good outfit; if not, nothing McCall could do would ever make the 22d anything but a mob. Sergeant Winslow was a mature bull with a big head, big jaws, and a twisted nose, all with the certain solidity of a block of wood. Where his cap should have been was a pale stubbled field that had given up seeing the sun. He was self-conscious about his condition, ruffled as a wet bird, but the pride and essential righteousness were intact, leaving the impression that had he been naked before a crowd his composure would have been exactly the same.

"Where are the others?" McCall said.

"I don't know, sir. I hope they're with the aircraft."

"The officers?"

"Beats the hell out of me, sir."

McCall turned to Corporal Acres. "Go on to the jeep," he said. He led Winslow across the lawn. They stopped beneath a huge tree, its gray trunk drawn in supporting blades around its base. Rankin gave Acres a smoke and a light. "Just the basics," McCall said.

"We didn't start unloading until late yesterday, sir, but the officers were already gone."

"Gone?"

"All except a warrant named Dukemire. A Frenchman came out in a boat just after noon and got them—said they needed Lieutenant Atherton to fill out some papers, took the others along for the ride. It was getting dark by the time everything was offloaded. The Frogs had some kind of plan. They divided the gear to split us up, then started a fight and stole the jeeps." Winslow stared angrily at the ground, then back at McCall. "We did what we could, sir," he said.

"I can see that," McCall replied. It was plain enough that not all of Winslow's fights had yet been fought. "Let's get on down to the docks and see what's left."

"Yes, sir!"

They jammed into the jeep, Rankin and West yielding their short seat to the wet men, sitting instead in the tight space behind. The corporal, a dark-haired young man with strong bones and a built-in tan, sat smashed against the big sergeant, smiling like a blind date. They all braced to keep their skulls from bashing with the bumpy ride.

They drove south two blocks, then east and north toward the river. Soon the walls of warehouses closed in, then opened again as they reached the docks. "That way," Winslow said, aiming a thick finger. Sperek turned, squeezed into a space against a corrugated wall, and killed the engine. Above the heads of milling coolies they could see rotor blades angling against the sky. "Let me out of this son of a bitch," Winslow muttered. Acres hurried ahead, shoving anybody that got in his way.

They found Jim Kinney, Joe Whitney, and Billy Mano with the birds, all three wearing signs of battle. Kinney jumped up and said, "Hot dog!" when he saw Acres. Dried blood rimmed his nostrils. His relief became dread when he saw Winslow, then dissolved to hopelessness as he spotted the major. "The shit's fixing to hit the proverbial fan," he mumbled to Acres, then said in a louder voice, "Never thought I was going to see you guys again. You look like you've been partying." Two Acres grinned and grabbed Kinney in a one-armed hug. The others gathered around, men shaking hands as if they had won the fight. Whitney's right eye was nearly shut, and every now and then Mano would gently test his front teeth. Rankin and West began going over the birds.

"Where's Tooler?" said Winslow.

"With the gear, First Sergeant," Kinney said. "What's left of it."

"They take the guns?"

"Yeah." Kinney looked at the pavement. "All eight machine guns, all the rifles, all the ammunition. That and the jeeps. They didn't lay a hand on the birds." He looked up at the big sergeant. "We did all we could."

"Where are the officers?" said McCall.

Kinney pointed toward a warehouse wall where nothing could be seen but coolies and crates. "Back there somewhere, sir," he said. "All except Mr. Dukemire, and he's gone." He turned to Winslow with a grin. "We *did* fuck over some French fries," he said. "That dude you took out had nothing but a hole for teeth." Two Acres, Whitney, and Billy Mano joined him in a painful laugh.

"Hold it," said McCall. The laughter died. "Gone where?"

"Just gone, sir. Mr. Dukemire went after the jeeps and didn't come back. Then about an hour ago a French Army dude came by, asking questions. As soon as he found out about Mr. Dukemire, he took off."

"Who was he?"

Kinney shrugged. "A Frenchman in a jeep, sir."

McCall looked around. There was still no sign of the officers. "Will the birds fly?" he said.

"Yes, sir," Kinney said. "They're fueled and ready to go, soon as we spread them out a bit."

"Mr. Rankin," McCall said. Rankin was still checking the ships, peering here and there, testing things with his hands. Two birds away, Cody West was doing the same.

"Yes, sir?"

"Get two birds moved out and ready to go."

"Yes, sir."

Winslow headed toward the containers to locate Tooler while the others helped Rankin. They tilted a bird on its heels, lowered the dollies, and began to roll it into the open. McCall watched, then started grimly toward the warehouse. He found the men around the corner at the entrance of an alley, all three asleep on wooden pallets. When he shook the lieutenant, the bewildered man looked up, slapped at the one at his side, and scrambled to his feet. He snapped to attention and saluted.

"Lieutenant Atherton reporting, *sir!*" he said. His cap was in the dirt, and his eyes were red and confused. The others were still flat on their butts, blinking and staring. One brought up a hand in salute, looked around stupidly, and got to his feet.

"Get ready to fly," McCall said, then walked away. He found Winslow at the four containers, examining the damage.

"They knew right where the guns were, sir," Winslow said, his voice a low, quiet growl. "They only busted one lock."

The major frowned. "Have the men eaten?"

"Yes, sir. We brought a week's rations."

McCall walked toward the birds, waving for the pilots to assemble. Atherton was strutting around, hands on his hips, giving orders that nobody heard. The others who had been asleep were helping with the aircraft, working fast and not talking. When all had gathered before the major, he asked the two bluntly, "What are your names?"

"David Brantley, sir."

"Mr. Cowan, sir." Both looked away, but Cowan quickly turned back in plaintive apology.

"Okay, we've got more birds than pilots," McCall said. "Rankin, West, Cowan, Brantley—each of you fly one to Lam Du, double up, and come back. Mr. Rankin, Mr. West—you retrieve the last two birds. Sergeant Winslow, assign two men to guard the remaining aircraft, then they'll make the second flight. Lieutenant Atherton—"

"Yes, *sir!*"

"Lieutenant Atherton, stay here overnight and guard the containers. Ride in with the convoy, then report to me."

Atherton was stunned. The enlisted men exchanged quick glances. More than one wounded lip began to quiver. Kinney looked at the ground, took a breath, and said airily, "Better get to work." He strode around an aircraft, but was overcome with convulsions of squelched laughter. "Oh, God, it hurts," he said, holding his injured mouth when Two Acres joined him. They both roared, no longer caring who heard.

"Sir . . . " Atherton managed, but McCall had turned to Winslow.

"We'll ride with Jack Sperek," he said. "It's a long, rough trip, but it'll give you time to dry off. We can discuss some things." He was thinking it would also give him time to go over his meeting in Saigon with Colonel Smith, looking for anything he might have missed.

"Just what I had in mind, sir," said Winslow.

Burd Rankin pulled a sheet of paper from a shirt pocket and moved among the other pilots. "Here's the tower frequency and a sketch of the field," he said. "There's supposed to be an American on duty sometimes. If not, we'll circle low to the south and west along the river, then cut back. Just follow me." He looked up at Brantley and Cowan. "Do you guys have a company VHF frequency?"

McCall watched until he was sure that Rankin had it under control. Sperek was waiting in the jeep, smoking in silence. When McCall climbed in behind Winslow, Sperek said, "And you want to know why I never went back to the Army?"

They watched as the birds began to crank. The coolies jumped, formed a wall, and stared. Rankin was first up, and he hovered along the dock, chasing coolies to clear a short path. Then one by one the birds moved into position and took off, passing in front of a freighter before skimming the water and climbing west. Atherton stood forlorn and furious, then marched to the containers he had been assigned to guard.

Chapter Four

SOLO JACOBÉ PULLED to the curb, feeling triumphant. It was noon of the fourth day, and he had begun to believe that the missing American was now bobbing against a pier somewhere, being slowly dissected by crabs. But instead, the one named Dukemire appeared to be doing okay. Jacobé watched as he paused at a vegetable cart just off Saint-Etienne, making humble gestures and turning out his pockets. The vendor groused, but bent and dug through a basket, handed something over, then shooed him away with annoyed words. Dukemire bowed three times before continuing along the sidewalk.

Jacobé was amazed, suddenly excited, thinking that perhaps there was a chance after all. The American was obviously worn, but also surviving, and after four nights on the streets was making no attempt to escape his predicament. Dukemire gnawed at something green, moving slowly like a person with no place to go. He peered into windows, checked driveways, and explored every alley—all patiently and slyly so that anyone watching might believe he was only looking for food. But clearly he was searching for clues, and in the right part of town. Jacobé watched another minute, checked the man's route so that he might find him again, then drove quickly toward a Cam Street bar, at once cursing and blessing his luck.

He might have found the man sooner had he not been required to return to Hanoi Monday to secure the assignment. But it was desperately important. He decided on the simple truth, telling his commander that he wanted to protect the missing American so that the affair might quickly blow over. Because Sécurité Intérieure's agenda often worked at cross-purpose to other authorities, it seemed a safe approach. The object was to avoid controversy which might force the gendarmes to get off their butts and do the job they were being ordered and sometimes paid to neglect. Jacobé's interpretation was correct: His assignment to Haiphong was approved without discussion.

Traveling back and forth had given him time to think. He knew who had ordered the assault on the Americans—one of the same men who he hoped to someday crucify—and he knew that much more was involved than just simple theft. He was even pretty sure where the stolen jeeps could be found. He knew practically everything, yet there was nothing he could do besides allow events to take their course—unless he could somehow lead Dukemire to discover the missing jeeps, providing clues to be carried to Marsh McCall. That meant finding a way to keep the pilot alive.

The doors of the Meo Cai bar were open, letting in the salty air and a black-and-white cat to stalk among the tables, swishing its tail. The bar was empty, abandoned in the whorehouse morning of midday. The bartender stuck his head around a corner as Jacobé passed through, smiled and nodded in recognition, then went on with some unhurried task. The lieutenant pushed aside a length of cheap printed cloth, then stepped out to a roofless hallway between crowded rows of doors. When he knocked at one, a drape moved aside from a high window, and a moment later the door came partway open, revealing a sleepy and slender woman, naked and rubbing her face. Her hair was dark and softly tangled.

"Ah, Sah-ko-be-san," she said, pulling him inside. "Good morning."

"Hi, Kim." He glanced over her body before looking away, wondering why a woman without clothes should embarrass a fully dressed man.

"I glad you come see me," she said.

He looked around the cramped room, dim in the window's poor light. An army bunk, some narrow shelves, an unplumbed sink with

72

a bucket below. Nothing was more hopeless than a whorehouse by day.

"I need to hire a woman," he said.

"This the place." She began to brush her hair, inserting combs to hold it from her face.

"No, not like that," he said, embarrassed again. "I need an old woman. One who will work for not much money." When she paused with her hands in her hair, he could not avoid admiring her breasts. Then he saw the arched brow, and waved his hands. "No, something else. An old woman to do a simple job. Is there somebody you know?"

"Yes, I think so." She slipped a cotton shift over her head, making her look more like the simple peasant girl she was, and allowing him to relax. She led him outside, down the passage, and around a corner to a small courtyard where an old woman in a conic hat was squatting over a basket of clams, turning them and talking softly. She squinted up at their approach, her mouth a black void of betel stains. She glanced at the girl, then gave Jacobé a speculative look. Her eyes began to grin and her vacant mouth grew wide. "We call her Ba," said Kim.

He eyed the woman helplessly. There was so much to do. "Is she the only one?" he said.

"She better than she looks," the girl replied. "She do what you want." Then she laughed. "She do *anything* you want."

There was no time to be selective. He needed to keep Dukemire in the right area. He turned to Kim. "Can you help me with some instructions?" he said. "I don't think my Vietnamese is good enough to tell her everything."

"Yes," she replied. "I help." Then her voice changed. "You stay Haiphong tonight, Sah-ko-be-san?"

There she was again, the old woman with the bread, looking in his direction. Dukemire glanced at the sky, afraid he had waited too long to make it to the shelter before dark. With considerable reluctance, he started in her direction.

After his first night when he collapsed in a near-coma of fatigue and was robbed of everything, he had searched for adequate shelter, settling at last on a coffin-sized space behind a mountain of pallets.

For the past five nights he had slept there undisturbed, protected by a warehouse wall and a bit of overhanging roof. It was a tight spot, but no one could reach him while he slept, and he was near the docks, where he was sure that help would eventually come. He made a bed of splintered lumber and wrapped himself against the dank night air with a pasteboard blanket.

By day he wandered the streets as if trying to locate the jeeps. But all he was actually doing was waiting for someone to find him. When he was forced by hunger to beg food, he damned his dumb luck. Things had been this way for two years, fumbling everything he touched, never comprehending a situation until it was too late. "I should have said . . . I should have done . . . " These were the private lines of his life. Maybe it was only a phase he was passing through, but in the meantime everyone in the outfit thought he was a bumbling fool. He had no hope at all of finding the jeeps—he was sure they were long gone—but if whoever found *him* could say that he had still been looking, it could make all the difference. He would stay on the streets forever before letting them know he had failed.

Even then, he had been almost ready to give up when the old woman appeared. At first it was simply the small burst of energy which comes with any intruder, but when she arrived the next day he began to wonder. Today was the third, and there was no longer a question that the old woman—ugly beyond words, a black empty mouth at least forty feet deep—was either nuts or had a purpose. She always gave him a baguette, and always pointed in some new direction for him to go.

As he approached her now, thinking of Macbeth, she gave him the bread and commenced to squeal like a midnight radio. He bowed in thanks, but shook his head at the claw aimed down the street. "Tomorrow," he said. But when he turned to go, she grabbed him with surprising strength. The streets were crowded with people going home, and some were beginning to notice. "Okay, old lady. Okay," he said. He frowned in irritation and set immediately off, planning to circle the block. Soon he came to an alley slicing through the tall buildings, and made a quick turn. The block was unusually wide. Above was a fading slot of sky, but in the narrow canyon itself it was growing quite dark. He began to jog, focusing on the ground ahead to avoid trash and potholes.

Suddenly he skidded to a halt and stared. Dimly in the dust at his feet was the imprint of tires. Jeep tires. He checked behind him, wondering about the woman, then pulled his cap low, moving ahead past shadows and doors. At the center of the block he came to another passage, a wide intersecting alley lined with crates and storage sheds. At his feet, tracks turned in each direction. He followed the new path, but after only fifty yards or so the light gave out. He bent and kept going, straining to see the ground. When he straightened he knew he was in trouble; the alley was completely black. A dim strip of sky was still overhead, but even objects close at hand were no more than vague shapes. It was a mile to the shelter, and even if he could find his way out of the alley, he was still facing the black hazardous streets of the waterfront, not a risk he wanted to take. He moved slowly to his left, back into the blackest shadows, then squatted between some crates to chew the bread and contemplate a miserable night.

He was deep in thought—wondering if the jeeps really could still be there, and if the old woman had known—when he heard a sound down the alley. He moved forward and saw a weak glow. The passage opened ahead in a bay at the heart of the buildings, and reflected from the far wall came the nervous dance of a lamp. Dukemire quickly broke the bread into chunks and stuffed his pockets, then moved into the alley.

He had taken only a few steps—the light faintly brighter, the bay gradually opening ahead—when a jeep rounded the corner behind him, catching him in the headlights. He leaped toward a black shape of machinery, but to his surprise the jeep only sped past. Something metallic and heavy bounced to the ground as it rounded the corner, but the driver kept going. Soon the brakes screeched near the source of the light.

He sat thinking about what he should do, certain that he had been seen. But behind him was nothing but darkness. He waited, and when it seemed that no one was coming to investigate, he advanced slowly toward the light.

Soon he heard voices, and quickly after that could see around the corner. On one side of the bay was a long metal shed where the driver and a man with a lamp were speaking in French. Then, to his astonishment, Dukemire saw that beneath the shed on either side were the outlines of jeeps. When he moved into the open for a better view, his foot struck something hard, a section of pipe. He picked it up and kept moving until the angle was right and he could see the stenciled letters: 22D TR DET.

The men were laughing. The driver returned to his jeep and found a small bottle, which he gave to the guard. When he signaled farewell, Dukemire rushed for the shadows of the shed. An old automobile was there, flat on the ground with no wheels, and he hid as the jeep turned about. The driver shifted gears, but slowed as if checking the ground for the missing length of pipe. Dukemire's heart was pounding. He crouched deeper into the shadows, afraid that his footprints might show. Then to his huge relief, the driver merely dropped a gear and went on, departing the way he had come.

Dukemire was suddenly exhausted. He took several slow, deep breaths, trying to decide what to do. He could not believe his fantastic luck. *He had actually located the jeeps.* God, what a coup that would be! He imagined himself returning triumphant, doing what nobody else had been able to do. Cowan and Brantley would eat buckets of shit.

He leaned from the hulk of the car until he could see the silhouette of the guard a hundred feet away. He thought about what that man had put him through in the past week. At the same moment came something else—not a thought but a sensation—a wordless awareness of all that had changed, a coiled strength which told of how hard he had been fighting to simply stay on the streets. He held his eyes on the shape of the man, and felt the pipe in his hands. There was nothing in life that he could not do.

He began unlacing his boots.

McCall stared at a blank tablet, waiting for the coffee in his belly to percolate. It had been an exhausting week. Construction of the camp had cost them time, but seemed to satisfy French High Command in its desire to demonstrate that a U.S. presence was not required. Six French pilots, their first students, were to begin orientation today.

The 22d Training Detachment was now housed in tents—one each for officers and enlisted men, and another divided into private quarters for McCall and First Sergeant Winslow. A fourth served as Operations and, beyond a wall, a narrow gun-cleaning room. Major Legère had saved old crates in anticipation of their arrival, enough to provide the quarters with plywood floors over pallets, plywood walls to four feet, partitions inside, and door sections at either end. Winslow had brought tools, and he set the men to breaking panels, cleaning lumber, straightening and saving the precious nails. Several French paratroops came over to watch, but on the second day when a couple who were carpenters volunteered to help, the pace of things picked up. Everyone, with the sole exception of Private Tooler, had performed heroically. Other than Winslow's shouting occasional orders, there was no rank distinction in the effort. To Major Legère's obvious dismay, McCall had stripped to his T-shirt to head the sandbag detail.

The only real structure of the camp was the orderly room. McCall's office sat at one end while Winslow ran shop beyond an alcove where they made coffee. McCall had to smile when he thought of Colonel Smith and *his* office. The building resembled a quilt: spliced studs and spliced rafters, walls patched with crating that sometimes had traveled halfway around the world. Inside and out were old shipping stencils, giving the building the look of a well-traveled suitcase. Judging from one on the end of his shipping-crate desk, McCall's office had been furnished by Ou River Traders, Luang Prabang.

He made a face, hating the paperwork ahead. There were two things to write—a note to Colonel Smith about Atherton, and a report on the disappearance of Dukemire. Not a word had yet been heard of the young warrant officer who had disappeared in Haiphong. At Major Legère's insistence, the gendarmes had searched every quarter, but nothing had turned up. Dukemire had now been missing a week, and according to Winslow did not seem the type to survive even a single night on the waterfront. It was a troubling idea, but McCall had to admit that losing a man he had never seen did have a certain appeal: war most efficient—join up and disappear, no one to tell how bad it had been, no bloating body to be such trouble. With a shake of his head, he forced himself from the subject. The French Air Force captain, Philippe Sarot, was due to arrive with his pilots in less than an hour, and there was still much to be done.

He addressed the issue of Atherton first. The young officer, weary and needing a bath, had been shocked and confused by his dismissal. McCall explained more forcefully, then had Winslow drive the soldier around the field to await the next military flight to Saigon. Beyond dereliction of duty, there was the puzzling fact that Atherton was not a qualified instructor pilot. But neither was Dukemire. McCall decided to ignore that detail for now. He asked Colonel Smith for only a single replacement, one who was a rated instructor pilot and a commissioned officer.

It had been good to see the Old Man again, but as McCall thought over their meeting he could not avoid a feeling of concern. It was plain enough that the one he had so respected in Korea—his battalion commander in those first bitter months until wounds forced the colonel to a desk job—had bowed remarkably to the workings of age. Smith was not without fault, but he had certainly been better than most. Now it seemed that much of what McCall admired— the mental quickness, the ability to plan ten moves ahead—had suddenly disappeared. Combined with the opulent surroundings, fresh from the shabby streets of Saigon, the impact was almost physical.

"It's all I have with Elizabeth gone," Smith said in spontaneous defense of his rich retreat.

"Sorry, Ezra," McCall replied, noting that her photograph stood beneath a table lamp. He had not known the woman, but had heard the colonel speak of her enough to feel as if he did. McCall sat unrelaxed in a deep leather chair. "You came straight here from Seoul?"

"More than two years ago. Same job, though, still chasing the black market. After all the reports of corruption, Congress decided we needed somebody here to watch over things. It took a while in Korea, but I finally got the market there under control. The Korean King was never identified, but I was able to make him move much of his operation elsewhere. Now it's the same problem all over again." The colonel allowed himself a smile. "In honor of all I learned in Korea, I've dubbed this one the Prince—the Prince of Tonkin."

"Not the King?"

"No, I think the King is still around somewhere."

McCall was watching closely. Smith's wavy hair had gone totally white, the skin softer and thin. But the greatest change was in the eyes, revealing a man no longer so certain of his course. Smith squirmed beneath the inspection, the eyes flashing false brightness.

"But let's get to your job," he said. He stood and poured drinks from a crystal decanter, handed one to McCall, then resumed his place at the magnificent desk.

"You're to head a small training detachment," he said. "Aviation—teaching French pilots at Hanoi to fly some two-place helicopters we're moving down from Korea, primarily for medical evacuation. I realize you're not a pilot, but you are amply suited for the job. It'll only take a couple of months, three at the outside. The detachment is aboard ship right now in Haiphong, except for two men diverted here en route who will accompany you tomorrow. The main part of the detachment—the mother unit—will arrive here in a few days, but they'll be under a separate command. When you're done up north, your men will rejoin the mother unit, and you can return to your precious infantry."

The two shared a smile. "The next part of your assignment, Marsh, is more in line with your talents. The DA wants an assessment. . . . " He paused for effect. "They want an assessment, an opinion, of what kinds of problems we'll be facing if we decide to commit troops."

McCall was unprepared. "We're putting troops here?" he said. In view of the outcome of Korea, unless the rules had been revised, the prospect sounded insane.

"No decision has been made," said Smith, "but it's in the air, and DA wants to be ready. If the president starts asking questions, they want to have answers. This place is crawling with CIA, so Washington has its own source. But the Army is always the last to be asked, and by then it's no longer a question. They want to be ready this time."

"They knew Korea was coming, and nobody was ready for that."

"Congress wouldn't give us the money."

"You can't blame it all on them. Truman, maybe, but the Army is just as responsible. Nobody was trying to be ready. They sent thousands of men to slaughter, knowing that they weren't trained, they weren't equipped, and they were grossly undermanned—*knowing* that most would be killed."

Ezra Smith said nothing while his eyes spoke volumes.

"I'd feel precisely the same if Brad had never gone," McCall said more calmly. "What's going to happen is that in their rush to be ready, they'll contribute to the decision."

"Is that worse than not being prepared?" When McCall did not reply, Smith added, "These things swing back and forth, you know that." He paused again. "Do I need to get another man?"

"Nope. But they might not like what I have to say."

"They want it in writing, Marsh. Six weeks or less."

"Good enough," McCall said, aware that such a report, containing wrong answers, and in the wrong hands, could terminate a career.

The colonel seemed to have mentally left the room. When he remembered McCall, he spoke quickly to hide his discomfort. "While you're up there, Marsh, there's something I'd like you to pay attention to, something personal for me," he said. He took a hard pull on his drink. "I'd like you to keep your eyes open for a system, any form of organized corruption, in U.S. military aid. An awful lot of our stuff is reaching the battlefield on the wrong side. This is not an official assignment—it's just that I've had a hard time getting a grip on it up there, and it's beginning to look like I never will."

"What about Capperson?"

"The Capperson Mission was a waste. The French kept resisting any kind of inspection until Congress threatened to cut them off. So they brought in General Capperson for a look-see, showed him around with sirens and flags, then whisked his ass out of here. Maybe the general didn't like what he saw, but he liked the alternative— putting in U.S. troops—even less. In any case, he went back and reported that the French were doing a hell of a job and Congress should increase aid. Nothing changed. The French still won't co-operate in an accounting of where all the supplies and equipment go. They know they don't have to. France is shouting that they're fighting Communism on our behalf when in fact they're doing no such a damn thing. We are not in a position to refuse to give aid, but neither are we sure that it's not all going to be a waste.

"For my part, what it gets down to is that I've already fought all my battles. I'm due to retire, but the black market here is still going strong. There's nothing that could make me happier than to cremate some of those crooked bastards before I leave. Anything you could turn up would be a help."

"I'll keep my eyes open, Ezra. That's about all I can say. I've got more than an average interest in the subject."

"I knew you did, Marsh. That's just one of the reasons I wanted you up there. I thought that your other experience, combined with what happened in Korea, made you the perfect choice."

McCall turned his head at that. The colonel had always been good at assessing a man's motivation, then using it ruthlessly to accomplish the job. If that was the case here, he was walking a very thin line.

"I have to tell you that you're not the first man I've sent to look into this—the black market part, I mean. George Tunnell, a major, went to Hanoi a few months ago as an adviser. He was killed by a sniper—Viet Minh, apparently, at the edge of town. I'm not sure I believe that story, so watch your step. You probably know, but I'll mention it anyway: Eber Walloon of *Le Monde* is there. With everything that's going on right now, he might not even notice us. I may send something your way now and then, but critical business will be conducted strictly in person. I'll be flying up to see you occasionally for that purpose. The rest of the time, you're completely on your own. If you happen to step on some toes, I'll back you all the way. But be careful. I don't care what MacArthur *or* the song says, old soldiers *do* die."

They had gone downtown after that, enjoying a tropical evening in Saigon. They laughed and talked and drank, catching up on the old times and the whereabouts of friends. But more than once Ezra Smith seemed to slip away, his mind somewhere else or simply gone, leaving McCall to wonder if his old friend might have recently had a small stroke.

He had just sealed the envelope when Calvin Winslow came through the door. The sergeant's face was yellowish-green with recovering bruises. The swelling was gone, but he constantly licked at the broken tooth. "That peckerwood is headed this way, sir," he said.

McCall frowned and replied, "Be out in a minute." He was slowly learning Winslow. The sergeant was organized, seemed a good soldier, and was completely without insolence. But this courtesy did not always extend to other nationalities.

From out front came the rattle and rumble of a truck, worn brakes and voices, something being unloaded. When McCall opened the door he saw Major Legère looking unhappy but satisfied. "I have come to pay my debt," he said, squatting among a collection of rifles, machine guns, and cans of ammunition. His bright beret was beaded red with drizzle.

McCall's stomach was a sudden knot. After Legère misled him about the *Saraffin*, he had imagined several explanations ranging from the French major's being directly involved to his being simply misinformed, perhaps manipulated by those who carried out the plan. But Legère was too upset to have been a participant. McCall had initially been mad enough to murder someone, but staring now at the gear his feelings were changed. Somewhere out in the bush were French soldiers who truly needed these weapons. To his surprise, he saw the same awareness on Winslow's pathetic face.

Legère got to his feet. "I am at last able to do more than merely apologize for the treatment you received," he said. Eight machine guns stood leaning against the sandbags, and next to them were a dozen M-1 carbines, used but in good condition. Six Colt automatics with new holsters and web belts, plus a half-dozen ammo cans, sat to one side.

"We don't need half that ammunition," Winslow said.

"That's right," said McCall. "Just leave half, then we'll let you know if we need more."

"Thank you, but I would prefer that you kept it all. This replaces everything except the jeeps. I am still working on that. In the meantime, if you require transportation you are welcome to use mine. This is all I can do, and I want very much for this matter to be settled. Besides, you may eventually need every round, and I cannot guarantee that I can later provide it. I am humiliated by your treatment. This is all I can do."

"None of it was your fault."

"I am responsible. Now if you will excuse me, we are building two convoys this morning. Another that left before dawn is trying to reach Hoa Binh, but there has been no word. If you require anything else, please stop by. I will be on the yard for most of the day."

When he was gone, Winslow said, "I'll get the men started on the weapons, sir," then headed toward the flight line.

McCall had barely resumed his place at his desk when the door opened to Captain Sarot, an ugly but exuberant man in his thirties. His nose formed a beak between birdlike eyes a finger width apart.

Sarot had been a spotter pilot until his Cricket was caught between guns up on the Lo River, crippling him with a chunk of shrapnel behind one knee. Now he employed a cane and spent his time on the ground. What the man lacked in looks he made up with enthusiasm, tempered by the fact that he had permanently misplaced his toothbrush. McCall reached for a defensive cigarette.

"Good morning!" Sarot said.

"Morning," McCall replied, absorbing the robust tone. It was hard to speak to Sarot another way.

"A small problem this morning," Sarot said, smiling as if the situation were both hopeless and amusing. Allowing room for his damaged leg, he sat on a steel chair, glancing at McCall's pack of smokes before reaching for his own. Soon a cloud was jetting toward the rafters. "No pilots," he said, raising black brows and looking astonished. When McCall only stared, he continued. "There's trouble down at Nam Dinh. That and the usual thing to Dien Bien Phu. We were forced to put the men in the air. I am sorry. Every day is a new catastrophe. Perhaps we can try this tomorrow or some other day."

McCall still said nothing. He had almost expected something like this. Sarot looked around the office. "An interesting place you have," he said wryly. "I've been watching all week. Sorry I could not be any help. You have made great progress. I was out on your flight line just now, and your men have their helicopters looking very good. I wish I could get my own to work so hard. They want only to fly, then go to town and play with the girls." He made a helpless gesture, then became serious. "But today they are earning their pay. One has already been shot down, rescued, traded aircraft with a man who took a small bullet, and has now gone back out. They are running back and forth, returning to Lanessan with the wounded." The smile was still there, but the brows had collapsed.

"But this is not your problem, is it, Major McCall?" he said. No smile could help now, so he no longer tried. "So why am I here, you wonder," Sarot said. A thought overtook him, and he said more quietly, "Why am I here?" Then he continued. "You heard the convoy leave this morning before daylight? They are trying to reach Hoa Binh, and have made it now to somewhere near Luong Son. From there they must cross a small group of mountains guarding the Black River. The trip so far has been without serious event, only light sniping. But this often precedes an attack, to slow them down, and perhaps to signal those ahead.

"So, what I am asking," Sarot said, "is if you would consider the loan of two small helicopters, with pilots and perhaps gunners, for the purpose of observation until the convoy has crossed the pass. It has taken the trucks two hours to make it this far. The distance can be covered by your aircraft in a mere twenty minutes."

McCall was far ahead. He wondered how long this moment had been planned. What Sarot wanted, more than aerial observation, was the potential of quick medical evacuation in an attack. A twenty-minute flight might save a man who could not survive a torturous two-hour trip by truck. The decision was strictly McCall's—Colonel Smith had given him free rein—but flying other types of missions could only jeopardize their purpose in Hanoi. McCall felt for the plight of the soldiers, particularly the wounded, but those few who could be saved today might cost the lives of many more. Once his birds were made available, the French would never find time for their pilots to train.

"I can't help you, Captain," he said, angered by his forced position. Anything that happened to the convoy would now be deemed his fault. It was an adolescent approach to war that he had seen before, someone wanting a quick fix to a problem that was strictly long-term.

"You are doing this because of Major Legère?"

"I'm doing it because I have a job, and I refuse to jeopardize my men and aircraft on a diversion."

"Then you are in agreement with Major Legère. But I can at least understand your view. His, I never will. The convoys are constantly chopped to pieces. If I were not here, and did not have to see it every day, perhaps it would not seem so important."

"Get me some pilots to transition. The sooner that happens, the sooner you'll have more pilots and aircraft. Maybe we can help you later, I don't know. Right now we need to stick to the program."

"Never mind, Major," Sarot said. He stalked from the office on his cane, colliding with Winslow at the door. The first sergeant gave a look of distress, and fanned the air when Sarot was gone. When he saw McCall, he broke into a smile.

"I always think of those squid-eating Okinawans," he said. "A man learned to lunge quick, hold tight, and not spend too much time kissing." He opened the door. "I just came back to say that some of those weapons we got are brand-new, still coated with Cosmoline. The men are tickled pink."

"That's fine, First Sergeant," McCall said, dwelling on Sarot and the convoys. It could be a quick couple of months, or the weeks could be endless. "How is the work lining out?" he asked.

"Real good, sir," Winslow said, reading his thoughts. "The men have had a full week, but no one's complained but Tooler. They'll be till noon on the weapons, and there are still some men working on the flight line with the pilots. Should be in shape by midafternoon."

"Fine. Tell them that everybody who wants to can go to town this evening. All but Cowan and Brantley—I'll have Mr. Rankin tell them."

Winslow left the office excited. McCall listened as the sergeant rounded the building toward the containers and bellowed. "Awright, you flatdicks . . ." Then his voice dropped. Half a minute later there arose a loud cheer.

A diesel haze began to smudge the low green sky where the road came off the highway. Far down the tarmac in the assembly area stood a handful of men in fatigues. "Somebody's going out," Rankin said. He took a quick turn around Cody's helicopter, pointed vaguely toward the mast, and moved to the next bird.

With Lieutenant Atherton gone, Rankin had taken charge of the platoon without anyone being told, ruling as much by age and experience as actual rank. As soon as they had learned that morning that the French pilots would not be arriving, he had assigned the men the simple but tedious task of wiping down every part of the aircraft, conducting a thorough cleaning and simultaneous inspection.

Before the trucks had circled the field, four C-47 Dakotas taxied across the runway, their engines stumbling at idle. They formed a line, then pivoted together so that the last was first. The trucks moved across the tarmac, paused to discharge men, then left the

barking sergeants to shape groups from confusion. Top-heavy silhouettes, four centipedes of men, climbed slowly through the
hatches.

"Glad I'm not going where they are," said Mano. He stepped
down from a strut and checked his nails. He had gotten into some
grease, and he reached for a rag at his hip. Billy Mano was the only
enlisted man besides Tooler who had joined the detachment from
a different outfit. When the men paired up into pilot–crew chief
teams, Mano and Cody West had wound up together, a fact that
suited them both. Mano had grown up near Rio Grande City, only
two hundred miles from Cody's hometown, making them practically
next-door neighbors in that uncrowded land. Mano's family had been
east of the border since long before the Alamo, but he nonetheless
spoke with a slow and heavy accent, a musical slurring of words
that sounded lazy to those who did not know him. He was short
and wide and had perfect teeth, a natural mechanic, but worried
about his nails. "Dien Bien Phu," he said. He dipped the rag in
solvent and wiped his hands as the airplanes taxied away.

The Dakotas turned at the end of the runway, then each came
screaming past with a Dopplered roar, the landing gear folding away
like hands against a chest. They circled the field and assembled,
then headed directly west.

The name Dien Bien Phu had already grown to mean the war
itself. The valley, which had been abandoned to Viet Minh troops
in November 1952, had been reoccupied by a larger French force one
year later. When it became apparent to Ho Chi Minh that the French
intended a set-piece battle, the challenge was accepted. By the following March, preparations were almost complete. The thirteen
thousand troops at Dien Bien Phu were by then surrounded by fifty
thousand Viet Minh. On the thirteenth day of the month, at 1700
hours, the battle commenced, led by an artillery barrage of such
intensity as to make the French suddenly aware that they had drast-
ically underestimated the capabilities of their enemy. Now, two
weeks later, the battle was an everyday and every-night event, the
focus of all attention. For the French, after so many years of pursuing
a decisive engagement, there seemed great appeal in having a corner
of the map where they could point and know that the war was there,
and believe it was where it might end. For the Americans, no more
was known about Dien Bien Phu than about the war itself, but it

was the place where everyone agreed the future would be determined. The maps that they were issued did not reach that far.

Cody climbed up on the frame, rag in hand, to inspect the mast, and to gaze across the camp. There seemed a sense of permanence to the collection of tents and sheds beyond the road. Besides the quarters, Operations, and the orderly room, there was a screened shower, a wooden privy, and a bulletin board with sheltering roof. A defensive bunker had been dug and covered with layers of sandbags, while close to the road stood a new sign lettered in black: 22D TR DET, US ARMY, LAM DU, VIETNAM.

Beyond the tents were abandoned fields, the berms of the ammo dump, and the perimeter of Lam Du. Cody envisioned the way it all looked from the air—the city, the river, the paddies and green villages, the lines of blackened concrete bunkers embedded like warts. He had flown that morning a second time with Burd Rankin, and was still experiencing the glow. All week Rankin had driven the men relentlessly, giving checkrides by rotation while the work progressed. Then, this morning when it was found that they had some extra time, he had insisted on an additional short session with each pilot. The two others—mainly Brantley, whose bitching conveyed the sentiments of his quieter sidekick Cowan—seemed resentful because they had arrived from a working outfit. Cody, however, a new instructor fresh from Stateside training, and with a lower rank, had been glad to get the extra time in the air. Besides, he had been quick to see that Rankin was no ordinary pilot, an observation which meant a lot from a kid who had grown up with an airplane in his yard. Rankin flew the way most people breathed, without conscious thought—a style which those of less ability were forced to condemn, particularly in a by-the-numbers Army. But it was hard to blame his critics; the man was frightening to watch, moving so smoothly, so imperceptibly that it seemed he had a pact with the aircraft, a black act of magic that yielded no clues.

Their flight had been different from the others, Rankin perhaps recognizing something in Cody as well. Other than clearing for turns, the CW3 hardly spoke. When he broke traffic, he let the chopper descend, just topping the levee before sliding on down to the rice fields. Peasants jumped and shouted as they hurtled past, but Rankin did not smile or even seem to be playing. The aircraft moved like a swallow, taking its exercise—brushing the rice tops, slipping past staves of bamboo, practically flying through thatched shanties—all to the urgent, gentle sound of a heartbeat.

When they reached the banks of the river, the bird moved down to its natural limit, the water's roiling, muddy surface. The river was busy with the morning commerce—sampans, fishing boats, barges, and an occasional military gunboat. Rankin found a path, passing traffic like a hurtling speedboat, leaving a wake of bulging eyes, gaping mouths. On an open stretch he let the bird wet its feet the smallest fraction, throwing a trail of vapor that looked like smoke. He held it for a time, then climbed a foot and shot beneath the bridge. When they climbed to altitude, Cody could see the entire city with its trees and many lakes, the curving river coming down from China, blue-white mountains to the north. South and east were paddies and lumpy hamlets, meandering streams and levees, all fading in a horizonless haze.

Then Rankin slowed the bird over the practice field along the pcrimeter and performed a zero-airspeed autorotation from five hundred feet, a maneuver that Cody had heard about, but never believed could be done. Rankin made it look simple. "Don't ever try that," he said as he gave Cody the controls. "I just wanted you to know what's possible."

Cody smiled now as he gazed along the row of aircraft, happy to be where he was. The OH-13s were ugly enough—he could see that sometimes when his eyes first fell upon them—squat and olive like insects, embryonic and incomplete with bulbous heads, skeletal tails, skinny wings that whirred in near-invisibility. But it also seemed that the helicopters looked precisely as they should. It was one of man's unwritten laws: Nothing that flies looks funny.

Beyond the last aircraft, Private Tooler was standing slouched, doing nothing, his buckle horizontal beneath a flaccid gut. Rankin passed without looking, then headed back up the line. Following him now was Roy Cowan, head down, turning to glare at each bird as if it might soon betray him. The 22d had been outfitted from the storage yard near Seoul known as the Bonepile, and it had fallen to Cowan, along with Whitney, Kinney, and Two Acres, to pick out six good birds from the shrapneled, worn-out hundreds. There had been no time to do more than read the logs, install new batteries and fluids, and give each craft a thirty-minute flight. Cowan was a competent instructor pilot, but hated being the one responsible for so much. He had seemed to feel better when Rankin initially inspected each bird, but quickly began to worry that something might have been missed. Each evening when the sun was gone and the blurry drapes of distance had turned purple, he put a clear lens in his flashlight and went out to examine the birds. It was better at night, he said, because a light in pure darkness could let a man see what he missed by day. The others brought their chairs outside and talked before the tents at night so that Cowan would not have to be alone.

Rankin completed his walkaround, returning to his own aircraft, which Two Acres was putting back together. As soon as the flight with Cody had ended, he had set to work with Acres, pulling the seat and floor panels, checking the linkage for each control, greasing fittings and testing for worn bearings. Nothing was found out of order, but Rankin wanted to *know*. It seemed a hobby of his, taking his aircraft apart.

Slowly the men wrapped up their work, then a migration began. Brantley was first, joined quickly by Tooler and Kinney, Joe Whitney and Cowan. Cody West and Billy Mano were almost ready when they passed. The group assembled near Rankin's bird just as a pair of B-26 bombers pulled away from the rearming point with fresh loads.

"Finished for the day?" Rankin said, snapping a seat cushion into place.

Nobody replied, then Tooler mumbled, "Yeah, we're done."

"We'd like to be," said Kinney. "Sergeant Winslow said we're getting the afternoon off to go to town."

Rankin looked at the group as if they had lost their minds. "Do you believe that crap?" he said.

The men looked at one another. "Yes, sir," said Sergeant Whitney. "We sure do."

The bombers taxied past, tires pooched, the pierced-steel surface popping and screeching beneath the load. One of the pilots gave a casual wave, and everyone but Tooler responded.

Brantley, who seemed to have had something stuck in his craw all morning, stepped forward with a deep frown. "Well, if you won't tell us about that, maybe you can tell us something about what we're doing here," he said.

Rankin was wiping down the instrument panel. He finished, then turned to silently face the CW2.

"Most of us came here volunteer," said Brantley. "All we were told was that we'd be training some Frenchmen to fly our birds, then we'd go somewhere else. That sounded fine at the time, but a couple of things aren't adding up." Bit by bit, those unfamiliar with Brantley were learning why Cowan simply called him Bitch.

Rankin wiped his hands and sat on a strut. "What doesn't add up?" he said.

"The machine guns, for one," said Brantley, getting nods of support. "First, we bring them over here, supposedly to give to the Frenchies. Then they steal 'em from us, and all hell breaks loose. So this French major in supply jumps through his ass. Now we've got guns and plenty of ammunition. But why?"

"We also brought stretcher rigs for the birds," Cowan said mildly. "Two apiece. Are these for the French, or are we here to use them?"

"And if we're flying medical evac," Brantley continued, "what do we need machine guns for? And if we're flying combat, why didn't anybody tell us? And why didn't they send more people? And if we came here as instructors, then why were all the pilots not IPs? And are we going to get replacements for those two men? And why were we told we'd be stationed in Saigon, but here we are in Hanoi? And how come we can't write letters home? The list goes on and on. We don't know *anything*, not the truth. Just that age-old Army mushroom method—keep 'em in the dark and feed 'em shit. I, for one, would appreciate some light."

"We're not complaining," Cowan said quickly. "We'd just like to know what's going on."

The first of the bombers roared past, and all the men turned to watch as the other followed, blasting off to their unseen war.

"You know exactly as much as I do," Rankin said. "But there's nothing to get worked up about. You don't want to be here, see the major. He'll trade you for somebody who does. I figure the reason we don't know much is that *he* doesn't know much. I also think that after we get some people trained we stand a reasonable chance of doing some evacuation, maybe more, depending on how bad it gets. But like you said, this is volunteer. You don't want to go out, I don't think anybody will make you. This is not our war, but that's not always the determining factor. We're in the environment, and anything can happen. All I can say is be patient, do what needs to be done, or pack your butt out." When Brantley flushed at the reprimand, Rankin added, "That's all I've got." He lifted a small ammo can filled with tools. "As far as town is concerned, it's my understanding that we have the afternoon off, everyone except two men, and they know who they are." He leveled gray eyes on Brantley.

A De Havilland Beaver landed, and two Bird Dogs took off. Then the sounds of aircraft were replaced by the drone and groan of diesel trucks, the returning remnants of the morning convoy. The men all turned to stare. "*Jesús Cristo*," Mano whispered. The trucks came slowly, painfully—windows shattered, tires and tops in rags, fist-sized holes in heavy steel. Only four had made it. The drivers stared in bleak accusation.

"Looks like the war is coming home," said Kinney.

Arriving convoys ordinarily turned along the fence, entering Lam Du far down at a side gate before driving up the center of the yard. But this one went straight ahead. The door of Legère's office opened, and Captain Sarot stepped out. He stood leaning on his cane, looking at each man that passed. When they were gone he turned and faced the orderly room of the 22d, where Marsh McCall now stood alone. Sarot threw a sharp salute, then disappeared inside.

The men on the flight line watched the scene in silence before starting across the road. Cowan was the first to see the approaching jeep, and he raised a hand like halting a patrol. "Son of a bitch," he muttered as if seeing a ghost. He looked around at the others. "Dukemire made it."

Chapter Five

FRESH AIR AND RUBBING lint balls from between his toes felt so good that he forgot all about removing his other boot. He used his pocketknife to scrape a dead callus, then to trim his nails. The sun had sunken enough to be strangled by haze, leaving the tent comfortably cool. Burd Rankin walked in, letting the plywood door slam. "Kid, you going to town?" he said as if Cowan were not there.

"Sure, when I get cleaned up."

"Better get it in gear if you're going with us. We've got the jeep." He walked into his partitioned space.

"Got time for a shower?"

"Haul ass."

While Rankin changed shirts, Cody lunged into action, ripping at laces, slinging sweaty clothes, then slowing when he remembered Cowan. Brantley had gone somewhere to sulk, but Cowan had merely stripped to his skivvies and stretched on his bunk, staring thoughtfully at the roof of the tent. Cody wrapped a towel around his hips, grabbed his soap, and went quickly down the corridor.

"How do you suppose he did it?" Cowan asked. Unlike Brantley, he was unconcerned about not going to town, but the return of Dukemire had him baffled. Cowan had never said so, but his

93

opinion—expressed by Brantley—had clearly been that Dukemire was dead. He had witnessed a resurrection.

"I don't know," Cody said. "But I didn't know him."

No one but the major had yet spoken with Dukemire. They were still holed up in the office after sending for food from the mess hall. Dukemire was apparently okay, just hungry.

"I don't see how he could have possibly done it."

Cody shrugged and hurried to the shower, a roofless structure served by a metal tank on a tall dirt berm. When he returned, he brushed his teeth in a cup, dabbed on deodorant, combed his short hair, and was dressed in three minutes. He had just tucked the strings into the tops of his boots when he heard the jeep.

Sergeant Winslow was behind the wheel, massive and out of place as a man on a tricycle. The sun was about to go down, but bright for the first time all day, sliding a deep orange glow across the flat land, turning Winslow's face to bruised fruit. He was rather dolled up for a first sergeant, his burr bright with fresh Wildroot. He seemed to have romance in mind. He polished the broken tooth with his tongue.

When Cody climbed in back, Winslow's feet found the pedals. They stopped for traffic on Depot Road, a pair of small trucks departing Lam Du, then Major Legère in his jeep. When he nodded stiffly, Rankin loosely lifted a hand.

"Must have a villa in town," Winslow said. Legère wore the same weary khakis he had been in all day. Even his beret looked tired.

Beyond Legère and the flight line, four B-26s were parked in a row, taking on bombs in the rearming area. Early morning was normally the busier time, but since midday the aircraft had been running constantly between Lam Du and the western mountains. The men had grown accustomed to the noise at night, sleeping through the crashing commotion.

Winslow waited for the dust to settle, then followed the French major. He drove in irritating spurts as if he enjoyed the sound of the motor. When they reached the highway, Legère looked back, then stomped the gas and pulled away. He passed a shuttle bus and disappeared.

"Been a busy week," Rankin said.

"That it has, sir. But you lucked out. Nothing has been as bad, not even Haiphong, as it was on that damned tub, waiting for a rivet to pop, a big wind, a sand spit, or just a hellacious shark with a taste for rust. I rode ship eight times in the Pacific, and nothing has changed. Water you can't even swim, stupid at the rail in somebody's periscope. Sailors have got to be dumber than shit."

Cody West absorbed the proclamation in silence, uncomfortable with the older men, wishing now that Cowan, or even Brantley, could have come along. No one had said where they were going. He sat back and watched the scenery, smelling hair oil and dust, a green leaf on a very old wind. He decided to watch Rankin, keep his mouth shut, and see what developed.

When they crossed the long bridge the sun was down. Low in the northern distance stood purple-pink fins of mountains. Along both sides of the bridge were peasants leaving the city, trousers gilded by the sky, the river below moving molten between dark shores. Up ahead the streetlamps flashed in progressive strings, and evening was suddenly night. The jeep dropped down from the levee, down into the city along a curving street.

Winslow seemed to know the way. He drove with confidence, dodging bicycles and babies and old men, cyclos and Lambrettas, like an old Hanoi hand. He had startled the enlisted men that afternoon by chauffeuring them across the river in two trips, dropping them wherever they pleased. The move was not so magnanimous as it seemed, giving him an excuse to learn the city. He circled Little Lake, then cut straight through the central business district on a street with four names.

"Thought you fellows might like to look around," he said. Rankin glanced over his shoulder at Cody. They crossed a wide plaza where a grand opera house gazed down, drove past the customs house and a school of archaeology, then turned south below the levee toward Lanessan Hospital. They went west to another lake, then north and west again. Rankin watched but said nothing. Cody watched them both.

At last Winslow stopped at a cyclo stand, a tremendous sandalwood tree surrounded by writhing roots and dirt. It was now pitch-dark in the city, but a faraway lamp provided a moon. The drivers dozed in their battered machines beneath the tree, colorless and limp as old rags.

"So much for the tour," said Winslow. He yanked the emergency brake, put the jeep into neutral, and stepped out. Rankin moved across without a word, motioning Cody forward. Winslow gave a clumsy little laugh. "Think I'll walk around a bit," he said. "See the city." Even in the dark his smile looked painful. When he drew in his stomach and looked around, one of the cyclo drivers raised his head like a sleepy hound. A sidewalk kitchen nearby was open for business: an old woman with a wooden red face squatting beside a blue-smoking grill, three meaty bones, four bottles of beer, and a dish of *nuóc mam*. "You men have a good time," Winslow said. "I'll find my own way back."

Rankin put the jeep into gear and immediately drove away. When Cody looked back, a cyclo was pedaling away, the hard knotted calves of the driver sharply carved in the lamplight.

Rankin turned twice, then stopped on a street full of shops: a haberdashery, a bakery, a soup kitchen, a store that sold spices and tree bark and candy. Each place was no more than ten feet wide, and above was another story or two in European style, shutters and balconies and curved wrought-iron rails. Gauzy drapes drew breath at the windows.

"What have you got planned, kid?"

"Oh, I don't know. Thought I'd look around a little," he said, doing just that. A man with suspenders and diminishing hair, watering pansies with a sprinkling can, glanced down without interest.

"You going with me?"

"I guess so, if that's okay."

"I'm not exactly sight-seeing."

Cody colored in spite of himself. "Well, of course not," he said. The balding man had returned inside, but the balcony doors were wide. When Rankin released the clutch, there came the faint chatter of dishes.

The streets of Hanoi were not easy, colliding at flat angles or wandering like cow paths, yielding a patternless quilt as if built at a bee, stubbornly sewn and forced to fit. Cody tried to keep track, but soon gave up. Even straighter routes changed names every block or so, tribute to some obscure person or place or circumstance.

They went down a dark lane, cut through a tunnel of bamboo with stone walls, and eventually emerged to a smear of pink neon. The street was lined with jeeps and automobiles, men in uniform and out. They turned into a gap between two clubs where a skinny

Vietnamese kid waved them toward a space. Rankin chained the wheel to a hanger bolt between the seats, then walked off as if he knew where he was going. Cody double-stepped to catch up.

The Coup de Feu was a shotgun club with tables down the middle, a bar on one side, and a bench stocked with girls. Above the door was a dull red light, but those inside were blue and cool, hidden by panels along the wall. At the back between two doors was a four-piece band and a small round dance floor. Rankin gave only a perfunctory glance at the girls, but Cody looked a little longer. They wore painted lips and painted eyes, some with hair straight and dark, others carefully coiffed in styles that might have been French. When he saw how young they were it gave him a twinge, his own private piece of masculine guilt. The girls were rigged in tight tops and short skirts, each with the leg near the door cocked over to display a portion of hip. Some smiled and tossed their heads. Others were bored.

Rankin bought them both beers, then searched the tables. All the customers were soldiers but one old civilian and two French sailors. "This your first time?" he said.

"Huh?"

"A place like this, a whorehouse. You seem to be doing lots of looking."

Cody shook his head. "No," he said, not exactly lying, but skirting the truth. "I guess there's a lot to see."

Rankin appraised the thighs and said, "Indeed." He sipped some beer. "I don't know if we'll be coming here again, or how often, but you might want to make use of the opportunity. Early's better than late."

Cody nodded but said nothing. He had known all afternoon where they would likely end up. There had been years enough to prepare: Whores were as much a part of the south Texas environment as rattlesnakes and prickly pear. It was taken for granted that sooner or later most young men partook, just as it was naturally assumed that by his age he already had.

"You want a girl?"

"Huh? No. Uh, not right now."

"Then you'd better stop looking."

It was too late. One who was thin, much taller than she appeared on the bench, had him already in her sights. She stalked him with catlike steps, never moving her eyes. Her blue-black hair was in a pageboy style, and she looked like a Chinese secretary. Cody glanced at Rankin, then she was there, dressed in a black leather bra, a leather scrap of a skirt, laces dangling beneath a neat navel. A doll's mouth was painted too wide, and her eyes were flecked with blue light. She was far and away too pretty to be a whore.

"'Ello, GI," she murmured, moving her brows. "You buy me drink?" She held up a long blood-red nail.

"Uh, no, thank you. I just came in here for a beer."

She cocked her head as if she did not believe him. "Maybe you change mind. W'at name you?"

"Cody," he said, feeling at once that he had given away a secret.

"My name Jo," she said.

"Nice to meet you. Jo." The words sounded stupid. He glanced around, feeling conspicuous. Then he realized the trap he was in. If he made her leave, he would seem less than a man, a fumbling adolescent; and if he bought her a drink and went with her to a room, everyone would see them go, and while he was with her they all would be mentally watching. Later, when the little deed was done, he would have to walk back into that crowded bar. He would no longer be friendly toward the girl, and she would return to her bench to wait for some man who had not been there. Cody would sit and have another beer before leaving, and maybe he would still be around when she went to the room again. By then he would know everything there ever was to know about whores, a lifetime vaccination like a tattoo or killing a man. He wished that they could just talk, and he could look at how pretty she was.

"You really—you really will do better talking to somebody else," he said firmly.

"No," she said, pouting her lips. Cody looked at Rankin for help. The CW3 only nodded, but that seemed to do it. The girl gave Cody a look that seemed to say "See you later," then carried her pretty hidebound butt to the bench. The other girls smiled with vicious satisfaction.

"Let's get a table," Rankin said. Cody bought fresh beers, then followed him to the edge of the dance floor. More men were arriving, and others moved up to fill adjacent tables. Cody looked around for the reason. To the right of the stage was a doorless *pissoir*, men plainly visible. Opposite was a beaded doorway giving a low glimpse of a narrow hall and the legs and bulging gut of a seated fat man.

The band had been playing a variety of tunes—German, Austrian, Polish, Algerian as well as French, and had even played an American song, Hank Williams's most enduring and a favorite of Cody's father, "Your Cheating Heart."

The guitarist took the microphone and made an announcement in French. A shout went up, and the girls smiled along the bench. The lights were quickly dimmed, a spotlight came on, and after an expectant few seconds a pulse of drums began. Then a naked woman burst between the beads and took the dance floor. Rankin lazily clapped his hands, drank some beer, and settled back in his chair.

She was tall and white, small at the waist, wide at the shoulders, wearing only silver sandals and a glittering blue string with a feathery fluff in back. She had a dizzy kind of beauty—drunken eyes, a small flat nose, ample lips, large teeth with space between. Honeybrown hair, tinged red and pinned with rhinestone combs, bounced in loose traces against her shoulders. But the only thing that Cody West saw was her ass. As she shuddered and spun and kicked, he kept forgetting to breathe. He tried to follow her other lines, but always returned to the enticing flare, the matching halves of important fruit. He recognized at once the apple of Eden, and that Adam was judged unfairly.

She paid more than average attention to Burd Rankin, then danced for Cody alone. He watched her butt and made his face placid, as if this happened all the time. But he lacked the control to take his eyes away for even a moment.

When the performance was over and she had taken her bows—deep in three directions, then to the band—she walked toward Cody in birdlike steps, wearing a superior smile. When she was inches away, and he could smell her, she turned and sat down on Burd Rankin. The CW3 grinned, casually cupping her hip with a practiced hand.

"Who is your young friend?" she said, nodding toward Cody. Her accent was part Spanish, part Oriental, but she had plainly known English for years. Her eyes were sleepy-lidded, and he could see the tip of her tongue. Sweat glistened on her breasts.

"His name is West," Rankin said. "My best pilot."

"But so young," she said.

Cody colored, embarrassed and unhappy. I'll show you young, he thought, but knew he didn't mean it.

"I'm sorry," she said, placing a hand on his knee, sending his heart toward his throat. "My name is Raphi."

He was angry now, hating the ways of women—them needing so little, so filled at birth with knowledge, while he needed so much and knew nothing at all. He noted the way Rankin's hand held the curve of her hip, not stroking or getting a feel the way he might have done, just resting there as if the outrageous ass were nothing. Then, with eyes so cruelly sympathetic, breasts surging like breakers, the naked woman leaned forward and asked ever so gently if he wanted to go someplace and fuck.

Cody's mouth moved like that of a fish thrown ashore.

"Everyone has a first time."

He stared, wondering if Rankin had heard. Suddenly all he wanted was out of there, away from this problem, his youth and inexperience. He was relieved when she drew back toward Rankin, brushing his chin with a breast before leaning to whisper in his ear. The hand shifted to her shoulder. Cody backed his chair around the table, and tried not to look.

"Maybe you should try the skinny one," Rankin said, nodding toward the bench.

"Is this what you did our first night here?"

"Precisely."

"Did you know her before?"

"Naw, we just met the other day."

"You act like old friends."

"Whores and soldiers. Raphi here is mostly Portuguese, one of those high-octane, all-weather models honed to perfection on the occupation army of the Philippines."

The woman smiled. "Occupation army? Yes? Well, I tell you, occupation army is no good for girls. Not much money. Men send money home to wives and girlfriends. Is better when somebody shoots at soldiers. Then soldiers *spend* money, buy what they need. Like this man here." She nodded toward Rankin. "He knows what money is for. So maybe you will be ready for me pretty soon when somebody shoots at you. Then you will be ready for me."

Cody looked toward the bench. "Aren't the other girls jealous of you?"

"Not too much. Many girls and many soldiers, but only one dancer. When I leave, all men who want bed with me find somebody else. Maybe they think it is me, I don't know, but I make girls much money."

"Say, kid," said Rankin. "We're gonna take a walk, see a man about a dog. If we don't come back, think you can find Lam Du? There's no rush. Take your time, get you a girl."

Cody glanced from Rankin to the woman, wishing he had more courage. He knew that if *he* had gone with Raphi, no one would see him again until tomorrow or maybe the next day. He held no better hope for Rankin. "I think I'll find a place to get something to eat," he said.

"Good idea," said Rankin. He looked relieved. "Food for the body, what a young man needs. Later it's companionship, that and conversation." He grinned when Raphi jabbed him with an elbow. "Turn right as you go out the door, there's a soup shop down a ways, got a yellow sign. You want to go back to Lam Du or anyplace else, just watch for a blue shuttle. They all get there sooner or later."

Raphi stood and stroked her butt as if straightening a skirt, then turned with long ostrich legs and stepped toward the door. Rankin was not far behind, languid and unimpressive, considerably less than a match for what he was willing to buy. Every man in the place saw them leave. The legs of the fat man moved, and the beads gave a chuckle.

Cody was instantly filled with terrible regret, suddenly certain that he could go boldly now with Raphi, even if some fool stood and shouted to the entire congregation, "Hey, look, everybody! That dumb kid is going to go fuck that beautiful woman!"

Without meaning to do so, he looked around for the Chinese girl. Only a few remained on the bench, but she was still there, starkly different from Raphi, but prettier. He caught a remembered glimpse of the Portuguese ass, how close it had been to his face, the very ass that Burd Rankin would soon be pounding to a lather. From out of the vision stepped a body, and the Chinese girl stood before him.

" 'Ello," she said with a pretty smile. She had applied new paint to her lips, but their form was still perfect. "You buy me drink now?" she said. As if on cue, a barmaid arrived.

"Sure," he said firmly, standing to pull out a chair. The girl nodded at the barmaid. When she sat down, her skirt barely covered the prize. The barmaid quickly returned with a vial much smaller than a shot glass, the price of two beers. When Cody paid, and the Chinese girl eyed his wallet, he remembered that Rankin kept a few bills in each pocket. He glanced around at the beaded curtain, and when he turned back to the girl her glass was empty. "You buy me another drink?" she said. The barmaid instantly appeared.

He stared at the empty thimble. "Not yet," he said.

She accepted his answer by gazing coolly across the room, her schoolgirl persona slipping. He drank some of his beer. The barmaid was still waiting, so he turned and said, "Go away." She glanced at the Chinese girl and left.

He looked around the bar, then at the girl. She did not seem so pretty anymore.

"I must have drink to sit at table," she said. "It is rule."

Girls at other tables were smiling and laughing, speaking charmingly with their men, and some were not so bad-looking. The girl raised a brow quite high. "Well?" she said. Darkening lines had begun to grow beneath her eyes, and her mouth was not so neat.

"Well, what?" he growled.

She stared at him. "Then let's go to the room," she said emphatically.

He looked her over carefully. The parts were generally the same as when he entered the bar—the lips, the eyes, the way the hair was done, the shape of her neck—but they no longer seemed to fit together so well. He could not explain it. "Just go on back to your bench," he said.

A place on her cheek began to twitch. She raised her brows, inclined her head, and the shapely lips slowly turned into a snarl. "You no want me? I the best. You funny boy?"

"Just go the hell away."

"Fuck you, United States *fuck!*" she screamed, lunging to her feet. "You no likee gull? We gottee big Chinee!" She pointed toward the beads. "Maybe you likee. W'at say you? Ehhh? You wantee, yes?"

People were staring, men smiling, women exchanging glances.

He did not know how much he had learned until he stood and left the bar, completely unembarrassed.

The street was choked with traffic now, men wandering across at angles, neon dust, belching smoke, competing music from the clubs. Surrounded by people, some of them perhaps from his own outfit, Cody felt very much alone, very much the foreign soldier who could not speak the language. He wished he had stayed at the tent, but there was also a feeling that what he was doing was somehow necessary. But it was lonely duty. Beyond a couple of clubs he saw a sign suspended from an iron tendril: *Pho.*

The place was plain and bright and vacant but for one sodden soldier, boots flat on the checkered floor, eating with careful strokes in search of a second chance. When he felt Cody's presence at the window, he raised bleary eyes in defense. A Vietnamese man in an apron stood beyond the counter with a plastered smile. A shuttle was making its way along the street, stopping every few feet. Cody stepped out and climbed aboard. "The Café Ho Tay," he said.

Soon they were in a squalid section of town, part slum, part rundown industrial, the glow of headlights revealing a dismal panorama. Humanity was everywhere, colorless as sparrows in a lifeless tree. People walked aimlessly down the dark streets, slumped against walls, curled and slept on sidewalks and in the throats of alleys. Thousands more filled doorways, hung from windows, stuffed the insides and even draped the rooftops of abandoned automobiles. They shuffled through filth at the curb, rode desperate bikes, pissed openly in the street, assuming the dimensions of lice. Cody thought of Winslow floating quietly along the dark pavement in his open cyclo, the driver's breath at his back, the rattle of chain, an exposed intruder going somewhere bright to rent the wonders of a girl. He thought about the angry whore.

They passed a place where five streets met beneath a tangle of electric wire. In the intersection sat an armored car with a mounted machine gun and two helmeted soldiers. From that point the streets were wider, the trees larger, and there were streetlamps at the corners. Soldiers walked in pairs with submachine guns, and the streets were empty.

Things began to look familiar. The bus turned a corner and stopped, and the driver opened the door without a word.

The Café Ho Tay was dimly lighted inside, but the gardens and grounds were bright as a cruise ship. European automobiles lined the drive and even the street out front. When Cody passed beneath the porte cochere he knew he had made a mistake. The evening was cool, and the glass doors were closed. Su Letei was standing beyond, wearing a dazzling blue dress which just touched the floor, close-fitting and lovely, slit between the breasts and hooked in a Chinese collar at the throat. On the lobes of her ears were diamonds. Through the windows he saw that the crowd was superbly dressed. It made him feel the sudden difference, the eternal apartness of soldiers and those who send them to war. An elderly couple appeared beside Su Letei, spoke amiably for a moment, then the doorman did his job. The gray man was a French officer, tall and groomed and excellent in a beribboned uniform. His wife was portly in red crepe, three loops of pearls in orbit of weary cleavage. They spotted Cody at once, and from the altitude of the porch gazed down in offended silence. The man muttered something to his wife, then led her by the elbow along the far edge of steps to a waiting Mercedes.

Cody gazed dumbly at his sorry fatigues, then toward the street, wondering how long he would have to wait for the next shuttle.

"Mr. West!"

He turned with embarrassment and dread to face Su Letei, impossibly lovely on the steps. He wanted to run and hide.

"Hello, Mr. West," she said, descending the steps. "It's so good to see you. Won't you please come inside?" Beneath her dress were the tips of silver shoes.

"I'm not exactly dressed," he said apologetically. He glanced around for the shuttle.

"You are a soldier, and you look like one. You are just fine." She lowered her voice. "The French like to dress up on weekends and pretend they are someplace else. I must always look nice for my guests. It has nothing to do with you. There are others here dressed as you are. Come, it is too cool to stand out here. I am happy you came. I have a small surprise." She touched his arm. "Please, come inside." She turned and went up the steps.

By then he would have gone with her anywhere. He forgot his fatigues, noting instead that her dress was split in back well above her knees.

"I hope you are hungry," she said, almost catching him looking.

"I'm starved."

"That's perfect. The cook has prepared some *bo xao hanh tay* that is exceptional. I am sure you will like it." She paused where the path divided between restaurant and bar. Several patrons observed him with disdain, all well dressed, but it no longer seemed so important. "If you prefer, I can seat you in the bar," she said. "We serve more food there than alcohol."

"Sure." He followed her toward the table. The old sailor was straddling a stool at the corner of the bar, speaking intently to a man wearing a canvas crush hat and a bulging, oversized coat. When the stranger turned to look at Cody, his eyes were bloody maps. Dirt was smudged on his arms and face. The sailor smiled and nodded, but kept talking.

Su Letei was gone only a minute when a waitress arrived with a tray of food. She arranged the table: a covered bowl of rice, a dish of thinly sliced meat marinated with lemon, wok-cooked with onions, garlic, and peppers; three small loaves of bread, butter, preserves, sliced carrots with cubes of tender bamboo, a steaming bowl of *pho*, a small ceramic pitcher of hot tea, and a tiny cup. The waitress seemed to be mostly French, but enough Vietnamese to darken her hair and eyes. She had done nothing to make herself pretty, but had her hair pinned on each side with cheap combs, loose strands framing an oval face. She seemed very serious about her work, moving quickly, hardly noticing her customer. When all was arranged, she straightened and spoke to him in French. Cody had been engrossed in watching her, and he stared blankly.

"Would you care for anything else?" she said in English.

"Uh, sure," he said. "Could I have a beer?" He did not want a beer, but it seemed he should ask for something.

"Hanoi beer?" she said.

"Yeah. I guess so."

He filled his plate from the several dishes, and began to eat. The meat was delicious, and he hardly noticed when the waitress returned, poured his beer, and departed. In a matter of minutes he had eaten everything but the plates, and had even drunk the tea, which was not very hot. He felt foolish with the little cup, and quickly set it down when the waitress returned. She surveyed the carnage in open astonishment.

"Do you always eat like that?" she said.

Cody frowned and looked at the table. Nothing was spilled, no crumbs scattered around, everything pretty much as it had been except without the food. "What's wrong with the way I eat?" he said.

"Nothing. But you did it so fast."

"I was hungry," he said, annoyed. "That's why I came here, to eat."

"You seem to have done just that," she said. "Would you care for anything else?"

He glanced around at the table, beginning to be irritated by her impertinent manner. "Yes," he said. "I would like another order of the meat and onions. And some rice to go with it, please."

She raised her chin, lowered her lids, and said, "Right away, sir." She sauntered away as Cody watched. He was no longer hungry, but he sure didn't like her attitude. She could just do her job and mind her own danged business, thank you very much, and he would eat as much or as fast as he chose. He wondered what the extra food would cost, and he mentally counted the bills in his wallet. But it was almost payday.

The girl quickly returned with the order. But this time, instead of separate dishes, the meat and onions were heaped over a mound of rice on a fresh plate. She moved several empty dishes aside, set the plate down before him, then stepped back without a word. Cody looked at the pile of food. He could eat it all, but he would certainly be full when he finished. The girl was still waiting. "I don't need anything else," he said brusquely.

"Very good, sir," she said in a clipped British accent.

He began to eat, then realized that she had not moved. "I said that's all I need."

"I heard you, sir."

The "sir" was beginning to grate. He wasn't old enough to be a sir to anyone, but he chose to ignore it now because she was being an ass. "Then why are you still here?" he said.

"I wanted to watch you do it."

He thought of all sorts of ugly and stupid things to say. Then, because she deserved it, he looked her rudely up and down two times, at last returning to her face. She was not really bad-looking, he decided—or she wouldn't be if she tried to fix herself up—but she sure had an attitude. On impulse, he stood and pulled out a chair.

"Please be my guest," he said. Her chin came up again, but she sat on the chair, hands in her lap around a dishtowel. Cody began to eat. He wanted to impress her now, to show her the difference between a woman and a man, so he went about it with machinelike precision, chewing each bite exactly three times before gulping it down, instantly ready for the next approaching mouthful. He glanced at his plate to arrange food and check his progress, but the remainder of the time he kept his eyes on hers, a few feet away. It took no more than three minutes to clean the plate, but by then he had decided that her eyes were really very nice, even if she did have an attitude. But like his own indignation, that attitude seemed to have softened with the long meeting of eyes. When the plate was polished they both were smiling.

"You will be a big man someday," she said, glancing at his shoulders.

"Yes, I will," he said. "As long as I get enough to eat."

"I must get back to work," she said. The smile disappeared and a shield descended, a defense that was more than just work.

"My name is Cody."

"And mine is Moni'," she replied. Then she added his plate to the others and walked away, leaving him stunned. A moment later, Su Letei appeared at his table wearing a knowing smile.

"Why didn't you tell me?" he said quietly.

"I assumed you would know. I said I had a surprise."

"I was hungry. I guess I forgot."

"Please excuse me, but I have to return to the front. Have you enjoyed your meal?"

"Yes, I have," he said, glancing toward the kitchen.

Su Letei was gone only a moment when Moni' returned with a dish of custard sprinkled with nutmeg. "I just realized who you are," he said. "I saw you here one day before."

She frowned. "I don't remember seeing you."

He decided not to mention the balcony. "I was here for only a minute, the day I arrived." She was distant again, the way she had been at first. He had liked it better the brief moment when they were almost friends. "Your aunt said you live outside the city."

"Yes. I help her sometimes on weekends. She does not really need me here, but she worries that I will not learn everything she thinks I should know to be a woman. And she is very nice. So I come here sometimes, when I am not at the hospital or on the farm."

"Where is the farm?"

"Just off the highway between the river and Gia Lam. A white house with a red roof, a long drive with trees on both sides."

"Oh, yeah! I've seen it from the air. I remember the roof. So what else do you do besides work here or at the hospital, or stay on the farm?"

"That is it mostly. It takes up my time."

"You don't do anything for fun?"

"There is war here," she said gravely.

"Yeah, I know," he said, sensing a deepening return of her attitude. "It's why I'm here."

"What do you do?"

"I'm a helicopter pilot, an instructor. My detachment is teaching some of the French pilots to fly our aircraft."

"Will you be fighting?"

"No, nothing like that. We're just here for a little while. So what do you do on the farm?"

"I cook and take care of my father."

"Is he sick?"

"No. He is only alone." She had begun to look slightly annoyed at the continuing questions, and she glanced toward the kitchen. "I should get back to work," she said.

"I don't know yet what my schedule will be—we're just starting—but maybe sometime I could stop by your farm. I go right past it on the way to town. Maybe you could show me around."

"No," she said. "Don't ever do that. My father is very strange, and he drinks."

"I know about drinking fathers," he said.

"You don't understand."

"Better than you'll ever know."

"No, you don't! My father *shoots* at people. Ask Aunt Su." She looked around the restaurant. "Ask anybody here. He has a sign out front, and he sits on the porch with a rifle. He is really a very good shot, even when he is drinking. He shoots only to drive people away, but I know someday he is going to kill somebody, or someone will kill him. So don't ever come to the farm. Don't *ever* come see me."

Cody watched her face, trying to understand. Then he quietly made a young guess. "That keeps you from having to talk to anybody except in a public place," he said.

She looked startled, exposed. "That's a stupid thing to say. Why would I want anything like that?"

"I don't know. Just the way it looks."

"It's stupid. Now I must work. Do you want anything else?"

"No," he said quietly, studying her face. She would not look directly at him now. "Nothing else. It's been real nice talking to you."

She went away then. In a little while a Vietnamese waiter brought his check and carried away the custard dish. He waited a long time, but Moni' did not come out of the kitchen again.

Chapter Six

THE DAY BEGAN with a heavy dew that made it seem it had rained. At one end of the runway, above a clear space tall as a truck, a narrow band of fog moved slowly past, dividing in opposing eddies each time a plane zoomed through. Birds on the flight line were glazed and streaked with moisture, and beneath were puddles. Later a drying breeze came through with the warmth of day, leaving a bluish sky of Sunday promise.

Dukemire was still on his bunk when Cody got in from flying. A lean kid with freckled skin, dullish hair that spilled in front, he was dressed in fatigues and a T-shirt, reading a comic book by the light of the screen door. Since his return from Haiphong, he had not been out of the tent except to shower and to use the latrine. Cowan, trying to make amends for having misjudged him, had brought him early breakfast from the mess hall, then hung around waiting for Dukemire to shed some light on the mystery of his survival and how he had recaptured the jeep. Finally, Cowan gave up the vigil, accompanying Brantley to the flight line to mess with the birds. Both were completely perplexed, still talking about it when Cody left them with Rankin.

He had risen early that morning to work on the aircraft with

Billy Mano, then had changed his plans when he found that his crew chief had been assigned to duty in the orderly room. He had returned to the tent to find Dukemire awake and dressed on his bunk, blinking at the ceiling. They had visited for more than an hour before Rankin came in with word that the fog had moved, and that they might as well spend a little more time in the air. That had suited Cody just fine. Now he was back, and Dukemire had not moved.

"It's gonna be a great day," he said. Their cubicles were on opposing sides of the tent. "It was really nice out there, you should have seen it. The paddies were pale blue, and when you looked east the sun was coming off of 'em, lighting low clouds underneath, shining back down on the water. The other direction, everything was the purest green you've ever seen, like the world was new, and for a while you could see the mountains, still dark but beginning to shine at the edges. You've really got to get out and do some flying. It'll let you know where you are."

"I'll do it later," Dukemire said. "I'm real tired, more than I thought. But there's no rush. That CW3—Rankin?—he seems a little chapped that I'm not an instructor, like it's my fault."

"He's okay. It's just that not a lot of planning went into putting this outfit together."

"I already knew that," Dukemire said. He tossed the comic book on the floor. "I'll be glad when it's lunchtime."

"It might be already. I hear it's different on Sunday. I saw some guys headed that way. Why don't we go see?"

When they stepped outside, Private Tooler was walking past in a bigger hurry than usual. He saluted and said, "Good morning, sir." He had a roll of screen wire tucked beneath one arm.

"Where'd you get the wire?" Cody said. He was thinking about making a window in the wooden wall beside his bunk, then rolling the tent outside for more air.

"I traded for it, sir," Tooler said. He had colorless brows, loose damp lips, and eyes that lied whenever he smiled. He was smiling now.

"What'd you trade?" Dukemire said, squinting at the sunlight, sizing up Tooler.

"Oh, personal items, sir," he said. "I'm going around, seeing if anybody would like some wire for windows." He turned to Cody. "How about you, sir?"

"Sure!"

"How much do you need?"

"About two feet," he said.

"Fine." Tooler produced a knife, unrolled a portion, and cut it smoothly against the door. He handed it to Cody. "That'll be two dollars, sir," he said.

"Two dollars?"

"Yes, sir. A dollar a foot."

Cody frowned, but reached for his wallet. He had just been paid not thirty minutes ago, four days early by a courier from Saigon who brought the payroll and a packet of papers to the major. Tooler had wasted no time.

"That's too much," Dukemire said. "Let him keep it."

But Cody produced the bills, paying for experience. With enough time and cash, he reasoned, he could someday buy himself some brains. He pitched the wire into the tent.

"You should have just beat him over the head and—" Dukemire stopped himself in midsentence, saying nothing else as they approached the mess hall.

Because they were a small detachment, the 22d was forced to rely on other outfits for support. Elements of the U.S. Air Force— mechanics who had arrived a few weeks ago—were housed directly across the airfield, but they were more than a mile distant along the road. It was much easier for the adjacent French paratroops, the 1st Colonials, to provide meals for the 22d, receiving extra rations as compensation.

The mess hall was a blue plywood building with a metal roof and a front of screened half-walls. As the men entered, they saw that things were indeed different on Sunday. Although lunchtime was not far away, breakfast was still being served. A buffet had been arranged along a table draped in cloth. The cooks and servers wore hats and clean aprons, and stood proudly, suddenly courteous, receiving their compliments. Some had even bathed.

Dukemire and West signed for their meals, then joined a casual line, loading their plates with croissants, fluffy brioche, string bread, and fresh fruit. When they looked for a table, a French lieutenant who had helped with the construction waved them over. Cody was glad to see him; he wanted to ask a favor.

"Good morning," the Frenchman said, speaking the unfamiliar

113

words with care. He was short and young and had blond hair.

"*Bonjour,*" Cody replied and grinned. He turned to Dukemire, already seated and eating. "His name is Marcel, but we call him Pepe the Paratroop. He's a lieutenant in First Company. These guys are reserves. They don't fight very often, but when they do they've had it. They even drop in at night. Can you imagine? Like the bombing crews who bailed out over Germany, all those steeples everywhere. I'll bet on the way down they were wishing like hell they'd leveled all the churches. Anyway, Pepe here got us some extra tools when we were setting up camp. He seems all right."

Dukemire looked up to verify the assessment, but he did not stop eating.

"I need to borrow a hammer and saw," Cody said to Pepe, enunciating his words and using signs. Pepe nodded and seemed to indicate it would be no problem. He was well ahead of the others with his meal, but went for seconds. Cody lowered his voice. "This is going to be really weird," he said. "They sent us here without teaching us French, and most of the pilots we're supposed to transition don't speak English. How do you use sign language and fly a helicopter at the same time? Should be fun."

Pepe returned, bringing them each a fresh cinnamon roll, fragrant and still steaming from the oven. It created a small stampede.

When they left the mess hall, Pepe led them through his company area to a supply shack that had long tables beneath an adjacent shed. He opened a lock on a flimsy hasp, then showed them to the tools. Cody did not really need anything—he could have gotten tools from Winslow—but he wanted to show Dukemire around. "There they are," he said. Lining each wall were rows of parachutes, all neatly hung and ready to go. Dukemire shook his head slowly. Pepe said something in French, then had himself a laugh.

"Not me, buddy," Dukemire said. "No way."

Pepe made a tight, rapid orbit with a finger, then shook the same finger from side to side, clearly stating that as far as he was concerned, riding in a helicopter was more dangerous than jumping out of one.

They watched him lock the door, then motioned that they would return the tools in two hours. Approaching the tent, Dukemire veered off course to climb the berm which supported the water tank. He seemed to be trying to get his bearings. Cody followed, turning immediately northwest to locate Moni's house. It was hidden by trees, but when the wind came in gusts he could see a bit of red roof. He had watched for the farm last night from the shuttle, seeing only a chain, a glimpse of a tree-lined drive, and a sign that he could not read. He had seen it again this morning with Rankin, just some color through the trees.

Throughout the morning he had thought about Moni', not with ideas of romance—he would not be here that long, and besides, there was something deeply unfriendly about her—but because she seemed to have a strange life. He wondered about her father. The man she described seemed a lot like his own father. But apart from that, he thought Moni' was about the loneliest person he had ever seen.

"Have you ever wondered what is going to happen here?" Dukemire said. He was surveying the camp, the compound of Lam Du, the airfield and adjacent units with a strange expression.

"Why would I wonder something like that?"

"Just curious."

Cody frowned and looked again in the direction of Moni's farm. Dukemire did not seem the way he had been described. He was soft on the surface, apparently indecisive, but the eyes did not always agree. There was a fearful determination there as if he understood his own weakness, hated it, and planned to beat it in battle. But despite how he looked, there was no denying that he had spent a week on the loose in Haiphong, then surfaced intact with a jeep.

"So what did you do in the week you were gone?"

"I don't know," said Dukemire. "The first night is mostly blank. I slept somewhere. Then I just wandered around, looking for jeeps."

"You see any cops—gendarmes? They were supposed to be looking for you."

"Sure, I saw some. They saw me."

"How did you eat? Did you buy food?"

"No. I got robbed the first night."

"What did you do?"

"People fed me."

"What people?"

"Just people. Vendors on the street. More as the days went by and they got used to seeing me. Then this one old woman started bringing me bread."

"So how'd you find the jeep?"

"Jeeps. I found two, by accident, really. I just kept walking, up and down, in all the places that looked right. Then one day I saw some tracks going into an alley."

"Okay. Now how did you get the jeep?"

Dukemire looked at Cody, then away. "I killed a man," he said.

There was stunned silence. "You killed a man?"

Dukemire nodded, staring straight ahead.

"Wait a minute. You *killed* a man? Does anybody know?"

"Not anybody here."

"Jesus Christ!" Cody shouted. It was finally hitting home. They were less than a hundred feet from the nearest tent. He lowered his voice, hissing fiercely. "Why the hell did you tell me?"

"You asked."

"The major asked, too. Did you tell him?"

"No. Just you. You seemed like somebody I could trust."

"You just met me a few hours ago, and now you're telling me you murdered a man, and that I'm someone you can trust? Are you totally out of your fucking mind?"

"I didn't murder anybody. I killed a thief, a guy that put his life on the line for something that wasn't his. He had what belonged to me, to my outfit. And I'd had a really bad week."

"A bad week? That's all it takes? God almighty!"

"Look, I'm not happy about it, and I sure didn't enjoy it. The man is dead, and he's off the hook. *I'm* the one that's left to walk around with the consequences. I almost wish he were still alive so I could kill him again for doing this to me, the sorry shit. I only told you because I thought it might help."

"I'm still not believing this," Cody said. He looked Dukemire over. He didn't look like he could kill a rabbit, let alone a grown man. "How'd you do it?"

Dukemire sighed and his mouth grew grim. "I found a piece of pipe," he said. "I took my boots off and sneaked up on him and beat his brains out."

Cody was numb, not sure what to do. "The guy I bunk next to," he said slowly, "just walks up and beats a gook's brains out. Then he wants to share the moment, and tells me. Terrific."

"He wasn't a gook."

Cody's jaw fell. "You killed a Frenchman?"

116

"He was white."

"I've never seen you before in my life."

"They let me get away."

He did not stop thinking about Dukemire until he passed the house with the red roof. It was midafternoon, and the blue skies of late morning were covered now with a high listless layer of clouds. The winds had died and the haze had returned, leaving a balmy afternoon, sliding toward Monday. There were only a half-dozen other men on the shuttle, all French, a few lisping their effeminate language. Cody stared out the window, breathing the odors of Vietnam, the dust and water and feces and food. There was too little time to do more than walk through a park and maybe get something to eat, but he wanted to be away from Dukemire, wanted time to decide what to do.

After the bombshell, they had spent a silent two hours breaking down crates, fashioning them into two sets of shelves. Cody studied Dukemire, watching his face and hands, hearing his words again. He thought about what it must have been like, doing the killing, and it made him shudder. A piece of iron pipe was a far cry from popping sunburned melons in the fields with a .22, pretending they were the heads of evil Japanese. Maybe he could have shot the man, he decided; he felt he needed that distance. In any case, he wasn't sure about Dukemire's story. The bit about the French letting him get away was surely hallucination, a part of his brain looking everywhere to spread the guilt. But it threw the entire story into question. Still, there was no denying the jeep, proof positive that something had happened during that week. There was also the consideration that for whatever reason, provided he was honest, Dukemire had decided that Cody was someone he could trust. He needed help and was asking for it the only way he could, asking someone to simply share the weighty load. Before they completed the shelves, Cody had decided on a solo trip to town.

When he signed out at the orderly room, Billy Mano, still on duty at the desk, had issued the reminder that the major was having head count at 1800. The French had assured McCall that their pilots would be present first thing in the morning, and he did not have time to search the soup shops and whorehouses to find his men. He wanted everybody there. *"No chiquitas, señor,"* Billy Mano had said with a smile.

Cody turned his head as the shuttle sped past the farm, but could see little more than was visible last night. The house and a few white outbuildings stood two hundred yards off the road at the end of a narrow drive, rice paddies all around. Large trees along the drive led to giant ones around the house. The gravel path dipped from the elevation of the road down through the boughs, and the house itself could not be seen. Beyond a chain, a white sign was lettered black in French, Vietnamese, and Chinese characters. A young French soldier tapped the arm of one older and asked a question. The man only shook his head.

A narrow slant of sun was building the colors of afternoon as the bus rolled off the long bridge, down into the dusky shade of Hanoi. Soon they arrived at Little Lake, three or four blocks of murky green water where colorful trolleys began their regular runs. Beyond the arch of a red wooden bridge stood an ancient island pagoda. Down the middle of the lake a man rowed a sampan with his feet.

Cody had planned to walk around the lake, perhaps get something to eat in one of the facing cafés, but when he stepped down from the shuttle and saw the couples hand in hand on the walks, he decided to wait. The afternoon was winding down, picnics long ago completed. Women sat on blankets, talking and watching babies and daughters while fat bald men slept apart on the grass. Scattered about were soldiers, a few with girls, but more sitting alone near the water, silently flipping pebbles.

Cody moved around to where most of the people were, then stepped down the slope to a polished tree. Nearby, an old bent Frenchman sat on a bench, hands stacked on the curve of a cane. He had white hair and a great white mustache, and though they looked nothing alike, his hair and his obvious interest in everything young reminded Cody of his grandpa.

Grandma West had always referred to her husband as an old fossil. Now it suddenly seemed that the label was quite appropriate, even honorable. An old fossil, permanent in form and purpose, something that once lived and is now dead but remains nonetheless worthwhile; something worthy of remembrance by the impression left behind; something that you are glad came before, even if it is impossible to comprehend its life.

118

The chain of thoughts brought him around to Dukemire and killing a man, trying to deny the connection, knowing where it would lead, either now or tonight in his bunk. Now was better than later; he could never know if he talked in his sleep.

It always began with a scream, one that everyone said he must have imagined—he could not possibly have remembered at that age. But he was certain that he did remember. It was where time itself began, regardless of where he wanted to start, all of a package—his father, Grandpa West, and what everyone referred to in hushed tones as the Accident. The spasm of impact was long ago gone, but it remained the door he was forced to pass through to reach childhood. He closed his eyes and took a slow breath, letting it grow in piercing crescendo, shadows of arms in the air. Then came the inevitable silence.

Cody Bentline West was named by his father. Propelled by his own last name, Beatty West had always dreamed of Wyoming. But he never made it. It turned out to be Texas instead, a fact which in honest moments he attributed to laziness and gravity, moving westward from Kentucky, all right, but sinking slowly toward the bottom of the map, following the easier, beaten path. It was a matter of trajectory; had he begun at a greater distance he might have settled even lower, the very tip of Texas, perhaps, or even Mexico. He came close enough as it was, settling on a mesquite-bottom farm on the edge of Batesville, sixty miles from the border. What struck his fancy about that particular hole nobody ever knew, but it was less than a year before his parents sold their place and auctioned off their junk to join him with his strapping teenage brother, saying that Beatty shouldn't be down there all alone.

But he was not alone. He had a young wife named Mary who had spent most of two years crying because of his mother, and who cried again when she learned that Mother West had followed her to the isolated farm. There were four hundred acres to choose from, but the elder Wests built their frame house at the edge of the property beside the highway, in full open view of the window above Mary's kitchen sink.

Mary cried still more when the baby came. She had agreed that if the child was a boy they would name him Cody in concession to her husband's dream. "You never know about a name," he said. "You hear it every day. Maybe he'll grow up and go there, the way I never did." For a middle name, Mary thought that Hawthorne was good. Hawthorne West sounded like a man who would be somebody when the youthful name of Cody had been outgrown. But Mother West thought the name ridiculous, saying it sounded like a movie part that the grinning, lop-eared fool named Gable might have played. Bentline was a family name neglected for two generations, and Mother West wanted it revived, never bothering to explain why she had not hung it on one of her own three sons. Mary and Beatty should do that much for her, she said, since she had sold her treasured things and moved all the way to Texas just for them.

In frantic, tearful nights Mary made her husband promise, and he did so willingly enough. But Beatty was drunk the morning Cody came, despite the fact that his every dime had already been paid to the doctor. Mary understood at once, of course, but by then it was much too late; her baby had a name.

Beatty tried for a while to make her laugh with an ironic joke about Bentline West, but it never worked.

There were those who called it fate, that were it not for the Accident, it would have been lightning or a rattlesnake, a flash flood or tornado. Something would have come along to retrieve her. Mary was just too unhappy to live very long, and there seemed little doubt that Grandma West was making no plans to pass on. The biddies who still mouthed these words in later years made Cody foaming mad. *Nothing* had come to take his mother; she had been murdered by a drunken old son of a bitch who also happened to be his father. Facts were facts, and people could all go to hell.

It was a wet and starless night on the highway out of Hondo when Cody was three, coming the long way home from San Antone. Four hundred pounds of bristling, stinking, charcoal feral boar, trailing sows and pigs. The guts dropped out, the carcass rolled, and the car bounced over, wrecked underneath, to skid and turn and sit upon the center stripe in darkness. No one was injured, and there was no reason in the world why they could not have all piled out to stand on the shoulders in either direction to warn and try to stop the next motorist. But not Beatty West, no sir. No goddamned pig was going to turn him from his appointed course; they would all stay right there in the car until he got the son of a bitch running. While Mary turned to wrap the baby and rearrange the pillows in the backseat, her husband sat with his car door open, drunkenly determined that a ruptured battery would start a vehicle with a smashed-in radiator, a displaced axle, and a crankshaft scraping the pan. Then came the big lights and big horn, protective shadows and a mother's eternal scream. Cody's father jumped and ran.

He was a teenager before he pieced it together in the framework of a story where all the loose confusion could finally jell as rage. That was when he began to understand that his father's every move toward him was an ongoing apology. Except for the drinking. But all that was later.

For a time, Cody believed that he had been born without a mother. Then, when he grew old enough to question, he decided that he had been abandoned. "She has gone away," he was invariably told, as if the phrase had been agreed upon. Never was it acknowledged that his mother was simply dead. Only later did he hear the term "the Accident," and no one would ever explain.

Even when Cody was just a little squirt his father would sit on the porch and drink and talk about a man's responsibilities.

Those first few years, he was raised by his grandparents—not as their son, since his father was still present, but as a grandchild. It was a puzzling period which grew even more so with the passage of years, until he learned the entire story. He was never close to Grandma West, nor did she want him to be. She performed every duty of a mother, but it was plainly nothing but that. There was no mention or pretense of love. The only time Cody could ever remember hearing her utter the word was with derision. They had gone to a birthday party in town, and some of the mothers were observing the first puppy-love notions of their children. Grandma West was the oldest woman present. Cody had gone into the house to use the bathroom, and as he emerged, hands still wet from washing, he caught the tail of a question that one of the younger women asked of Grandma West, inquiring about physical love at her age. "Humph!" she said, enormous breasts on folded arms. "I'm through with all that! When I was a girl, my mother said that when a man was in love, he would want to poke something in you. But she told it backwards. She should have said that when he wanted to poke something in you, a man was in love!"

Accordingly, Grandpa West spent a lot of time sitting in a spring-steel chair beneath a live oak tree, or wandering the four hundred acres with his Parker sixteen or a single-shot .22. As soon as Cody was tall enough so the strike of a rattlesnake wouldn't hit him between the eyes, he began to go along on those treks. It was Grandpa West who taught him how to shoot.

Then one day Uncle Ned came home in a J-3 Cub, and changed everything forever. He buzzed the house to get their attention, then landed on the highway and taxied right up the drive. While the hugs were bestowed, the smiles and backslaps and exclamations, seven-year-old Cody stood shyly back, staring in wonder at the airplane and at the golden, perfect image of his uncle—muscles and teeth and gleaming hair—knowing everything now that he needed to know about his future: Someday he would be a pilot.

They were still standing there in the yard—Cody now in the cockpit, unable to see over the dash, but sloshing the stick around, wondering if an airplane was pedaled like a bicycle—when his father came in from Cotulla. For the past two years the rains had been poor, and his efforts at farming the lower portions of the patch were practically futile. He had begun supplementing his income with short-term jobs on some of the area ranches. Beatty West was not much of a cowboy, but he could usually stay astride a horse. He knew about windmills, and was a fair mechanic, so never had much trouble finding work, just getting there. He climbed out of the pickup sunburned and dusty, the problem he was having with his smile mostly hidden by a huge black mustache that always reminded Cody of a movie character named Handsome Dan.

Ned had been gone in the Army more than a year, and though he arrived in uniform, he had exciting news. He was being allowed to resign from the Air Corps in order to join a civilian aviation outfit forming up to go to the Far East to fight Japs. The Cub was a gift from a pilot friend, he said, one who had been killed in a crash. He wanted to leave it in his brother's care until he got back.

Uncle Ned was the second to go. Another brother, Alfred, who Cody did not remember ever seeing, had been in the Navy for several years. He seldom wrote, and never came to visit. In the tightening secrecy of approaching war, his parents no longer heard from him at all. They only knew that he was aboard ship somewhere in the Pacific.

Ned stayed with them three weeks, and in that time there was hardly a moment that he and the boy were not together. By the time he left, Cody was in love with Uncle Ned as only a small child can be with a dashing, adventurous adult. Ned said he would send souvenirs, and he was true to his word. Cody used the things to decorate the walls of the bedroom in his father's house.

Even at that age, Cody had already learned the benefits of having two homes. The house up the slope was never locked, even when his father was gone overnight, and Cody went there sometimes to play. It was not long until he realized that under no circumstances would Grandma West ever set foot through the door of that house. From that moment forward, the place became a sanctuary. The old woman would stand and scream from the corner of her porch, but she never came near. When his father was there in the summertime, usually drinking out on the front porch, Cody slept in his own bed, in his own house. Grandma West tried for a time to prevent this, but Cody got unexpected support. His grandpa seldom crossed her, but this time he interceded. "Leave the boy alone," he said. "He needs to know his father."

Then that winter, when they had already cut and decorated a cedar tree for Christmas, war began. The Wests of Batesville became one of several Texas families to bear the distinction of having lost a son at Pearl Harbor. Uncle Alfred was dead, entombed belowdecks in the battleship *Arizona*.

A pall of silence fell over the farm. Grandpa West began to change. Uncle Ned, the youngest, had always seemed the favorite, and Alfred had never been close to his parents, but the death hit Hiram West awfully hard. It was years before Cody understood that a lot more died at Pearl Harbor than just a distant son.

For weeks the old man spent his days in isolation in the cold chair beneath the tree, remaining there even when a freezing wind came through and threatened sleet. That was when Grandma West began to crack, and she spent the afternoon carrying quilts and steaming mugs of coffee out to her husband.

When Grandpa West finally came inside, he had it all worked out in words. "The whole damn thing was planned," he said. "That's why nobody can understand how the United States got caught with her britches down: The buttons were fingered by the man at the top." He sat at the kitchen table, looking older, his hair and mustache whiter than Cody had ever seen. "It would have been a tough decision for a less cutthroat son of a bitch," he said. "But not him, by God. The man held his own counsel. Smart and crazy, dangerous as a mad dog."

Cody's grandmother disagreed, saying that Roosevelt was a good man and wise, a kind man who never would have considered such a horrid thing, and didn't deserve such talk. He couldn't help it if their baby had been killed. She puckered and dabbed her cheeks with her apron. "Don't listen to him," she said. "He's just a bitter old man and don't know what he's talking about!"

But Alfred's father never gave up. He hung a long sign on the barbed wire along the highway, "Remember December 7, 1941," realizing that passersby would believe him crazy. It might take years, he said, but sooner or later everyone who saw that sign would understand that it had nothing at all to do with Japanese.

After that, on the warmer days of declining winter, Cody's training with the rifle began in earnest. "You need to learn to shoot," his grandpa said, "in case the sonsabitches ever come. Keep plenty of bullets around, and don't ever let yourself run out. Always save one for the mad dog."

Then, in the spring, Uncle Ned was shot down in Burma, removing the likelihood that Cody's father would ever have to go. They inherited the airplane. The years went by, and many things changed, but never so much as when he was nearly fourteen and heard the story about his mother.

Cody pushed himself away from the polished tree, blinked, and checked his watch. He had fallen asleep, but for only a little while. The old man was gone from the bench. Then he remembered his grandpa, his father, and what later occurred, and the recent problems of his new friend, John Dukemire. It seemed that everybody he knew had at least one story that he didn't want told.

He looked again for the old man with the cane, and when he couldn't find him he thought of the sailor named Larkin and what his life was like. He decided to try the Café Ho Tay, see if the old fellow might be there. It would mean buying at least one beer, but that was better than wasting what was left of the afternoon.

He was the only remaining passenger when the shuttle took the turn beside the lagoon called Truc Bach, heading toward the garrison on the edge of Big Lake. When he signaled that he wanted to get off, the driver looked surprised, but shrugged and stopped and opened the door. The bus was pulling away when Cody looked up and saw that the Café Ho Tay was closed. Of course, he thought, it's Sunday. He laughed at himself and decided to walk the half mile to the bridge. There he would have his choice of many shuttles heading back to Gia Lam. He turned with energy and set off down a sidewalk lined with tremendous trees.

"Mr West," a woman's voice called.

He turned and was shocked to see Su Letei standing on a small porch in front of a house. Then he remembered that she lived next door to the Café Ho Tay. She was dressed in a creamy lace *ao dai* over a white silk blouse and white trousers. She had braided her hair, rolled it into a coil, and pinned it in back with two long picks of carved ivory. Her ears were adorned with ivory cubes. Because she was not in her usual place, he could not remember her name.

"Oh, hi," he said. "How're you doing?"

Su Letei smiled with mild amusement. "I am doing just fine, Mr. West," she said with a gracious nod. In her hands were scissors and a single pink rose.

"Why don't you call me Cody?" he said. "I'm not old enough to be a mister."

"But that is how you were introduced."

"It's my rank. They call warrant officers 'mister.' I don't know why."

"Very well, Cody. What brings you to this part of town on such a beautiful afternoon?" She stepped from the porch and walked slowly toward him. He saw she was wearing white sandals.

"Uh, well, the shuttle, actually," he said, then smiled. "I guess I forgot it was Sunday."

She studied him a moment. "Moni' is not here today," she said.

"Who? Oh yeah. Moni'." He could feel the blood rising in his cheeks. Su Letei was now only a few feet away.

"They sent for her last night," she said. "There was an attack on three bunkers of the De Lattre Line to the north, and reinforcements went out. Many were wounded. Then a planeload of casualties from Dien Bien Phu came in, and Moni' was needed at Lanessan. She returned only after daylight, completely exhausted. She cleaned up, then went to the farm to rest."

"Seems like she could have done that better here."

"She told you about him?"

"A little."

"She will be fine there. It is where she wants to be."

"Why . . ." He paused, and she waited for his question. "It's none of my business, but why does she live out there with him instead of here with you?"

"He is her father. She is all he has. She takes care of him, and in her way she takes care of herself. It is not what I would like, but it is for her to decide. I am pleased for the time she spends with me."

"Yes, but . . ."

"There is nothing else to consider." Her tone was a bit abrupt, impossible to say if she was annoyed, or if she simply knew the futility of discussion.

"What happened to her mother?"

"My sister was killed four years ago."

"How?"

He had asked too much. "In the war," she said.

He nodded gravely. "Well, I guess I'd better be going."

"In case she forgot to warn you, do not ever go see her out there. Her father is a madman who begs to be killed."

He walked away frowning, hands in his pockets, eyes on the path ahead. He did not see the trees or handsome houses or any of the few people he passed. He spaced his steps to avoid the rooted cracks.

fingers of one hand. There was another shout from the house, then he saw Moni' beyond the screen, and heard her gasp. The gun bucked and roared, and the smoke shot out, and she screamed again, lunging from the door, hysterical. Her father smiled and drew back the bolt. Cody's mouth was cotton now. He moved forward, saw that he had more time, and moved again. But the old man was watching. He checked the breech, slid the bolt, and brought the handle down. Then he spoke to Cody in French and took aim.

"No, no, *no!*" Moni' leaped from the porch, charging toward Cody. "Go away!" she yelled. "Are you crazy? Go away! What are you doing here?"

"I came—" He was having trouble with his throat. "I am here to see you."

"I don't *want* to be seen!" She was barefoot and wearing faded peasant garb, rusty brown and lifeless.

"I'd like to go for a walk with you."

"A *walk?* You *are* crazy! Get out of here before he kills you!"

Cody was quite close now, within fifty feet of the porch. He looked past her shoulder to her father. His mustache was ropy black, causing Cody to remember the name Handsome Dan Blackweed. "Hello, old man," he said, clearing his throat. "Good to see you again."

"Again?" Moni' turned toward her father, then back. "You've never seen him before!"

"He reminds me of somebody."

The man looked at him, adjusted his eyes, and smiled. *"T'es venu ici pour baiser ma fille?"* he said.

Moni' turned and screamed a torrent of French.

"What did he say?"

"Nothing! He said nothing! Now leave! Go from this place and never return!" Behind her back, her father was giving Cody a leering smile.

"Tell him I said to kiss my hairy ass."

"I will tell him *nothing!* Go away, you fool!"

"Not until you walk with me. I will stay all night."

She blinked at him, turned and shouted at her father, and took a deep breath. "Very well," she said. "We will walk. To the end of the drive. Then you will go. And you will never come here again. Agreed?"

"No."

"Yes. It *is* agreed." She marched past him toward the road, turned, and said, "Well? You wanted to walk? Let's walk!"

He turned toward her father. The rifle was resting across his knees. The man gave Cody a grotesque smile and gestured toward the drive. Cody followed Moni', stopped when she surged ahead, then followed again. When they were halfway to the road, well within the tunnel of trees, he stepped to the side to lean against a mossy trunk. Moni' continued a little farther before stalking back, hands on her narrow hips.

"You're not walking! You said you wanted to walk!"

"Now I want to talk." He took a slow, deep breath, trying to keep her from seeing. He had been able to get the trembling under control, but it was still everywhere inside. He released it now with the long gulp of air.

"I don't have time to talk. I have things to do."

He glanced toward her father. "Yeah, it looks pretty busy around here."

"That is none of your business," she said. "What was it you wanted to talk about?"

"I don't know," he said. "Just talk. Just visit. I thought maybe if you weren't doing anything we could go into town. Eat some dog meat or something."

"That's not funny," she said.

"You're right. I'm sorry. But it would be nice to have a simple visit without the hostility."

She studied him a moment. "Why did you come here?" she said.

"No particular reason." He looked toward the porch. "I thought you might like some company."

"You came to do me a favor?"

"No, I didn't mean it that way. I just thought we might be friends. I don't know anybody here but the guys in the outfit, and I don't really know them. I thought maybe we could go into town, that's all. You could show me around."

"I am not a guide for wealthy Americans."

"I'm not wealthy."

"You're all wealthy, so wealthy you don't even know. Then you come here expecting people to bow down."

"I didn't come here expecting a thing. In fact, I didn't even expect to come here. We were sent, supposedly to help out."

"And who are you helping?"

"The French, I suppose."

"And how do you think you are doing that?"

"By giving them aircraft. Teaching them how to fly them."

"So they can bomb people?"

"No! They're not even armed. The birds will be used to evacuate wounded men."

"I heard that you brought machine guns and bullets."

"Who told you that?"

"You hear things in the city without listening."

"All I can say is there's a war going on, and we're here in the middle of it, not fighting, but here. It would seem kind of dumb to show up without guns."

"Do you realize how many guns you have brought?" He stared at her, not understanding. "This country is sinking beneath the weight of your bombs, your tanks and trucks and aircraft. Your nation runs a retail store for war."

"That's ridiculous."

"Is it? Then go into town, into the Chinese quarter, have a look around. You can buy anything you want, new American equipment, anything from canteens to howitzer shells, in the tiny Chinese shops of Hanoi."

"That's impossible. No way. Besides, the French would never permit it. It's absurd."

"Go see for yourself. I have with my own eyes seen hand grenades, little apples of death, displayed in a glass cabinet. As for the French, who do you think sold them to the Chinese? Then the Chinese sell them to the Viet Minh. And sometimes, when an American shipment is late and the French are in a really bad way, they buy the weapons *back* from the Chinese! What do you think of that, Mr. American?"

"I don't believe any of it."

"Of course not. Neither do your generals. They come here, have a look around, can't believe it, and go home and order more guns for the French. Without America, the war would have already been over."

"So you're on the other side?"

"I am on *no* side," she said. "All I want, all I have ever wanted, is for the war to be over. Everyone has already lost. I am waiting only for it to be over so we all can begin to win."

"But your parents are French."

"My father is French. My mother was half Vietnamese. But now she is dead."

"I'm sorry."

"Are you? She was killed with an American machine gun, murdered in a village not far from here. The Foreign Legion went through in four trucks—American trucks, American machine guns, American bullets—and killed everybody they could find because a patrol had been ambushed nearby. It was a day like today, a Sunday, and my mother was visiting relatives in the village. It was before we lost the plantation on the road to Tam Dao, and I was with my father to see the harvest."

Cody had watched closely as she told the story, but now he turned toward the house. Her father was still there, the rifle standing brown against the wall. The man turned the bottle up, then leaned and smashed it among the shrubs in what sounded like a mound of glass.

"You said you wanted to talk," she said. "This is what my stories are like, the parts of my life, just as you would talk about yours. But different."

"So what do you do around here for fun?" he said.

"Fun? I tell you about the murder of my mother, and you want to know about *fun*?"

"Okay," he said. "How 'bout if I tell you about the time I killed my daddy. Maybe that'll make us even."

"You are making a terrible joke. I don't want to hear your story."

"Good enough. Now what do you do for fun?"

"Not very much anymore," she said with less anger. "It has been difficult for a long time. When I was very small, and my mother was alive, we had a place at Bai Chay. It is across from Hon Gay on Ha Long Bay. A beautiful place with pine trees right down to the water, a veranda all around a house on a little hill with gardens—bougainvillea, frangipani, so many wonderful flowers."

Cody watched Moni' in wonder. Her voice had softened, and despite her drab clothing she seemed to have blossomed with the colors of the place she spoke about.

"It is less than one hundred twenty kilometers from here, but the climate is mild. The breezes are cool in summer, and winters are warm without the drizzle or *crachin*. There is not much to do but sail around the bay, or catch fish, or look for shells, or climb mountains for a view. At night you can count the lanterns of the boats all around the bay, drifting across like stars, and in the morning they catch the wind and you can see them with their brown sails like Chinese junks, coming closer and closer. Then the women wade ashore with baskets of shrimp and squid and little hammerhead sharks, and men walk down with weighing scales and fat rolls of piasters." She stopped as the vision disappeared. "It was a beautiful place when I was young."

"Sounds like it. What about now? Around here."

"Here and now is war," she said.

"Okay, there's war, but is that it? You help out at the hospital, then spend the rest of your time taking care of an old reprobate who has lost everything but a loyal daughter and a run-down house?"

"Do not speak of my father that way!"

"I've earned the right," he said calmly, ignoring the challenge. He looked through the trees toward the sky. "I flew over your house this morning," he said.

"Yes, you woke me. I thought it might be you."

When he looked at her she turned away. "Why don't we go into town?" he said. "To one of the lakes. I've only got about an hour before I have to be back, but we could get something to eat, chunk some rocks at the ducks or something."

She started to smile, but quickly covered it with a frown. "No," she said. "I cannot go with you anyplace. Not now, not ever. Not until the war is over."

"So that's it? You just suspend your life for as long as the war lasts?"

"You can say it that way."

"And what happens if it lasts for the rest of your life?"

"Then that will be my life."

He left her then with the promise, against her protestations, that he would come to see her again, and that they would go and do something fun. He turned to her father, who was still watching, and held up a middle finger as if it were a toast, forward and high above his head. "Tell that old son of a bitch I'll be back," he said, and walked down the drive.

He had taken less than a dozen steps when the bullet sang past and he heard the report of the gun. Moni' screamed and ran toward the house.

When he reached the road he waited for a shuttle returning from town. But as one approached, he waved it past and stepped across the highway. He checked his watch. There might not be enough time, but he had to know for sure. It was no consolation at all, but if what she had told him was true, at least he would be able to explain to the major.

Marsh McCall's grandmother—his father's mother—had many sayings—reliable lines of limited range that defined the parameters of her life. One which impressed him as a child by the explicit image it evoked was what she would say when she was completely disgusted—usually by a thing his grandfather had done. She would knot her apron and choose a hard chair to scratch a note to her sister, but invariably she got bogged down. Her nose would crinkle and her lips draw tight until her chin was the pit of a peach, then her brows came down like a predatory bird's. When it seemed as if steam should emit from all ports, she would twist her lips and announce, "I'm so gutty-blamed mad I could just *poot!*"

McCall would have given it a try if he believed it would help. The immediate cause of his mood was Cody West, but the warrant officer's absence from the evening formation had been merely the crowning event of a day of disgust. He had finally acknowledged that he had accepted a questionable assignment directed largely by the quixotic fantasies of a friend grown suddenly old. Except for the military assessment and report, a man of less rank could have easily handled the job. But that was normal enough. The Army was a lot like a machine gun—98 percent of the bullets were wasted, but a great deal of noise was made, and it was unquestionably scary as hell when it happened to be pointed at you.

It seemed to McCall that this little detachment had as many problems as an entire battalion. A note from the colonel had arrived via courier, explaining that it had been decided to keep the men's records down south. If the major needed specific information on anyone, Smith would be pleased to coordinate things with Major Hadley, commanding the mother portion of 22d at Tan Son Nhut.

So McCall conducted interviews, learning little more about the men than he already knew. Most were above average, a couple were outstanding, and one—Tooler—would not be missed. McCall's most immediate concern was a lack of qualified pilots, which the tardiness of Cody West had suddenly pointed up. It had not been until McCall had sent Lieutenant Atherton packing that he had discovered the twin holes in the organization—that not all of the men had volunteered, and that two of the pilots were not qualified instructors. It was only luck that Atherton had been one of those two. The other, Dukemire, arrived with his own set of problems. McCall was still puzzling over the kid, how he had managed to survive his ordeal. There was the temptation to write it off as dumb luck, but nobody was that lucky, even if Dukemire did possess the proper sense of unconsciousness.

Dukemire reminded McCall of a rifleman he had known in Korea, a kid named Gitch whom everybody called Dizzy. Dizzy's favorite trick was stepping into foxholes in broad daylight. One day, after a patrol had been sniped all morning, the men settled into a crater for lunch. "Hey, Diz, what happened to your steel pot?" somebody said. Dizzy pulled off his helmet and stared at a couple of grooves where bullets had been deflected. Then he said with a gentle smile of amazement, "I wondered why it kept falling off."

Thoughts of Korea forced McCall to pause. He blinked and moved firmly ahead, determined to stay on course.

Something about Dukemire's story had struck him as strange, causing him to call the weary man in for another hour-long session. Dukemire's experience, tied to the robbery, was a solid lead toward the organized corruption that Colonel Smith wanted pursued. But nothing new had been discovered. Dukemire was exhausted and nervous, clearly believing that he was suspected of something. McCall tried to reassure him, but without much effect.

Near 1900 hours McCall heard someone enter the orderly room, not carrying enough beef to be Winslow. Something bumped against the wall, then Cody West appeared in the door, looking sheepish but with something to say. It was an expression the major had seen so many times he had dubbed it the one-and-a-half—one hour late, a half-hour excuse. The warrant officer waited to be recognized.

"Yes, Mr. West?"

Cody marched three steps to the desk, came to attention, and saluted. "Mr. West reporting late for duty, sir."

"At ease," McCall said, returning the salute, shuffling some things on his desk. "I suppose you have a story of some kind," he said as he studied the pilot's face. West was a sincere kid—the best of the pilots, according to Rankin. There was something quaintly naive about him, as if he assumed that everyone should believe what he said.

"Yes, sir, I do," West said firmly.

McCall looked at his watch. "Where were you at seventeen hundred?"

"Sir? Wasn't the formation at eighteen hundred?"

"That's right. But I have a feeling that what you were doing an hour before that will tell me everything I need to know."

"No, sir, it sure won't," Cody said. "There's a lot more." When McCall just looked at him, he swallowed and said, "At seventeen hundred I was visiting a lady, sir."

"A lady?"

"Yes, sir. A lady."

So much in a word, McCall thought. "And where did you meet this lady?"

"At the Café Ho Tay, sir. She's Miss Letei's niece. I went to her house."

"Were those the shots we heard?"

"Most likely, sir."

He leaned back, looking anew at Cody West. "Did you enjoy the visit?"

"Not the word I would choose, sir, but it was interesting."

"I'll just bet it was," McCall said. He had heard the stories of the crazy old man, and had read the sign beside the highway: KEEP OUT. TRESPASSERS WILL BE SHOT. SURVIVORS WILL BE PROSECUTED. "Was it worth getting shot at?"

"I think so, sir."

"What do you think I should do?"

"Nothing, sir."

"Nothing?"

"No, sir. I mean, I'll go along with whatever you decide, but you need to hear the rest of what happened. It's why I was late."

"You do realize that we are beginning classes tomorrow, and

that anyone who is late or absent will throw the entire schedule out of kilter."

"Yes, sir. I'm sorry I was late, but it was unavoidable." When McCall raised a brow, he added, "Well, not exactly unavoidable, sir. Just required. I was late on purpose."

McCall heard Winslow enter the building. "Okay, let's have it. Make it short."

"I went to town and bought a machine gun."

McCall's frown developed by layers. "Not that short," he growled. "What kind of machine gun? Who from? Why? You'd better get to explaining yourself, soldier."

"That's what I'm trying to do, sir. I bought an American machine gun, brand-new."

The full import of the statement swept McCall. Then he heard Sergeant Winslow's rumbling voice touched with rage: "Good God-almighty damn!"

"Sergeant Winslow?"

Winslow appeared in the doorway, a dull weapon in his hands, still partially wrapped in a gunnysack. He looked stunned. "It's one of ours," he said. "One they stole in Haiphong."

It was the next evening when they boarded the jeep—Winslow driving, his mouth set, the tight belly of his shirt putting a shine on the steering wheel; McCall relaxed, solemnly thinking things through; Two Acres in back with the weapons, looking happy but not friendly, wind working the black feathered hair above his ears.

They moved down Depot Road without a word. Scattered cells of rain clouds drifted around the sky, trying to muster energy to get together. It had been a busy week for convoys, and the road was showing wear. Wide, shallow craters as large as the jeep had begun to develop. Winslow sawed at the wheel, neglecting the brake, weaving smoothly from ditch to ditch as he picked out a course.

McCall was absorbed with all the possibilities, every repercussion that might result from what they were about to do. Given the right conditions, it could end his career and go even beyond that. But Colonel Smith had known exactly how he would respond to this sort of thing—the experience of Korea waiting only to be stirred.

McCall was increasingly convinced that it was the one reason, beyond all others, that he had been sent to Hanoi. If the black market situation was as bad as he suspected, the official reaction would be almost nonexistent. The unofficial aspect, however, might be something else entirely.

It was pointless to try to do anything through the French. A call to the authorities would only ensure that everything would be swept from view until McCall was safely gone. There was nothing else to do. Beyond the satisfaction of the act itself, he would enjoy seeing who it flushed from the woods.

He glanced around at the others as they made the turn to Route 5. Winslow was staring ahead, his righteous jaw projecting like the prow of a ship, gray stubble spiking his chin. Two Acres sat relaxed, ready for whatever might come, heavy hands and lumberjack frame bouncing easily with the motions of the jeep. When his eyes met McCall's, the major knew that Winslow had chosen well.

As they passed the Frenchman's farm, McCall looked left and read the sign, then had to turn away to suppress a chuckle. Last evening, after Winslow left the orderly room to have the machine gun cleaned, Cody West had frowned with a pained expression. "Was there something else?" McCall asked.

"Yes, sir. Two things. First, will I be able to get my money back?" When McCall assured him that he would, and even handed him partial payment, Cody thanked him, then frowned again. "The other thing, sir—I was wondering if you could translate something for me—something that Moni's father said."

"I'll try."

The warrant officer thought a moment, reciting the phrase to himself before saying it aloud. "What does '*T'es venu ici pour baiser ma fille?*' mean, sir?"

It required all the control that McCall could muster, but he drew a breath and released it, then solemnly said, "Yes, Mr. West, I believe that phrase means 'Have you come here to fuck my daughter?'"

McCall had laughed about it for most of an hour after the embarrassed young man was gone.

There was a vague rumble of thunder as they entered the city. A brief shower had passed through, settling the dust, enhancing the odors, leaving the sidewalks washed.

As they passed along a curving section of street, a narrow canyon of stacked habitations and clotheslines, McCall saw a girl of about thirteen emerge from a blistered door. Two floors up, a mother watched. The girl was dressed in a spotless *ao dai*, pink over white, as pretty and perfect as any little girl in all the history of the world. She walked primly along, black eyes liquid and lowered, smiling shyly. McCall was transfixed, and for that moment the little-boy part of him was once again heartbreakingly in love. He had seen it before in other places, but never did he cease to be amazed. In the evenings in the poorest parts of the poorest places on earth, flawless beauty emerged from the dust and grime to tiptoe out in delicate bloom at the instant of life's brief apex. It was less than a moment, and a man had to count himself lucky to be permitted to see it at all.

The Chinese shop was in the crowded west portion of the city beyond the rail station, not far from the whorehouses. Before World War II, wealthy Chinese had bought a number of fine houses in the central district, as well as resorts at Hon Gay, only to lose their investments when the Japanese moved into Tonkin. Then, during the postwar occupation ordered by the Potsdam Conference, the Chinese forced many of Hanoi's citizens to relinquish property in exchange for worthless currency. But by 1954, these were not the same Chinese. These had no other homes to go to, and had come to Hanoi to stay. They clustered in an enclave of tinkers and tailors, jewelers and laundries, groceries and cheap cafés.

Winslow had done the scouting that morning with Two Acres, and said he did not like the looks of the place. They had purchased a Colt automatic, not new, but in excellent condition, and had spent enough time inside to observe the layout, the potential defenses, and to plan an escape. They drove around and checked the back door, which opened onto a very long trash-filled alley. Winslow returned to Lam Du to report they would be needing a measure of luck, and perhaps another man.

Now, as they passed the location, McCall could see the assessment had been correct. The shop sat in the back of a tiny courtyard surrounded on all sides by three-story tenements, each with wrought-ironed porches draped in laundry, half of them staring down on the door of the shop. Access to the courtyard was by a narrow tunnel that penetrated the storefronts at street level, leaving a gap like a missing tooth. The place was a perfect trap, an ideal defensive position which the Chinese had probably selected for that reason. When they drove around back, the alley was only slightly better. On one side were the backs of the buildings, each with an open door, and on the other was a solid stone wall that was ten feet tall. Trash was everywhere. The only redeeming aspect was that tall bamboo lined much of the alley, screening it from balconies and windows behind the tenements, possibly providing a place to hide.

When they dropped Two Acres off, Winslow held up eight fingers to remind him which door. The corporal slung his carbine, grinned and waved as if thanking them for a lift, and strode easily down the alley like someone headed home. When he had gone a safe distance, he sidestepped and disappeared.

Winslow parked, leaving the tires turned toward the street, an unlocked chain draped through the steering wheel. The two walked into the tunnel, carrying their rifles impersonally, as if they brought them only to trade. While Winslow led the way, McCall relaxed his face and deadened his eyes so that when they emerged from the tunnel and crossed the courtyard he looked as down-home as any hick from the hills. "*Chào*," he said loudly when he entered the shop. Winslow stopped at a side counter, nodding and smiling as if he were brain damaged, the slanted gap of his tooth leaving a triangular hole. He placed his rifle on the counter and walked away from the weapon.

"*Chào anh,*" the shop owner said. He was about sixty, dry parchment on bones, thin hair that was long and wispy. A dozen white whiskers fell from his chin, shifting with the slightest motion of air. He was smiling like Winslow, so happy to see them and their wallets. Behind him to one side was his wife, a small, suspicious soul who stood with her back at the edge of a thinly draped door. She gave only the faintest twitch of her lips, the slightest tilt of her head when McCall nodded. He turned to the old man.

"Good afternoon," he said. The man smiled and bowed. McCall let his eyes fall to the glass counters where lay a selection of sidearms. Against the wall at counter level, linked by chains, stood an equal assortment of rifles. "We trade?" he said. The old man smiled and nodded, but with doubtful comprehension. McCall knew only a smattering of Chinese, so opted for pidgin and sign.

"You, me, trade?" he said. He pulled the slung firearm from his shoulder and held it out, motioning back and forth from the old man to himself, pointing generally at all the guns. The old man's smile broadened, and he nodded rapidly. He had only four upper teeth. "Tlade," he said. "Tlade." His wife was very still, rapidly shifting her eyes from McCall to Winslow to the courtyard. McCall reslung the weapon, walked over and peered at the rifles, then looked all around, briefly toward the doorway beyond the woman. He raised his hands as if holding a machine gun, frowned hard, and made a soft shooting sound as he bounced his arms. "Machine gun?" he said, then made the sounds and sign again. "Machine gun?"

The old man smiled and started to nod, then noticed his wife's fierce stare. He smiled helplessly at McCall and shook his head. "No," he said. "No shingung." He glanced at his wife.

McCall pleasantly frowned and approached the woman, smiling and altering his tone to one persuasive and pleading, as if there were nothing he wanted so much as to get in her arid pants. "Machine gun?" he said, then held up his fingers. "Four machine guns." The old woman gazed back with dry speculation, then slowly shook her head. Her hair was not yet all white, pulled to a tight little bun. Her ears were laced with onionskin creases. She eased from the jamb and stood squarely blocking the door.

McCall produced a wad of bills that he and Winslow had wrung from every man in the outfit. He held the money up, shaking it so she would know it was real. The old man joined her at the door, glancing from the money to his wife. When her eyes softened, McCall handed her the wad. "Four machine guns," he said. "Or trade, some-some." He pointed again at the carbines.

She looked at the money, then at the rifles. "No tlade," she said. She thumbed disdainfully through the bills, looked up and added, "Two shingung."

McCall smiled sadly and shook his head. Winslow was down on one knee, studying the weapons in the cabinet, working his way toward where he had left his rifle. "Four," McCall said, then wavered and looked doubtful. "You bring me one machine gun," he said, holding up a finger, then pointed toward his eyes and nodded. "I look one time."

The old man looked at the woman with a pleading smile. He

141

seemed to want to hold the money, but she lowered it to her side. Winslow stood, stretched and yawned, then walked past his weapon to join McCall. When her husband was not watching, he smiled warmly at the woman. She lowered her eyes, raised one brow, and pushed past the drapery. The old man followed.

"Ma'am?" McCall said abruptly. The drapery moved aside, and the major held out his hand. "My money." The face turned sour, but she forked over the cash. He dropped it on the counter, then watched for light in the darkened room. He had already seen that the shelves beyond the drape were stacked with gear, not weapons. Far back a dim light appeared, as if from an outside door. The drapery bent with a breeze, relaxed, then was immediately replaced by the dim incandescence of a bulb. Finally, the old man emerged with a battered Browning. McCall refused to even touch it.

"I said machine guns," he said, still smiling, but beginning to look angry. "*Good* machine guns. Not junk. Four good machine guns. You show me one. We go 'nother place." He reached for the money, but did not put it away.

Winslow glanced at his watch. "We're late, sir," he said. "We need to leave right away."

McCall checked his own watch. "Okay," he said. "Another minute or two, then we'll go." He turned back to the couple, held his hands in a questioning gesture, still holding the wad of bills. "No good machine guns?" he asked.

The Chinese glanced at one another, then returned to the back room. A few minutes passed, then there were sounds against the wall. Winslow casually reached for his rifle, then stood gazing around the room and checking his watch. Then the old man appeared with a new weapon, followed at once by the woman.

"We really need to go, sir," Winslow said, looking again at his watch.

McCall frowned with irritation. "Just a minute, Sergeant," he said. He placed the money on the counter and turned to examine the weapon. It was one of their own. He fought to hide his anger. He hefted the weapon, raised the cover, drew back the bolt, examined the breech, and peered down the barrel. He managed to smile at the shopkeepers. "Good machine gun," he said. "You have four?"

"Fo' gun, sis hunded dollah," the woman said.

"Excuse me, sir, but we've got to go. Now!"

"You're right, Sergeant."

With a nimbleness McCall would not have believed, Winslow vaulted the counter, his rifle leveled at the old man while he grabbed the woman by the knot of hair. She started to squeal and go to her knees, but he jerked her to silence, then pushed them both clear of the door. McCall stuffed the money inside his shirt, then rushed past the counter and stuck his head through the curtain. Against the wall were three matching machine guns. Winslow shoved the old ones ahead, then tossed his rifle to McCall and bound them with cord. He tore strips from the curtain for gags. Then they spread apart and rushed along opposing sides of the room.

The place was a narrow military warehouse, but nowhere were weapons in sight. The men circled the room, checked all the shelves, and looked for trap doors. That left only some stairs leading up to a door.

"I don't like it," Winslow said. "Let's take the four guns and get the hell out."

"Not yet," said McCall. This was as close as he had ever come to one of the worst enemies he had ever faced, and he was not about to leave until he had a look. He checked his .45 and started up the stairs. They groaned beneath his weight.

He stopped a few feet from the door to listen. There was no landing up top; when he got to that point he would be committed. He thought he could hear a shuffling. He looked down at Winslow, and when the sergeant nodded, he rushed the door, bashing it with a shoulder. It bumped and gave way, shoving something aside, then swung open to an armory displayed in the light of a dusty window. He got only a glimpse—row upon row of weapons and cases—before he heard the sound and saw the rush, and the animal was in his face. His .45 roared, the belch of flame blinding, then he was backward down the stairs, end over end. He tumbled twice before his legs could snag the rail, and he pushed against the wall and swung the pistol around. Above him on the stairs lay a yellow pit bull, head down, chest ripped open and belching blood. The jaws were gnashing, chewing the wooden step to splinters while its glinting eyes stayed fixed on Marsh McCall.

"You okay?" Winslow yelled.

"Yeah." McCall gazed dumbly down at himself. His chest and

arms were covered with blood. He hurried to his feet.

"Let's get the hell out of here!"

"I've got to check these weapons," McCall said, starting up the stairs.

"Bullshit!" Winslow roared. "Get the fuck down here! *Now!*"

McCall stopped, astonished. It had been a long time since he had known a real sergeant. He looked back up the stairs, and knew that Winslow was right. All the illicit weapons in the world would not help a thing if they both were dead. He hurried downstairs. "Watch 'em while I move the guns out back," he said. He holstered his .45 and carried the four machine guns to the rear door. The Chinese were on the floor, bound and gagged, eyes darting. "Okay," he said, "let's try to get you out the front."

He checked beyond the curtain and around the counters, then watched as the amazing Winslow strode calmly into the courtyard, his carbine dangling like a toy. People were on the balconies, peeking past the laundry, but no one seemed alarmed. When Winslow entered the tunnel, McCall rushed back to the Chinese. They had thought the men were gone, and were struggling to free themselves. McCall grimaced toward the top of the stairs. It would have required a five-ton truck to empty that room, perhaps enough weapons to arm a battalion. All they could do was leave it. He ran for the back door.

Two Acres had secured a position in a natural bunker of bamboo. McCall barely saw him. When the jeep rounded the corner, he signaled the corporal and began bringing out the guns. Two Acres came in a rush, rifle ready, checking all doors. Then Winslow was there. They threw the goods aboard, the bloody major climbed in back, and they drove slowly away from the alley.

It began to rain as they crossed the darkening city, lightning fluorescent in the clouds, brief green flashes of daylight. All three men were silent until far in the center of Doumer's proud bridge where Winslow halted the jeep. The muddy river was dim and gray-green below, and they could just make out the shape of the island. There was no traffic at all, and they sat a long time in the dark pouring rain, releasing the adrenaline with a roaring great laugh.

★

Two police wagons without sirens—only winking red lights to show they meant business—made their winding way past the pools on Depot Road. The bar ditch was full, and there was no place for the water to go.

"Here they come," said Two Acres.

The MPs pulled up before the orderly room in their doorless vehicles. One swung and turned, then backed toward the door as two men emerged from the other. The men had donned their ponchos with reluctance, their authority draped in green plastic. Only the white helmets remained.

No one moved when the two entered the room. Winslow was in his chair, arms on his desk, studying them quietly. Two Acres stood in a corner near the door, and Marsh McCall was in the passage to his office. He had washed and changed, leaving his bloody fatigues to soak in a bucket behind the shower. The MPs stomped their boots, then a lieutenant pulled his poncho over his head. He looked around for a place to hang it, and found himself staring at Two Acres, a carbine in his hands. Neither acknowledged the other. The lieutenant grunted, and the sergeant who was with him put his back to the door.

"Major McCall?" he said. He had churlish lips, jaws thick with muscle, and eyes of a man who had learned that he could be a thug *and* a policeman.

"I'm McCall."

"My name is Lieutenant Larieux," he said in careful English. "I am here on a matter of police business. Can we speak in private?"

"I'm afraid not, Lieutenant. As you can see, this building is small. When you leave I will be discussing our conversation with my first sergeant. Corporal Acres is a trusted aide. What can I do for you?"

Blood rushed to the lieutenant's face. He glanced at Winslow, then over his shoulder at Two Acres. Suddenly he seemed to realize what he had seen, and snapped his head around. Leaning against the wall beside Winslow's desk were four machine guns.

"A robbery occurred a short time ago in a Chinese shop in town," he said. "The owners said it was done by Americans whose descriptions happen to fit yours. A jeep from your unit was observed crossing the bridge at about the same time."

"That's unfortunate. What sort of things were taken?"

145

The Frenchman looked at the weapons. "Money," he said. "More than three thousand piasters. An expensive pet was killed, senselessly gunned down while the old people watched." He was carefully studying McCall. His eyes narrowed.

"You've got the wrong outfit," McCall said. "My men were just paid. We don't entertain ourselves with petty robberies."

"We do not consider such a matter petty in Hanoi, Major."

"It's good to know that you have developed a concern for the welfare of Chinese."

"My government is concerned with maintaining order."

"I share that interest. There is nothing I enjoy more than making things right."

The lieutenant moved his eyes to Winslow, then to the weapons. "You have some nice machine guns," he said.

"Glad you noticed. I happen to think they look especially fine. As a matter of fact, we just found those a short while ago. They are some of the weapons that were stolen from us in Haiphong."

Comprehension slowly came to the lieutenant's face. He smiled in recognition of the daring step. "And how did you come by them?"

"We found them."

"Where?"

"There. Leaning against that wall."

"That is absurd."

"Nonetheless, Lieutenant."

The jaw tightened. "With your permission I will search the premises, Major."

"Denied."

"I have the authority to arrest all of you. At the very least, Major, I can see that you are removed from the region."

"Then do so, Lieutenant. Now get out of my office."

Winslow had been sitting motionless, moving his eyes between the two Frenchmen, but now he glanced at Two Acres. He casually reached over and lifted one of the machine guns, and with a slow motion, drew back the bolt and opened the cover. A short belt of bullets appeared from his lap, and he clamped it in place. The lieutenant looked sharply at McCall; his sergeant groped at his poncho for his sidearm.

"I do not think you realize what you are dealing with, Major,"

Larieux said. "This is not some little combat action that you will be able to win by luck and aggressiveness. You would be wise to leave this country, and have them send in your place a man who can mind his own business."

"That will be up to my superiors."

"Perhaps not," said Larieux. He nodded at his sergeant, who opened the door, then he turned once more to McCall. "By the way, Major," he said, "you have blood in your ear."

Chapter Eight

SU LETEI WAS LOVELY in a black *ao dai* with opposing dragons cut in the material above her breasts. Beneath the flapping tails were purple slacks and black-heeled sandals. "Good evening, Major McCall," she said, a smile beneath her smile. "It is good to see you. You have chosen an interesting time to come. There is always much here to learn."

When she led him to a table, he dropped his eyes briefly to her bottom, which had benefited from the French influence, then casually scanned the room while pondering her words. He recalled that she had made a similar remark during his previous visit. A number of patrons were scattered about, but the place was not nearly so crowded as he expected for a Friday. The white-haired retired colonel named Gereau was seated in the same spot at the long table, and across sat Major Legère's boss, Colonel de Matrin. In the bar the old sailor named Larkin was on his roost, speaking intently to a civilian. The doors to the patio were closed to the evening air, but two kerosene lamps on posts spread a comfortable glow beneath the trees. A pair of men were seated there in hats and light jackets, their backs to the Café Ho Tay.

Su Letei seated the major in the same spot as before, then served a pretty smile with the menu. "I must congratulate you," she said softly. "You have made a number of important enemies in an extremely short time."

"That's always been one of my talents," he said with a wry grin. "Maybe I'm doing something right."

"It is likely that you are," she said, "so long as you understand the rules. You will know more once you have had your visit with Mr. Pearbone. He made an inquiry about you. Would you like something to drink?"

"Just some coffee, please," he said. "Black."

McCall frowned mildly, thinking about Walter Pearbone. Had he not been so busy, it was still uncertain that he would have gone to see the diplomat. It seemed likely that Pearbone had as many questions as rules, and McCall wanted to avoid giving the answers. Perhaps he would see him tomorrow.

It had been a busy four days since the raid. As McCall expected, after the French MPs went away, nothing else happened. The pilot training was proceeding, impeded slightly by communication, but not so much as expected. It helped a great deal that all of the students were experienced helicopter pilots. The sessions were coordinated so that Rankin could go over everything in French before each flight, then again to answer questions when they returned. Rankin handled the role calmly, seemingly unaware of how hard he was working. He also managed to find time each day for training Dukemire. Between periods he gave brief classes on useful phrases in French and English. McCall sat in on some of the sessions, but there was little he could do. He had begun to realize the difference it could have made if he were a pilot.

The one surprise of the week had been the complete absence of Major Legère. McCall had thought that Legère would be most interested in the news that some of the guns had been recovered. He at least expected Legère to ask for the return of four of the replacement weapons. But until an hour ago when McCall had seen him pass in his jeep, Legère had not set foot out of Lam Du all week.

Rather than sending a waiter, Su Letei delivered the coffee herself. "Your sergeant stopped by this afternoon," she said.

"Oh?"

"Yes. First Sergeant Calvin Winslow, a very big, very charming man."

"Charming?"

"Yes. Very much so."

She walked away, leaving him to wonder what Winslow's charm would look like. He determined to watch for it. His thoughts were interrupted by the harsh scrape of a chair, and he looked up to see Colonel Gereau pushing angrily away from his table, followed by a concerned Colonel de Matrin. Gereau marched directly up to McCall, clearly furious. He had bushy black brows, a thick nose, and thinning white hair swept back from his forehead. He stood beside the table, unable to speak, glaring down at McCall. Finally, he said in French, "You are an idiot!" He then stalked out of the restaurant, leaving Colonel de Matrin looking embarrassed. De Matrin was not tall, but the mass of his head and shoulders and an air of authority lent the man dignity. He smiled uncomfortably and nodded at McCall.

"Please allow me to apologize for Colonel Gereau," he said, turning to follow Gereau with his eyes. He extended his hand to McCall who stood to take it. "My name is Maurice de Matrin," he said. "Head of Northern Vietnam Matériel Command. I am sorry for the disturbance, but much of Hanoi is aware of the incident at the Chinese shop. I do not blame you at all—I probably would have done the same myself—but I must warn you that there are many here who do not feel that way. They have many reasons. You are alive right now because you took only what was yours." When McCall started to speak, de Matrin held up his hand. "I know that you believe we condone such places as that shop, but it is not true. We simply cannot raid every place in Hanoi. The one you struck, by the way, has been cleaned out by the authorities. There was talk of your arrest, but I think it was decided to let the matter drop for now. But French authorities will be the least of your troubles should you pursue this sort of activity in the future. I hope you do not misunderstand. I have no part in this. But if you are to remain here, and remain alive, you have a great deal to learn."

"Would you care to sit down?" McCall said.

"I am sorry, but I cannot," he said. "Anyone who speaks to you becomes suspected of something. I can get away with it to an extent because it is assumed that a man my age has developed some judgment. I can tell you there is much talk about you, and you will not find many friends in Hanoi. Now I must go."

When de Matrin had left the Ho Tay, Su Letei arrived with more coffee. "Have you learned anything yet?" she said.

"You said it would be interesting."

"The evening has only begun."

He looked around. "Why so slow tonight?"

"This is an average Friday," she said. "The customers are mostly men. They gather briefly in the late afternoon, then wander away to their homes or posts. Some stop by again for a drink or two about eight o'clock to get ready for the fights. They return Saturday afternoon when they have recovered. Saturday night is not the same problem. There are fights then as well, but many of the older officers and civilians bring their wives here for a nice dinner. It has been this way for almost four years."

"Boxing?"

"The fights? Oh, no, not boxing. Much worse, and the men seem to love it. You know of the Chinaman Chang Wu. Four years ago when he began to make much money he built an arena at the edge of town which he calls Le Profond Bleu—the Blue Deep. That is a bit of a joke, as you will see. The Blue Deep is positioned inside the levee, so each year when the waters come in August it is filled with mud and rats and poisonous snakes. They climb and make nests in the thatch. They do not leave when the waters recede, but remain to live in the filth, and they eat one another. At the beginning of summer, just before the Blue Deep is closed, the roof's population is lowest. Only the smartest and most terribly desperate survive. Then the rains come again, and the rising flood brings a new feast of creatures, drowning and unaware, believing that they climb upward to safety."

McCall smiled. She had forgotten his question. He was about to ask again when she looked toward the door and said, "Excuse me. I have spoken too long. I assume you are hungry, I'll have something sent out." She took the menu and went to the front to greet three men, apparently pilots for Civil Air Transport. McCall watched her go, then tested the coffee. A procession of waiters and waitresses began to arrive, bringing a plate of mounded white rice, a large bowl of soup, sautéed pork with red peppers and chives, seasoned bean sprouts with thin strips of cucumber, a dish of boiled turnips and greens, and the usual loaves of bread, *nuóc mam*, iced butter and preserves. They laid out black lacquered chopsticks, a ceramic spoon for the soup, and European utensils. McCall placed the turnips at the far edge of the table, then began with the soup. It was slender black eel the size of pencils, cooked whole with bits of onion in a thickened broth. He sucked up the wormy food with relish.

Su Letei returned to the table. "You do not eat turnips?" she said in the tone of an offended mother.

"Not since I got big enough to use a rifle," he said.

She suppressed a smile. "Mealtimes must have been eventful at your house," she said, looking him over. "It appears that you ate something during those years." She carried the dish away.

McCall was ladling pork and peppers over rice when the two men came in from the patio. One was a blond, crewcut American with blue eyes who walked like a soldier out of uniform. The other was Jack Sperek. As the crewcut left the restaurant, Sperek approached the table, grinning as if he had rabies. McCall was not sure if Sperek was thinner, or if not seeing him for a few days simply renewed the shock. Sperek had injured a forearm, and a large bubble of blood had collected beneath the skin. His grin was hideous as he slid into a chair. He jerked a thumb toward the door.

"That's what they're replacing us with," he said. "The CIA's new generation, educated little pricks, brainwashed, ready to rid the world of Commies."

McCall understood Sperek's view, but no longer cared. His perspective had slowly changed until he came at last to regard his time in the OSS with a mixture of pride and embarrassment. As he matured, he had become more the straight soldier, inclined to view the OSS as an organization for large and capable adolescents. But in its new manifestation as the CIA, it seemed to attract the grown-up kids less for adventure than for the opportunity of unpunished nastiness.

"Sound old, don't I?" Sperek said.

"You *are* old, Jack. You look ninety. Here, eat something." McCall shoved forward the remaining portion of pork, but Sperek waved it away.

"I'm not hungry," he said. He watched as two men entered and went to the bar.

"You ought to eat anyway, hungry or not."

Sperek ignored him. "You decided to come out and test the waters, huh? Well, this is a good place," he said. "You pulled a real

153

coup, fella. Pissed off more people at a single stroke than I'd have thought possible. And you did it with style. You know what made the big shots mad? That you had the balls to do it, and the brains to leave all those weapons. Like you pulled down their drawers, laughed at what you saw, and walked off. 'Course, if you'd taken everything, the Chinese would have been on your butt, and since they are not the government they don't have so many restrictions."

McCall thought about Winslow and continued to eat. "How much do you know, Jack?"

"More than anybody. The part I don't, I'm working on."

"So who runs it?"

"Chang Wu. Everybody knows. It's just that I'm one of the few who'll tell you, or even talk about it. But above him is somebody else, and maybe somebody above that."

"Why don't they stop it?"

"They just went through this last fall, Congress holding funds because of reports of black market dealings among French officials. If the French fight it, they get a lot of bad publicity, and the funds are reduced. But if they keep quiet, and simply show that the war is consuming everything, they get more U.S. weapons."

"But they're arming the enemy, killing themselves."

"That's the price of getting on the tit in the first place: It's too hard to get off. With the system like it is, it all comes down to who gets to the battlefield first with the gear. In the meantime, somebody like you slops a finger in the punchbowl, even to dip out a turd, nobody's going to be happy. If the Chinese don't kill you, the French will."

"Is that what happened to George Tunnell?"

Sperek looked surprised. "Yeah, that's what happened, more than likely. They said the Minh got him, but maybe that's what happened instead."

"So we're supposed to just sit and watch?"

"I don't know what anybody's supposed to do. I'm just telling you the rules of the game."

"And what position do you play?"

"I'm a spectator, just trying to stay alive." Sperek's eyes brightened, and he smiled. "But I do enjoy a grandstand play every now and then." He clapped his bony hands together. "Good show."

"Who else is playing?"

"There are lots of opinions."

"What about Major Legère?"

"He's in a good position, but he got his job by busting a ring himself. Legère's daddy is a banker, he stands to inherit a ton. The old man was pissed when the boy signed up, and doubly so when he asked for Indochina. Daddy used his influence to keep him out of combat. That's why Legère wound up at Lam Du, assistant to a Major Villouise. Villy was a tough old nut, eccentric as hell, should have been retired, but he had a job that nobody wanted. So Legère showed up, thinking that if he did good in this shit assignment, maybe he could get into a paratroop outfit where he belonged. Villouise cooperated by dumping more on Legère. Then one day Legère realized that not everything was reaching the troops. He started keeping separate records, then took the evidence to Villy's boss, Colonel de Matrin. The colonel said he would work something out. Three days later, Villouise was shot in his jeep on the highway. Legère was thinking he's on his way to the paratroops, but what he got was promoted to major and put in charge of Lam Du. Meanwhile, Daddy was trying to get him to come home. Started cutting his allowance. But so far Legère hasn't budged. He's taken up gambling instead."

"So you think he's clean?"

"I don't know," Sperek said. "It's kind of ironic, though—de Matrin won't let him have an assistant. Maybe Legère has gotten a little careless, but he also has a hell of a job, and he's working alone." He paused and studied McCall. "What made Smith decide to send you?" he asked.

"We shared some bad times in Korea."

"Did it have anything to do with the military black market?" When McCall did not reply, he continued, "You're thinking about pursuing this further, aren't you?"

"There's no way I can, Jack. But no, I wouldn't mind being in that position."

"When you got here, I suggested you turn your tail around and get out. So I'm saying it again, Marsh. I know you—you won't give up until you're dead, and you'll *be* dead if you hang around here too long."

"You always went for the drama, Jack."

"And you always had a hard head." Sperek stared across the

restaurant, suddenly withdrawn. "I'm telling you the only way I can. Get out. Tunnell died because he was an idiot. You'll die because you're not."

McCall studied his old buddy, wondering where the lines might eventually be drawn. It seemed appropriate to change the subject. "So what's happening at Dien Bien Phu?" he asked. "Nobody talks to me anymore."

"Well, the Viet Minh are dug in, fifty thousand troops, artillery embedded on the reverse slopes, siege trenches closing in, picking off the scattered French positions one by one. The French bunkers are worthless, their hospital is inadequate, all resupplies have to come by air, and now—today—the airfield is closed. Nothing's a secret anymore. Like I said, this is the big conclusion. I don't know if I'm right about the motives, but I am right about the results. And everybody knows. There's not a banker or diplomat in town who doesn't have a suitcase packed."

"What happens out at the Blue Deep?"

Sperek made a terrible smile. "There you are, back on it again." He moved back from the table. "It's been real nice knowing you, Marsh."

"What are you talking about?"

"I just wanted to say goodbye while you're still alive. Nothing I can do for you now." With that, Jack Sperek pushed himself to his feet, wobbled a moment, then left the Café Ho Tay in what for him was a hurry.

He was barely out of sight when the man talking with Larkin stepped down from the bar. He was of medium size, underfed, and balding slightly in front. He carried himself with an effacing air that seemed more than fatigue. He wore khakis, and on one arm was a soiled jacket with pockets all over, stuffed to capacity as if it were a suitcase. They had never met, but McCall knew him at once.

"Major McCall?"

"Yes."

"My name is Eber Walloon. I am with *Le Monde*."

McCall stood and shook the small hand with reserve. "Marsh McCall," he said. He knew the reporter by reputation. Walloon had written the article for *Time* which Roach Harman had succeeded in squashing. Born in France of French-American parents—both university professors—he had earned considerable respect for his diligence, evenhandedness, and unerring honesty, even when the facts were not those he wished to report.

"I wondered if we might talk a few minutes."

"Join the parade," McCall said, motioning toward a chair. "Care for a beer?"

"I would, but I don't think I could stay awake."

"You know I can't give you what would be called an interview."

"I had hoped for something less. Or more." He hung the jacket over the back of his chair. "I am faced with the need, common to war, to be quickly intimate with strangers, Major McCall. My visit has nothing to do with a story. But that may not be true. A week ago, when I became aware of your arrival, I wanted to ask why you were here. Since that time I have been to Saigon and to Dien Bien Phu. I got back this morning...no, I'm sorry, it was yesterday. I have not been to bed. Returning on the airplane I fell asleep with my eyes open, then had to ask someone where we were going—I could not remember."

McCall had expected something more aggressive. He began to relax. "Everything I can tell you, you already know."

Eber Walloon looked around the room. "There are many stories here, but most will never be written. It is how those connect which interests me—how the vignettes lock together like parts of a puzzle. I know about your detachment, Major McCall. I know what it does. I also learned in Saigon that your outfit is not officially here, but is stationed instead down south. Combined with what I have learned today, I find that the question I thought was stale is still valid: Why are you here?"

"To train French pilots in U.S. choppers for medical evacuation."

"What I mean is, why are *you* here? You are too qualified to remain unnoticed. Until Monday, everyone seemed to take the attitude of watch and wait. Now that has changed. No man without authority, without some reasonable assurance that he would not end up on a penal island—regardless how courageous he might be— would attempt the act attributed to you. My opinion does not count, and I try not to voice it often, but Colonel Smith would have been wise to select a more delicate instrument for this particular piece of surgery. I hope you do not misunderstand. I am not hostile to your work—in fact, if it is what I believe, I support its intent—so long as it does nothing to harm France."

"Does that allow you to remain impartial?"

"It is becoming difficult. I am a reporter, but I am a *French* reporter. My countrymen are being deliberately slaughtered by their own commanders." Walloon's face was immediately filled with images of Dien Bien Phu. "Excuse me, Major McCall," he said. "I will go. I will probably never hear, but it would be interesting to know what discoveries you make in the coming weeks. Good luck to you, sir." He lifted his lumpy jacket and walked away in a slumped, traveling gait that carried him quickly outside.

"Good evening to you," Larkin said. When McCall looked, the old sailor was wearing a smile that only a half million cigarettes could have produced. Without waiting for an invitation, he sat down. Larkin was a small man in his seventies with pissy-white hair and eyes like a worn-out ocean. Four front teeth were gone, missing staves in a picket gate, no longer guarding the threshold. It had been only a week since McCall had seen him, but the sailor seemed to wear the same ten-day growth of beard. "Would you care to buy me a beer, sir, Mr. New-man-in-town?" Larkin said. "Then we can talk and get acquainted." His voice was nasal and whining from thirty years in Asia, less like an American than a Vietnamese who had learned English.

McCall eyed the man benevolently. He was hoping to get a chance to speak to Su Letei again, but Larkin was bound to know something. "Be happy to," he said, "just as soon as I finish my meal. How about if I join you in the bar?"

Larkin worked his lips. "Yes, sir," he said. "That sounds fair. I would rather talk there anyway." But he did not move. He pushed his tongue against his lips, producing a sucking sound as he scanned the room. "You don't seem to be average," he said. "How long did you plan to be in this vicinity, sir?"

Su Letei was looking in their direction. "Tell you what," McCall said. "Let's talk in a little bit. For now, tell the bartender to give you a beer, and charge it to me."

The sailor's smile was insincere. "I thank you," he said, "but I came for more than a drink." He got to his feet and returned to the bar without a backward glance. He straddled a stool and waved a finger at the bartender.

"Did you enjoy your meal?"

McCall looked up at Su Letei. "Yes, very much. It was delicious."

"So are you going?"

"Where's that?"

"To the fights."

"You forgot to say what sort of fights they were."

"Dogs, of course. I am sure it is sickening, but I also think you should see it at least once."

"I had hoped we might talk."

She leveled her eyes on his with understanding. "This would be as good a time as any if it were possible at all, but it is not."

"You said I could learn a lot here."

"And have you not?"

"Well, yes."

"And you will learn more." She paused. "I lead a fragile existence here. My business exists because I am perceived as being on nobody's side. I have served French, Japanese, Chinese, British, and American generals here. I have served leaders of the Viet Minh, and may serve them yet again. The Café Ho Tay is neutral ground, and as its proprietress, I must also be neutral. Someday that may no longer be possible. Sometimes when I am tired I think of moving south, perhaps to Vung Tau, where the weather is pleasant and life is not so delicately balanced. But I have been here many years, and will probably be here more. Everything that can be learned about Hanoi can be learned within these walls, and since you wish to learn many things, I encourage you to come here often. As for a long conversation with you, I am sure I would enjoy that very much. Perhaps we can do that someday in Vung Tau. But never in Hanoi.

"Now. You must go to the fights at once. Do not worry about the check, you can pay the next time you come. Good night, Major McCall. Be careful, and pay attention to everything."

Finding the Blue Deep was not hard. He simply drove to the levee and followed the traffic. A half mile north of Truc Bach lagoon, just south of the barricades which closed the road each night, the loose line of vehicles descended into the river proper, directly through the village of Tu Lien. The dirt streets of Tu Lien were heaved in ridges and ruts, dried marks of damp struggle between pools renewed by the recent rain. Beams of headlights wallowed through dust, past children hawking cigarettes and fruit.

Beyond the village, down low on land that nobody claimed, Chang Wu had erected his arena. It was a round structure with forty-foot walls, four layers of handmade brick pierced all around by butts of wooden beams supporting the bleachers. Vehicles lined the river bottom in irregular rows. McCall parked beside the beached white hulk of a tree abandoned by last year's flood. He secured the wheel with the chain, and joined the converging throng.

The last thing that he had any desire to see was dogs killing one another in a pit, but it seemed that Su Letei had wanted him to come. He weaved between the vehicles, remembering that it had been a pit bull—a fighting dog such as he would see tonight—that had attacked him in the Chinese shop.

A loud roar rolled out from the Blue Deep, and he looked ahead. Beneath the round thatched roof a ring of lights was aimed outward across the field, suspending a haze of smoke and red dust so dense the air resembled dirty water. He stopped to look. Standing between the levee and the sunken heart of the river it was easy to imagine the land in flood, the surface at the limit of light forty feet above his head. The Blue Deep. Maybe so, he thought, but it should have been the Muddy Deep instead. Far off, boosted by brake lights of trucks, the air that seemed like water was completely red. That made him think of the Bloody Deep, then the Deep Bloody, and he knew that he had it right. The Blue Deep was, after all, positioned on the banks of the Red River. The Chinaman Chang Wu, who fought dogs to the death in the midst of war, had something of a sense of humor.

Though taller than most of the crowd, McCall soon felt carried along by the tightening crush, as if he might raise both feet without impeding his progress. Others were moving in the opposite direction, anger or disillusionment or simple drunkenness in their eyes. Thanks to the Foreign Legion, the port of Haiphong, and the cross-roads influence of Hanoi, McCall counted what he believed were more than fifteen nationalities. Black, brown, yellow, white, various shades between—they smashed against one another through the gates.

Once inside the circular walls, McCall paused to orient himself. Ahead were stairs leading up into the arena, while to his right, beneath the beams that supported the tiers of seats, were concessions and an open *pissoir*. In the other direction, tucked beneath the stands, was a long enclosed room where men were placing bets at a dozen windows. Opposite were four French guards, gendarmes with submachine guns.

He went first to the *pissoir*, a curved trench against a forty-foot concrete wall. Directly across was a concession selling programs in six languages, beer and cigarettes, fruit and dried fish, pocket sandwiches and link sausages on buns. The blend of odors was spectacular. From inside the arena came the sound of a gong and another loud cheer.

At the top of the stairs, a wire fence and guarded gates enclosed the ringside rows where prosperous civilians, old French officers, wealthy Chinese, and a few minor diplomats were seated. A fight was in progress, but McCall ignored it as he searched for a seat. He climbed a few rows and took a space between a fat German in khakis and a well-groomed Indian wearing a white embroidered shirt. He nodded at both, then jerked as a bearded Legionnaire shifted and sat on his feet.

He was cramped and claustrophobic, still paying no attention to the fight, but fascinated with the spectacle. The Blue Deep smelled of piss and shit and dust and blood, sweaty men, dry grass, and damp decay. He glanced at the roof, but saw nothing there but straw thatch and cobwebs. The building was not as large as it seemed, the top row of seats forming a circle no more than a hundred feet across, funncling steeply to a twenty-foot ring. The walls were facing crescents, like a pair of cupped hands, rows of windows at the top. Four central posts supported the roof, and from them a few hooded lights were aimed at a sandy ring. Within eight-foot walls at ground level were two cubicles connected to corridors, doors with bars opening into the pit. Smoke bluely hazed the arena, and the lights beamed down in concentrating focus while the walls contained a collective moan. A yellow dog was being dragged away.

"There is a very important fight tonight," the Indian said in precise English. His skin was charcoal-brown, and he held himself primly erect, black-lashed eyes alert, like an interviewing secretary. Below his starched and spotless shirt were brown cotton trousers and dusty, gleaming black shoes. "Is this your first time?" When McCall nodded, he continued. "Then you *are* in for a treat. Everyone gambles on the outcome, but unless you do it at the windows, you have to be careful. So many languages, so many kinds of money, there are terrible misunderstandings. One or two men are always killed. But no need to worry; such things usually occur outside." He broke into a strange and sudden smile that quickly vanished.

McCall responded vaguely, unsure if it had been a joke. The Indian turned earnestly toward the ring. The German dug into the huge pockets in his shirt, producing a bottle of beer and a package of greasy newsprint containing an enormous long sandwich of sausage and sauerkraut and mustard. It smelled wonderful, but watching him eat it was not. The Legionnaire—his beard signifying that he was a sapper and not to be messed with—checked for drops of mustard, turning to give the German a warning look.

The next fight began without fanfare, so much so that McCall almost missed it. Less than half the crowd seemed to be watching. The German focused on his sandwich.

"This is only for warm-up," the Indian said, not taking his eyes off the ring. That may have been true for one of the dogs, but in less than a minute the other was dead. The winner, a black mottled beast with a flat, square head, lay with its jaws clamped around the lifeless throat. The pit doors opened, and two small men emerged from each with wooden staves, a chain, and a canvas sack. While two gripped the winner's collar and secured the chain, another reached back and gave a sharp tap to the gonads. When the dog came free, the sack was instantly over its head. The winner was led from the ring, and the loser dragged by its back legs, leaving a stain on the sand. There was no roar for the victor, no hush for the dead. Just a bunch of men talking, most oblivious to what was going on.

"Local talent," the Indian said, making another quick smile. "The winner is very old, four years in the ring. From Kwangsi. The winners can make lots of money for their owners, but most are killed in their first season. Then they are nothing but soup bones. Few survive two seasons, and three is a rarity. That one made it four, so now he makes the girl dogs smile, and they bring him in sometimes for an easy kill. It is a superstition that without the occasional taste of blood, the little sperm will not remember what to do when they make their happy swim. And the exhibition helps the owner sell the offspring. The next fight will be better, and the one after that is why everyone came. Except you, of course, and you are here because you do not know better." He flashed another weird smile.

As promised, the next fight was better; at least it was longer and bloodier and involved the crowd. The German had finished his sandwich and beer. He wiped his face on the back of his arm, then his arm on his pants, and leaned forward until his gut was touching his thighs. It was growing much warmer in the arena. The Indian peered intently toward the ring, a thin mist beginning to grow on his lip like a mustache.

One of the pit doors opened, and a Chinese handler stepped into the ring behind a pure-black dog that had a limp. Attached to its collar was a thick chain secured to a hook in the door. The handler lifted the chain from the hook, then held it close to the collar and spoke softly while the dog locked his eyes on the opposite door. When it opened, the black leaned forward and lowered its head, but did not growl or make any other sign. He widened his stance in the sand.

The other dog was tan-and-white, and had a scar that ran from its pale nose across the top of its head. Its eyes were pale and cold, instantly fixed on the black enemy a dozen feet away. Its body seemed to thicken as it prepared for battle in a world too small.

Upon seeing the tan-and-white, the crowd went into a frenzy— strangers betting with strangers, clusters of bills in the air. To McCall's surprise, the Indian leaned across his legs and began rattling in Vietnamese at the German. The German sputtered and shook his fat face, then nodded with a growl. McCall leaned back to make room, and was kicked in the head. Then the Indian got off his lap. Slowly, the fury eased as the bets were made, though the shouts continued. A man dressed all in white leaned over the wall, holding a short stick beside a suspended bronze gong. The handlers gripped the collars and carefully released the chains, leaving them draped across the animals' shoulders. Though McCall had eaten a good meal at the Café Ho Tay, he was suddenly hungry. The gong sounded, the handlers yelled and jumped for the doors, and the killers collided. Both dogs fell back, then scrambled again to the attack.

This was like nothing McCall had ever seen. Any revulsion he may have felt was quickly overcome by the hypnotic power of the scene. The crowd became fused in one hellish snarl like the animals themselves, contributing as much to the battle as the beasts in the ring. The black was the bigger animal, powerful and unimpeded now by any limp. He overwhelmed his enemy with pure strength. But the tan-and-white was younger, quicker, easily eluding the traplike jaws, still able to turn with each assault to inflict small but slashing wounds down low, then high again as the slower beast came down in defense. Both were quickly frothed with blood. There was never the slightest pause in battle, each animal aware of what losing would mean. Dust boiled and spread in a mushroom above the crowd. The men yelled, and Marsh McCall yelled with them.

Suddenly it ended. The tan-and-white feinted high, then very low, and as the black came down for the exposed neck, the smaller dog caught the supporting foot, clamped and pulled, and the black came crashing down. The tan-and-white was waiting, and locked his jaws on the heavy throat. They flopped a few seconds, then the great black dog was dead.

McCall was starving. The Indian had won from the German, and leaned across to collect. The German sputtered and worked his lips, but finally paid the little man. When he could break away, McCall headed down the stairs. The animals were gone from the ring. He paused to stare, feeling only a strange twinge before continuing to ground level.

He used the *pissoir* again, then waited in line for food. The crowd began to roar, louder and more frenzied each moment. McCall fidgeted and turned his head toward the stairs. Finally, he had his beer and sandwich, but as he hurried for the stairs a hush fell upon the crowd. Men were standing on the steps above, pressing against the wire. McCall dug himself a path to see.

Near the center of the ring, a few feet from a dead and bloody animal, stood a tan dog mottled in brown, densely covered with blood. Protruding from one hip was a large chunk of meat, and his neck was gashed between his shoulders. A piece of lip hung loose. The tan dog stumbled, then something caught his eye, and he stared blankly up at the crowd. A column of blood marched along his shoulder to the sand. He sniffed the place where it fell, moved painfully around to view the enemy dead, then sighed and lay down for the handlers.

McCall looked at the dog, and he looked at himself, and he looked all around at the crowd. He saw the lathered Indian smiling madly, shaking a great wad of bills; he saw the diplomats and businessmen in their unlocked cage, the ones who never bled; he saw the handlers drag away the corpse and lead away the victor, neither good for anything now but meaty bones for soup.

With a sudden motion he dropped the food and beer and spun about to leave. But at the foot of the stairs he was trapped by the wagering lines at the windows. Past the glass on a low dais, he saw a table of cash beneath a bright lamp. Beyond, in the safe edge of darkness, sat the shape of the Chinaman Chang Wu. The big head swayed, making dark glasses flash like false golden eyes. McCall pushed to find a way out, but had barely moved when he saw something that stopped him cold: Major René Legère of Lam Du Depot was stepping away from a window, staring at thousands of piasters in his hands.

Chapter Nine

THE PRIVATE RESIDENCE of the vice-consul lay on a shady side street off the Boulevard Ham Nghi at the edge of the diplomatic quarter. The trees were old, and the sun seldom touched earth except in artful splashes.

McCall closed an iron gate and stood admiring the house, thinking he might like to have one similar someday, one in the country, but not this country. It was a handsome two-story, square and white, with a green metal roof and a wide wooden porch, all trimmed in a pleasing light green. Near the door sat a pair of rocking chairs. Beyond an oval glass, etched in a pattern of morning glories, lay a wide hall with dark stairs and white balustrades. He could see straight through to a veranda. It was the home of a man with few secrets, or one who knew to keep them from view.

McCall pulled the chime, waited, and rang again. When no one appeared, he descended the steps and went around the side of the house, down a drive through overgrown shrubs. Beyond a wooden gate he heard a voice.

The American vice-consul to Tonkin had his butt in the air in the classic pose of gardening old ladies. Dressed in frayed khakis and a huge white shirt of comfortable weave, he was working amid an array of colorful iris, holding animated conversation with himself. When McCall cleared his throat and said, "Hello," Walter Pearbone rose as from a hole, face red and flustered. He stared at the major as if he had never seen him before. "Good morning," McCall said. "You asked that I stop by."

The consul's face was resuming its normal pallor, but the red-rimmed eyes were bright. He held a trowel and a few weeds. "That was two weeks ago," he said vacantly. He looked at McCall, then down at his clothes and the things in his hands. "I'm sorry, Major," he said. "I was immersed in something. I am glad you have come." He paused with a distressed expression, and turned to survey his gardens. The yard was quite large, covered with hundreds of iris in countless shades, set in oval and crescent beds divided by brick walks, all within a walled enclosure topped with spears of broken glass. "If you do not mind waiting, Major, I won't be but a few minutes," he said. He dropped the weeds, stabbed the trowel into the earth, and rubbed his hands.

"No problem," said McCall. He admired the grounds. The houses left and right had shaded yards, but Pearbone's was completely open, making it seem he might have selected the place for that reason alone. Other flowers—mainly roses, gladiolus, periwinkles, and climbing morning glories—filled a banked and trellised garden beneath a spacious porch. Along the fences where neighboring shade was shared were beds of begonias, caladiums, lush ferns, and ivy. In the middle of the yard lay a vegetable plot, tilled but unplanted.

"On the front porch, if you don't mind," Pearbone said with sudden stiffness.

McCall returned down the drive and made himself comfortable, pleased to have caught Pearbone talking to himself. He knew enough about the man to believe he might be an interesting old bird to know, but only if he could penetrate the official facade.

Walter J. Pearbone was a lifelong diplomat who had grown attached to one part of Asia, turning down positions that could have led to an ambassadorship simply so he might serve where he wished. His trouble was in finding a woman who shared his interests. When his American wife left him in Taipei, he had married the sister-in-law of a Taiwanese shipping magnate. But even she had declined to accompany him to Vietnam, and their marriage had subsequently

168

been annulled. For three years he had been consul in Hanoi, but as plans were made to send an ambassador to Vietnam, his position had been reduced, a clear invitation to retire. The new men, however, were not quite ready to be rid of him. He was fluent in several languages and knew lots of important people. He was out of the mainstream now, dusty but too valuable to discard, an obsolete encyclopedia.

Twenty minutes passed before the vice-consul received his guest. He had dressed in casual gray trousers and a loose white shirt, open at the throat and exposing a dense patch of gray. "Excuse the informality," he said, "but this is the weekend." He was freshly shaven, skin thin and vaguely pink. The soaring brows had been brushed.

He led McCall to a study that had French doors opening to the veranda, windows draped in yellowing lace. Three old and very fine Persian rugs covered the planks. He motioned toward a chair, then took his place behind an imposing desk. The room reminded McCall of Smith's Saigon office, but smaller and brighter, older and more comfortable. The view of the veranda and gardens through the windows was inviting. McCall took a seat, then caught himself as the cushion sank too deep.

Pearbone seemed to be working himself into an indignant anger. He gave McCall a disapproving glare. "Pardon me for not offering you refreshment, Major," he said, "but the girl who attends such things is off today. I'll try not to detain you long."

McCall just stared. The chair was too low, Pearbone's desk too commanding. He stood and stepped back to the center of the room, where he glanced out the doors. "Okay, Mr. Pearbone," he said, noting that the frown had deepened with the altered perspective. "Let's get to it."

"Let's do," Pearbone replied. He rocked back, braided his fingers, and assumed the expression of a high school principal. "I had hoped that a discussion such as this could be avoided, Major McCall. Which, of course, is why I invited you here for a briefing when you arrived. I wanted to familiarize you with the ground rules, to introduce you to the way things operate in Tonkin. You delayed the visit, and we see the results. Nothing can be altered, but I do hope that today I can make you aware of the damage you may have done. I might add that you are also in extreme personal danger, but that is strictly your concern. Mine is only for my government and its relationships."

He paused, changed his face to meditative wisdom, and moved on. "It is my understanding, Major McCall, that you and some of your men recently conducted an armed robbery of a Hanoi business. Is that information correct?"

"I didn't come here for this."

"I can have your job, Major."

"That's right, sir, you sure can. But nobody said I had to dance with you."

"And what is your job, Major?"

"You need to speak to my commanding officer."

"As a matter of fact, I have already been in communication with Colonel Smith. All he mentioned was that you were in charge of a training detachment. That assignment would not seem to encompass armed robbery." He waited for a response, then continued, "I have learned through other channels that something more is involved. What, exactly, I don't yet know. But back to the robbery—excuse me—the raid, we'll call it. Did you lead such a venture?"

"Mr. Pearbone, I am not going to discuss anything on this subject. It's that simple."

Pearbone came out of his chair. "I will not tolerate your insulting tone, Major!"

McCall eyed him calmly. "And I don't need the condescension, Mr. Pearbone. We can start this conversation over, or I can leave."

Pearbone braced his hands on his desk and lowered his head as in prayer. When he looked up, the professional face was gone, and in its place was one relaxed but terribly fatigued. He sighed and stepped around the desk. "If you'll sit down, Major McCall, I will make us some coffee."

"If you don't mind, I'll just stand here at the windows and enjoy the view."

Pearbone looked out at his yard. On the porch were a pair of unpainted, oversized wicker chairs with cushions and a matching glass-topped table. He stepped over and opened a door. "Make yourself at home," he said.

When Pearbone returned, McCall was relaxed. He had spent the minutes admiring the flowers, enjoying the morning. The air had been filled with a warm, wreathy fog—what the French called *cra-*

chin, or spit—until just before he crossed the river. Then the fog had literally lifted. It was now scooting along a hundred feet above the trees, pushed by an eastern wind, causing a hazy sun to dim and blink. He watched Pearbone arrange the cups, then pour from a common blue granite kettle. That seemed a good sign. Pearbone went to his office and returned with a blank tablet and pencil. Before he sat down, he frowned and extended his hand across the table. "You may call me Walter," he said with only slight embarrassment.

The major stood, and they shook hands. "Marsh McCall," he said without smiling. "Use either name. I go by both."

"Very well. Marsh." Pearbone sampled the coffee, then sat back and scratched at the pad. "Major McCall—Marsh—you've come to an unusual place," he said. "The arrangements here are like none other in the world."

"You mean the condoned corruption?"

Pearbone winced. "In your language, I suppose that's what it is."

"And in yours?"

Pearbone's head was lowered, and when he looked up, his eyes were as the major had seen them at the Café Ho Tay, fretful in their sockets, watching for any loose bit of enthusiasm. "It is a necessity," he said slowly, then hurried ahead. "It's unconscionable, and I'm sure from your position it is quite incomprehensible. But it is temporary."

"It looks rather permanent."

"The war will soon be over."

"You're saying it's too late to interfere?"

Pearbone let his eyes follow a vine embracing a white porch post. He paused on a single blue trumpet. "No," he said. "It's not too late. But there are other considerations."

"I need to know them."

The diplomat turned sharply. "You cannot," he said. "Not even if you were able to survive the information." When McCall began to shake his head, Pearbone continued, "The damage that would result could be worse than that already being done by the system. I have looked at this in every way, and I am sure I am right. When the war ends, the system will end with it. At the very least it will move into other hands and will no longer be our concern."

"I can't accept that without an awfully good reason."

Pearbone glanced at his tablet. "All I can tell you is that your interference will not be tolerated, and I do not mean officially. You are under observation by more than one group, any of which is quite capable of having you killed."

"Which groups?"

"Considering what you already seem to know, I'd say that you should be able to guess at least two of them."

"The French and Chang Wu. Who else?"

"I can tell you nothing else, Marsh. Only that it would be virtually impossible for you to survive long enough to cause damage to the system. Nothing can be achieved by one man alone, and you will not find anyone in Tonkin who will help, least of all someone from your own government."

McCall finished his coffee, held his cup out for more, then gulped it down. "I am glad we got to talk," he said. "I'll keep everything you've said in mind."

"You're leaving?"

"Yes. I'll be in touch." He looked all around the yard. "This place is very nice. I can see all the work."

"The flowers are at their peak just now," Pearbone said. He tore the top sheet from the tablet and absently handed it across the table. McCall glanced at the paper, folded it, and put it away. "You are not backing off, are you?"

"There is nothing I can do," McCall said.

"I wish I believed you. I may as well tell you now that I intend to try to have you transferred south. In the meanwhile, be extremely careful, Marsh. You are welcome here anytime. You've already caught me talking to myself, and there is nothing else you are likely to interrupt. I am usually here on weekends, and many afternoons, working in the garden."

When McCall got to his jeep, he unfolded the paper, then drove through the pleasantly shaded city feeling sorry for Walter Pearbone and his wilting flowers. The American vice-consul had given him a note that was nothing more than mindless scribbles.

The men trained until noon. Only four students showed up, so while Rankin finished out the morning with a two-hour session with Dukemire, he had everyone else spend time on the aircraft. When Rankin and Dukemire finished their flight, all but Rankin called it a day and headed for the tents. He sent Two Acres on his way, then set to work cleaning his bird alone. It seemed that the CW3's interests in life were restricted to helicopters and whores. He spent Friday and Saturday nights in town, and the rest of his time either flying, giving classroom instruction, or reading a technical manual on how to take a helicopter apart.

Cody hung around to assuage his guilt about leaving Rankin alone, but the older pilot seemed not to notice. Finally, he followed the others. He found Dukemire stretched on his bunk, boots off, reading *Of Human Bondage*.

"Where are the guys?"

"Out back cleaning up." Dukemire did not take his eyes off the page.

"You eaten yet?"

"Not hungry."

Cody sat on his bunk, unlaced his boots, and put on dry socks, trying to decide what to do. Since sharing his secret, and experiencing Cody's thoughtless reaction, Dukemire had withdrawn even more. He had become almost obsessive about flying, apparently on the theory that when someone came for him he might be gone and the problem would then go away. Other times he seemed to give up. Then he would hole up in the tent, read his books, and wait for the police to come. That had almost had disastrous results the night the MPs came to see McCall. When Dukemire saw the flash of red lights, he ran out of the tent in a thunderstorm. Cody found him hiding behind the water tank, half drowned in the pouring rain. Dukemire sat shuddering, then suddenly ran inside and jumped into bed. He pulled a blanket over his head and pretended to be asleep.

"What the fuck's with him?" said Brantley.

A minute later Dukemire muttered, "To hell with it." He changed clothes, then put on the polished boots he kept beneath his bunk. He dumped everything from his pockets into a footlocker, then handed Cody the keys. "There's money in there," he said in a low voice. "In the first-aid kit is a ring worth a hundred dollars—I thought I was getting married. Anyway, it's yours. Be sure you get it before they do inventory." Then he went out the door.

"Wait!" Cody yelled. Cowan poked his head around the corner as Cody ran from the tent. Dukemire was already standing beside one of the vehicles, saying, "I'm the one you're looking for." The French MPs just stared at him, then looked at one another. Cody grabbed Dukemire's arm.

"C'mon, let's go back inside. They might be here for something else."

"I don't care. I want this over with."

Just then the door of the orderly room sprang open, and two more MPs stepped out. They glanced at the Americans, then got hurriedly into their jeep and drove away. The others gave a brusque wave, then followed. Cody still had hold of Dukemire's arm. "Let's go back inside," he said, leading him toward the tent like an invalid.

Thinking about that night helped Cody come to a decision. "Get your boots on," he said. He lowered his voice as Cowan entered the tent carrying a towel. He disappeared into his cubicle. "Let's go to town."

"Nah, you go ahead."

"I don't want to go by myself. C'mon, go with me. I'll introduce you to a couple of people I know."

"Get Cowan to go."

"I don't want Cowan to go, I want you to go," he whispered.

Cowan emerged from his cube and stepped into the gangroom area at the center of the tent. "You guys going to town?"

Cody gave Dukemire a look. "Yeah, we're going to the Café Ho Tay, get something to eat."

"Sounds good. Hang on a minute, I'll see if Bitch wants to go."

When Cowan went out, Cody turned to Dukemire. "Okay, butt-head, you've just ruined my afternoon. Get your tail up from there. You are definitely going." When Dukemire looked up and saw his face, he lowered his book and swung his feet to the floor.

"Okay. I'm getting ready," he said with a wan smile. "You don't take rejection too gracefully, you know. You need to work on that." He began lacing his boots. "I'm not going to a whorehouse."

"Don't worry about it, neither am I."

Brantley came in with Cowan. "Who's going?" he said.

"All of us," Cody replied.

Brantley considered a moment, and when he saw that no one cared if he went or not, he said, "I guess I'll go."

"Gee, thanks, Bitch," Cody said with a grin. He got special satisfaction from the nickname because the CW2 outranked him. But

Brantley was not so bad, he had decided. He griped a lot, but much of what he said made sense, especially his comments about the Army. His biggest problem was in swallowing the military theory that rank was reason enough to accept a man's judgment, particularly in matters that could get people killed. But if things made sense, Brantley kept quiet; if not, somebody was going to hear from him.

They signed out with Sergeant Winslow, then went to wait at the turnaround at Lam Du's gate, where a thatched hut and a split-log bench served as bus stop. They watched the activity on the ramp—the working men, the constant coming and going of aircraft. Only Dukemire ignored it all, scratching the hard-packed earth with a twig. Cody tried to see the farm, but the elevation was too low. He had flown over it again that morning, as he did every day he flew, but had seen nothing but treetops, the red roof, and the empty balcony. He never knew if Moni' was there.

A three-quarter-ton truck emerged from Lam Du, and they hitched a ride as far as the causeway road dividing the lagoon of Truc Bach from the body of Big Lake. As they walked, a small boy checked a gill net in the lagoon, pulling himself along in a dugout, pausing to extract a few flopping white fish.

Approaching the café, Cody halted the group. "Hold it, fellas," he said. "Fix yourselves up. You're about to meet a beautiful woman. I don't want you embarrassing me."

Cowan laughed, and Brantley sniped, "Sure we are." He checked himself anyway.

Dukemire looked intently toward the restaurant beneath the spreading trees. "Nice place," he said.

Cody ran his hands down both sides of his head, cleaned the corners of his eyes, checked his nostrils, and flicked a subtle finger across his fly—the last a trick he had learned from a ten-year-old woman named Melissa. Melissa had bouncing tubes of hair like Goldilocks, and Cody was sure they would someday marry. After Sunday school one day he stood for her in his best catalog pose, hoping she would notice his new slacks. But all Melissa could find for him was a furious look of disapproval. She crossed her arms and snapped, *"Your barn door's open,"* and ran to her waiting mother, losing a fiancé and teaching Cody all about women and about the subtle finger.

"A beautiful woman, huh?" Brantley said as they mounted the

steps. Cody felt a pang of disappointment. Nothing greeted them beyond the open doors but a vacant teakwood desk. But when they rounded the corner, there was Su Letei in a simple emerald dress graced with dangling earrings and a necklace of gold and soft jade pebbles. Her lips were ruby and full.

"Oh my God," Cowan whispered.

"A beautiful woman," said Brantley.

Su Letei sized up the situation instantly. She gave Cody her warmest smile and reached for his hand. "What a wonderful surprise, Cody," she murmured, stressing her accent to make his name sound like an intimate part of his body. "Are these your friends?"

"Well, sort of," Cody said, checking the guys' reactions. "But I can't remember their names right now."

"Brantley. David Brantley."

"Roy Cowan."

Each stepped boldly forward. Dukemire kept his head lowered, but he met the female eyes, reached for the tender hand, and said quietly and firmly, "John Dukemire, ma'am."

"So nice to meet all of you. May I seat you in the restaurant or bar?"

Cody glanced at Dukemire. "We came to eat, but how about a table back in the bar?"

"Of course. I have a place available."

She led them along the elevated portion past the bar, seating them at a round table in the darkened alcove. They had missed lunchtime rush by two hours, but the Ho Tay was a popular place on Saturday afternoon. A few patrons—some civilian, some military—glanced up from meals or drinks as the small procession trooped past. Brantley walked behind Su Letei, suddenly silent, followed by a whispering Cowan, then Dukemire and West. Cody nodded at Larkin. The sailor was slumped on a stool, loose as a length of old rope, talking to a balding civilian. Larkin's eyes brightened, and he stopped and raised a finger toward Cody. Then the light burned out, leaving him frowning. He continued telling his story to the civilian.

The others were seated when Cody reached the table. Su Letei was helping Brantley with the menu. The CW2 watched her face in adulation, then lowered his eyes as if toward the place she was pointing, mapping her breasts and body. The fool was even smelling of her, taking slow, deep breaths as if she were a breeze from a field of flowers. Cody was pissed. He had not been eager to share the café and Su Letei, but he had wanted to show them off. Now he knew it was a big mistake. The way Brantley was behaving, the obnoxious ass would soon be a permanent fixture in Cody's hangout.

When Su Letei walked away, Brantley watched her hips and rolled his eyes. "Mercy," he said.

"Grow up, Brantley," Cody said. "She's old enough to be your mother."

"Mothering's not what I had in mind."

Cowan grinned. "Yeah, grow up!"

"Besides, I think the major's sweet on her."

"A couchside coronary."

Dukemire was watching Cody with a hint of a smile. When the waiter came, then departed with their orders, Cody looked up to see Su Letei motioning to him near the bar. He stood with a noisy scrape of his chair. The others watched him go.

Looking at Su Letei, Cody could not blame Brantley too much. He was beginning to believe that he was in love with the woman himself. She smiled, then her face became somber.

"I wanted to tell you that Moni' is not here," she said. "There has been action to the south, and a great many casualties have come in. She is working almost around the clock. She stops by for a nap, then she is gone again. There has also been action on the road to Lang Son. They are unable to get any of the wounded out of Dien Bien Phu just now, but Lanessan is filled to overflowing."

"If you see her, will you tell her I said hello?"

"Of course."

He started to turn, then stopped and said, "Tell her I said to try to remember what it was like at Bai Chay. Tell her to think about that." As he walked away, Su Letei watched him with a startled expression.

He returned to the table to find Cowan and Brantley involved in a rather heated discussion about the potentials of direct involvement in the war. "If they want me to die in another war," Brantley was saying, "they're going to have to do better than some slimeball politician telling me I owe it to my country, and that if I don't fight his goddamned war he'll have to get a job and his kids might have to go to school with mine."

"I agree with that, but it doesn't change what's happening. It doesn't keep me from feeling sorry for these poor dumb bleeding bastards. Like that convoy the other day. We might have prevented it if we'd been out there. At least we could have gone with litters and brought back the wounded. That's all I'm saying. I wish we could help."

"I guess I'm just not the helping kind."

"Then why'd you go back to Korea?"

Brantley gave him a sour look and turned away. When he caught sight of Su Letei, his expression changed. "What was that all about?" he said to Cody.

"She and I are friends. We have things to discuss."

"*Touché,*" said Dukemire.

Their meals came, and the four plowed into the food with gusto. With increasing numbers of Americans coming to Hanoi—the CAT pilots and crews, the Air Force mechanics, the various liaisons and would-be advisers—the Café Ho Tay had broadened its menu to include steak and French fries. All four men ordered T-bones, and washed them down with beer.

As they were finishing, Larkin's last free beer got up and left. Within thirty seconds the fuzzy old man sidled up to the table. "Mind if I join you boys?" he said.

The young men looked up with amusement, the accidental insolence of youth. "Sure," Cody said. "Sit down, Mr. Larkin."

Larkin pulled a chair from another table and sat between Cowan and Brantley. "You fellows have the afternoon off, do you?" he said. When they nodded, he added, "That's good." He scanned their plates and smiled, exposing the gap of his missing teeth. The prickle of his projecting chin resembled cactus, and his eyes were red and blue and old.

"Would you like a beer, Mr. Larkin?" Cody said, turning to signal to the bartender.

"Indeed I would, young man. And I appreciate it, too. I live on a very small pension." He looked around the table. "Helicopter pilots, are you? Does that mean you're helping the Frenchies out, carrying in their wounded?"

Cowan looked at Brantley. "No," he said. "We're just giving them some aircraft, showing them how to fly them."

"That's right," Larkin said, looking at Cody. "I remember now."

178

Then he paused and raised a finger. "There's something I need to tell you, something important. Can't remember what it was." He smiled as if it were hopeless. "That's just one of the things that goes when you get to be my age."

"What age is that, Mr. Larkin?" said Cowan.

"Seventy-four, I think. Maybe seventy-five. I stopped counting when I realized that getting old was not an achievement." His beer arrived, and he gave a silent toast before turning the bottle, taking a thirsty drink. He scraped a trickle from his whiskers. "What made you young men decide you wanted to be part of what's happening in this strange corner of the world?"

The pilots looked at one another. "We didn't exactly decide it," Dukemire said. "Some of us just got sent. How about you? Why are you here?"

Larkin blinked and thought. "I spent twenty-four years in the Navy—signed up in 1898. Went all over the Atlantic and the Pacific, the Indian Ocean, too. Something about this part of the world seemed right."

"Had you spent time here?"

"No, I had never been here before I retired. I hired out on a freighter in Singapore with the agreement that when I got here—Haiphong, it was—I would stay."

"Why would you come to a place you'd never seen, planning to stay?"

The sailor blinked and worked his lips. "I wanted to be different than I was," he said. "I wanted to do something nobody would expect, not even me. People move somewhere and think they've started over, but all that's changed is the surroundings. They still have family and letters, they still go back. I didn't want to be a changed person, I wanted to be a *different* person, somebody else. So I picked a place I had never been, bought and married a woman I didn't know, and began to learn the language."

"Did it work? Did it make you somebody else?"

"No. The only thing that changed was where I grew old."

An awkward silence followed the blunt admission. "Were the French here then?" said Cowan.

"Oh, yes. They colonized this country, stole it in the late 1800s, the southern part first, then later up here. France wanted a foothold here as a trade route to China's interior, since Britain had the

Yangtze. But then they found that the Mekong was not what they thought. So they decided to try the Red, but it wasn't much better. There wasn't anything here that anybody in France needed, but the people were poor and ignorant, and that's always a temptation to a civilized man. Leaving would have meant they'd made a mistake, so they stayed. Visions of empire, trying to hold on to what no longer existed. It's cost them a thousand times what it's worth, but they're still here. They may not be brilliant, but you can't say they're not willful."

"Kind of rotten of them to just come in and steal it."

"Sure. Sort of like the United States and the American West— slaughtered men, women, and kids. Invaded Mexico for no damned reason, machine-gunned a few of them for good measure, and there wasn't anything there but cactus, billy goats, and hungry kids. Same damn thing, over and over, big dogs eating little ones, the only difference being that the U.S. is more arrogant, God being on her side and all."

The four young men were silent as Larkin ended his diatribe. All wore different expressions: Brantley seemed to agree, Cowan looked mildly insulted, Dukemire was puzzled, and Cody West plainly thought it was all hot air. He had grown up around an old man, and understood that they were not necessarily all liars, just that the truth was sometimes less entertaining.

"You don't believe me, do you?"

"Huh?" Cody was not sure that Larkin was talking to him.

"You don't believe me," he said again, resting his ancient eyes on Cody's.

"Sure," Cody said, glancing at the others. "Why not?"

"Someday you'll be old like me, if you don't get killed in that helicrapter. Then let's see how *you* tell the story." He was completely serious, leaving Cody embarrassed. Then the moment passed, and Larkin again looked like nothing more than a slightly intoxicated old man. He rubbed the white stubble, and the skin rolled beneath his hand. "Still got something I need to tell you," he said, "if I can just remember."

Something caught his attention beyond Cody's shoulder, and his eyes were instantly alert. Cody turned and saw Jack Sperek walking through the restaurant. He stopped to speak to a man in French uniform.

"Who's that?" Dukemire asked. "God, he looks terrible."

"Sort of an ex-commando," Cody replied.

"That's not what I'd call him," Larkin said.

"What would you call him?" said Cowan.

"A doer of dastardly deeds." Larkin pushed back from the table and shook a finger at Cody. "That's what I've been trying to remember." He stood and headed toward the rest room, weaving slightly.

Cowan watched, singing softly, "Sailing, sailing..."

Everyone chuckled but Cody. He was puzzled over what Larkin had said, wondering if it was worth pursuing. He decided to go find out.

The rest room was through a narrow door at the end of the bar, then outside beneath a canopy and back again, opposite the kitchen wall. It was small with a single stall and the usual concrete gully with a dripping pipe. Larkin was there, his pants open, fumbling around. Cody stood beside him, pulled out his penis, and strained, but nothing would happen. Larkin was still digging around, head down and looking. Finally he turned to Cody, worked his lips, and said, "I know the son of a bitch is in there somewhere."

Cody began to laugh, and almost peed on himself. Larkin finally found his withered root. He talked as he pissed. "You laugh, young fellow. Before you know it, that pony of yours will be pissing in two different directions. Pretty soon after that you'll be someplace like this where there's lots of people, and when you think you're through it'll give another little squirt. You'll be walking out and feel something warm and think, 'No, it can't be,' but it will, and you'll look down and there'll be piss halfway to your knees. Then all you've got to do is figure out how to get out of there, and if there's a woman with you you'll just go ahead and kill yourself. You go right on and laugh. You're thinking it won't ever happen to you, but it's like a low limb on a tree, it'll die and fall off just when the part that everybody sees is looking the finest." He worked his lips again and stared down at the puny trickle, squeezing to build up pressure, but with little result. "When I was your age, my eyes were blue and my dick was red. Now my eyes are red..." He squinted to focus on what he held in his hand. "Now my eyes are red and my dick looks like a boiled gizzard."

Cody laughed, but he was thinking about Jack Sperek. "You said there was something you wanted to tell me."

Larkin still had his mind on other things. "We had pissing contests when I was a kid, but these days it's a contest just to piss."

"Come on, Grandpa!"

Larkin closed his pants, leaned against the wall, and worked his empty lips. "I can't imagine what it was."

"I think it was about Jack Sperek."

At the mention of Sperek, Larkin's eyes narrowed. "He's poison," he said.

"That's it? That's what you wanted to tell me?" Larkin looked at him, blinking as if to loosen his lids. "Jack Sperek," Cody said. "What about Sperek?"

"He's an assassin."

"Come on, Grandpa. He's a sick commando."

"He was. Now he's an assassin."

"So what's that supposed to mean to me?"

"Sperek is who killed the last man who had your major's job. A real likable fella named George Tunnell."

Chapter Ten

THE SHIP WAS FRESHLY refurbished, and had the fat, impotent look of an aircraft assigned beneath its purpose. When the feathered blades lurched backward, McCall pulled alongside, remembering similar meetings with Smith in Korea. They had known each other a little too well, blurring the boundaries of friendship and rank. But not completely. Smith was a colonel, McCall a major, and regardless how any conversation might go, neither ever forgot those facts.

When the stairs were in place, three men in black caps and gray flight suits stepped out. One moved beneath the aircraft with a set of wooden chocks while another approached the jeep, a lean, serious man who carried himself with military bearing. He held his cap as a Boxcar rumbled past, headed toward a slot between pallets. "The colonel said he will see you inside, sir," he said. "He asked if we might use your jeep to get a bite to eat while you talk."

"Sure." McCall stepped from the vehicle, and watched the three speed away.

Ezra Smith was standing between groups of plush airline seats, bending over a fold-down table, chopping at a bucket of ice with a miniature pocketknife. A sunny beam had the blinding force of a spotlight when it struck his hair. He filled ceramic mugs with chips of ice, then smiled and grabbed a towel for a handshake. "Hello, Marsh," he said warmly. He looked happy and healthy, tired from the trip, but not nearly so worn as the last time they had met. "Good to see you. Have a seat while I build us a couple of drinks." He stepped behind the seats, dug in a duffel bag, and finally came up with a bottle, napkins, and soda. From outside came the sounds of equipment arriving from the supply yard at Lam Du. Aft of the seats, the C-47 was divided by a bulkhead and a narrow door where a small window yielded a view of a cargo hold. There was a bang against the side of the aircraft as a pair of doors opened. Two men climbed aboard and began shoving at crates.

"I borrowed this bird," Smith said, "but only this portion, and with the provision that it continue its duties. The accommodations are pretty nice, but I have to put up with seeing some extra country." He poured the drinks, then held the bottle against the light of the open door. "I was tempted to drink this entire jug on the trip," he said. "We crossed some mountains where the turbulence damn near flipped us. I had a feeling it might be like that, so I packed it where it would be hard to reach." He gave a wide grin and handed McCall his drink. The aircraft shook, and the odor of exhaust fumes swirled through the door.

As usual, seeing Ezra Smith made McCall feel better; the white-haired man had a reassuring presence, a majestic calmness that found a man's secret doubts and soothed them. For one as self-assured as McCall, the old man's power produced a certain edginess as well.

"It's nice to get up and move around a bit," Smith said, immediately sitting down. "So how goes the war in the north?"

"I'm sure you know more about that than I do. I get rumors and thirdhand reports, but the closest I get to the real thing is what I see happening on this ramp."

"They're busy, are they?"

"Round the clock. I thought they were going hard at it before, but nothing compared to this week."

"The situation at Dien Bien Phu is damn serious," Smith said. "The French have underestimated Uncle Ho all along, and now it's almost too late to make up the difference. I don't know if they're that dumb, or if they are so blindly determined they're willing to bet the entire farm that we're going to pull their nuts out of the fire again. Washington is getting a crawful. If it weren't for the Communists, we'd be out of here in ten minutes flat." He paused to down half his drink. "But right now, that's not our concern," he said. "How're things going here for you?"

"There was some confusion at first—we lost a week setting up camp—but we're rolling now. We've put the training on a two-week syllabus, and except for two instructors, we're halfway through the first batch of pilots."

A doubtful expression crossed Smith's face. "What about other aspects?"

"The market? It's more or less condoned. They're doing nothing to stop it. Which makes it twice as hard to find out anything. I'm picking it up a piece at a time."

"What have you learned?"

"Nothing I'd feel comfortable reporting," McCall said. "No real facts. I think that in a little while I will have a better idea where the pieces fit."

"I heard you ran into some trouble."

McCall was unsure if he was referring to Haiphong or the raid on the shop. "Some of our equipment was stolen when we arrived," he said. "We managed to locate a few of our guns, and we stole them back."

"No serious repercussions?"

"Not yet."

"Did it yield any leads?"

"A couple. I'll have to see if they pan out."

"Well, keep after it, but don't risk too much. I'll keep the pressure on from my end. They're suspicious of everybody, and they're especially suspicious of you. I realize there is not going to be a lot you can do, Marsh, but you're here, you're a set of eyes, and you know what to look for. I can help reduce official interference, but I can't do anything about what they might do unofficially. In the meantime, I'm trying to put together a group to track the military gear around Hanoi. But it has to have official sanction to be effective. I'm having a tough time getting it past General Sanfield. He seems to think it's too late, and in any event it should have the cooperation of the French. We could do it another way, but there's resistance from the CIA. They won't work the turf, but don't want us doing it." He downed his drink in a gulp, and began making another.

McCall understood the sentiment about the CIA. In only a few short years Washington had stripped the Army of much of its intelligence capability, producing a military that was a dictator's dream. The Army also had to endure the fact that the group, operating within military operations for cover, also spied on the Army itself. The arrangement left the president and his secret police in control while condemning the Army to the status of boneheads.

Smith began his second drink, and continued, "Dien Bien Phu has changed the complexion of everything. There's a feeling that nothing is likely to matter unless the president gives the okay for full air support. Nixon wants to put in two hundred thousand troops, but Ike is having none of it. The French are hopeful, but I'm not. On the other hand, if France is able to survive the summer, anything you've learned could be of great use." He paused and looked at his drink. "And I knew you'd want a chance to even the score."

McCall was instantly furious. The skin of his face drew tight and his ears moved closer to his head. "That's a hell of a thing to say," he shot back.

"Sorry, Marsh. I didn't mean that the way it came out."

McCall was too angry to trust himself to respond. He knew that Smith *did* intend it exactly as he had said it. Quite apart from rank, that was the one characteristic that had always stood in the way of complete friendship. Ezra Smith was a sly manipulator of men; nobody ever reached the inner realm. At last McCall's anger came under control. "How do you get even for the death of a son, Ezra?" he said.

The older man assumed an injured look, one that McCall had never seen. "I said I was sorry, Marsh. What more can I say? But the fact remains that Bradley and a lot of other men were killed with American weapons—some captured, but a hell of a lot, particularly the ammunition, procured on the black market. The same thing is happening here. Nothing can ever make up for the loss of a son, but at least something can be done to fight the situation. That's all I meant. For that and several other reasons I thought you'd be the man for the job. But maybe you're not."

McCall began to cool. Perhaps he had overreacted, misinterpreted what he believed he saw.

"You're not drinking," Smith said.

"Stomach's been giving me trouble."

"I know about that myself." He dumped down half a glass. "So what else is going on from your end?"

"I fielded an interview with the vice-consul."

"Pearbone? Don't worry about him. He's being replaced. They'll keep him around awhile, but he's got no authority. This operation would be beyond his reach anyway. What about the assessment?"

"Too early to have anything. That's going to be the hardest part. I can nose around, try to pick up the way it feels, but in the end a lot will come down to nothing more than my opinion."

"No one expected anything else."

"I still have not received written orders from Saigon. Every man in this outfit, including my first sergeant, shipped out of Inchon with nothing but a kiss and a promise."

"I'll get the orders. Your men got paid, didn't they?"

"Yes, sir."

"Fine. What else?"

"I assume Lieutenant Atherton made it to Saigon."

Smith looked surprised, then amused. "He's been reassigned. You were a bit hard on the boy, weren't you?"

"Not at all, sir. What about a replacement?"

Smith's face changed completely, as if he could put off an unhappy task no longer. "I had been saving that for last," he said. "There's been a bit of a change in the nature of things." He paused to take a significant sip from his drink. "What's happened is that with the war situation the way it is, Washington is having second thoughts on how many aircraft they want to give the French. They're stalling, in other words. Officially, what they're saying is that they overcommitted themselves and failed to fully account for agreements already made with South Korea. A hold has been put on the other shipments of helicopters. It's temporary right now, but could become permanent. I'm fighting to keep you here, as much to do your report and to look further into the corruption as anything. General Sanfield is arguing our case, but there's no telling how things will turn out. Meanwhile, I need you to go on with your duties. We need your instructors to train enough men to at least take over your aircraft if no more show up. Plus, something has been added."

This time the pause was longer. "We've been getting requests from French Expeditionary Headquarters to fly some observation missions over convoys—not regular combat, just the eyes-in-the-sky kind of thing. I told you when you came up that this would later be your option if the men wanted to do it. Now it's not so optional."

McCall's eyes grew dark. "You can't do that. This is a volunteer outfit, here to train pilots. Nobody said anything about combat."

"I'm not talking combat, Marsh. Just observation."

"And we both know that's crap. The only difference between aerial observation and combat is a bullet, and there are plenty out there. This may be an afterthought by Saigon, but from here it looks like a shitty trick. The boys are not even receiving mail."

"Wait a minute, Marsh. I guess I didn't make things clear. It's still volunteer. You brief the men, explain the situation. Anybody who wants out can transfer to Saigon, no problem. And no pressure. As far as the mail is concerned, that condition will end as soon as they're through up here. They knew that when they volunteered. I don't like to say this because it sounds like I'm shirking responsibility, but the truth is I'm just passing along what's been passed to me. I don't blame you a bit for your feelings."

"It's not me," McCall said. "I'll do what I'm ordered to do. But I've got a responsibility to my men. I'm the only thing between them and whatever comes down the pike. If we had some air support, if we had some troops of our own, if we had some kind of broad-based commitment, it would all be different. They'd be part of it, and they'd take orders like anyone else."

"I agree. So there's no problem. Present it to your men. Let them decide. Nobody is going to make them fly combat."

"How long is this going to last?"

"Not long. A month, two at most. Just until we see which way things are going to go. We'll either get a commitment from Washington, or the French will lose. In any case, your job will be finished."

"How do we handle it if we lose some men?"

"They'll be shipped back through Saigon. It may have to be reported as an accident."

McCall stared out the door. He did not like the sound of this at all. "Why do I get the overwhelming feeling that I'm not hearing the entire story?"

Ezra Smith stared at his drink. "Because I'm not getting it, Marsh. The truth is, I don't know everything that's coming down.

All I can say is that I've always done the best by you in the past. If that's not good enough, there'll be no hard feelings."

McCall clamped his jaw. There was no way out, and Smith knew it. But it was different for the men. This was not their fight, and it wouldn't be until someone made a commitment. "I'll talk to the men," he said.

"Good. Tell them that if any of them decide they want out, they can catch a ride to Saigon next Saturday on this airplane. I won't be on it—I'll be back in two weeks—but it'll be making this stop at about the same time. They can ride south in style. But I think you're going to be surprised, Marsh. When I was the age that most of them are, I'd have traded my left nut for a chance to be here."

McCall was sure he was right, just as he was also sure that at age twenty or twenty-two, nothing in the world could have stood between him and the experience. Whose war it was would not have mattered so long as someone older and wiser had assured him that it was a place where America should be.

He stepped down from the airplane frowning, thinking that in all the time he had known the colonel, he had never once heard him say that he was sorry for anything. Coming from anyone else it would have been a welcome change. But with Ezra Smith it was impossible to distinguish the difference between careful calculation and a cautionary signpost on the route to old age.

"He doesn't believe me," Dukemire whispered.

Cody frowned and shook his head. He was concerned about Dukemire, but right now he had his own situation to think about. The tent was slowly filling with men—officers on the right, enlisted men on the left. Winslow had spread word that afternoon that in lieu of the Sunday-evening formation there would be a briefing in Operations. No one, including Rankin, seemed to know what it was about, and Winslow understood the functions of authority too well to let anything go.

"He called me in for another interrogation—what he calls an 'interview,'" Dukemire continued. "Went through the whole thing again, beginning to end, taking notes all the time. He kept saying it was just routine, but that's baloney. He kept asking for the tiniest detail, insignificant stuff, trying to trip me up."

"Take it easy, Duke," Cody said. "It doesn't mean a thing. He's just trying to figure out what happened, probably would like to catch the guys who stole the jeeps."

"He knows something, I tell you."

"Learn to live with it, like everybody else," he whispered fiercely. "You're not the first person to ever—" He stopped. "Just shut the fuck up about it!" Others had begun to wonder what they were talking about. When Dukemire got like this, it drove Cody crazy. Besides, he was still stinging from his own recent "interview."

He looked all around the tent. It was a GP Medium, much like the ones where the men lived, but the floor was dirt except for a small area in back—a table, a desk with an FM base radio, a bulletin board, a plywood counter, and a section of wooden floor built up on pallets. The Ops tent was also the ground school classroom where the French pilots and the instructors gathered to go over things before and following each flight.

The men took their places on rows of short benches. First Sergeant Winslow walked down the center aisle, taking count and checking faces. He frowned, made a note on a clipboard, and sat on a folding metal chair in front.

"I wonder where Major McCall is," said Cowan.

"Who gives a flying fuck?" Cody said in a low voice.

"What put your pud in the pepper?"

"Nothing."

That was not quite true. After pondering Mr. Larkin's rest-room revelation overnight, Cody had finally decided to take it to the major. He went cautiously, not wanting to appear a fool, feeling there was a possibility that Larkin was telling a tale at Sperek's expense. The starving, unlikable man was an easy target, and in his present condition certainly looked capable of any treachery. Larkin's memory was clearly weak, and the rest of his mind might be in the same pickled condition. But what if the old man was right? Besides what it could mean to McCall personally, the idea carried implications about the entire unit. It was all too much for Cody to work out. Maybe McCall would know what to make of it.

The major was busy preparing for the briefing and did not have time to see him, Winslow said. When Cody explained that it was important and could not wait, Winslow gave him an okay-you-asked-for-it look and stepped into McCall's office. He returned in a moment and gave a grim nod.

Cody was already uncomfortable, wondering how he was going to put this without sounding like an idiot, but as he entered the office he could see the entire scene shaping up as a mistake. McCall had his head down, working on some papers, and he continued to work for some time while Cody stood a mere two feet away. When he finally looked up, he had the distant glaze of a stranger, one with authority. McCall responded to Cody's salute with an impatient wave at his brow, a pencil still in his hand.

"Sir, I heard something at the Café Ho Tay yesterday that it seemed like might be important." McCall made no response, but simply stared, his mind on other things. "I was talking to Mr. Larkin," Cody continued.

McCall lowered his pencil. Ironic lines shaped his weary eyes. "And what did Mr. Larkin have to say that could wait all night but now can't wait another hour?"

Cody had never seen the major like this. He decided that under certain conditions, ones similar to these, McCall could be a real butthole. "It was about your friend Mr. Sperek." Cody paused. Suddenly, everything he had to say seemed dramatic and stupid. But it was too late to back out. "He said that Sperek killed a man, the last man—"

"He killed a man?" McCall interrupted. He gave a cruel smile. "I expect that by now Jack Sperek has killed hundreds of men. What else?"

Cody took a breath. He had to find a way to penetrate the barriers, to get past whatever was eating on McCall and make him listen. When he spoke, his voice was growing husky. "Sir, I thought about this all night. I stayed up late, and woke up early. I knew how dumb this would sound, but I thought you might make some sense of it."

McCall rubbed his face, then his eyes. "Make sense of what?" he said more softly.

"That Larkin said Jack Sperek is an assassin."

McCall looked at the various shipping labels stenciled on the walls. When his eyes again met Cody's, they seemed almost black beneath the brows. Lines cut downward between them. "I have known Jack Sperek for twenty years," he said. "He is a killer, no question about it. I have known Mr. Larkin a few days. He is an old mooching drunk with nobody in this world but people he can corner, people like Su Letei, too nice to tell him to go away, and no place left but a last-ditch bar. You, Mr. West, are young and gullible, precisely the sort of person that an old guzzler like Larkin wants to impress, the only kind he can impress. Putting it as plainly as I can, the man is full of crap." He paused to study Cody's eyes, now pink with anger and humiliation. "I am sorry to have to say it so bluntly, but I am short on time and have a great deal to do. You will just have to learn how to judge old men."

Damned if I'm not, Cody thought. But what he said was, "Yes, sir. Sorry to bother you, sir." Then he saluted and left the room and left Marsh McCall to learn a few things for himself.

As he thought about the scene again, Cody decided it would serve McCall right if he got his head blown off. Just like that other butthole major named Tunnell, whoever he was.

"A-ten-*hut!*" Winslow roared. The room jumped to its feet.

"At ease," McCall said. He walked down the center aisle, stepped up to the wooden floor, and took a position behind a skeletal podium. He spread some papers, and was about to begin when Private Tooler wandered in and sat two rows behind the others. Winslow noted his presence, and returned his attention to McCall.

"As many of you know, I had a meeting today with Colonel Smith from Saigon. That meeting is the primary reason for this briefing, but before we get to that I want to cover some other things.

"First, I want to tell you that you have done a tremendous job. You began under considerably less than ideal circumstances . . ." He paused while several men laughed. " . . . but you recovered quickly, put in a lot of hard hours, and things are now going smoothly as a result. I want you to know that your efforts have not gone unnoticed. In an outfit this small, everything you do—and don't do—is visible, and with few exceptions your performance has been outstanding." He glanced at Winslow, who in turned looked at Tooler.

"That said, next is the current situation at Dien Bien Phu. Although what happens out there has not yet affected us directly, it may eventually. A number of you have begun to develop friendships with some of the potential combatants as well as some of the locals, and they *will* be affected." His eyes tried to catch Cody's, without

192

success. "This is day twenty-nine of the siege. The Viet Minh appear determined to take this battle to the end. From a tactical standpoint, most of the advantages lie with them. Which side eventually comes out the winner may get down to nothing more than seeing which side is willing to pay the greatest price. Reports and rumors and word from Civil Air Transport crews seem to indicate that the enemy is growing stronger every day while the French are going the other way. As many of you may have observed, there appears to be a lack of recognition in Hanoi as to just how serious this battle is. Take my word for it, it is serious. There are between thirteen and fifteen thousand men in several divided positions within a seven-mile-diameter area which can only be resupplied and reinforced by air after a flight of almost two hundred miles. They are surrounded by at least fifty thousand Viet Minh supported by a hundred thousand peasant porters. Dien Bien Phu is in a valley in jungled mountains, all roads are closed, and the monsoon rains have started there, meaning that there are now days that the flights are unable to drop supplies or men. All of which both sides knew from the beginning.

"As I receive information that seems more than mere rumor, I will make further reports. Again, I don't know how this battle is going to affect us, but it will affect us. All of you need to remain alert to the potentials.

"Now, the reason for this briefing: Colonel Smith has informed me that there has been a substantial change in the nature of our mission. We are still a training detachment, but apparently due to confusion higher up the line, it is now not certain if all the promised helicopters will be arriving from Korea. Things seem to be in a state of flux, someone trying to make a decision, or maybe trying to get out of one they've already made.

"For us, this means two things. First, when the present group of French pilots has completed training—next week for some, a couple of weeks longer for the two instructors Mr. Rankin is working with—our schedule will be reduced considerably. If more aircraft are not coming, there will be no need to transition more pilots. This will be on a wait-and-see basis. After this week, we will likely cut back from the present ten students to a maximum of four or five, to be determined later."

McCall paused and looked at all the faces. "The second thing this means is that in lieu of the training we will begin flying a limited number of missions in support of French forces, primarily observation missions over convoys." He watched as a stir went through the group, some excited and smiling, others waiting to hear the rest. "As you know," he continued, "most of you volunteered to come here, but in a training capacity, noncombat. That is about to change. But there is no reason to kid anybody about what is about to happen. Observation missions over hostile forces are combat, pure and simple. They are defensive in nature, as opposed to offensive, but when you catch a bullet it feels the same. Some of you have considerable experience in that type environment, some do not. The usual combat problems will be aggravated by difficulties in communication and a lack of supporting U.S. units. Therefore, each of you, as a volunteer, will have the option of transferring south, returning to the mother unit at Tan Son Nhut if you wish. Colonel Smith has made his airplane available for those who elect to leave. It will be on the ramp next Saturday afternoon.

"I want it to be perfectly clear that there will be no pressure on anyone. You are *all* free to go. It is up to the individual. Technically, you have until Saturday to decide, but as you each make your decision, please let either Mr. Rankin or Sergeant Whitney know. There will also be a short training period involved, preparing for the new missions. We will go over those details as soon as they are worked out. That is all I have to say. Are there questions?"

Brantley's hand went immediately into the air. He had listened to the briefing with his arms crossed, ignoring Cowan's glances. "Yes, sir," he said. "What will we be doing if we elect to go to Saigon?"

"You will either continue the same job there with the rest of the unit, perform some other noncombat duty, or be assigned somewhere other than Vietnam. I have not been in contact with them directly, but it is my understanding from Colonel Smith that the southern element of the 22d is conducting essentially the same training we are, so I expect they are in the same limbo situation."

"I thought U.S. troops couldn't be committed to combat without instructions from the president."

"First, I have no way of knowing to what degree the president has been involved in this decision, but I am sure he is aware of it. Second, it's a matter of semantics. I said earlier that observation missions are combat, and they are. However, because the missions are defensive, they do at times stretch it and call it noncombat. This is the reason that you are being given the option to go south."

McCall looked around the tent for other questions, but Brantley was not finished.

"Sir, was this planned?"

McCall looked at him, trying to decide on an answer. Finally he said, "Not by me."

There were no other questions. McCall looked at Winslow, pointed a finger toward the orderly room, picked up his papers, and left. The men immediately began talking excitedly. Above it all came the clear voice of Brantley.

"I don't know about you guys, but I'm out of this son of a bitch."

They waited as long as they could, milling around outside the officers' tent, sitting on sandbags, and wishing that something would change. Every man in the outfit was there—all but Private Tooler, straddling his duffel bag out on the ramp, smoking and looking around like nothing mattered. A silence covered the men like a smothering blanket, each knowing the wrongness of the situation, each hoping that someone would think of words to make it right. Finally Cowan, who had already talked himself hoarse, lifted Brantley's bag to his shoulder and headed across the road toward the waiting airplane. Watching him go, perhaps catching a glimpse of what it must feel like to be Cowan, Brantley's resolve seemed to slip. But it was too late. He glanced around without seeing anyone, then stood and followed Cowan. After a couple of seconds, everyone followed.

The argument which had begun at the Café Ho Tay as a simple airing of views had become a complete rupture between the two men, emphatically displayed in a tattooed mouse beneath Brantley's eye. They still were friends, but not the same way. The friendship itself had been one of the points of contention: Cowan was incensed that Brantley would put it so easily and unexpectedly on the line; Brantley resented the intrusion into his right of personal decision, and that Cowan would try to employ their friendship as a swaying force. Each man was right, neither wrong, but both were losing. Since it had fallen to Brantley to be the one to take a stand, and to make the hard decision, he also bore the accompanying weight of guilt. That only served to make him angrier, more determined not to veer from a course he believed to be right. It cemented his vaguest feelings into hard conviction. "I'm not fighting anybody else's war again," he kept saying.

"Nobody's asking you to," Cowan replied.

The two had gone at it on and off all week, Brantley maintaining that it had been a trick, getting them all to come to Vietnam for false reasons. He kept saying that if he had learned one thing from Korea, it was that governments did not have accidents, they had carefully planned fuckups. The entire situation was a setup; all that remained to be determined was why.

It had not taken Brantley long to voice his opinion. He had stated it loudly and firmly for all to hear the moment McCall left the Ops tent, ignoring the disapproving stare of Rankin and the outraged but silent countenance of the first sergeant. Winslow began hustling the enlisted men from the tent. After announcing that he would be heading south, Brantley added, "What are they going to do if we all decide to leave?" Everyone listened, but no one replied.

All week he went on like that, perhaps hoping to recruit support. But no one joined him. What made it so exasperating for Brantley was he understood that most of the men—probably all but Cowan— were electing to stay in Tonkin for every sort of reason but the one that seemed apparent. Some stayed because they lacked experience; Cody West and John Dukemire fell into this category. Jim Kinney and Two Acres were a team, the way Cowan and Brantley had been; they stayed for one another and for the hell of it. Joe Whitney stayed because Kinney and Acres did, and Billy Mano didn't care one way or another, but only wanted to be with men he knew. Burd Rankin and Calvin Winslow, different in every way, stayed for the same reasons; they were career men, experienced soldiers with obligations in both directions, but mainly they stayed because it would have been unthinkable for either to leave; they took orders, and that was that. Tooler did not count at all, except to sully what Brantley was doing, sending him off in the company of a lazy scumbag. The first thing Winslow had said when McCall told him about the change in mission was "I want Tooler out of here." Tooler would have probably gone anyway, and nobody would have ever been willing to fly with him as his gunner. At least the two men did not share an attitude; neither looked at the other as they waited apart on the tarmac.

Another thing weighing on Brantley was that he was breaking up a partnership. Though he and Cowan were opposites in many ways—Brantley thin and loud, slightly belligerent, quick to point out any injustice; Cowan big and typically quiet, prepared to accept what came along, rarely critical of another man—each had found some balancing element in the other, and so had been friends. The agreement to come to Vietnam directly from Korea had been their joint decision. Neither would have made the trip without the other. Now, because of Brantley, the marriage was falling apart. They might later be in the same outfit in Saigon, but nothing would ever be the same; the trust was destroyed.

One at a time, the plane's engines belched to life, then quickly settled down to a businesslike drone. The civilian crew had returned only minutes ago, and while the pilots disappeared inside the plane's gray hold, a burly crew chief in a dirty jumpsuit went briskly about his business. Soon he signaled to the men. The aging, directionless Tooler stood and moved slowly toward the aircraft, duffel bag banging against his leg, while the others watched. Brantley looked around at each man, then finally came to Cowan. "Take care of yourself," he said.

"You, too. Sorry about the eye."

"I deserved it."

Brantley shook his head almost imperceptibly. He had talked himself into the circumstance, and there was no way out. He shook Cowan's hand, then hefted his bag and walked toward the plane. When Brantley was almost there, Tooler already aboard, Winslow and the major drove up in the jeep. McCall got out, shook Brantley's hand, and gave him some papers. Brantley climbed the steps, the hatch closed behind him, and the C-47 began to taxi. The others wandered away, but Roy Cowan stayed behind on the hard steel ramp to watch his obstinate friend disappear in a pale gray sky.

Chapter Eleven

MCCALL HAD THE OFFICE to himself, enjoying the freedom of meditation without worry of anyone finding him staring into space. Once the aircraft were gone on their missions, Sergeant Winslow had asked if he might take the jeep into town. It was an odd request at midweek, but in his present mood McCall frankly did not care if Winslow spent the entire day in a whorehouse.

He made fresh coffee, then drank a cup at the front window. There was a lull in the usual noise of the airfield, allowing him to note the growing balminess of the weather, a day for shorts and beer and bare feet. He thought about the pilots out on their first convoy mission, and envied them their freedom. He was beginning to understand how glad he would be when this assignment was completed.

He watched a convoy pull out, led by a jeep, then shifted his eyes through the gates of Lam Du, noting that Major Legère had still not made it to work. The fishbowl location of the 22d, intended to provide the French major with a view of everything McCall did, had produced a reverse effect. Not that there was much to see: Legère spent an occasional night in the city, and went to the Blue Deep on weekends. That was about it.

He poured more coffee, then returned to his desk to scratch a few notes. Several things were eating on him, all vaguely connected, and he wanted them worked out. He was always careful to burn such notes, but had found that it helped to think with a pencil. Seeing his thoughts on paper allowed him to follow a trail directly to his subconscious, permitting discoveries unavailable another way.

First was John Dukemire. Something had been omitted from the young man's story. Anyone with daring enough to go on a self-assigned mission, and the ability to successfully complete it, should not have been intimidated by questions. During their second session, one small detail had been unearthed: Dukemire had been fed. The pilot mentioned it innocently, as if it were unsurprising in a land where people starved.

Suddenly everything looked different. If Dukemire was fed, it implied that somebody wanted him to find the stolen jeeps. It naturally followed that somebody let him get away, meaning that the assault had been staged with specific purpose, the most likely reason being as a diversion, something to draw attention to someone like Major Legère. This would certainly explain the Frenchman's frantic befuddlement about Haiphong, and it tied neatly with McCall's impression that although Legère was probably involved, what was happening in Tonkin was a great deal larger than one frustrated major.

But regardless who was behind it, the effort would be for naught. Despite the fantasies of Colonel Smith, and as much as he might like to pursue it, McCall was in no position to do anything but observe and report. Ezra Smith was dreaming, probably faced with the conflict of wanting to retire, yet still hoping to leave a mark for someone to remember.

Next on his mind was Jack Sperek, and through him, Roach Harman. Since its inception from the remains of the OSS, the CIA had steadily grown, but not so much as to avoid the budget knife under Truman, debilitating its efforts in the increasing heat of the Cold War, particularly in Europe. The damage in the Far East was less severe, mainly because of the resourcefulness of Harman. When his funds were cut, he set his men to trading cash on the black market exchange, producing an income to support operations. It was also rumored that there had been dealings in drugs. McCall doubted that story, but whatever the source of funds, it was a neat arrangement for everyone. The president was completely oblivious, some members of Congress had heard about it but were unconcerned so long as no tax revenues were involved, and Roach Harman was able to conduct his work with little or no oversight.

Another aspect was more difficult to ignore. Increasingly, to provide cover for operations, the CIA had begun to operate within less obtrusive organizations, with or without their cooperation, and sometimes without their knowledge. Almost all aid and cultural assistance programs had been penetrated for varying durations. Agents had posed as doctors, scientists, surveyors, engineers, architects, reporters, and photographers. Though operatives were sometimes put in Army uniform, the more usual method was simply for orders to come down from the top, requiring cooperation by senior officers. By the end of the Korean War, Harman had so many men in so many places that it became imprudent to discuss him at all. Thus the man who was practically invisible became unmentionable as well, culminating in the summer of '53 with the killing of the story in *Time.* It was now commonly understood that Colonel Smith's organization, the Military Assistance Advisory Group in Saigon, was actively involved in CIA operations.

McCall set his papers aside, feeling suddenly weary. His thoughts had completed a circle. That was the danger of delving into the subconscious—he then had to worry about what was unearthed. He went to the alcove for more coffee, regretting that he had not stuck to a straighter course. He checked a sack that Winslow had left and found a few golden croissants, but he no longer had an appetite. He returned to his desk to stare bleakly at the wall, wondering if he had fallen face-first on a trail he had deliberately ignored. He was suddenly sorry for Ezra Smith. If Roach Harman held the strings—if their assignment had been bent to his fuzzy purpose—it could only mean that the colonel had degenerated to complete helplessness.

The door to the orderly room opened. "Hello?"

The voice was that of Major Legère. McCall checked his watch: exactly 1000 hours. For more than two weeks, Legère had remained out of sight. Occasionally, McCall would see him pass in his jeep, standing in the Lam Du yard, or sometimes meeting an airplane to receive a shipment, but the last time the two had made eye contact was the day Legère replaced the stolen weapons. Through the French

Air Force liaison, Captain Sarot, Legère had continued to express his belief that convoy cover by the choppers would only endanger the lives of the crewmen. He had only reluctantly agreed to cooperate with the missions. McCall stood and looked around the corner. "Good morning," he said.

Legère heartily returned the greeting. "I was wondering if you had seen Captain Sarot," he asked. His expression was pleasant and relaxed, the eyes shaded slightly with concern.

"Not since early this morning," McCall said. He stepped out into the orderly room.

"Did he mention the disposition of your aircraft?"

"Yes. In fact, he briefed my pilots. He was trying to locate you to get confirmation of convoy time."

"I was at breakfast. In the city." He frowned. "I noticed that half of your aircraft are gone. Are they training already?"

"No, they're covering a convoy as planned. They will be giving instruction this afternoon."

"Oh." The lines of Legère's face relaxed. "Then they have already departed for Phu Ly. So everything is all right. I was afraid we might have missed—"

"No, they didn't go to Phu Ly. That was apparently the plan, but since Captain Sarot couldn't find you, he said he could not confirm when or even if that particular convoy would go. Rather than lose the aircraft time, he sent them on another mission."

"Another mission? To where?"

"Haiphong. That was the only thing he was sure about. They're escorting a convoy up Route Five."

The French major had lost all color, and seemed ready to faint. He turned, fumbled at the door, and rushed from the office. When McCall stepped to the window, Legère was supporting himself on the sandbag wall, vomiting a yellow breakfast. He spat and wiped his mouth, then hurried unsteadily toward the gates of Lam Du.

Billy Mano was wearing a furious frown. Brown hands loose on the machine gun, wind whipping his fatigues through the open door, he had not said a word since leaving the ground. All week, as Rankin drove them in training for the new mission, Mano had acted that way. Cody wondered what he was mad about, but now he understood. Mano liked the aircraft, and was a mechanical talent, but he accepted flying only because it went with the territory. He was relaxed, but having a hard time. Cody watched the two aircraft ahead bobbing in the currents rising off the fields, and was sorry for Mano. He felt the controls in his hands and beneath his feet, felt the floating, shifting motion of flight, the muted vibration at his back, heard the engine's low growl and the airy thump overhead, and knew that he, at least, was where he belonged.

The countryside was patterned with canals and meandering blue streams that turned muddy below, rows of eucalyptus, irregular paddies, villages scattered as if dropped from the sky. Fat clouds shuffled along overhead. Along the crests of the nearest mountains, through a weird warpage of light, shapes of trees stood oversized like sentinels in blue.

The flight was cleared at fifteen hundred feet along the highway to Haiphong, Rankin at lead, Dukemire flying as his wingman. Cody had at first been incensed at being assigned as chase bird, the spare in case anything happened, but now he was enjoying the flight. Even flat land was pretty from altitude. Between checking the instruments, he swung his eyes around the wide delta.

The Tonkin delta had once been ocean, an intruding triangle at the edge of the continent, slowly filled over eons by sediment from the several rivers, primarily the Red. The backbone of the land was limestone, white when broken, but normally weathered to deep charcoal and pocked with countless caves. The remains of this spine stood now in boulders several hundred feet tall, projecting above the surrounding ocean of water, and at various places inland above the delta. These same formations in concentration had created the mystical and mazelike Ha Long Bay that Moni' had spoken about. He hoped to see it today.

Rankin had pushed them all week, insisting that the men were not prepared for combat. Captain Sarot was anxious to begin, but McCall held him at bay until Rankin said the men were ready. The CW3 had spent the evenings gathering information about their area of operation—airfields, refueling points, medical facilities, convoy routes, enemy concentrations, common ambush sites, artillery, radio frequencies, and which places had people on duty who spoke

English. Then he briefed the pilots—Cowan, West, and Dukemire—and began going over the methods of operation. Meanwhile, the crew chiefs were working on the aircraft. Because they were now to be engaged in three types of missions—training, aerial observation, and medical evacuation—it was decided to permanently rig each bird with a single litter on the right while a gunner would ride on the left—removing, then later installing the extra collective control stick for afternoon sessions with French pilots.

Rankin then held classes at the flight line, briefing the men on techniques, what to expect and what would be expected of them. They then took to the air, three helicopters at a time, for hands-on practice. McCall had wanted to restrict each flight to two birds, but Rankin pointed out that if one went down with two men, a single OH-13 with a pilot and gunner would not be able to retrieve them both. He also insisted that for at least the first couple of weeks he would be leading all missions. This put another burden on him, since he was still engaged in training the two French instructors in the afternoons, but he said it was the only way to ensure that the two inexperienced men—West and Dukemire—would survive. Finally, the pilots had taken their gunners to an aerial firing range a few miles east. Only then did Rankin declare the unit ready to accept the new missions.

Unexpectedly, their first nontraining mission now looked to be a milk run. Captain Sarot had appeared at Operations before dawn, saying that he had hoped to cover one of Legère's convoys to a fort beyond Phu Ly, thirty miles south. Viet Minh elements had established camps in the mountains along the Boi River. Nam Dinh, east in the delta, had long been a center of enemy support, and was now funneling rice westward to the Boi, and from there to Ho Chi Minh's troops at Dien Bien Phu. The French had reinforced the fortress to try to intercept this flow, and in response, Viet Minh sappers had attacked the position three consecutive nights. Supplies were desperately needed, and a convoy was scheduled. But that was where Sarot's information stopped. He had checked the depot and called a few places, but could not locate Major Legère. When he was unable to confirm when or even if the convoy would go, he had decided to send the helicopters to Haiphong instead. They would refuel at Cat Bi Field, then pick up a convoy on the outskirts of town at 1000 hours, escorting it toward Lam Du as far as one load of fuel would allow.

Cat Bi Field, four miles south of Haiphong, was busy when they arrived, mainly with fighters and small bombers supporting the struggle at Dien Bien Phu. When they had refueled, Rankin held the flight on the ground for a few minutes, then led an eastern departure, turning slowly back north. Because the mission had not been scheduled, there would be no radio contact between the aircraft and the convoy elements. The convoy might not even be aware at first that cover was being provided.

They climbed to five hundred feet and held a course that took them out over the river bay. Below were a few meager paddies, then none at all nearer the river, then empty mud and dead gray brush in the tidal flats. Ahead, the delta lay spread before them, more water than land. They were within twenty miles now of Ha Long Bay and the waterside village of Bai Chay. Cody looked for a long time in that direction, trying to interpret what he could see. The distance was marked by a fading progression of stone formations. Amid the boulder-mountains there was an open space, blue sky and blue water, surely the place off Bai Chay. He wished that he could fly there, escape the boring mission, and maybe even take Moni'.

She had been on his mind all morning. Though he had continued to fly past her house, it had been more than two weeks since he had been to the farm. He wanted to be able to say, the next time he saw her, that he had actually seen Bai Chay.

When the flight of three was above the river, Rankin began a slow turn westward which took them past the northern edge of Haiphong. The city from that perspective resembled Hanoi with its great trees and colorful stucco, but smaller and without all the lakes. A couple of curving canals cut through the city, and around them were parks.

The flight passed a petroleum depot along the southern bank of the river, then Rankin led them inland toward Route 5. The convoy had departed on schedule, and was strung out now along the highway. From a wide assembly area on the shoulder just short of a guardhouse and bunker, the last tractor-trailer was just pulling away, followed by an armored car.

"Two-three, this is Two-five," Rankin called. "You may as well take it up another five hundred feet. Hang well to the rear, but keep us in sight. We'll move on ahead, drop down, and start checking the road. Maintain clearance with Gia Lam and Cat Bi Artillery. And if you have to come down low or do any shooting, keep clear of these rigs. All eighteen are loaded with nothing but crates of artillery shells."

"Two-three, roger," Cody said. Billy Mano, monitoring the transmission, swung his machine gun, aimed at the last truck, and pretended to burn off a few rounds. As Rankin and Dukemire began to descend, Cody put the OH-13 into a spiraling climb, the Tonkin delta pivoting around them in endless panorama. The angle of sun had steepened, and to the southwest it cooked through the scattered clouds in splayed rays, yellow and white, accenting the blueness of the air. Far away down the coast were more mountains, but all they could see was a wall of deep blue.

Rankin had said that thirty thousand Viet Minh were now known to be in the Red River delta. Staring across it, Cody thought that seemed an incredible figure. There was no place at all to hide, no place except in the villages among the people. That thought gave Cody a jolt; if the enemy was able to hide among the people, then the people must also be the enemy. He frowned and refused to think about it.

When they had completed the turn and leveled off, Rankin and Dukemire were far ahead, blades flashing dimly against the greenness of the paddies. As the two worked the roadway and surrounding dikes and hamlets, Rankin issued a stream of terse instructions, Dukemire responding with double clicks of his mike. Then Cody looked down and saw a problem. The last truck in the convoy had stopped. The driver was standing in the roadway, kicking at a trailer tire. The armored vehicle at the rear of the procession came up and waited. Finally, the truck pulled away, escorted by the armored car, while the driver looked for a place to turn around.

Cody watched, then returned his attention to the other birds, far ahead now, difficult to see when they crossed the cloud shadows. The trailing semi was still moving slowly, approaching a turnoff to a village. Once the rig was able to turn around, it would be only a short mile's drive back to the guardhouse and bunker. The armored car seemed to have everything under control, so Cody closed the distance with the other birds, calling Cat Bi Arty for updated clearance.

He kept thinking about Brantley, making the sudden decision and sticking with it. It left an empty bunk in the tent. But a bit of Brantley was still with them. He had given the unit its call sign, Dragonflies, explaining that it was a blend of the dragon of Vietnamese lore and the modern aircraft; besides, it was what the 13s resembled—dragonflies, with their bulbous heads, blurred wings, and slender tails. Even Rankin agreed, his only stipulation being that though they might be Dragonflies on the ground, in the air they would always be Dragons.

When the two other choppers were directly below, Cody turned and headed back, counting the trucks as he went. The armored car had resumed its place at the tail of the convoy.

"Where'd the last one go?" said Mano.

"Back to town," Cody replied, looking far down the highway. There was no sign of the truck.

"I don't see how he could have made it that fast."

Mano had a point. "Two-five, Two-three," Cody called.

"Two-five, go."

"Roger, Two-five, we've got a truck with a problem at the tail of the convoy. We're going to drop down to five hundred and check it out. Should take only a minute."

"Two-three, go ahead, but maintain one thousand. Don't spend more than a couple of minutes, then call me back."

"Two-three, roger."

Soon they were above the side road leading to the village, but there was no sign of the truck. There was a clear view of the highway into Haiphong, but all they could see was a string of bicycles and a few overloaded Lambrettas. Mano leaned out and stared below, then turned back inside and keyed his mike. "Take a look down there. See those women? Look what they're doing." There were four of them there, all bent over with short brooms, sweeping the dusty road.

Cody turned toward the village. It looked like any other, a few stucco structures, but mostly thatched houses sheltered by the ordinary thicket of ubiquitous bamboo. Bare patches of earth could be seen, but most of the village was hidden. What Mano was suggesting seemed impossible. "Naw, they just beat it back to Haiphong," he said.

"Two-three, Two-five, what's the situation?"

Cody hesitated, then keyed his mike. "Two-five, the truck has returned to Haiphong. We're headed your direction."

"Two-five, roger."

As they turned again toward Hanoi, Mano hung his head out the door, gazing down the side of the aircraft for a long time. When he came back inside, all he said was, "No way."

Cody did not reply. He was wondering if he should risk another bloody visit to the major, and he was thinking maybe Brantley was right—maybe they'd really screwed up, getting involved in this idiot war.

McCall was sitting outside, boots off, scrubbing his tired, damp feet in the sand. Because that end of the tent faced away from the dust and commotion of the road and airfield, he and Winslow had rigged a tarpaulin awning on tall steel posts. No other structure lay to the west, and it made a good place to watch the evening sky above the ammo dump.

He already knew what he was going to say in his report, that what the French had not been able to achieve in eight years was even less likely to be accomplished by the United States. What cemented his views was the specter of limited war. Most of the United States' wars had been limited, but always there was the understanding from the outset that whatever it took to win would be done—until Korea in the new world of nuclear weapons. Just as in Korea, it seemed likely to McCall that future wars would be high in casualties and limited in goals, engaged with less than thoughtful consideration. Just as in Korea: One day we were not at war; the next day we were. All because Mr. Truman said so.

Winslow rounded the corner carrying two sweating beers. He handed one to McCall. "Thought you might like a drink before you set off to slay the philistines," he said.

"You bet." The first sergeant took a seat beside a small table of plywood and sand-filled 105 shells. "Looks like they're already warming up," he said. The low sky beyond the tent city immediately north was smudged by a pale thumbprint, the lights of the Blue Deep guiding early arrivals to vicarious battle. "You still planning on going?"

"A little later."

Winslow looked toward the lights. "You could take Two Acres with you," he said.

"No." McCall shook his head.

"I guess it's no secret that I'll be glad when we're out of this son of a bitch. I've never been anyplace like this. I can't explain it, but it just doesn't feel right. Maybe it'll be okay down south. If it was up to me, I'd give Hanoi to the gooks and never look back."

McCall agreed, but saw no point in saying so.

"In any case, this will give me something interesting to write to my wife."

"You're married?"

"Don't I act like it?"

McCall smiled. "I guess I never thought about it."

"Well, I'm kidding. I'm not really married. I mean, I am, but I'm not. It was a mistake, I'm just not the material. My wife said she didn't want to be called a divorcée, that she'd rather have a man who never came home than to go through life with that label. So I send her a picture now and then, and let her know where I've been so she'll have something to say if anyone asks. And if I'm ever killed, she'll get the insurance. She keeps my photograph on the mantel."

McCall was thinking about his own marriage, a different kind of tragedy, and the subsequent divorce. His wife was unconcerned with labels. Though they were married for twenty-two years, she didn't keep his picture on the mantel, and for the final seven—since the day he decided for sure to remain in the Army—she kept it nowhere at all.

Winslow sensed that something unpleasant had been stirred. He tossed down the last of his drink. "I think I'll go clean up while the shower is empty," he said. "Want another?"

"No, thanks."

He stood and gathered his things, then frowned and made a decision. "I've been wanting to ask, sir—are you the same McCall who lost a boy in the Munsan Massacre?"

"That's right."

"I've always wondered—we were on the move at the time, and I never heard—did they ever catch any of the men responsible?"

"I don't know," McCall said evenly. "Some said they did." That was a lie. Winslow's penetrating look said that he knew it.

"Well, anyway, I just wanted to say that I hope they did, and if they did I wish I'd been there. I know it's more personal to you, but it wouldn't have had to be my boy for me to cut that bastard's liver out—in public, accepting all the consequences."

"Good night, Sergeant Winslow."

"Good night, sir."

The Munsan Massacre had not occurred at Munsan, but northwest of there along the lower reaches of the Hantan River. It was a relatively small action which occurred well into the second year of the war when things had settled down to grinding, back-and-forth, everyday work. The battle made the news only because of the number of casualties. What did not make it was the way it came about or the incident that followed.

Baker Company, 3d of the 401st—attached to Task Force White Horse, charged with making a night sweep of the valley to counter Chinese action in another part of the peninsula—ran into trouble with its radios and became separated from its battalion. The unit wandered into a dead-end ravine before discovering the mistake, doubling back in the dark. That was the moment the Chinese launched an attack on the isolated outfit, and Baker was wiped out to a man. Bradley McCall had been among that group of soldiers. It was only the discovery of a dud mortar round beneath a body that led to the revelation that all of the weapons and ammunition employed in the attack had been of U.S. manufacture.

It took a while to find out how it had happened, and the event would have been overlooked completely had it not been for a sergeant major in Headquarters Company who remembered a small detail: Baker's radios had all been switched by Regimental Supply immediately prior to the action. No equipment was recovered from the battlefield, but the sergeant major, a twenty-eight-year veteran named Will Wockie, began his own investigation. He never reached the top man, but got as far as a master sergeant whose guilt was undeniable. Wockie literally sliced a confession from the man, revealing that Baker, the means to destroy it, and the maneuver plans had all been sold for cash. Realizing he could take it no further, Wockie slowly disemboweled the man before turning himself in to his commanding officer. The court-martial was kept quiet. Wockie was found guilty of manslaughter, sentence suspended with forfeiture of benefits, then discharged from the service. Unable to receive regular retirement, he was nonetheless paid a monthly cash stipend by an unofficial association. Marsh McCall made regular contributions to the fund.

He sipped the last of the beer, wishing he had taken Winslow up on the second. Thinking about Bradley always left a nauseating emptiness, the place where all the conflicts came together.

He had joined the Army in 1940, long before the United States was at war, telling his wife that he wanted to get his military service behind him. Besides being unhappy with the development, Bess was a little embarrassed to be married to a soldier. Training required that he be gone for much of the first year. When he finally came home, excited that his family could now move to his duty post and be together, the course of the future was set. Bess was stiff, on guard, clearly determined to not rely on him too much. He saw a deep anger in her, a desire to punish which caught him unprepared. They did not share a bed his first night home—he slept on the sofa. That alone would have made the next night more difficult, the chasm less likely to be crossed. She seemed to be waiting for him to say what he would not say, that he had made a mistake and could hardly wait to be out of the Army. In a short and calculated moment, it forever assigned sex between them the high and worthless status of withheld reward.

In the morning, young Bradley was there, eight years old and his mother's little man, watching him when he awoke. "How long are you going to stay?" he solemnly asked.

So the family did not move, and for a while it stopped being a family. Marsh McCall came home as often as he could, until one day he arrived to find that Bradley had been sent to summer camp. The timing was mere coincidence, Bess said.

Then war began, and it was stylish to have a husband who was an officer, off fighting the Nazis somewhere. He wrote and sent money home.

Bradley was twelve when he saw him again—a fine-looking boy and a stranger. The war was over and styles had changed. Bess had moved their home in his absence. The sofa was gone, and there was no place to sleep. He sat on a stiff upholstered chair, holding a cup that was too small for his fingers, and made the announcement.

211

"I'm going to stay in the Army."

"No kidding?" said Bradley. "Wow! My dad's a permanent soldier!"

Bess was across the room at the table, still wearing her robe. "That's fine," she said quietly. "When will you be leaving?"

He looked at Bradley, jumping around the room. A fine-looking boy. "This evening," he said.

It took another year to convince himself that it had not been a mistake. Following a brief stint overseas, he again returned to Fort Bragg. And as before, he made the monthly trips. There were scheduling problems again, then Bess began seeing another man, and things improved. He was the vice-president of a midsized insurance firm who had somehow missed out on the war. McCall met him once, and they had a brief conversation.

"Pardon me for asking," the man said boldly—his name was Filmore Banks— "but when do you plan to give Bess a divorce?"

"Whenever she asks for one," he replied, noting the blank surprise.

Bradley was changing fast by then. It grew increasingly difficult for his mother to tell him what he should think, but she let no opportunity pass to establish her view that being a soldier in time of no war was irresponsible.

When Brad was sixteen he got his license, then surprised his father by driving down one weekend with a friend, not mentioning it to his mother until he called her to say that he would be spending the night. It should have come as no surprise, but it hit McCall with jarring force when Bradley told his friend in front of him, "When I finish college I'm going to be a career soldier, just like my dad."

McCall began the necessary preparations, and by the spring of 1950, just before Bradley got out of school, had secured his son an appointment to West Point. Then the Korean War began, and Marsh McCall was among the first to go. He was there only three months when he received a letter from his wife stating that Bradley had joined the Army. The boy was afraid that the war would be over before he could complete four years at the academy. Like his dad, he wanted to be in the infantry.

Marsh McCall escorted the body of his son back to the States, a time beyond words. During the first part of the trip he alternately cursed and prayed, but before he returned the two were combined.

When the casket was lowered into the ground, the velvet ropes not yet retrieved, Bess had screamed and slapped him across the face with folded papers of divorce.

He came away from Korea still sorting things out. It never got any better. The nation which not long ago had considered war an unhappy necessity—an aberration—had quietly and completely changed. War was policy now, but aimlessly so, committing an army with no plan to win.

He dusted his feet and pulled on his dry socks. The dark of the evening was almost complete, the lights of the Blue Deep shone bright. He bent and grimly laced his boots, thinking that if he had been Colonel Smith, the war-burned soldier named Marsh McCall was the last man on earth he would have sent to Vietnam.

Chapter Twelve

HE PARKED FAR DOWN among the gray snags where the bleeding light was dim and ancient dirt from China hung suspended in the air. Scanning the hundreds of vehicles lined up in the field, he stepped into a hole and almost fell. He kept his eyes on the rough ground ahead, listening to the roar of the crowd, hearing and feeling the roar of Dien Bien Phu.

The situation there was now beyond desperate. The airfield had been closed for more than two weeks, and the casualty rate far exceeded the rate of replacements. Many of the French positions scattered around the field had already fallen, with the only good news being that one of several composing the complex called Elaine had been retaken from the Viet Minh. Improved weather over the valley had permitted a recent increase in the volume of parachuted supplies, but the proximity of encircling trenches meant that much of this material—food and ammunition—fell into enemy hands. It was no longer a question of whether the defenders of Dien Bien Phu would be able to prevail. They were already lost. They knew it, and the men following the battle from the safety of French Expeditionary Headquarters knew it. All that remained was for both sides to continue the grinding, bloody struggle until enough had died to make surrender permissible. The men were still being ordered to hold positions at all costs, though by then they would have done so anyway. Nobody was fighting for France anymore; they were fighting for one another, for those who lived and those who died, for all the bleeding and dying that had already been done, and for the possibility of reason. They were fighting because there was nothing else left to do.

Reduced to nothing but symbols, French High Command had notified the surrounded men that most of the senior officers among them were being promoted in rank, and that every soldier was awarded the Croix de Guerre.

In spite of all this, there continued to be a slow but steady stream of volunteers dropping into Dien Bien Phu by parachute. The drop zone was now quite small, the aircraft were battered as they ran the gauntlet, and the drops took place at night. Many men parachuted into enemy trenches, and even more were dead before they hit the ground.

It was not his war, not his enemy, and he would not be going, but Marsh McCall could feel the pull to battle. The more desperate the situation became, the more the defenders of Dien Bien Phu were a part of his daily thoughts. It seemed that every Frenchman in the country should have been clawing for a chance to go west and help the others, futile though the effort might be. Many were doing exactly that, but a great many more were fighting their fights beneath the infested roof of the Blue Deep.

The outer ring, with concessions and betting windows, was packed with men, apparently at intermission. McCall worked his way through the crowd, slowly circling until he could see beyond the glass. Chang Wu was seated upon his dais, flanked by guards and with his wealth before him, plainly enjoying himself. He wore dark glasses, small and round, and when he leaned from the shadows his smile came into the lamplight. Beads of sweat adorned his face like jewels.

McCall stood for a time and watched the transactions. As each man approached the window with cash, the teller reached overhead for a ticket. He then wrote upon it in ink, and took it and the cash to Chang Wu's table. Either Chang Wu or an assistant would then examine the ticket and check the amount. When all was correct, the ticket was inserted into one of two small presses armed with ivory teeth—one for the previous fight, the other for the fight about to take place. A third press sat to one side. When all the new bets were taken, and the old redeemed, the teeth were drawn from the third press, then randomly rearranged to produce another pattern. When a bettor returned to claim a winner, the teller checked the ticket against the appropriate press. If the holes aligned, the man was paid. If not, he was led away by guards.

McCall moved away from the windows, around the curve of the building to a place where the crowd was thinner and the wall was cool. He was not sure what he hoped to gain by being here, except to confirm what he already knew: that Major Legère was guilty, that Chang Wu was getting rich, that someone he could never touch was making it happen, and that the lives of men fighting for France were being sold at market. There was no reason to delude himself about what he might accomplish, but he was compelled to grope around in the dim hope that something important might come. And he wanted to see Legère get paid, and to let him know that he knew.

Following yesterday's vomiting performance by Legère, McCall had waited to meet the returning helicopters. The information the men gave was less than conclusive, but it was enough to convince McCall he was right. Cody West was reticent, plainly recalling their last discussion. But he told enough to make McCall sure there was a connection between the truck's return to Haiphong and Legère's sudden illness.

An increased volume of voices signaled the approach of another fight. McCall started back, catching a glimpse of snow-white hair that was quickly lost in the crowd.

He stayed for only the one fight—apparently the main event. The stands were packed when he reached the top of the stairs, the building trembling with anticipation. Through the smoke and sweat and beer and dust he could smell the rot of rice-straw thatch. He worked his way forward until he was near the wire enclosure and could see past other men. No one in the stadium was seated except those at ringside. The noise of the crowd became a pressured moan.

The warriors were already in the pit with their handlers—one a blue-gray brindle with pale eyes and random black patches; the other pure copper. Maybe he only imagined it, but it seemed to McCall that as the animals stared at one another, there passed a mutual comprehension, a respect beyond the cultured hatred, a remorseless sort of sympathy. Gladiators of the narrow ring, born to kill, to reproduce and die. He saw the rabid faces of the crowd, and wondered if the dogs might not be trained another way.

When he lowered his gaze, he saw Major René Legère directly across the pit. The Frenchman was leaning out over the wall, fists clenched, mouth wet and open. On one side sat a thin Chinese in a frosted stupor, and on the other was a decrepit old man with a cane and black beret who looked like a woman. The roar of the crowd was suddenly complete, and the battle commenced. Legère lunged with such force that he almost tumbled into the pit. The senile old man and the drugged Chinese traded smiles.

McCall pushed toward the stairs. The outer ring was nearly vacant, and he quickly circled until he reached the windows. Chang Wu was sitting back from his table where the light was very dim, enjoying a cigarette with a large-breasted woman who seemed to be French. McCall proceeded to the long *pissoir*, then took a position on the outside wall and waited.

The fight was unusually long, but eventually the winner won and the loser lost and the future was decided. Those who had made a profit gave a victorious, slightly disappointed cheer. The arguments about what had happened began, and the Blue Deep shuddered.

Minutes passed before René Legère appeared, looking fatigued but satisfied. He inched along, checking two tickets. He cut quickly to the front of the line, said something to the second man, then waited for the one ahead to complete his transaction. McCall began working his way toward Legère just as the man at the window—a few dissolute hairs screening baldness, pale damp eyes of a molester—stepped away with a spent smile.

Legère shoved the two tickets facedown toward the teller. The young Chinese glanced at the tickets, and at Legère, then took them to the table of cash. Chang Wu accepted them without expression, dropped them into a shirt pocket, and reached for a banded stack of bills. When he aimed his dark glasses toward the French major a sardonic smile touched his face. He fanned himself with the bundle so the muttering bills could all be seen.

The instant Legère accepted the cash, McCall put a hand on his shoulder. "How many sons of France?" he said. Legère turned with a face of pale death as two guards appeared. One motioned McCall to wait while the other escorted Legère outside. Chang Wu laughed and slapped at the table.

There was no sign at all of the Frenchman when the guard walked McCall outside, gazing out over the field before motioning that he could go. A dense fog was moving downriver like a sluggish stream as McCall began the long walk toward his jeep. A loose arm of fog reached over the field, slowly increasing the effect of the floodlights before suddenly descending, snuffing them almost completely. McCall stared ahead, trying to fix the position of his jeep in his mind.

When he had passed the last row of vehicles, the lights of the Blue Deep now only a dim smear, he turned back and tried again. Soon he found the gray snags, then his vehicle. He unlocked the wheel, and had just started the engine when the windshield exploded in his face.

Folded double, he frantically groped for the gearshift, found reverse and tromped the throttle. Blood was spraying about, hitting him in the face. He stabbed first gear and sped away, bouncing wildly across rough ground. He heard men shout as he almost ran them down. The jeep spun sideways, made the turn, then leaped ahead toward the brightening lights. When he burst from the fog and roared past the Blue Deep, the guard was still there on the steps, staring placidly across the foggy field.

The shape of Calvin Winslow blocked the light. "Thought you could use this," he said, holding a cup of coffee. "I don't know what all you did last night, but if it's gonna turn out like this the next time, I'd sure like to go along."

McCall finished lacing his boots, then grimaced with a throbbing headache as he straightened. He touched the stitches on his face, glanced at his wrist, and slowly worked a shoulder. "It's pretty pitiful," he said, "when you pull a muscle just getting shot at." He reached for the cup.

"I'd say they connected," Winslow said. "You lost a lot of blood. I checked you over this morning when I saw the jeep. Thought for sure you'd had a leg shot off. All that come from your wrist?" McCall nodded and dipped his head toward the cup. Winslow's tone deepened. "You know who did it?"

"Got a couple of ideas, not enough to shoot at."

"If you find something out, need somebody for a special assignment, Two Acres has already volunteered. And me with him. Who sewed you up?"

"A girl in town," he said, yawning. "A nurse." He sobered with the memory, frowned, and cocked one eyebrow. "Without anesthetic." It had taken only one stitch each on his cheek and forehead, and two to close the hole in his wrist, but that meant a curved needle through live flesh eight times. If the doctoring had been done by a man he could have at least groaned or made a face, but with the young lady, Moni', doing the job, and none too gently, he had been compelled to sit unperturbed as a dozing bull. But, *damnation*, it hurt.

"She was young, but I believe she enjoyed it."

Winslow grinned. "I had a hole in my leg one time you could have dropped a lemon in, waiting to get sewed up, and in walks this darling with a pan of soap and a twisted-wire scrubber like a mop. Didn't say 'Good morning,' 'Kiss my ass,' nothing. Just poked that mop in that meaty hole and scrubbed around like it was a commode. That's how I got this blood vessel here on my nose. Anyway, I thought you might want to use the jeep today. The men have her cleaned up, and they fixed the windshield. Wanted to see if you were up to coming out to take a look."

McCall stared dumbly, then glanced at his watch. It was almost 1000. "Thanks, Calvin," he said. "Yes, I'll come look. I need to get on my feet anyway. Be out in a couple of minutes."

Winslow backed out and quietly closed the screen door.

McCall sipped the coffee, carefully touching each of the stitches and wondering about Su Letei's niece. She had been more than simply not gentle. Such fiery purpose was always a surprise in one her age, such lucid definition; when she finally found a target, she stabbed with relish. He thought of Cody West, wondering if anything was developing between those two. The boy had sure better enjoy it quick, he thought; this Moni' was a lady of pain. He winced, recalling his own brief encounter, the probing false motions, then the quick snap of her wrist to bring the needle through. It was more than masculinity that made him sit calmly and take it. Somebody owed this woman; it was simply given to him to make one of many due payments. It seemed likely that any man who got within reach

220

of her in the near future could expect to come away with stitches.

He had approached the Café Ho Tay with headlights doused. He was still bleeding, but had finally found the source—a narrow sliver of glass had penetrated an artery on the back of one wrist. Once beyond the Blue Deep, he had stopped to locate the wound, then drove slowly and clumsily toward the Ho Tay. His hands, the wheel, and even the floor beneath his boots were slick with blood.

He stopped on the darkened curve of the drive where he could watch for Su Letei. When at last he saw her in the foyer, looking with puzzlement in his direction, he moved the jeep into the edge of light, still holding his wrist. Then he learned the worth of the woman. In view of several customers, she took only a casual step forward. She recognized him through the blood, and with no display of alarm, turned her eyes toward her house. He found reverse, parked around the corner, and went quickly up the sidewalk.

He heard voices of two women inside, one angry, the other quiet and insistent. Then the door opened, and without a word the girl named Moni' led him to the kitchen, seated him at the table, and went to work. There was no sign of Su Letei. Moni' washed him, sewed his skin, and applied the iodine without speaking. But as she was completing the job, taping squares of gauze in place, they had a terse conversation.

"You are the commander of the helicopter pilot named Cody West?"

"That's right."

"He is very foolish. My father almost killed him."

"He's a fine young man, a good pilot with a good head. Maybe he's just less concerned with appearing a fool than with being friendly. Maybe he has courage."

"He's immature, like all Americans."

"He's young, not yet burned to a crisp."

Her cheeks colored, but she plunged ahead. "Like you?"

"Yes," he replied. "Like me. Like your father. And a little like you, although I think you are just tired."

She was silent as she worked with the tape. "I did not ask for life to be this way."

"No one did."

"Some are more fortunate."

"That's true. And some are much less." He looked her over.

"You need to go home and rest. Someone will do your job." When she only blinked and vaguely shook her head, avoiding his eyes, he continued, "Go on home. You are a fine-looking young woman, and you have character. The war will be over soon."

She suddenly sat in a chair with her eyes toward the floor, still holding the scissors. She tried to speak, but all she could manage was a breathless whisper. McCall leaned and took her empty hand. She was trembling. "I couldn't hear you," he said.

Again a whisper was all she could find. "You are all going to be killed," she said. "Everybody is going to be killed. I don't want to know any of you. Please go away."

"Thanks for sewing me up," he said. "Tomorrow is Saturday. We were busy last weekend, and I wouldn't let the men go to town. I can't say for sure, but I would not be surprised if tomorrow you had a visitor." He showed himself to the door, leaving her staring at her scissors.

Thinking about the girl, his coffee had gotten cold. He combed his hair before a mirror taped inside a cabinet, pulled on his cap, and emptied the cup outside.

The jeep looked brand-new. It had been cleaned from top to bottom, paste-waxed, and polished. Kinney was buffing it down with a towel, and Two Acres was going over the glass a final time. The other men and all the officers were out on the flight line, working on the aircraft, but a couple were watching in the major's direction. He walked around the jeep, smiling with admiration while the men watched. All the bits of shattered glass were gone, all the blood except what had fallen on the canvas seats. He looked toward the flight line, then at the two men. "Thanks a lot," he said. "Tell the others." He turned to Winslow. "Where'd you find the new glass?"

"Major Legère, sir."

McCall only nodded. "Well, thanks again, fellas," he said. "Sergeant Winslow, if there's still coffee in the office, I think I'll go complete my transfusion."

"Still half a pot, sir."

McCall headed toward the orderly room, feeling the beginnings of regret that he would not be serving with this group of men much longer. He swept his eyes across the yard and through the gates of Lam Du. At that distance it was hard to say for sure, but it appeared that the jeep belonging to René Legère just might be missing a windshield.

Su Letei had a smile for him, amused and warm and inexplicably sad. "You are an interesting man," she said softly, "but you begin to worry me too much."

The traditional all-male clientele of early Saturday afternoon gave the Café Ho Tay the appearance of necessity. It was the beginning of the day for the less genteel, the men who had recovered sufficiently from their Friday night with the dogs of the Blue Deep or the women of the Chinese quarter or the grueling flights of sudden illumination past the hills of Dien Bien Phu. Just after noon they began to wander into the café for breakfast. Meanwhile, the planters and landlords and merchants who arrived at late morning, avoiding plans of frustrated women, slowly took leave. They mumbled of trivial business, mundane tasks they had saved to keep them away from home until dark. And by now, somewhere on the streets of the city, dealing with peasants and vendors, were the gratified wives who knew the techniques of preserving a day for themselves.

Su Letei checked over the little cuts. The stitches were holding well. The tape and gauze had been removed, and most of the iodine carefully washed away. "Those places should be covered," she said.

"I heal better with air and sunlight."

"Germs could penetrate your bloodstream."

"They did that a long time ago. We have an agreement—I let them eat me a little at a time with the understanding that they can later have the whole mess. In return, they kill any new critters that show up." When she smiled at his nonsense, he added, "I'd like to thank your niece. Is she still at your house?"

"No. She has gone to the farm, and I would like to thank you for that. She will not listen to me. She was very angry with you last night—I do not know why—but this morning she took your advice and went home for some rest. They have worked her to near exhaustion at Lanessan, but there are others—wives and daughters of officers and civilians as well—who could help. Some do, but the majority will do nothing so long as Moni' and others are willing to shoulder the load. They have still not accepted the reality of what is to come...." Her voice trailed off, and she glanced around the restaurant. "You were seen here last night," she said quietly. Then she switched to her professional smile and spoke louder. "It is very pleasant today, Major. Would you care for a seat outside?"

"No, I think that inside would be better. Don't you agree?"

"Yes," she said, though it was plain she did not. "There are two things I need to tell you. First, your sergeant was here again this week, a most persistent man. Second, Mr. Pearbone, a friend, was here only an hour ago. He asked that I tell you that if you happen to be in town tomorrow afternoon, please feel free to drop in."

"Thank you," McCall said, surprised. Considering that Pearbone seemed beyond reproach, this seemed to say much for Su Letei. He did not know what to say about the reference to Winslow, so he chose to ignore it. "Have you thought any more about Vung Tau?" he said.

"Yes," she replied with the faintest smile. "I think about it more every day."

She turned quickly and led him through the restaurant to his table. McCall noted that although the gathering of men was about the usual, there was an extra air of tension. He saw that Lieutenant Solo Jacobé was talking with the white-haired Colonel Gereau. Jacobé looked away, but Gereau stared with fixed anger.

Su Letei seated him at his usual table near the doors in the corner where he could observe most of the room, and it could observe him. The doors to the garden were open, and the scent of rich soil moved into the room. Slow fans turned at the ceiling.

When she handed him a menu, McCall waved it away and said, "Surprise me, as you continue to do." She gave him a look that was quietly flirtatious before walking away. He checked her backside, then looked around the room and out toward the gardens, considering possibilities of Vung Tau.

He noticed that Lieutenant Jacobé was still avoiding his glance. His attitude was a puzzle. The young man McCall had known as Lapeste had always been a survivor, with the orphan's talent for reading things that were not said, and it was certainly no surprise to find him now doing police work. Even as a teenager in the maquis, he had been a natural detective, always asking questions, always anticipating what was to come. Later, when his face was on so many

224

posters, wanted by the Nazis, it was Lapeste who was asked the questions, and who dropped his youthful act and assumed his place as a man. There seemed little doubt that had the war lasted another six months, Lapeste would have been leading men twice his age.

The memory was reassuring. It seemed likely that the adult Solo Jacobé still possessed the same perceptive intelligence as had the teenager Lapeste. McCall wondered what relationship might exist between Jacobé and the retired Colonel Gereau.

A waiter arrived with bread and coffee, a covered plate of white rice, and a large deep bowl of chicken soup prepared with garlic and floating bits of scallions. McCall spread a linen napkin and began to eat. From the opposite corner of the Café Ho Tay, Su Letei was watching. She turned to greet Solo Jacobé as he approached to pay his bill while the scowling Colonel Gereau watched his back with undisguised fury.

The soup was delicious. In a small side dish were a couple of scalding red peppers in a bath of *nuóc mam.* These he shredded and added to the soup, then dumped in some rice, and ate with the short ceramic spoon.

The message from Pearbone was intriguing. Weird as the man was, and despite his announced intention to try to get McCall ejected from Tonkin, he seemed like a decent sort. Had he been successful in his efforts, no meeting would now be required. But if he had failed, a face-to-face encounter might seem embarrassing. Colonel Smith was due to arrive tomorrow for the scheduled Sunday briefing, but once that was done, McCall decided, an afternoon with Walter Pearbone might be worthwhile. He had no delusions of getting anything more from the diplomat than he wanted to give, but the man undoubtedly knew where a lot of the pieces fit.

He finished the soup and had a mouthful of bread when Colonel Gereau strode forcefully across the room, abruptly pulled out a chair, and sat down. McCall stared, chewing slowly on the bread.

"You, sir, are a damnable fool," Gereau said. McCall reached for his coffee to wash down the bread. "I warned you what was to come, Major. Now you see the results. It is far too late to tell you again to mind your own business. Nothing less than your immediate departure from Hanoi will save you."

A dark flash caught McCall's attention, and he shifted his eyes to the front windows, where a black Mercedes had stopped. "I am not an enemy of France, Colonel," he said. "My record proves that. So what makes me an enemy of yours?"

"You are not my enemy," Gereau said, his features flat with anger. "You are only a fool who can do more damage than your life is worth. I was just discussing your past with Lieutenant Jacobé. He is a courageous young man, very polished for one his age. I was not supposed to perceive that his purpose was to make me understand why you should not be killed." The colonel swung his dark eyes around the restaurant, the lids thick and weighted. "I respect what you have done in the past," he said, "but that can no longer be allowed its importance. In your blundering sincerity you threaten to destroy everything I have worked a lifetime to build. I will kill you myself rather than allow that to happen. I am old, and it would be a worthwhile way to end my life. You, on the other hand, are just now hitting your prime. You could still have many productive years. Your death would be a waste."

McCall took a breath and released it. The man before him was an old soldier who had been a leader of men, not the type who made such statements without purpose. "Colonel Gereau," he said, "when I was in France during the war, I heard of you everywhere. In both world wars you were a hero of the people. When I came to Saigon in 1946, there you were again, leading your men through a difficult time. You have my complete respect and admiration as a soldier. But as a soldier, you must also know that I will not be frightened away by threats to my life, no more than you would be."

There was a teetering moment between acquired wisdom and the frustration of encroaching age. McCall knew the turn before the old man opened his mouth.

"You know what I am talking about," Gereau said. "You cannot possibly be that ignorant. But you need not worry about me. There is great competition for your corpse." He pointed a finger. "I can tell you, Major, I am an old hand at such things. If I have to do the job, it will be done correctly."

McCall sat in silence as younger men watched. Gereau blinked and withdrew the impotent finger, then stood and walked out of the restaurant, neglecting to pay for his meal, almost colliding with two men at the door. Su Letei emerged from the kitchen, smiling as she reached the table. She stopped at the sight of the men in the foyer, and her face changed in a way that McCall had not yet seen.

A big Chinese man had entered the Café Ho Tay and was standing in the reception area, aiming an offensive smile in her direction. He was dressed in a white suit and white straw hat, and carried a black cane of polished bamboo. McCall knew him at once as Chang Wu. At the end of a leather lead was a gray pit bull in a silver-spiked collar, squarely on four legs with its mouth clamped shut, eyeing the men in the room. Near the alcove a thin guard with splayed teeth and quick eyes watched everyone. Chang Wu still wore the dark glasses, black round lenses in wire frames.

"Is he blind?" McCall said.

"He sees everything," she replied. "Excuse me." She walked toward the men, her body rigid. When she had spoken to them for a time, she gave her most formal nod, turned about, and led them through the restaurant and out the garden doors, passing within inches of McCall without a glance.

When she reached a round table at the far edge of the patio, she waited with a menu tight against her breasts, her features brittle as porcelain. Slowly came Chang Wu, tilting carefully down the steps as if his feet were asleep. All the restaurant watched. The dog seemed to know the way, what pace to keep, and strode along with muscular purpose to the cadenced click of nails. Chang Wu smiled with Buddhistic contentment, black lenses fixed on the woman. His hands were dimpled at the knuckles, the free one flapping at his side. The procession passed McCall with the gargantuan presence of a steamship passing a small craft. Several feet behind came the skinny escort—loose jacket and darting eyes. Beyond the double doors, he moved left to check the patio and gardens, then backtracked swiftly toward the toilets.

Chang Wu's chair was specially made of strong wicker and heavy cushions. The guard suddenly arrived, seated his boss, and moved off toward a far section of the gardens. The dog stood to one side, grinning, until Chang Wu dropped the lead, then lowered its butt to its haunches and stared straight ahead at McCall.

Su Letei presented a menu, listened a moment, gave another quick bow, and again passed McCall's table. Soon a covey of waiters emerged from the kitchen with several trays, hustling around Chang Wu beneath the gaze of the watchful guard. Su Letei returned, made as if to leave, then sat with reluctance on the edge of a chair, her back rigid while Chang Wu smiled and spoke. The dog ignored the woman, but glanced around at the patrolling guard. After several minutes, Su Letei stood and moved swiftly past McCall to the front of the restaurant, where two men were waiting to pay. A minute later she appeared at McCall's table.

"Chang Wu has asked if you might join him at his table," she said, her face still frozen.

McCall looked deeply, and saw a helpless flicker. "You are very lovely," he murmured, ignoring the fear in those deep dark eyes. "Tell Mr. Wu that nothing would please me more than to have him as a guest at my table."

"He has anticipated your words, and makes his apologies, saying it would be much easier for you to change positions than for him."

McCall reached for his cap. "I will bring coffee," she said. He nodded and walked out to the patio, where Chang Wu was smiling like a happy frog. The bodyguard suddenly appeared at McCall's side, snapped a finger, and held out an expectant hand toward the major's automatic.

"Forget it."

Sudden fury filled the face. He flicked his eyes toward Chang Wu and was sent away with a casual toss of a small fat finger. McCall pulled a chair from the table, turning it so that Chang Wu was to one side and he could observe the roving guard, the restaurant, and the dog. Neither spoke until Su Letei arrived with cups and a pot of coffee on a small tray, arranged them on the table, and walked away.

Chang Wu watched her go, resting a hand on the oblong head of his cane. "She is very lovely," he said. He leaned back in his chair and slowly removed his glasses, revealing eyes like small boiled onions. "I understand you experienced an unpleasantness last night, Major McCall. I wish to apologize for that. We try to avoid such things, but when passions of war and large sums of money are combined, they are perhaps inevitable."

McCall did not respond. He watched the fat fingers flutter along the arm of the chair. Chang Wu turned his creased neck.

"It is of no particular concern, Major McCall, but I am curious. What is it you hope to achieve by your efforts?"

"There is nothing that can be accomplished here."

"Then why do you persist in such a dangerous pastime?"

"I have an interest in such things."

Chang Wu nodded. "Do you believe that in Indochina you can settle the scores of Korea?"

McCall said nothing, but to a man like Chang Wu, even silence could be an answer.

"It is understandable, Major, when a man is compelled to do a dangerous thing, but only if he has a plan to ensure success. I wonder, do you have a plan? If so, it is not apparent." He paused, then continued. "You are no threat to me in my business. I believe you know that. There are others—such as Major Legère—who fear you intensely, and with reason. There are even a few who underestimate your potential. I wonder if you are among that group. As you have seen, the system that operates here involves everyone. No one wants it to stop, they are too afraid of life without it. They send their soldiers off and hope that they do not get too badly wounded, but the people are unwilling to make the small sacrifices to ensure their men victory. They believe it is better that soldiers die while life remains the same than to risk the many inconveniences of the alternative. So I prosper. They allow me to operate because I allow them to do the same. Like the colorful growth on rocks—half fungus, half algae—two organisms immutably bound, feeding upon one another for existence. The agreement produces the colors you see.

"I am a businessman, Major McCall, not a traitor. I deal in goods, not principles or morals. But even your own government has been involved in the trade."

McCall assumed he was referring to Roach Harman. "I believe that period has passed," he said.

Chang Wu moved his eyes and smiled. "Perhaps. In any case, it is rumored that your man now wishes to retire."

McCall raised a brow in spite of himself. He had always assumed that Harman would drop dead in his tracks, unwilling to yield power. But Chang Wu did not seem the type to be a merchant of rumors.

"The French are about to lose their long war," the fat man continued. "Nothing will change for me when that happens—a temporary inconvenience, but one that is inevitable. I have already prepared, and will continue trading opium and guns and influence. I will continue for the simple reason that I am needed. Men such as Major Legère are not, and they all will eventually perish. You, too, are not needed, and the same may happen to you, though probably not by my command. You can do me no harm unless you kill me. You have no reason for that. You would die, and others close to you would die. We are not opponents."

McCall was thinking that it would be a true pleasure to kill this bastard, but that it would do no good. The vacuum of power would be quickly filled by someone much like Chang Wu, and possibly by someone worse.

"I am in a position to give you part of what you want," said Chang Wu. "I do not yet know if I will do that, or if it will be necessary. For now, your efforts suit my purposes. There is but one way that you concern me, Major. I am a fat old man with few pleasures, but those few I consider to be most important. The Blue Deep is one of those pleasures. It is only now beginning to make money, but money is not a consideration. There seemed to be a need for such a place, a place where a man could experience a definite victory or a definite loss, and where he could know the difference. I was right, the men love it. All of life is to be found in that arena. Because I cannot travel to observe the world, I have devised a way to bring it within view."

He shifted his gaze toward the restaurant, where Su Letei was seating a group of men. "The woman you find so fascinating is also one of those pleasures," he said. He paused to think, or to give the words effect. "My interest in her is not romantic. She is much too beautiful for that." He turned toward McCall. "I can have all the women I want, when I want them, though that is not so often anymore. But they do make pretty ornaments, and sometimes they are pleasant to touch or hear speak." He glanced toward the Ho Tay, but the lady was gone. "This woman is not for that. She is in her perfect place. I prefer to admire her excellence for many years as opposed to possessing it for only a few moments. She is a flower that would surely wither and die if I took her home. I come to this place for no other reason than to admire her. She is the single flower in my garden, and I take every measure to ensure she is not disturbed."

Chang Wu reached for his glasses, and slipped them onto his face, taking care with the golden wires behind his sunken ears. "Now if you don't mind, Major, I shall continue my lunch and the admiration of the flower of the Café Ho Tay. I wish you luck in your other endeavors. The next few days should prove very interesting for you. If you survive, we may later be of use to one another."

Chapter Thirteen

HIS ENTIRE DAY had been ruined. He had done it himself, and with no other motivation than petty anger at an old coot who was not to blame for anything. It was a foolish moment, and it scared him.

He raised a hand for the blue shuttle, and the dull and dented hulk screeched to a halt at his feet. The driver gave a familiar smile, but Cody did not notice. He found a seat near the rear, and sprawled his legs across it.

He had no idea why he was so upset, any more than why he had said what he had. If it had been to get even for a brief humiliation, it had failed miserably. The disapproval of the major in no way compared to the pain in old Larkin's eyes. The man had been an easy target, small and slow-moving. Cody slumped in the seat, determined to punish himself by replacing the planned afternoon with a few sulking hours in the tent.

He had told himself he was going to the Café Ho Tay for no particular reason—just something to do—but he knew now that he had gone for precisely what he had found: a glimpse of the beautiful Su Letei, some word about Moni' and her crazy father, and a chance to take a shot at a harmless old man. Su Letei had met him at the door, and as he listened to her voice he knew he would do anything for this woman. There was no hope of romance, nor any such thought beyond outrageous, middle-of-the-night, lonely growing-up fantasy, but she was the quintessence of the other half. He stood with animal dumbness and only glanced at her eyes.

Larkin's legs were entwined with the stool as if they had grown that way. Cody ignored the sailor. Through the windows he saw Major McCall at a table with a fat Chinese. Several men in the restaurant were watching.

"Good morning, young fella."

Cody was still observing the major, feeling anew the undispelled anger. "Afternoon," he said to Larkin, his face tight, remembering that this foolish old man was the reason he had gotten his butt chewed out. He leaned against the bar, but did not take a stool.

Larkin came close and said in a low, urgent voice, "I'd been hoping to see you, young fella. Did you tell your major what I said?"

Cody frowned. "I told him," he said.

"Sperek tried to kill him last night. He's cut all to pieces."

Cody's expression was incredulous. He turned toward the patio. McCall was sitting relaxed in a chair, sunlight dappling his uniform, shaking his head at the Chinaman. The flight line had been abuzz that morning with news of what had happened. There was a lot of blood in the jeep, but Winslow had said it was only a scratch. Cody later saw McCall, and he seemed okay. Larkin was full of crap, just as McCall said. The major might have occasionally been a jerk, but he at least still had all his brains. Cody was not buying Larkin's tale a second time, and he was not buying him a beer.

"He's taking a terrible chance, talking to that Chink, especially here. You sure you told him about Sperek?"

"That's what I said."

"And what did he have to say about it?"

Cody looked at Larkin, then toward McCall, wondering why he should feel obliged to protect these two buzzards from the effects of their words while he was smashed in the middle. His lips formed a cruel smile. "He said you were an old drunk."

Larkin looked as if he had been stuck with a knife. Something left him like the rush of rancid air from a dead man's mouth. When it was gone he was smaller. His face began to twitch, and he cleared his throat. "Maybe I am," he said huskily. He moved his eyes around the floor.

Cody felt sudden regret, ashamed for landing a blow on a defenseless old man when who he wanted to hit was McCall. "I'm sorry," he said, his stomach empty. "Come on, I'll buy you a beer."

Larkin stared with eyes of amber oil. His lips bent downward. "I don't want your beer, you young punk," he said. "You think you're beyond all this, but you're not. You're part of it too. You're *all* part of it. You'll get yours just like McCall before it's done." The collapsed and stubbled face became a hideous grin, but the eyes were fearful and sad and faraway. "Mark my word, young man," he rasped. "Mark my word."

Cody left the Café Ho Tay unshaken, but angry at himself. He was confident that Larkin was blowing smoke, an ineffectual old man whose life was essentially over, still trying to impact a world quickly leaving him behind. But Cody's confidence slipped before he covered half a block, and doubt began to grow. Larkin had been in Tonkin an awfully long time. He might be practically senile, but he also might know a lot. By the time Cody reached the bridge, he was halfway convinced that Major McCall, and even he, might have made a really dangerous mistake.

As the bus moved over the long bridge, rising and falling in slow gallop with the road's undulations, Cody stared at the leveed basin and at the churning mud that chewed both shores. He dimly observed that the water was slightly deeper, and that portions of the sandy island beneath the bridge had disappeared.

Larkin always made him think of his grandpa, and that reminded him of his father. Now that he had been to the farm and encountered the twin of the man whose death he had caused, there seemed nothing to do but go back, to face the reincarnation head on. He had planned all week to return to the farm and give the tormented man a few more free shots. They both deserved it. And if Moni' happened to be there, it might be nice to see her too. Maybe they could go into town and mess around. But Larkin had changed his course; he was mad at the old man all over again.

Up ahead he could see a bit of red roof and the rows of trees that lined the long drive, and he imagined a man with a green bottle and wretched eyes, watching that drive and waiting. Waiting for him. He saw the lined face, the way the fingers plucked at the mustache; he saw the dark rifle against a white wall.

"Hold it!" he yelled.

The driver looked in the mirror, touched the pedal, then pressed harder as Cody lunged down the aisle, walking his hands between seats. The brakes gave a thin wobbling cry. As he stepped down from the bus, the driver said something smart, and a few men laughed, but Cody paid no attention. He heard only the crunch of gravel beneath his boots, then the *vroom* of exhaust behind him and the sounds of changing gears. He studied the inscrutable sign, and stepped over the chain, feeling better now and on the right course. Larkin, McCall, the Chinaman, Sperek—none of them mattered a damn compared to what happened right here. With slow measured steps, feeling each one and watching himself as if from a distance, he moved firmly into the trees.

Handsome Dan Blackweed was in his chair, small in his corner of the porch. He had heard the bus stop and pull away, and was watching the driveway intently, tugging at his twisted mustache. An overturned bottle lay near his feet. Cody paused, smiling as he spotted the man. Blackweed really did look like his dad from that distance, just older, maybe a little bit uglier. The hand reached for the rifle. He moved slowly and firmly ahead until the slender weapon became a narrow black hole.

The bullet was extremely close, close enough to make him wonder how drunk the man was, close enough to make him believe he might have made a mistake. He wanted to turn and run, but knew that if he did he would never be able to make the trip again, not this or any other. It was nothing like the first day when he had been a young stud out to impress a girl who was about to become a woman. The miracle of that could work only once. He tried to remember why he was there. With a groan that was more like a whimper, he moved slowly ahead.

The second round sailed past his ear, a ragged chunk of lead so close he could hear its spinning song and feel the heat. A shuddering moan rose up from the region of his bowels, a hard tremble ran through him, and he was unable to move his feet. The old man squinted, a knowing smile beginning to grow.

"*Qu'est-ce qui se passe!*" he called. "*On ne bouge plus!*"

He did not know when it began, but he became aware of Moni's scream. It gave him strength enough to move, but not enough to stop a groan that slowly grew into a roar as he approached the house. Moni' burst from the door. "Stop it!" she yelled. She bent and grasped the green bottle and drew it back, aiming for her father's head.

"Moni'!" Cody yelled.

"*What?*" she screamed, the arm still cocked. Slowly she moved her eyes, and he saw how completely terrified she was.

"Did you forget to tell him we have a date?"

She jerked her head toward him, back toward her father, then to Cody again. She looked exhausted, much older than when he last saw her, but she seemed glad to see him. Her chest was heaving for breath.

"We were supposed to go to town," he said.

She glanced at her father. "That's right," she said. "That's right, I forgot." A weight seemed to lift from her then, and the years peeled away. She lowered the bottle and reached for the rifle. Her father let her take it, and she leaned it against the wall. "Give me a few minutes, and I'll get ready." She paused at the door, and a smile suddenly spread. "You can visit with Daddy while I am gone."

The two men stared at each other. Cody glanced toward the weapon, wishing that for just one minute they could trade places and he could show the Frenchman what it meant to really be good with a rifle. He had begun shooting at six; by eleven he was saving the bits of brass of .22 shorts, using them as bright targets in the afternoon sun. It didn't count if the bullet's breeze blew them away.

Not knowing what else to do, he looked around at the house and the neglected yard with the spectacular trees. It had once been magnificent, but now all he could see was the many jobs that needed to be done. "Nice place," he said. Handsome Dan Blackweed just looked at him. In his corner of the porch between the peeled rail and peeling wall, the old man matched his surroundings like a camouflaged moth. His khakis were clean, but the collar and sleeves were frayed, most of the color was gone. He had not shaved for several days, and to Cody's surprise the stubble was mostly black. Only the mustache and fanning sideburns showed white. Then he saw that the long curling ends of the mustache were practically gone. Only a few long hairs remained. The rest had been twisted in nervous spirals like ropy cigars. Blackweed observed the inspection while conducting one of his own.

A few uncomfortable minutes passed, Cody standing in the yard, not sure what to do. Then a slow smile began, and his eyes brightened. "I think you're an asshole," he said cheerily. When Blackweed showed no comprehension, Cody's smile grew broader. He climbed up and took a seat at the top step, then looked around at the trees and house admiringly. "In fact, I think you're a real smelly turd," he said. Handsome Dan seemed to agree. He nodded and followed Cody's gaze, eventually giving a hesitant but polite smile. "This is a beautiful place," Cody said, "and I think you should have your sorry ass kicked for letting it go to hell. And furthermore, I wish you were younger so I could stomp the few brown-caked teeth you have left right out of your old snail-sucking mouth. What do you think of that, Weed? And if you didn't have that rifle, oh Rectal One, I'd even wish you could understand what I am saying, ha-ha."

"You are very stupid," said Moni' from directly behind him beyond the screen. The spring groaned as she stepped out wearing sandals, a white cotton blouse, and the flowered skirt he had seen on the balcony at the Café Ho Tay. She had done something subtle to her hair. As he looked at her, he believed he saw a glow that had not been there before, but it vanished so quickly he could not be sure. She said something to her father, then moved past Cody and down the steps. He could not help glancing at her legs and the motion of the skirt. "Well," she said from the bottom of the steps, "are you coming?"

Cody could feel the eyes upon him as they walked away, and when he turned, Dan Blackweed was watching. It was impossible to read his expression, but the fingers of one hand tugged unconsciously at his mustache.

They did not speak as they passed through the tunnel of trees. Cody felt strangely conspicuous, mildly embarrassed, but glad she had agreed to go. It was not really a date, just something to do. He became conscious of his fatigues and boots, and of her simple skirt, and the differences between them. It made him feel awkward and manly, as if the two were the same.

When they neared the end of the arbor he saw that the wind had changed, and that a thousand white clouds were moving in from the coast. They stood beneath the last trees and waited for the civilian bus that made the rounds between the villages. Moni' leaned against a thick trunk. Cody squatted a few feet away, trimming his nails with his pocketknife, glancing up at the clouds, and trying to think of something to say, burdened now with the obligation to entertain. Moni' was apparently content to touch the rough bark and be away from the house in the breeze and say nothing at all. That was the thing about girls, Cody thought, always so patient that way. But he guessed they could afford to be. He thought of things they could talk about—her work, his work, the war, what was happening to the entire country and to the both of them. Nothing seemed to fit for a boy-girl afternoon that really was not that way. He gave up and trimmed his nails until they spotted the bus. "I'm glad you came with me," he said, and she smiled.

There were many stares from the people. The bus was in terrible shape, completely packed with Vietnamese. Cody and Moni' stood in the aisle, swaying and bouncing between the people and the things they carried. In a rack on the roof were baskets and cages of produce and worried creatures, and inside the bus were still more. One old woman, her eyes Manchurian and her face a study in vertical lines, held four scrawny brown hens that were lashed by their feet in pairs. Opposite was a man who had no teeth and looked two hundred years old. In his lap was a basket of loose weave, and he held it up so they could better see a green python in new skin. The bus moved onto the bridge, across the swirling brown water, and into the city. A smiling boy showed them the tightly rolled hide of an iguana, but another waved and shook his head as if that were nothing, then raised one leg and showed them a stump. The wound was not new, and seemed not to cause pain, but the gauze was caked in old blood. Moni' frowned and stared through the crowd, bending to give the boy instructions. She did not smile again until they got off the bus at Little Lake, and then only briefly as she touched the child's head and spoke with a warning finger in his face. Cody watched, in awe at the years she had gained in the short trip. When he compared her world to his, everything he had ever done seemed insufficient and dumb.

Moni' led the way, unconsciously becoming the tour guide she said she would not be. From the northeast corner of the lake where the trolleys made their stops, they circled left and crossed the arched bridge to the ancient pagoda. The building was constructed of timbers and tile, all centuries old, and looked good for at least a few more. The roof was covered with moss, and the sturdy beams were twisted and checked. Joss sticks smoldered in a sand-filled urn, the slender stems dyed pink and yellow and green. Wrapping the outside walls and writhing all over the roof was a serpent of bougainvillea as thick as Cody's arm. Directly in front of the pagoda was a raised pavilion where two old Vietnamese men with skin like lizards were playing Chinese chess. Around them squatted several others, all talking excitedly, pointing at pieces and giving advice. "It takes hours to finish a game," Moni' said. "No one can think with that noise going on, but the old men can never resist telling each other how to play." She smiled again, the child on the bus forgotten, and again she looked young.

They sat upon a low wall beyond the pavilion and watched Vietnamese boys wading and fishing. The children came and showed them their catch, three tiny perch no larger than coins. One of the boys reached out and stroked Cody's light hair, then they all ran away to the water.

Cody had until now said very little, and only in short sentences. He studied Moni' in quick glances, the smallness of her arms, the shape of her neck, the color of hair against her skin. As they recrossed the red bridge, he decided it would be okay to talk about work.

"Why don't you show me Lanessan?" he said. "I think I've seen it from the air, but on the ground I'm a little lost. It's not that far, is it?"

"No, it is not far," she said, "but I do not want to go there. It is that way." She gave a nod southward, then was silent, continuing to look in that direction. She seemed older again.

"Maybe we could go to Bai Chay," he said. She looked startled, then saw that he was joking. But the lines of her face relaxed a bit. "Why not?" he said. "Let's go steal a helicopter and fly down there. We can take our swimsuits and blankets, maybe some things for a picnic."

Her eyes were smiling now. "Perhaps we can do that another day, when the war is over," she said. "But then you will no longer be here."

He caught his frown before it formed. "Well, let's go somewhere," he said.

"Have you seen the Botanical Garden?"

"Up near the Café Ho Tay?"

"Across and down."

"Just a glimpse from a distance. Is it this crowded?"

"No. The garden is large, and you must pay. But it is very beautiful there."

"Sounds good to me," he said. "Why don't we take something to eat? I'm starving to death."

She led him around the walk, past the benches and stops and across the street to a shop that specialized in picnic preparations. As they walked, and people noticed them, Cody was struck by the thought that in the eyes of strangers, they were probably a couple. The idea caught him by surprise, but when he looked at Moni' he decided that maybe that was not so bad. The more time they spent together, the more he enjoyed being around her. Already he was looking forward to seeing her the next time.

They bought a few small loaves of bread and two stuffed sandwiches which the shop owner, a fawning little Frenchman with a waxed mustache and wire-rimmed glasses, prepared on the spot. He gave them a nauseating smile as if they all shared some lurid secret. Then he made an unfortunate mistake: He tried to overcharge the ignorant American.

The transformation in Moni' was instant and unbelievable. She lunged at the man like a rabid dog, her eyes red, face contorted, screaming in French. People outside stopped to stare. Cody stood holding his wallet, astonished and completely embarrassed. "It's okay," he said, hoping to make her quiet.

"No, it's not! Nothing is okay! These bastards are bleeding my country in the same way he tried to bleed you!" She picked some bills from the open wallet, crumpled them in her hand, then hurled them at the pale man. "*Sangsue!*" she screamed, then stalked from the shop with the food.

Cody glanced at the shopkeeper, then followed, puzzled anew by Moni'. She was three-quarters French, yet railed at the man as at an invader. Somewhere in the native fourth of her lay something stronger than love or family or anything taught in school, something all her own and not a happy possession.

They boarded a red-and-white trolley and moved off through the city. Among the people again—her people—Moni' seemed to relax. The years peeled away and she again was nineteen.

When they reached the gardens, they were only a block from the Café Ho Tay and a few hundred feet from the lake for which the restaurant was named. The sky to the north was open, its development exposed. The afternoon heat and gathering clouds had brewed a far storm, and the lake was a ruffled pallet—algae-green nearby, quickly shading through near-white to steely gray at the distant shore.

They strolled deep into the park, veering as the trail divided. The trees were exceptionally tall, and on the occasional pools were rafts of water hyacinths and lily pads. Where a stream emptied into a small lake, French boys were swimming naked. Soon the forest formed a high ceiling. They saw a couple making love in a distant copse, and Cody was only surprised that he was not embarrassed. They came to a table and sat on its top and had lunch, flicking chunks of bread to fat golden carp in a leaf-lined brook.

"I dreamed last night about Bai Chay," she said. She paused as if fighting a decision. "Our house there was on a small hill, and overlooked the road and beach beyond. I dreamed that the house was empty, and... and I was there to visit again, and no one knew. The trees had hidden everything, but from the second floor you could see Hon Gay and the really steep hills behind, and you could see twenty miles across the bay. My room was exactly the same. It faced the water and opened to a veranda of checkered tile, and the table and chairs were still there where the breeze comes cool up the stairs. Someone had prepared breakfast, and we ate at the table, and drank juice and looked out over—" She abruptly halted, blushing intensely.

"I wish we could go there sometime," he said, as if he had missed what she meant.

"You are very foolish."

"I know we can't. I just wish we could."

"It is the same, dreaming of the imposs—" She stopped again, trapped by her words.

Through the space above a meadow they could see a group of circling birds. Moni' watched, entranced by the effortless motion. "They say that when they fly like that their wings are locked," she said. "They can dream or sleep and remain aloft, moving with the wind without thought or worry." Her face darkened. "They say that in the forest there is a place where they always roost, and you cannot walk beneath the trees, and nothing grows."

Cody only glanced at the birds. Vultures were nothing new, useful only as idle entertainment to a kid with a .22 lying on his back in a pasture. When the bullets were close the scavengers awoke and flapped their big wings. Until one day when the tiny bit of lead connected, and the big wings folded, loose and trailing in a rapidly rising wind. There was plenty of time to watch, to know regret before the hard thudding crunch in the pasture. He did not go look, and he did not clean his rifle when he went to the house.

"Did you really kill your father?" she asked.

It caught him by surprise, but not completely. No one ever believed him. "No," he said. "I was only kidding."

"But he is dead?"

"Yes."

"How?"

"In an airplane."

"And you saw it."

It was not a question. Maybe she did believe him. "Yes," he replied.

"Will you tell me about it?"

"No. I won't." He threw the last chunk of bread to the fish. They formed mottled rays around it. The bread bounced and slowly disappeared.

"I think I will see my father die," she said.

"We have a new mission," he said, wanting to change the subject. She frowned, not following. "My outfit. We're going to start helping in another way."

"What do you mean?" She gripped the edge of the table.

"We're going to start flying observation missions."

"Observing what? I do not understand."

"The enemy, I suppose. We're going to be flying over French units, helping them spot ambushes, that kind of thing."

"You're going into combat? You can't! You *can't!*"

Cody was confused. He thought she would be pleased by the news; he had saved it for that reason. "It's not going to be combat," he said. "We're just going out to look around."

"That's combat! We don't need you! We don't need more men fighting this stupid war! We need everyone to leave! You cannot do this thing! This is not your war!"

Cody straightened, his face solemn as he studied the baffling woman. "They gave us a choice," he said. "I wanted to help."

"A choice? I bandage men every day who believe they had a choice. But they were brought up on stories of war. From the time they were very small they were told that war is the manly thing and the route to glory. Then one day when they were old enough, someone said to them, 'Who will fight for France? Who here has courage to be a man?' Only the very bravest can resist such a challenge to die."

The blood was gone from Moni's face, and the tender places beneath her eyes were dark. "I wanted to help," Cody said, turning away. "I still want to help."

"You are the most foolish person I have ever known."

He turned to face her. "I'm getting tired of hearing that," he said. "One guy in my outfit did what you said. He walked away. He said he would be glad to go on teaching men to fly, but that it was not his war. They shipped his butt south, and no one has heard from him since."

"That is what you should have done," she said. "That is what you must do."

He searched for compassion and found nothing. "I guess everybody is on his own," he said. But it sounded so final, he tried to soften it with a small joke. "If I go south," he said, "you can forget about us ever going to Bai Chay."

"That is what you must do."

"It's not your decision to make. I'm staying."

"Very well." She slid from the table and dusted her hands. "If you insist on fighting, I don't ever want to see you again."

"You're supposed to save big bombs for big targets," he said. She just looked at him. He was beginning to be angry. "I guess that makes it real simple. If I didn't fly the missions, I wouldn't be seeing you again anyway. But that's not the point. I'm staying, that's all there is to it."

Moni' looked startled, realizing she had left him no way out. She whirled and marched in the direction of the Café Ho Tay. Cody waited to see if she would change her mind, then with his hands stuffed into his pockets, he went in another direction. Dimly in the distance he heard thunder.

The French boys were still in the water. They waved for him to join them, but he only shook his head. Moni' was nowhere in sight when he arrived at the gate. With one final hope, he walked to the Café Ho Tay, then in front of Su Letei's house. He kept his eyes on the sidewalk, but all he heard was the sound of his boots and his own angry thoughts. Things could sure change fast where women were concerned.

He had almost reached the bridge when he heard skidding tires. Rankin, Cowan, and Dukemire were in the major's jeep. "Hey, kid, you want to go to town?" Rankin said.

Cody glanced over his shoulder. They were already *in* town, but he knew what Rankin meant. Even Dukemire was smiling. "Sure," he said. "Why not?"

Chapter Fourteen

THEY DROVE DOWN SINH TU to check traffic. Things seemed normal for Saturday night. The thunderstorm was still rumbling in the distance, its wide flashing panels beginning now to affect the city, though failing to penetrate the neon dust of Sinh Tu. The air was filthy and damp and full of odors. Bluish smoke of sidewalk grills was strung before the headlights.

He was uncertain at first, but Cody was quickly glad that the guys had come along to rescue him. It was good to be in the company of males again; women were so exhausting. The age-old female complaint about men being interested only in their bodies was largely true; it was the only female part that men were innately equipped to handle.

He was still slightly angry at Moni', but she suddenly didn't matter so much. Even though he was sitting next to the normally gloomy Dukemire, they had covered only a few blocks before he was smiling again, happy to be out on a Saturday night.

"So where the hell have you been all afternoon, West?" said Cowan. He had shed ten pounds, his cheekbones emerging, the lines of his face showing more character. Now that Brantley was gone, he also talked a lot more.

"He's been chasing that homely girl," Rankin said. He dropped a gear, crossed De Lattre, and headed downtown.

"The crazy man's daughter? Is that right?"

"We heard the rifle," Dukemire said.

"Yeah, he only shot at you twice this time," said Cowan. "You guys must be buddies by now."

"Why do you go out there?" said Dukemire.

"She must have some awful good pussy," said Rankin.

Cody waited for the remark to fall flat, then said simply, "She's a nurse."

"Nurse! Nurse! Oh, nurse!" Cowan yelled, causing them all to laugh.

There was a Vietnamese restaurant on Dinh Le Street, almost directly behind the French officers' club, which served hamburgers and French fries, American-style coffee, and American beer. Rankin had heard about it from one of the Civil Air Transport pilots. It sat on a frontless second level of a typical three-level in a jammed section of shops. The men trooped down a narrow hall and climbed a square set of stairs steep as a ladder. A thin old Vietnamese man seated them, and in a moment his grandchildren began bringing water, utensils, and napkins to the table. A skittish teenage girl took their orders, and soon returned with what appeared to be American hamburgers with lettuce and onions.

Cowan eyed the patty suspiciously. "I wonder what kind of meat this is," he said.

"Don't interrogate it, eat it," said Rankin. The sounds and fumes of the street below flowed in through the missing wall.

"Anybody hear any more about what's happening out west?" Cody asked.

"This pilot I talked to said that two positions north and west of the field have been under attack for three days. One of 'em the Viets almost took, then the French took it back only to abandon it this morning. They're picking off the positions one at a time. They've got coolies digging trenches all around each camp, slowly moving closer and closer."

"Sergeant Whitney said that Winslow told him that French Headquarters has already acknowledged they probably can't hold out for more than ten days or so," said Cowan.

"I heard the same thing from the pilot. They're losing men faster than they can be replaced. Right this minute they've got planes going out with about three hundred more volunteers, but that won't make any difference. Those new guys won't last a week."

"I don't understand," said Dukemire. "If they know they are going to lose, why do they keep sending out more men to get killed?"

"They're hoping the United States will send in bombers. And I guess they're looking at it as having lost too much already to quit. They know that if they do quit, the entire shooting match is probably over. On top of that, the ones that are there are trapped. They can't even get the wounded out now. And I heard today that they just had their first case of gangrene."

"Moni' says they've got a hospital there that's nothing but a bunch of bunkers connected by tunnels filled with rats and mud and dirt."

"What are we talking about this for?" said Cowan. He stabbed some fries. They ate for a time in silence.

When the young waitress again tiptoed up to the table, Cowan asked if he might have a little more catsup. She explained in halting English that there was no more, that the American units at Gia Lam had gotten all that was available, and that there likely would be no more until the GIs either went home or came over in large numbers.

"Which do you think is going to happen?" Rankin asked.

She gave a shy and pretty smile, and slowly said, "Fathah say is good I lun Engliss."

They stayed two hours, drinking beer when the food was gone, and telling stories. As their voices grew louder, the little waitress became increasingly frightened. Finally she disappeared, and the grandpa with his ancient thin hair presented the bill gravely in both hands. One of his eyelids drooped. Rankin insisted on paying the entire check. He looked at his watch. "Should be about right," he said. They tumbled down the stairs and headed for the Coup de Feu.

When they passed Little Lake with its arched bridge and island pagoda, Cody thought of Moni'—not with anger, but with unexpected regret. For a time it had seemed she might emerge from her cocoon, but that possibility was gone. Thinking of Moni' was like watching a woman drown herself, the struggle between halves—one wanting life, flailing for the surface; the other withdrawing, pulling the arms against the chest, expelling air, and sending the body downward. He was beginning to understand that he had gone to the farm for no other reason than to see her. The image of the girl in a house with a drunken old man who shot at anyone who might take her away had drawn him as surely as a magnet draws steel, unconscious and denying, even as he slipped forward.

Half the heavens were erupting greenish-white—wide stuttering moments that could now be seen without looking toward the sky, but the rumble of thunder was still vague, even when the jeep had stopped. A slow breeze had begun to feed the storm, and on that same wind came the sound of heavy aircraft headed west. Listening as he walked, Rankin almost fell. The men hurried down the alley toward the neon.

Sinh Tu Street was churning like a factory at the city's elbow, giving off a glow that wiped away the warning sky. Smoke and dust and fumes and vapor; odors, light, and pulsing beat. Men crossed the street at smiling angles, far away from war.

Raphi was just beginning her act, but they found a table near the wall that was occupied by a single soldier. When Rankin produced some bills, the man smiled, grabbed them, and found a place at the bar. When they were seated, he waved for four beers and announced that tonight he was buying all drinks. When Cowan suggested that at his age he should be saving something for retirement, Rankin merely smiled. "Things may be changing Monday," he said, glancing around the table. "I don't mean to worry anybody, but if you fellas want a girl, tonight's the night. I'm talking especially to you two," he said, nodding at West and Dukemire. "And by the way," he said to Cody, "the major gave us passes—you're signed out until tomorrow at 1700."

Cody nodded solemnly, then managed a smile. He looked at Dukemire, but Duke was dividing his attention between the dancing Raphi and the girls on the bench. He had loosened a lot in the past few days, finally admitting to Cody that what he felt was not guilt, but fear of being caught. There was a big difference. For whatever reason, those in Haiphong who knew about what he had done were not planning to tell.

Cody thought again of Moni', wishing that things were different. Raphi smiled toward the table. He took a long pull from the bottle, settled back in his chair, and focused on the oiled motions of Raphi's ass.

Two girls arrived at the table—one taller and plump, the other young and plainly frightened. The older one suddenly sat on Cowan's lap. He seemed to expect it; he slipped a hand around her waist and smiled. The younger one stood between Cody and Dukemire and looked back over her shoulder. To Cody's amazement, Dukemire reached out and touched a thigh. The girl jumped, but held her ground and tried to smile. Anyone could see that Dukemire was just as scared as she, but he kept his hand on her leg. When he led her down to his lap, they gave each other strange smiles.

Cody quickly forgot them, watching the tall and lithesome Raphi dance. He wondered if it was true that some were born to be whores. Surely there had never been a possibility that Raphi would be anything else.

Rankin suddenly threw an arm around Cody's neck, drawing him close. He had not eaten much at the café, but had been drinking fast all evening, sinking deeper into a mood. "I saw twelve hundred men in a field one day," he said hoarsely. "A parade I was in. Some asshole on a stand. Left and right, left and right, we covered the field." He paused with his eyes on Raphi. "We didn't parade the next year," he said. "Nobody asked. Four hundred missing and four hundred limping would have made a mess of our formation. And wheelchairs are goddamned unsightly." When Cody squeezed his wrist, Rankin released the hammerlock, staring blankly at a vision somewhere near the floor.

When her dance was finished and she had made her bows, Raphi approached the table in her peacock strut. She smiled, then stood talking to Rankin with her butt mere inches from Cody's face. He could feel it all coming together—the beer, the storm, the threat of war, even the fight with Moni'. Then Raphi bent at the waist to whisper with Rankin, and Cody was left to stare at a vertical line between cheeks. To his uncertain disgust, he thought of doing things with his tongue. When the woman turned and put her lips against his ear and said, "Are you ready now for me?" there was nothing left to do but nod.

★

He could just imagine what Grandma West would think.

The cyclo moved down the dark and winding street, bumping gently, squeaking with the orbits of the chain. The thunderstorm had receded, and the streets were dry, though clouds were still overhead. Exposed in the open clamshell for all Hanoi to see, Cody West, the brave and famous helicopter pilot, leaned back into the shadows. He heard the huffing labor of the man behind his back, and saw again the pumping calves of wood. The threatening street came slowly forward, each black door a sudden danger, each unknown turn a place he didn't want to go. He wondered if he was the world's greatest fool, on a snipe hunt arranged by Rankin, sent on a cyclo ride to the city dump or to a gravel barge or some infected den of bony addicts sucking pipes. He was embarrassed by what would be said when they found his body. He thought of Dukemire, afoot in the trackless gutters of Haiphong, and was filled anew with awe at what he had achieved. The cracks and crumbling asphalt came inexorably toward him, passing just beneath his boots. At the roots of trees and on the open sidewalks he saw loose black shapes of people murdered or asleep. He alternately wished for a weapon so that he might kill the driver and fight his way across the city, then made himself small, thinking what a stupid if popular way he had chosen to die. He even once considered praying, but decided that God was already in hysterics. He could hear the chastising words of Grandma West: "Got what you deserved, didn't you, Bentline? I told you. Little boys shouldn't be playing with whores."

Rather than taking Cody to one of the rooms as he expected, Raphi had led him out behind the Coup de Feu and loaded him aboard the waiting cart. She gave the driver money and instructions to which he wordlessly nodded before pedaling away. "Number nine," she called. "I take taxi, meet you there." When Cody had looked back, the alley behind the club was dark and empty.

They came to a slight rise, then turned on a short curved street where the lights were suddenly brighter. The driver stopped before a white two-story whose front steps rose directly from the curb. Cody gave the house an appraising look. It was sure no dump. The door was etched glass, and from a clean white wall hung a bright brass fixture. Abutting on either side were similar houses, different only in color. When he stepped from the cyclo, the driver turned the vehicle about and moved immediately away.

He looked all around, wondering if he was supposed to wait. The street formed a sloped horseshoe that opened onto a private park, and he could see the curved fronts of many houses, all neat and seemingly new, all sterile and silent and bright. A bell chain hung near the door marked 9, but he tried a discreet knock instead.

To his surprise and relief, the woman named Raphi answered the door. She was wearing a robe and slippers, and had apparently just stepped from a bath. Her hair was wet and dark, and though the lights were bright and her makeup gone, she was even more attractive than in the club—the basic beauty that most women possess. Cody stared, believing he must have gotten the wrong door, but she smiled and led him up the polished stairs.

The second level was small, intended only as extra space and to give access to the front balcony for a view of the city, but Raphi's bed was there, large and alone at the center of the room, made only with sheets and pillows. The walls were white plaster and the ceiling was peaked and lined with scorched bamboo. The back wall was black windows and doors of glass. To one side stood an inexpensive armoire and a dresser, and beside the bed was a table and lamp. "Nice place," he said.

Raphi looked around and shrugged. "It is a place," she said. Her voice was melodious and throaty and warm, and he could smell the wet fragrance of her hair. She let her eyes settle on his. "I decide to take the night off," she said. She opened her robe. "Come, I teach you things you never forget."

Grandma West made one last sputtering attempt, then the old gal wheezed and collapsed and left him alone.

He was thinking about Moni' when they heard voices downstairs. He reached for his pants, but Raphi held out a hand. "It's okay," she said.

"Who is it?"

"I don't know. It does not matter." When Cody looked confused, she said, "This is not my house. I rent only upstairs. Sometimes I go down and use the bath, sometimes I must go outside. Others have the lower part."

"Who owns it?"

"A man named Chang Wu."

"The guy that owns the place where the dogs fight?"

"Yes, as well as the Coup de Feu. But I have never seen him either place. He owns much of the city." She listened for a moment. A door closed downstairs and all was quiet. "Come," she said. "We must wash."

She led him to the glass doors, which opened to a landing behind the house. When she reached for a switch, a floodlight revealed a narrow yard abutting a tall cliff. Suddenly he realized he was standing naked in full view of anyone outside, and he hurried for his pants.

"It's okay," she said. "You do not need your clothes." He stared at her dumbly, but she was as naked as he. Anyone outside had already seen them.

A set of white stairs led down a white wall in the floodlight. Cody watched as the naked woman stepped calmly down, statuesque and beautiful. When she turned at the landing and made a beckoning gesture, the sharp light and shadows spelled the symmetry of her breasts. Her body was all curves, her face was all angles. "It's okay," she said. "Come." Every bit as scared as he had been in the dark cyclo on the unfamiliar streets, he glanced uselessly around and went carefully down the stairs. By the time he was halfway he felt better, more at ease and no longer afraid; he was naked outdoors for the world to see if it wanted to look, and if it did, it was no longer so important.

A cistern fed from the roof by a long black pipe was at the foot of the stairs, and he stood while she lifted the lid and dipped at the nervous reflection and washed him.

He was worried in the morning, sunlight burning through the glass. He thought of Moni' asleep on the farm, and felt a guilt he could not explain. He wondered if he had the clap. Life sure had a lot more problems at twenty than he ever would have believed at nineteen.

Carefully, he drew back the sheet. Raphi was half on her side, one leg drawn and a hand beneath her pillow, her upper breast just touching the bed. He ran his eyes all over her. A woman was a most incredible thing, a naked one more incredible yet. He wanted to touch her, and he wanted to jump from the bed and throw on his clothes and run quickly through Hanoi's morning. It scared him to want anything so much, to give so much away.

Contemplating Raphi quickly brought another view—the sense of being a product in skilled hands. Despite the favored image of men and their whores, this woman was more the consumer than he—the spider that reeled its victim to the web, sucked it dry, and discarded the carcass. The kid named West was one bit of raw material on which an industry survived. He frowned at the new perspective.

"Good morning," she whispered, and looked up and smiled.

He was embarrassed at being caught, but surprised himself by saying, "I like looking at you."

"Of course."

"I guess I need to go."

"In a little while. What were you thinking about?"

"I was wondering if I might have caught something."

"Something you can do nothing about."

"I could have done plenty about it by not going to bed with you."

"Something you can do nothing about . . ."

"Can I use your bathroom?"

"There is none here, but you can go there," she said, pointing toward the glass doors. When he looked doubtful, she added, "You don't need clothes, and you don't need to go downstairs."

He frowned and got dressed. The landing was bright, the sun looming above the tall cliff. He squinted at the yellow sky and at the silhouettes of palms and structure. Through dense growth below he could see adjacent yards, and when he looked down the stairs he saw himself there naked, not believing he had ever done such a crazy thing. At least it had been nighttime; no way now could he piss from a balcony in daylight. He went downstairs and found a private place beyond the cistern.

He could not stop thinking about Moni'. He did not regret his time with Raphi—he was not *that* remorseful—but it bothered him that she was not Moni'. As soon as he recognized the thought, he was bothered even more. He felt that if he had only been smarter or older, or if he had more experience with women, he would have known what to say or what to do to make things different in the park. That was one of the rotten things about life—no one told you a damn thing until you screwed up so badly and so often that you knew it all for yourself. Then you were too old to use it.

He looked around at the cliff and the houses and windows nearby, and he knew that Raphi was waiting. He went quietly upstairs, no longer so bold as a naked kid in the night.

The streets so scary by night were harmless in the honeyed haze of morning. The ancient colors of the city glowed, and the narrow lanes were pleasant. He set off at an easy pace, free for the moment of all worry, no longer a soldier or inept lover or beer-drinking chaser of whores. Raphi had shown him some landmarks through the front window. From the elevation of the two-story and the slope surrounding the limestone projection he could see the flags of French Headquarters at the Citadel, the standards of Doumer Bridge beyond, and in another direction, part of the golden roof of the opera house downtown. He paused on the front steps to listen, and all he could hear was the raucous crowing of a rooster. The sky was vacant. He wandered the city, observing the slow routines of Sunday.

At a corner grocery he paused to watch an aproned man clean heads of cabbage with a knife. Stacked against a turquoise wall were crates of produce, and on the walk was a growing pile of wilted leaves. The grocer looked up, and in that glance was everything he knew.

He saw a boy of about three, wearing nothing but a pink shirt above a protruding navel, pissing from the curb. The child turned as Cody passed, staring up with huge black eyes, the stream of piss unbroken.

Farther along, a man in bare feet and trousers, wearing no shirt and scratching at his white and sagging chest, reached down for his morning paper. He looked Cody over and said, *"Qu'est-ce qu'un Américain vient foutre dans ces parages si tôt le matin!"* Not comprehending, Cody smiled and wished him good day.

He saw an old woman, a Vietnamese in rusty-brown trousers, stringy gray hair becoming unpinned, walk out from a door and step partway off the curb. She pulled a pant leg higher and higher until the entire withered stalk was exposed, the material gathered in both hands. Then, with her head down, still standing, she began to piss. Cody kept walking, not sure where he was, but positive it was one long way from Batesville, Texas.

★

Su Letei was working the perimeter of her porch, clipping old growth with her scissors, placing the pieces in precise stacks beside the steps. Dressed in a pink *ao dai*, she looked as fragile as the flowers she grew. She placed a red rosebud in a slender vase on the rail, and glanced angrily down the street toward an automobile.

Cody was surprised when he saw her. He looked around. He had wandered unconsciously to her place, but it was too late now to avoid being seen. "Good morning," he said quietly, and was taken aback when she turned her furious eyes. The look vanished in an instant, but not before he believed that the anger was meant for him.

"Good morning, Cody," she said softly. Her smile was warm, but also a little sad. When she did not ask what brought him there again on Sunday morning, he was sure that she knew all about his evening, perhaps even the part on the stairs. There was nothing to say, no place to hide, so he just looked at her and thought how pretty she was and wondered about Moni'.

"Come help me with these chairs," she said, "and we will sit out beneath the trees where they can see." She nodded toward two men in the car, their faces indistinct behind the shining glass.

"Who are they?" he asked. He hurried up a walk of weathered brick as she shoved at two wicker chairs.

"Out there, beneath the tree," she said. "Take the little table as well, and I will bring some tea."

When he had the furniture arranged, he sat and watched the men, wondering what it was all about. He fantasized he had their glassy heads within a rifle's sight. Pop, pop; broken glass, ruptured melon heads. Then Su Letei arrived with a black lacquered tray, a ceramic teapot, and two nervous cups on saucers.

"They work for Chang Wu," she said. She lowered the tray.

"The guy with the dogs ...?" The name was everywhere.

"Yes," she said tightly. She poured tea, and they settled back into the chairs.

"What's he got to do with you?"

"Nothing, but he thinks he does. He is a sick but powerful man who believes I need to be watched. His men are always nearby."

"Is there nothing you can do?"

She blinked and stared toward the car. "Not just yet," she said. Then the worried and unhappy lines of her face dissolved, and she turned to face him. "But these things are not important. I am pleased that you have come to see me. It is a beautiful morning, and now that you are here it will be a day to remember." Her eyes were warm with familiar light. Cody blushed at her extravagance.

"Moni' told me about what happened in the park," she said. She turned her gaze up through the treetops. "I am glad that the storm turned back last evening. It does that often, building up to the north, then surging toward us before backing away—just a reminder, I suppose. The worst storms come from the east, much later in the year. Farther south, beyond Vinh, they are sometimes truly terrible, rising from the South China Sea, coming up along the continental edge, then turning inland there. Here we are more fortunate. The big Chinese island of Hainan Dao, two hundred miles in that direction, shields us from the season's worst typhoons, sends them sliding north or south, or depletes their strength. She is very lonely, but I do not know if anyone can reach her now."

"She said she never wanted to see me again."

"I know. She has said the same to me. It is the way she fights her war."

"I don't think for her there's anything else."

"She fights her war by embracing it. She fights you by turning you away because what she sees in you would take her partly from the war, and the war from her, and she wants that very much. You remind her of what she has missed, and what she thinks she cannot have."

"I think I understand that part. My mother was killed in an accident when I was three. Later, whenever my father brought a woman to the house, I always behaved like a monster so she would go away. I wanted a mother, and none of them could be that to me. So I guess in that way I was fighting Moni's war."

"You know much for your age."

"I don't know anything at all. But I think it is the reason she stays with her father."

"I believe this is true. How does he act toward you?"

"He shoots at me."

"And you face him when he does that?"

"I have twice, but I'm not sure I could do it again."

"No one else has ever faced him."

"He reminds me of my father. He is exactly like my father. The first time I saw him, I thought he *was* my father."

"But your father is dead."

"Yes."

"And you killed him?"

Cody stared. She was completely inside him now.

"Moni' said she thought you must have been responsible for his death."

"That's right, I was."

"Then that is why you let him shoot at you?"

"It's why I didn't run."

"You impressed her very much. Especially the second time, because she knew you really came to see her, and not just to show off."

Cody smiled. "It sounds like Moni' knows a little herself."

"Children without parents—or with one parent, or with parents that fight—must always see more. They are wise in ways that they do not know." She looked at her cup. "Our tea has grown cool. I will make more."

"I probably need to go."

"Where? Back to Lam Du? Do you have work today?"

"No. Not really."

"Then you can stay here and visit with me. Have you had breakfast? I see that you have not. Good. I have some pineapple pastries that will practically make you ill. But first I will bring tea and bread and juice and whatever else I can find. I will bring everything to the door, and you can come and put it on the table. I would invite you inside, but those Chinese curs might get the wrong idea. I will be right back. We will enjoy this morning. When we finish breakfast you can tell me all about yourself and what happened to your father."

When she was gone, Cody sat watching the two men from his chair, thinking that Su Letei knew a few things herself. He wondered if Major McCall had noticed her, but decided that the old boy was probably too stuffy for that. On impulse, he raised both hands, leveled an imaginary rifle, and squeezed off two quick rounds that could not possibly have missed the heads in the windshield. A few seconds later, the engine started; the car backed a few feet down the street, then stopped again at the curb.

But Cody had already forgotten the men. He was thinking instead about his father, Beatty West, and wondering how he could tell the story in a way that would make sense.

The second most important event in the life of Beatty West was the discovery of his considerable talent as a pilot. All during the war years his brother's airplane sat on blocks in the yard just off the front porch, covered with tarps, tied and staked to the ground. Never one to neglect a piece of equipment, even one that he could not use, Beatty had removed the three tires and stored them inside, against the wall of the living room. At least four times a year he and Cody would spend a day with rags and buckets, dusting and washing. Cody enjoyed these times, dreaming about the day he would fly. When the work was done, he got to spend a half hour inside, pretending he was flying. He stretched himself, but little by little he grew taller in the seat, his feet grew nearer the pedals. He would stand on the porch while his father started the engine and allowed it to run to lubricate parts and moisten gaskets. Cody could feel the sound, the tenor vibration, the beat of wooden blades in his chest. Someday, he said. Someday.

When he was twelve they put the wheels back on the airplane. The war was over and times were improving. It was a few days later that his father flew past the window of the school bus. "That's my dad," Cody said, prouder than he had ever been.

It was almost two years later when Cody heard something terrible at school, and whipped a kid for saying it, then came home with a question for Grandpa West. Beatty's father told Cody to wait beneath the live oak tree while he climbed the rise to speak to his son. "You've put it off too long," he said. "You need to tell the boy the truth about the accident."

But Beatty said he just couldn't do it. So while he went inside to find a bottle, then drove away in his truck, Grandpa West limped down the slope to answer all the boy's questions.

Beatty was gone four days. He came home unwashed and unshaven, drunk enough to build the belligerence he thought he was going to need. But he could have saved the alcohol. Cody avoided him for a time, but never deliberately so, and no more than he usually did when his father was drinking. Beatty was quietly amazed, deeply relieved, enough to wonder if Grandpa West had not changed his mind about telling the story. It took a few weeks, even a few months, but it wasn't long until any trace of doubt was completely and permanently dispelled.

For most of two weeks Beatty worked with the tractor, slowly building a crown and diversion ditch down the center of a field that grew maize. He borrowed a sheepfoot from the highway crew at La Pryor, hauled in caliche from the Deutcher place, then topped the compacted soil with fossilized gravel from the bend at the end of the arroyo. It set him back a bit, he said to Cody with a grin, but it was going to be an investment.

Cody didn't know about that, just that nothing was going to stand in the way of becoming a pilot. He kept his thoughts to himself, observed his father's efforts, and waited. He never mentioned his new knowledge, or had to. He wore it like a uniform of thorns, and his father cringed. At night he listened to the trucks out on the highway, big tires headed west to Mexico, shrill as stringed instruments, sometimes like a mother's scream.

Beatty West began teaching his son to fly. Cody was a quick talent, as quick as his father had been. With the help of pillows, it could have happened sooner, but Cody soloed at fourteen.

Then deep water began to be found in much of the area, cavernous reservoirs fed for millennia by basins and traps in the limestone desert. Vast flats of mesquite were soon cleared, and farming became a viable concern. Rather than leasing raw land, breaking his back to develop another man's property, Beatty West saw another potential. He would become a crop duster, and have a breeze in his face while men riding tractors were sweating below.

By his eighteenth birthday, Cody had long been an accomplished pilot. Though Uncle Ned's Cub no longer sat in the yard, in its place stood a silver Pawnee, a low-slung duster that Cody could fly as if he had been born at the controls. He had been working illegally for more than a year, but as he approached eighteen he drove to Del Rio to buy the study manuals. On his birthday he went back and took the tests for commercial pilot.

"It might keep you from having to go to Korea," his father said, "filling a need in the area agriculture." Cody didn't know about that, but he kept his thoughts to himself.

A lot more was learned in his teenage years than just how to fly. Little by little, day by careful day, he began to collect on his father's debt, sometimes in ways that were subtle, sometimes in ways that were not. Slowly he grew aware of his power to employ the levels of his mother's memory to control and even to destroy his father. Soon he had built a lasting image of the man on the porch: long periods of silence, then a low, directionless mutter of profanity that eventually rumbled and broke in claps like thunder; again would come silence, then an explosive swing at a fly. Cody always secretly smiled.

By sixteen, he was a ruthless shit and knew it. By eighteen, he was hell on wheels, or more precisely, hell on wings. He did as he pleased, and nothing else.

He came home one Friday after spending the morning line-shooting the heads off dove, leaving them for the coyotes, then the afternoon shooting pool at the Crooked Taco in Uvalde. His dad was on the porch, wearing a grin that could be seen from the highway. When he slammed the door of the Dodge, Cody's father called out, "We've done it, boy! By God, we've done it!" An empty bottle lay at his feet. Cody didn't ask, but his father shook a fist and told him anyway. "We've got the Barbee Ranch."

Barbara Brigham, the daughter of the lieutenant governor, held title to forty-six sections along the Nueces, north and east of Carrizo, a patch she called the Bar B. The land was largely untouched, but it had long been rumored that someday the wooded bottom would be made into fields, the mesquite-and-cactus hills converted to pasture. Now it had happened. All winter the Rome plows worked, and when the slash was set ablaze in spring, the smoky fog reached upstream for eighty miles, spoiling wet clothes on the line beyond Camp Wood.

When his father said that they had gotten the ranch, he meant that they had a spraying job that could make all the difference, maybe even a new airplane. Cody was secretly pleased. When his daddy wasn't drinking, he could talk the bark off a cedar post. Cody had to wonder if along with the deal, he might not have managed to talk the blue jeans off of Bar Brigham; if he hadn't yet, he was bound to be working on it. Cody nodded begrudgingly. "When does it start?"

he said. He had only come home to change and clean up, then he was going to a rodeo in Eagle Pass. He had heard in Uvalde that Trent Pascal had had a fight with his girlfriend and joined the Army, and that Shelly would be working the concession stand with her aunts. Cody had been watching her for two years—watching the shape of her butt, the titties that pushed at the pearl snaps; watching an interesting glance that she sometimes gave when Trent was looking away. Everybody said that Trent had been poking her for more than a year. Cody had avoided the whores in Piedras, but a girl with experience seemed like a good idea, at least for a time or two.

"In the morning," said his father. "I've been working on things all day. Everything's set for you to fly. S'posed to be there at daylight. Start at Chigger Bend, right along the road."

Cody just looked at him. He didn't say yes, and he didn't say no, figuring the old man could find out in the morning. He stepped inside and began stripping off his smelly clothes.

Harry Barnes had a deputy named Luci Carbón, a green-eyed Mexican from La Pryor, six years older than Cody. Within the area communities, Cody had developed a small reputation for nastiness that he had carefully nurtured. But he also knew his limitations. He enjoyed having a reputation, but half the task of maintaining it involved tactical discretion—knowing places to avoid, and keeping track of the habits of dangerous opponents. Luci Carbón, on the other hand, was the genuine item. He avoided no one. While he was still a teenager, Luci had whipped all of the toughs in the adjoining four counties, and more than half of them were grown men at the time. It was joked that Luci had a death wish—a lot of men wished he were dead—but when he pinned on a badge for Harry Barnes, the joking ceased. Anytime there was trouble that needed the law, Luci was who you hoped they would send—unless you happened to *be* the trouble. Then he was the last thing on earth you wanted to see.

Luci was there, leaning against the wall in his leather coat, the next morning when Harry Barnes let Cody out of jail. For a while he just watched, those killer green eyes burning holes while the sheriff handed Cody his things. "You know what a punk is?" Luci finally said. Cody did not answer. "A punk is something made of dried cow shit that smokes and burns slow and gives a bad odor, and all it ever does in life is burn itself up and destroy things. Nothing but shit on a stick."

Cody glanced at him a couple of times, showing a little anger, a little rebellion, but not too much. He halfway expected the sheriff to come to his defense, put the deputy in his place, but that was not what happened.

"I saw your daddy out on the highway a few minutes ago," Harry Barnes said. "He passed me in his airplane, just scraping the fence posts. Looked like he was headed for the Brigham place." He turned a clipboard and had Cody sign, then handed him the keys to his truck. "That was your job, wasn't it?"

Cody choked, and pocketed his change. "Yeah, well, I had other things to do."

"He taught you better than that. He's drunk, you know."

Cody pulled his crumpled hat down on his head. As he turned, his eyes met those of the deputy, solid as an anvil, still standing against the wall. Luci's lips barely moved. "Scum."

Things hadn't worked out so well in Eagle Pass. The sun was down beyond the river when he dropped off the hill. With just two paved streets—both U.S. highways—the entire town was wallowing in a fog of adobe dust as dense as cotton candy. He drove out past Seco Mines and killed a couple of hours at Lewellen's, where he teamed up with a junk hauler from Midland to win twenty-five dollars from some customs clerks on the shuffleboard. When he finally moseyed out to the rodeo, he discovered a cowboy from Fort Stockton practically nailed to the concession stand. Worse was everything he read in Shelly's smile. It wasn't long until he ran into Holler Johnson, a halfback from Pearsall with a broken nose and a case of Falstaff, and they began to get seriously drunk. It was two in the morning before he headed home, and almost three when Luci Carbón waved him over at the crossing in La Pryor.

"Three of my friends have already died in Korea," Luci said as they drove toward Crystal City, Cody in front like a regular passenger. Luci almost never cuffed a prisoner; everybody said it was because he hoped one would try something. "Two more I know are still there," he continued. "Your daddy has fixed things for you so you'll never have to go, and you think that's nothing. He does everything for you. Even the pickup you drive he paid for."

"I work."

"You fly. You call that work?"

There was no use mentioning the accident. Luci Carbón knew it all. It was Harry Barnes who had carried Cody home that night, wrapped in his brown leather jacket with the red quilted lining, to spend the rest of the night in Mrs. Barnes's bed while the sheriff went back to do all the things that needed doing. Luci was probably hoping he would say something about it, so Cody kept quiet. He leaned back in the seat and pretended to sleep.

He had been asleep in the cell no more than three hours when Harry Barnes's deep voice said, "Wake up." When he went up front, stumbling from lack of sleep and the beer that hadn't yet worn off, Sheriff Barnes had his things on the counter, and Luci was holding the wall.

"You're the reason he's out there," the sheriff said when he followed him out to his truck. "You're the reason he wanted the job in the first place. Doing the best he knows how to hang on to all he's got left of Mary West."

It was the wrong time of day. He saw that even before he pulled his truck into the shallow, grassy ditch. Half the runs were straight into the sun. And Beatty West was definitely drunk. The lines along the highway had not yet been changed—the light company had agreed to shift them to the other side—but that was not the problem. He would make the turns okay, line himself up for the next run, then drop down over the wires in good shape. But he was judging the distance poorly, misgauging the weight of the load, literally busting the heads of cabbage with his tires. He had to know it was happening; Cody could almost hear him laugh as he banked too low beyond the far side, wingtips close to the trees—left, then right, then back again and down.

He got out of the truck, and stood in the road and hopelessly tried to wave his father to land. At last he gave up, and leaned against the fender and watched and held his breath, feeling exactly like what he was. Luci Carbón said it right—shit on a stick.

He swung his head around, admiring the groomed field. It sat back from the river a mile, land that not so long ago had been covered with two-hundred-year-old mesquites, big around as he could reach. August Kohl, his wife and eight kids, once had a homestead there. Now the house and barns were burned and plowed under, the farm flat and clean, planted in either direction along the highway as far as Cody could see. He squinted and shaded his eyes, looking toward something dim across the field. It gleamed and disappeared in the movement of air and the low angle of sun above the trees.

Then he saw it, the old Kohl homestead. It had not been bull-dozed after all, but sat tucked in the tallest mesquites in the far edge of the field, the house with its roof caved in and a tilting barn. Between them sagged the single strand that Cody saw, the deadly filament, a spider's web of wire.

With a shout, he ran into the roadway, right into the path of a rancher driving along with his head out the window, watching the airplane. The rancher yanked the wheel and left the road, the tailgate and tools and a length of loose pipe banging loudly in the bed. He shook his fist and kept going.

Lifting both arms, Cody jerked his shirt off over his head, and used it as a flag, jumping up and down, and waving wildly. He could see his dad looking straight at him, not moving or acknowledging, just doing the job, turning the plane, flying into the sun. When he banked beyond the field, he passed close to the wire while Cody held his breath. Then he was back again at eye level, then up and over and around.

"Wire, wire, wire!" Cody screamed and pointed. His father ignored him, flying straight toward August Kohl's barn.

For a moment it seemed he would miss it, climbing left enough to clear the trees. But when he flopped the wings, he dropped back down too early, watching the rows ahead, lining up his run. The wing sliced neatly through the space dividing the buildings.

It was all afire before anything touched the ground, a spewing cartwheel of fuel and flame. Then it hit the trees and scattered like a napalm bomb. A bubble of black and red went up, and he heard the crack and trailing *Hu-oof!* Then silence and the sound of distant flames. Cody screamed and ran into the field.

Chapter Fifteen

WINSLOW DREW BACK the bolt, peered down the barrel, and worked the action a few times. He squinted and listened, completely unable to resist his role. When the first sergeant poked a finger into the breech, then checked beneath the light for carbon, Kinney whispered, "Brother."

"It'll do, sir," Winslow said. He lifted the machine gun and a small can of ammo.

"Thank you, First Sergeant," said McCall. "I'll take it."

Winslow mutely handed over the weapon. Kinney grabbed for the ammo can. "I don't know about the major," he said, "but I sure feel a whole lot better, knowing that you've checked things over." He grinned, then jumped for the door to avoid the boot aimed at his butt.

They walked in silence toward the flight line, McCall enjoying the weight of the weapon, being up and starting something important early in the day. The air was moist and cool, and he could smell approaching dawn, an odor like no other time. Behind them, someone slammed a door.

In a moment rare for Gia Lam, there were no fighters or spotters or cargo planes landing or taking off, none careening down the taxiways, none loading up beside Lam Du. For just that time it seemed the war had ended, and there was the feel of how the land might someday be.

Dukemire had the blades untied, and was going over the bird with a red flashlight. The dome light made the cabin bubble glow. "Good morning, sir," he said.

"Morning."

Kinney placed the can on the left floor, removed the lid, and unfolded a length of ammo. He took the weapon from McCall and clipped it to a length of cotton rope suspended from the doorframe, then showed him how the headset worked and where to place his feet to avoid the extra cyclic stick, and how, with the left collective removed, he could slide out to the edge of the seat within a loose belt, one leg hooked inside the door. McCall tried the position, hefting the gun, and only realized he was grinning when the stitches pulled.

"Don't have too much fun today, sir," Kinney said. "I don't want you trying to take my job." He disappeared into the darkness and returned a moment later with a few smoke grenades, which he hung along a wire beside the door. "And don't get blood on my aircraft."

When Dukemire completed his preflight, he climbed into the right side of the cockpit, nodded respectfully to McCall, and continued his careful preparations. The sky had begun to brighten, and the dome light was no longer needed. Jim Kinney stepped back from the ship and waited. McCall checked over his shoulder toward the shacks of Lam Du. There was still no light in the quarters of Major Legère. He shifted in his seat and watched Legère's windows.

"Clear!" Dukemire yelled.

"Clear!" yelled Kinney.

The Franklin cranked, then growled like an awakened creature before settling down to a healthy motor drone. The aircraft seemed to breathe. McCall could feel the engine at his back, and he thought about its cast-iron weight, the plastic bubble where they sat, and what a sudden stop would mean. Just another bullet—a slow, fat projectile that happened to be strapped to his butt. The blades that spun above his head like deadly scythes became a blur, and a churning wind moved through the doorless bird. Dukemire tuned his radios and ran his checks, then signaled Kinney with a thumb. The crew chief backed away, then stopped beside Rankin, who had just arrived to solemnly watch.

McCall showed Dukemire on his map where he wanted to go, then turned his attention outside, ignoring the pilot as he called the tower. He would have preferred to fly with Cody West, who had seen the village, but Dukemire—not yet an instructor—was the better choice for an irregular mission. Dukemire was okay on the controls, but not nearly so steady as the more experienced pilots, feeling for balance as he brought the craft off the ground. He was tense with concentration as they hovered into position and made the next call to the tower. As the bird moved forward with the takeoff, there was a short, stomach-sinking moment as it settled toward the earth before beginning to climb, smoothly and without effort. The blades beat a steady cadence.

McCall was still not too sure about these whirligigs. The word "contraption" came to mind. Helicopters were extraordinarily useful, particularly in the evacuation of wounded men, but the sense of contrivance was unavoidable—an assemblage of parts that served a mechanical purpose, but in a way that seemed unnatural. Helicopters struck McCall as just too tentative, too fragile, to be taken seriously as war machines. He would never let it be known, but he felt almost the same way about pilots. There was something about just flying away when their bombs were gone or when their fuel or courage ran low that made their commitment seem much too shallow for them to be called soldiers. The kamikazes of Japan—taught to take off but not to land—*those* pilots were soldiers. The rest he wasn't sure about.

As the helicopter gained altitude, the morning seemed to accelerate. The sky grew brighter all along its eastern edge, and the mountains in that direction stood apart—midnight blue trimmed in haze. The streams and rivers and big canals, the stagnant swamps and old oxbows, took on the graded hues and sent them skyward.

Rankin had disapproved of the flight, but would have objected more had he known what it was about. McCall told him only that he wanted to make a trip along the road to Haiphong to have a look around. Rankin clearly suspected more. Sergeant Winslow would be in operations to intercept Major Legère when he looked out his window this morning and noticed that one of the birds was gone.

Winslow was the only one who knew the entire story, though Cody West had to be running a close second. After three days of thinking about it, West had finally come to his office to say that he did not believe that the convoy's missing truck had returned to Haiphong; it may have stopped instead at the village of Cong My. It seemed the kid was perceptive enough, but nothing happened too quickly between his ears.

They flew in silence—the static calls of other aircraft squelching in their ears—and watched the changing colors followed by a flaming sunrise, the first McCall had ever seen from the air.

Perhaps it was the doubtful presence of Dukemire or only the new perspective of altitude, but before they reached the village— almost a thirty-minute flight—Marsh McCall was worried. He told the pilot to continue to Cat Bi for fuel, gazing down at Cong My as they passed. The narrow path connecting it to the highway was vacant, save for a few walking peasants with loads.

He had finally begun to acknowledge that his little band might have wandered into something with serious potential. With every day that passed, the impression grew stronger, as ominous as it was unshakable. Ezra Smith's failure to arrive for yesterday's meeting had begun a chain of thoughts. It seemed increasingly likely that Smith—and by extension, the northern element of the 22d—had fallen victim to the tangled workings of the CIA. Ezra was near retirement, vulnerable, and had clearly lost much of his quickness. But more than that was gone. It was a rare man who could jump all the fences on the way to bird colonel without snagging at least one nut on the wire. That was why old generals always smiled for photographs. For every man who made it intact, there were dozens whose growl was gone, traded for position and bits of ribbon never won.

Ezra's flight had landed at Gia Lam, carrying only a few small crates and some papers, all received in person by René Legère. Before McCall walked out, Legère had his men hustle the crates aboard a truck, then beat a retreat through the gates of Lam Du. When McCall spoke briefly with the pilot, a scruffy civilian who seemed to have slept in his clothes, all the man said was that the colonel would be in touch.

Cat Bi Field was swarming with activity, fighters hustling back and forth to the rearming point. Many were making the tiring run to Dien Bien Phu, but in the rugged mountains fifteen miles north stood a column of smoke, gray and black and white, bursts of red flashing below. To avoid traffic, Dukemire made his call, then dropped slightly lower and made a doglegged approach directly to the refueling point.

When they departed, McCall's attention was again with the helicopter. He had grown accustomed to the motions of the aircraft, rising and falling with currents, buffeted by the gentlest wind. Somewhat to his surprise, he was beginning to enjoy himself. The view was spectacular. The patterns of land and silty water surrounding Haiphong, the ships and little boats upon the river, the city itself and all the green villages, the suspended blue mountains and patterns of clouds—all seemed too much for just one set of eyes. He thought he could understand why pilots always seemed so excited. Flying was just plain fun.

"Beautiful, isn't it?" he said.

The aircraft lurched with Dukemire's reaction. Haiphong was passing below, and he had been gazing down toward its streets, completely lost to his duties in the air. "Yes, sir," he managed, eyes big and blinking and dumb.

McCall was strongly considering recommending Dukemire for psychiatric evaluation whenever the unit moved south.

The village of Cong My lay just off the highway, a bulbous green growth on a narrow dirt lane that wandered among the leafy hamlets like a connecting vine. Surrounded by rice paddies, the village was sheltered by tall, fanning bamboo, shielding it from strong coastal winds and harsh summer sky. Only a few shanties lay exposed among the frazzled palms.

McCall had Dukemire hold his course along the highway until they were two miles beyond the village. People were in the fields, but the dirt lane was empty, no vehicle tracks upon it. It hardly looked wide enough to support a big truck; he was sure that West had been mistaken.

"We need to go back and take another look," McCall said. "This time, hold your altitude until we're almost there, then come down fast right on top of the village, do a slow hover through the middle, just above the bamboo. Stay over the road if you can."

"Yes, sir," said Dukemire crisply. He brought the helicopter around, blades slapping sharply through the turn. They went straight for the village. Just when McCall decided that Dukemire had mis-understood, the pilot lowered the collective, allowing the aircraft to descend steeply. Dukemire's moves were positive and smooth, guiding the OH-13 to within fifty feet of the dirt lane, then turning sharply above the surprised peasants. When they reached the bamboo of the village, the path disappeared, but as the helicopter came to hover and the wind from its blades took effect, the fronds swayed and parted. They eased ahead. Many of the staring villagers turned and ran, and all the babies cried. Chickens went beating insanely across the packed earth. Then the bamboo closed and they could see no more.

Dukemire immediately kicked in right pedal and brought the aircraft about to the place where the road had disappeared, then came to a hover until he could see. Again they moved ahead, and again the path disappeared.

"Hold it!" McCall said. He loosened the belt and leaned out from the aircraft. "A little back and to the right." When Dukemire complied, the major twisted about, peering beneath them. The bamboo clacked and swayed, but he was unable to get perspective on what he could see. Dukemire now had the idea. Gazing out the opposite door, he began to move the ship from side to side. Finally the maneuver worked. The shifting wind bent open the bamboo, and both men saw the green banana thatch.

"Back up," McCall said. He could see an open doorway, and just beyond, new wooden crates that he instantly recognized. "A little more," he said, but the words were no sooner uttered than a man stepped boldly from the shadows, swung a submachine gun, and opened fire.

When he finished instructing he stopped by the tent for some water, then went back out to check the progress on the damaged bird. Sergeant Winslow had a block of ice wrapped up in a tarp in the major's jeep, so Cody helped himself to a chunk, iced down the jug in the tent, then carried a sweating quart can out to Mano, working alone in the burnished sun.

Following the loss of the bird at Cong My, Captain Sarot had agreed that all the aircraft of the 22d—five now—should be pulled from nontraining missions until the end of the week, when the present group of pilots would complete the course. There had been no further word on the promised helicopters from Korea, and by week's end a sufficient number of French pilots, plus Rankin's two instructors, would be qualified to take over the remaining birds whenever the 22d went south. It seemed pointless to continue training.

For three days the shattered hulk of the OH-13 had sat on the edge of the ramp beside Depot Road. Occasionally, a few of the French paratroopers would come to gawk and point and laugh. The bird was pretty well peppered. The radios had escaped damage, but the wiring had not. The plastic windshield had a number of holes below and overhead, and was beginning to split. One main rotor blade had taken a round close to the leading edge, and the cyclic-control jackshaft was almost severed. Another bullet had changed course after penetrating the floor and a structural support, and so far its remaining route was unknown. Counting entries and exits, the men had found twenty-three holes, but not a drop of blood. After a doubtful moment, McCall and Dukemire had made it out okay.

Kinney, Mano, and Whitney had done their best—the sergeant running back and forth in the jeep, borrowing tools and looking for parts, while the others took things apart. Whitney didn't have much luck. The only two places to try were the maintenance sheds of the French helicopter units, and the U.S. Air Force mechanics across the field. All were sympathetic and offered to help all they could, but the fact was they were not equipped to work on the Bell aircraft—those materials were supposed to arrive with the next shipment of birds. Rankin and Sergeant Winslow stopped by from time to time to give advice or to assess progress, but neither was hopeful. The head mechanic of the Air Force contingent, a can-do, cigar-chewing sergeant named Tanner, had said there might be a possibility of scrounging parts from the Philippines or Japan or Korea. He hinted that he knew men in all those places who were not beyond stealing an entire aircraft—though perhaps a damaged one—and shoving it aboard a C-119 on some dark night. It had happened more than once, he said. He would see what he could do.

"¡Qué pasó!" Cody said. He liked Billy Mano, perhaps because they had both grown up in the same part of the country. Mano was from Rio Grande City and had four sisters. It seemed odd that each could travel clear around the world and end up in the same hole.

"*Que pasa nada*," Mano said, shaking his head as he reached for the can. In anticipation of getting new parts, he and Kinney had borrowed a hoist and removed the main rotor assembly. It rested now on four low crates, long and ungainly, no longer a thing that could fly. Mano knelt in the narrow shade between the blades and the aircraft. "'Preciate it," he said as he began to drink. Bloody scratches marked knuckles and forearms.

"Where's Kinney?"

"Working the orderly room."

Cody began going over the bird for the twentieth time, counting holes, peering beneath plates. When he straightened, he was grinning. "Did you see his face?" he said.

"Who's that, sir?"

"Dukemire. Seriously scared."

"Who wouldn't be?"

"An hour after it happened?"

"Maybe. Maybe longer," Mano said quietly. He glanced at the ship, hid his face in the can, then wiped his mouth. "Winslow says things are fixing to change."

"What do you mean?"

"He says it's going to get bad for us now."

"How does he know that?"

"I don't know, but I think he's right. I'm just as scared as Mr. Dukemire."

The smile slowly slipped from Cody's face. He saw that Mano was not kidding, and he was not sure how to respond. He watched an Otter enter downwind, and thought about going back to the tent.

"But that's nothing new," Mano said, staring past the road toward the ammo dump. "Thing is, my old man was brave. He had scars all over—a long one here, and another here and here, a big crescent on this cheek, six teeth gone, lips sewed, part of an ear bitten off. Scars all over. He went around without a shirt."

Cody looked toward the tent, pale in the bright sunlight. A low stream of dust scurried around the corner past the door.

"I was always a big embarrassment, the macho's little sissy. And nothing changed. I was scared in Korea, I was scared on the boat coming here, I'm scared every time I fly. I'm scared right now about next week."

He poured water in a hand and wiped it across his face. Drops clung to his nose and eyebrows. "There was this kid in school one time named Koonce, always slapping me around. One day he was coming down the hall, and all the kids just stepped back to watch me get it. Something really weird happened. I kind of got a flash of my old man, what he would do. Before Koonce could make a move, I dropped my books and went at him. Pretty soon he was just a bloody worm on the floor. And you know what? I was still scared, scared I was going to get in trouble, scared that now I'd have to fight somebody else, scared that maybe I could never do that again. I *did* do it again, but I was always scared.

"So, I guess that makes me a coward. Every time I fly, I'm fighting hard just being there. So if Mr. Dukemire is scared, I know all about it. You looking for a hero, it'll have to be somebody else, sir. I'm just too damn scared."

Cody didn't know what to say. He surveyed the bullet holes and thought about what it must have been like. Sure, it was scary, but the bullets went by real fast, and when they were gone there was nothing to worry about—you were wounded or dead or okay. Then he thought about Moni's father, how scary it had been the second time, and he understood. It was not the getting shot at that was bad, it was the anticipation, thinking about it. If a guy could avoid thinking, if he could somehow learn without losing his ignorance...

He realized then that part of the story was missing. "What happened to your old man?" he asked.

Mano was waiting. "One night a wetback who wasn't brave at all connected all the scars with a little bitty knife." He smiled sadly toward the paddies. "My old man would have been so proud," he said. "Bet he would have run around naked."

Cody wished that he could tell the story of his own father's death with that same manly irony. Still, he knew what Mano meant. The south Texas border was the land of *machacado:* flint and limestone and dust, cactus, mesquite, and creosote. A place where men smiled and ordered dried donkey dick with their scrambled eggs; where rattlesnakes were real, women were dark and mean as the men, and being a man was a contest every day; where fights sprang up from lazy conversations, and people died on unexpected afternoons; where *macho* was the measure of a man, and not just a word, and many had died finding that out, even some like Mano's father who already knew. That was where the value seemed to lie, men willing to kill or die just to spell the definition. It left a lot of young widows and orphans, but nobody was ever confused by social subtleties.

They watched a jeep come down the road, laying a thick cloud. It pulled up beside the wreck, and Tanner got out, shaking his head. "I'm sorry, boys," he said. "Uh, 'scuse me, sir," he added when he saw Cody's rank. He pulled the cigar from his mouth, the end wet and frayed and green. "I did the best I could. There's nothing to be found unless we do an airlift straight out of the collection yard at Inchon. You'll just have to leave her like she is."

Mano looked around at the pieces of the dead aircraft. The cockpit was half apart, and looked suddenly as if it could never be together again. "Humpty Dumpty," he said.

Tanner got back in his jeep and chomped his cigar. "Look at it this way," he said, grinning. "Now you've got some spare parts." He drove away down Depot Road, hanging a fresh cloud in the sky.

Marsh McCall read the letter again, searching for any clue he might have missed. It had arrived while he was at lunch, placed on his desk in a tan sealed envelope while the orderly room was vacant. Sergeant Winslow had taken the jeep into town for a Friday noontime meal or tryst or whatever he did there, and would not be back until midafternoon. Aircraft and couriers were always running back and forth between Hanoi and Saigon, and the letter could have arrived in any trusted hand.

Ezra made apologies for missing the last meeting, adding that he had been caught by a sudden virus and had spent several days in bed. He had now recovered, and would be arriving at noon Sunday. For no apparent reason, before closing he added that two U.S. carriers, both armed with atomic weapons, had been ordered into the Gulf of Tonkin.

That was it.

McCall was unsure if he wanted Ezra to come or not. If he was bringing word that they would be leaving Hanoi, that was fine. But if, as he suspected, all he wanted was to learn what had been discovered about the black market, McCall would prefer that he stayed in Saigon.

Following the incident at Cong My, McCall was convinced that he had all the proof he needed to put Major Legère away for years. But in the same way that he had held his fire in the village as they made good their escape, then later made a misleading report to Sarot about the encounter, he could see no advantage of firing his big guns now. Smith would just screw things up, making conditions even more difficult. It was plain enough that Legère was dealing in military goods, trading with the enemy or with a middleman who did—Chang Wu—but there was a growing feeling that Legère was only what showed on the surface. For him to function so clumsily and successfully, there had to be higher officials involved. Nobody cared but the men in the field, those being killed by their own weapons, unaware that some of their leaders were part of the deal.

McCall was not kidding himself about the prospects; whoever the responsible persons might be, they were safely beyond reach of an American major with practically no authority. But they would also be beyond reach of Ezra Smith.

There was the sound of someone entering the orderly room, then the thump of a cane. McCall glanced around the doorway. "Hello, Major McCall," said Captain Sarot in a voice close to his usual exuberance. "Are you busy?"

"No. Come on back," McCall replied. He returned the letter to its envelope.

Philippe Sarot had become a familiar face at the 22d. Always coming around for one reason or another, he had slowly made himself indispensable. His role was simply as coordinating liaison, primarily in connection with French helicopter units, but he had adopted the 22d in spirit, taking over many of the duties which once had belonged to Legère. Though his injured knee prevented him from flying, he joked about taking the transition course himself, then stealing one of the birds and winging his way to Dien Bien Phu. His perpetual enthusiasm seemed able to solve almost any problem, and was the primary reason that the 22d had been able to settle so neatly into its surroundings. He still had not found his toothbrush, but every man in the outfit liked Sarot and knew something about his family.

The French captain moved slowly into the office, frowning briefly as if in pain. He placed a carton on the desk. "Here are the cigarettes you wanted."

"I didn't say anything about cigarettes."

"No, but I noticed you had switched brands, and there could only be one reason."

McCall smiled and produced his wallet. Sarot waved as if it were nothing, then accepted the bills. "Everything is set for next week," he said. "Unless some change comes from Saigon, or we get word that the helos are on their way from Korea, you will be having an easy time of it. I learned only this morning that another company of the 1st Helicopter Battalion is being transferred west. They are going to be stationed at Muong Khoua in Laos, and are going to begin a concentrated effort to get some of the wounded out of Dien Bien Phu. So the timing could not be better. Your pilots will fill part of the gap made by their departure. And a surprise. Major Legère has reversed his position completely. He now fully supports the idea of your birds covering the convoys." He paused for half a second. "But you haven't said anything. What do you think, Major McCall?"

McCall was thinking that Sarot was a likable guy, that his leg was probably bothering him, and that he had eaten too much *nuóc mam* with lunch. Catching the full blast in the tiny room, he knew now why the fishy fluid was called tiger piss. He tilted his chair toward the window. "It all sounds fine with me," he said. "We'll have to see what Colonel Smith has to say on Sunday. If anything changes, I'll let you know."

Sarot nodded while something like a smile bent his face. He got slowly to his feet, losing color. "If I do not hear from you sooner, I will see you Monday morning."

McCall watched him go, thinking that it was a damn hard thing to appear enthusiastic when your army was being chopped to pieces. He checked his watch and wondered about Winslow.

Chapter Sixteen

HE STOOD BEFORE the forbidding house, wishing there were someone else. All week he had thought about it, and kept coming up with Jack Sperek.

From the look of the place, the man could have died. The front windows were still boarded, and the iron gate still hung askew, but tall grass stood erect in the drive, and there were no recent tracks. Cody walked up the path and around the back corner, almost hoping that Sperek's jeep would be gone. But it was there, looking as dead and abandoned as the house. *Help me, Maria,* he read. From the look of things, whoever Maria was, she had been no help at all.

"Hello!" he called. He stepped up on the porch in the alcove beneath the stairs. There was no answer. He looked through the glass, tried the handle, and slowly opened the kitchen door. The house smelled old and foul, exactly like Jack Sperek. "Hello!" he yelled. "Anybody here?" He stepped inside and left the door ajar. The kitchen was just as scabby and filthy—empty bottles and dirty plates in the sink, smashed cigarettes on the floor, scattered newspapers. Huge roaches were cleaning the dishes. On the table was a basket of bread wrapped in off-white cloth. He leaned and peered into the dim dining room, felt for a switch, then remembered the overhead light did not work. He stepped cautiously into the room and found the lamp.

Cody was suddenly filled with dread. The room was empty, but the odor there was much worse. Surely Jack Sperek was dead. He didn't want to be the one to find him, to carry that image for the rest of his life, to see it when he closed his eyes at night or anytime he smelled something bad.

There was a sound in the next room, and a husky moan. Cody moved the lamp to the end of its cord. "Hello," he said, and leaned around the corner. He could barely see across the hall into the bedroom. Jack Sperek lay on a cot, gazing toward the door, extending a hand that was all bone. "Help me up," he said. A chunk of phlegm broke loose, and his body convulsed with weak coughing spasms.

Cody moved forward, looking all around, and jumped as several fat roaches ran madly away. "Where's a light?" he said. He found a switch that worked a single bulb dangling from two wires jammed into an outlet.

"Help me up," Sperek said, more firmly. "Got to go to the toilet." On the floor beside his cot lay an ashtray and a hundred scattered butts, a fork and a broken plate, a collection of empty bottles, and a small overturned table. The odor was overwhelming.

Cody reached out to help, astounded and disgusted by the feel of bones and withered flesh. He held his breath, helped Sperek to his feet, and with his arm around him for support, led him through the house and outside to the toilet. He stood at the edge of the porch, breathing fresh air and wishing that he had not come. But the man would have been dead in a couple of days.

Sperek emerged from the bathroom, weaving but moving under his own power. He tottered back to the kitchen, and carefully sat down at the table.

"You got any food?" Cody asked.

Sperek looked puzzled. "You hungry?" he said. His teeth were long and ratlike.

"No, I'm not hungry. *You're* hungry!"

Sperek nodded and looked at his hands lying limp on the table. "Yes, I suppose I must be. Better eat something." He stared dumbly at the table, head tilted to one side, then groped at the basket of bread. A loaf slipped from his hands and skittered across the floor toward the roaches. He shoved the basket toward Cody. "Want some bread, kid? It'll keep you healthy."

"No," Cody said, trying to think what to do. He found canned beans in the pantry, an opener on a tilting shelf, and a dirty spoon. He let the water run until it cleared the rust from the pipes, then washed the spoon and set the open can before Jack Sperek. He washed a glass and served plain water.

The sick man stared at the basket of bread, then slowly began to eat. The mere taste of food seemed to give him strength. "I was hungry," he said.

"No shit." Cody watched the revolting process, completely disgusted. He hardly knew this detestable man, yet he was nursing him back to life, serving him food, smelling his filth. Larkin had to be out of his gourd. There was nothing about Jack Sperek to inspire fear, just loathing. He stared at the grotesque goiter. "Why don't you get that thing cut off?" he said.

"Kind of grown attached to it," Sperek replied. "Get used to it, kid. You're gonna see a lot of men like me. Atomic mutations, you might say." When he grinned, a stream of chewed beans dribbled from his mouth.

Sperek had closed the kitchen door. Cody walked over and opened it for air, but the wet sounds behind him made him still see Sperek. He stepped outside, around the corner and into the bathroom. Sperek had forgotten to flush, and in the toilet was something awful, red and black, the stench straight from hell. Quickly he pulled the handle, then went reeling outside where the fetid odors of the city seemed suddenly fresh. When he went back into the kitchen, Sperek had stopped eating. He seemed to look stronger.

"So what are you doing here?" he said.

Cody wanted to forget the entire thing, but he got a sudden vision of microscopic monsters squirming along and gnashing their teeth in bloody darkness. He searched the miserable room. It was a horrible joke to ask such a question of a dying man, but he did it anyway. "I thought you might know a doctor I could see."

Dr. François Sapeine had pink blue eyes in a thousand folds bracketing a hornlike nose—the eyes of a rhinoceros or Moby Dick. Only a few stubborn hairs protruded from his meaty brow. Farther down were blue onionskin lips and a hopeful white mustache that flipped at the ends but did nothing to alter the eyes.

His office was in his home, accessible through a small porch which had been added to one side. The neighborhood was old French, respectable in decline, sidewalks broken by roots.

Cody had taken a trolley, then walked the last three blocks. En route, he had almost decided to wait, but he kept seeing the dream, squiggly spirochetes creeping slowly toward his brain. It seemed a really rotten deal: nature making a person want it, then making them pay for liking it. Life was beginning to be a mess.

He approached the house with hesitation, certain that anyone who saw him would know precisely why he was there. The anteroom was small and empty. He rang a bell on a shelf, and before he could sit, heard a shuffling of shoes. A door opened, and Dr. Sapeine peered out like a puzzled prehistoric bird. He looked Cody over and said, "Yes? What do you want?"

"Are you the doctor?"

"I am."

"Well, I need to see you about something."

"Mmmmm. You need to see me about something. Of course." He turned and went down a narrow hall, leaving Cody to wonder if he was supposed to follow. Finally he did. The man wore a limp white shirt, sleeves rolled halfway to the elbow, and black, dusty slacks. His waist was thick, but the trousers hung in loose gathers.

They passed two small rooms, dark but with doors open, then proceeded into a crowded corner office. Two windows were covered with blinds, casting an off-white light through the room. Two badly worn armchairs shared a badly worn rug with a tall amber lamp and an ashtray on a stand. Behind the desk were framed credentials, but every remaining inch was a library. The room smelled of books and spilled whiskey.

The doctor motioned toward a chair, then went behind his desk. He picked up some spectacles, carefully placed them on his nose, and raised his meaty brows. "I assume you have seen a girl," he said.

"Uh, yes, sir."

The doctor nodded. "And now you have a problem."

"Well, I'm not sure. Maybe, but I can't really tell."

"How long has it been?"

"One week, sir."

The doctor lowered the glasses on his nose, and gazed across at Cody with God's weary eyes. His thoughts seemed to wander, then he said, "Mmmmm."

Cody looked around the room. There was a path through the dust on the floor.

"It is very unlikely that you have a problem," the doctor said. "If you did you would know, and there would be no doubt. It is still possible that something could develop in the next few days. If it does, come back to see me. I assume that you also have a girlfriend you are concerned about."

"Well, sort of, but not really."

"Mmmmm," the doctor said. "Come, I want to show you something." He led Cody across the hall to a room that was spotless and had new furnishings. "This is where I examine the ladies," he said. "They never come on Saturdays." He crossed the room and opened a door which led outside. At the far end of a brick walk along a hedge was an alley. "They enter discreetly through this door, wives of soldiers who entertain officials and other soldiers, wives of officials who entertain soldiers and other officials. They are my only business now. There is much clandestine screwing in Hanoi right now, perhaps more than any other kind. I added this room four years ago because I suspected there was a need, but I had no idea. The ladies told their friends, and before a year had passed, much of white female Hanoi was my client. Trouble was, they stopped entering the front door entirely. They stopped recommending me to anyone who did not share their secret, and they found other doctors for their children. Now all I do is treat such women, plus a few loyal old men and a few young ones like you, worried about their wives and girlfriends, who I may already be seeing." The doctor sighed, closed the door, and turned again to Cody.

"I was always told that knowledge is comfort. That is a lie. Take care to preserve your ignorance, young man. Once it is gone, it is gone forever."

"Sure," Cody said, looking toward the hall. "That's what I'll do."

"Mmmmm."

★

When he left the doctor's office, Cody walked back to Boulevard Phung and found a European market. He still thought that Jack Sperek was a detestable character, but the man was starving. There was food in his pantry, but only a little. What he seemed to need most was someone around to force him to eat. And he needed to see a doctor.

He bought more canned beans, crackers and cheese, a tin of peanut butter, several bananas, a loaf of sliced bread, a tin of sardines that cost twice what they should, and a bottle of milk. Then he caught the trolley, and walked the last few blocks to the house.

Sperek had gone back to bed, but he got up without help and came into the kitchen. "What are you doing?" he said.

"Brought you some food."

Sperek watched, bent over and weak, as Cody put groceries into the pantry. When he was done, Cody emptied the water glass, poured it half full of milk, and handed it to Sperek. The man sat down and drank without speaking, his throat working grotesquely.

"You got any clean clothes?"

"Might be some back there."

"You need to take a bath. You smell."

Sperek gave him a startled, lingering look. "The hell you say," he replied, but he got up from the table and went out to the bathroom. When he was gone, Cody went back to Sperek's room. To his surprise, in a closet that had no door he found two suits of khakis on hangers, both of them clean. In a chest were clean socks and clean underwear. Despite the look of everything else, someone obviously took care of the man's laundry. If whoever it was would only make him bathe and eat.

He hung the clothes on the bathroom door, yelled to Sperek, then checked the oil in the jeep and got it started, leaving it to run to charge the battery. Then he went upstairs and sat in a chair on the balcony. After a minute he stood and stepped inside the room where he had spent his first night in Hanoi. The armoire stood open, and the stranger's things were gone. Because it was afternoon, the light was not the same, but the room still held the same appealing presence, the sheltered, shuttered comfort. It was a strange thing about the house, the two halves so different—the lower so full of Sperek, his evil odors and aura, while the upper was a place of promise.

He walked to the window, looked out, and thought of Moni'. It seemed so long since the time he had first seen her on the balcony at the Café Ho Tay, but he still could see the way the sunlight touched her face, the playful skirt against her legs. He had tried hard to avoid it, but thoughts of Moni' always came around. Standing now in the pleasant room where he had thought of her the first time, he began to realize that he missed her very much. He had to see her again.

Sperek emerged from the bathroom, still a deathly sick man, but one that looked good for a few more days. He stared at the running vehicle, then watched Cody descend the stairs. "I didn't ask you to do anything," he said.

Cody stopped to stare. It may have been the beans and milk, or it may have been nothing but the contrast of renewed vision coming down from upstairs, but something was terribly different. He knew in that instant that Larkin was right. Sperek was dying, but dying like a poisonous snake, still able to kill until its own dying breath. With nothing to say, Cody walked past Sperek and his obscene jeep, around the house, and down the weedy drive.

It wasn't so bad this time at first, then it was worse than ever. It wasn't so bad because for the first time he knew why he was there, and was willing to admit it. Then it was so much worse because he could see that Moni' understood, and she still left it all up to him. It didn't mean she didn't love him, or that she didn't want to someday go with him to Bai Chay—only that what she said was true, that there was war.

Her father did not shoot until he was less than fifty yards away and Cody could see the details of his face. The mustache was different again, the great curling ends pulled completely away. The old man seemed glad to see him, firing the first shot almost as a formality. Then Moni' came out in a sackcloth robe and stood on the porch. She had been asleep and looked awful, but made no attempt at disguise. She rubbed her face and sat heavily in an old wicker chair while her father watched. When she looked at Cody without expression, the man drew back the bolt, ejected the empty shell, slowly shoved another home, and took aim and fired.

Cody flinched as the bullet passed. He looked at Moni', not sure what to say. He tried to joke with himself, thinking that perhaps later when she had fixed her hair...But it didn't work, there was no smile to be found anywhere. When he turned and made the long trip down the drive, he didn't laugh or call any names or shoot anybody the finger, but he was no longer afraid.

Calvin Winslow prepared himself with fastidious attention, aware that he was breaking some ironclad rules: never do too much, never try too hard, always neglect something. Don't touch up the boots, don't trim the frayed cuticles, don't wear clothes too fresh, perhaps even forget to shave. In younger years he had found that rumpled hair would work so long as it did not appear the result of sleep. A small injury on a forearm and a dried trickle of blood were always good; he kept his pocketknife sharp, and a quick, backward scrape of the tip would usually suffice. The idea was to look strong but a bit weathered, a man in a man's world, a capable bull with plenty to do, places to spend his time. If the day had not been too hot or he had not worked too hard, he would simply go as he was, slightly dusty, slightly sweaty, smelling like a man. For those occasions he showered in the morning, applied the usual doses of deodorant and after-shave, then allowed the mechanics of manhood and a long day to take effect. The scent of a woman, especially after a long abstinence when the senses were finely attuned, could drive a man mad; it made equal sense that the smell of a man, so long as he was clean, was not without equal effect. It was a careful balance, sometimes requiring a subtle stroke like washing his rear and armpits, dabbing lightly of fresh deodorant, changing his drawers, and conducting a quick sniff test before donning his dirty shirt.

The thing to remember was that each encounter—no matter how remote the prospect, how short the likely duration, or how completely aware both parties were that there would never be more than those few minutes—*always* had to be staged with meticulous care. Many times he had seen a disappointing evening turn suddenly productive in the company of an unexpected, appreciative witness. Sometimes it happened later, sometimes there were signs and it never happened at all. But the moments of doubt which afflicted other men never bothered Calvin Winslow. He missed like everyone else, but he hit often enough to know what he knew, and to know that when dealing with women no detail was unimportant, no deliberate action frivolous. The key was first to avoid detection of the art, but if it was detected, to inspire such admiration of style as to stir the female desire to reward.

Winslow the artist, bedsheets for canvas, dabbing with careful strokes. He licked his broken tooth and smiled. Tonight he was breaking some rules—showering, shaving carefully with a new blade until his face was as smooth as a baby's butt, shining his boots and clipping the thick hairs from nostrils and ears. He had even stopped at a florist that afternoon to pick out a white orchid, and he paid extra to be allowed to disturb the owner near midnight when he would pick it up. He was breaking some rules, but he had done this long enough to operate on instinct, and his instinct said that for this particular woman he should go the whole nine yards. He thought about himself between Su Letei's legs, and was quite certain she would prove worth the trouble.

But he could be wrong. Nothing but pride would be lost, and after an appropriate period during which each had supposedly learned a lesson, he would give them both another chance. In the meantime, there was tiny Thi Linh, a clerk at French Customs. She had not been easy to find, and had required a little training—just what he preferred. What she lacked in experience was more than made up for with pure youth, a diminutive body, and a willingness to do absolutely anything. She was employed each day until noon, then in two hour-long sessions each week in a narrow room on Rue Yen Bay, she more than doubled her salary.

But Winslow did not believe he was wrong. He had watched Su Letei closely, observed the way she carried herself and all the little things she kept concealed. They had had several conversations, usually brief but always moving on more than one level. He had also carefully checked around to learn more about her. Su Letei was twice married, twice divorced by death. More recently there had been another liaison, though brief. The man who told him this, an American mechanic on contract at Gia Lam, knew nothing except that the lover had also been killed in the war. With that one exception, Su Letei had in recent years developed a reputation for being unapproachable. There was even a ridiculous rumor that she was the chattel of a Chinaman. Winslow sneered at both ideas, but was not surprised. There were always mythical tales surrounding beautiful women in Asia. Men liked to believe them because such stories explained their own failures. It had been his experience that beauty could make for a lonely existence, the place of a vulnerable soul. On at least two occasions, he had discovered such ladies merely waiting for someone to ask.

Whether she was waiting or not, tonight he intended to ask Su Letei. Her restaurant would be closing at midnight. He would wait out front with the orchid and a bottle of chilled wine, and when the light came on in her house he would go to her door. Even in the unlikely event that he did not succeed, he might at least spend a couple of hours in the company of a beautiful and interesting woman.

When Rankin called a break, he and Cowan and Joe Whitney immediately moved away from the aircraft to squat on the steel ramp and smoke while the others finished up. All day it had been threatening to rain—fat, black-bottomed clouds moving ponderously from the south, flashing lightning where they gathered in a slot at the head of the delta—but the men stayed on the flight line, watching for stray lightning and keeping an eye on Depot Road while they got things ready for Monday. As the noon hour approached, the men grew neater in their work, returning each tool to its box, keeping the tiedowns and port covers handy so things could be quickly wrapped up. There was work to take them well past lunchtime, but they planned to eat in rotation unless Winslow arrived. In which case they would break at once to assemble for lunch outdoors in the group of chairs now arranged beside the orderly room. A fresh breeze was moving across the camp in punctuated gusts, and it felt good to be out in it, breathing the green flavor of a hundred miles of damp fields.

"He did this twice in Korea," Whitney said. He sat on a gray seat cushion from the damaged bird.

"That's right," said Kinney. He lowered a cyclic stick, and sat with the others to light a smoke. Now that the training mission was complete, the extra aircraft controls were being permanently removed. "If we hadn't had such a pansy for a commanding officer, he'd have lost some stripes."

"Too bad, so sad," said Mano. He wiped his hands on a rag and sat near Whitney. He did not smoke, but he liked the aroma. "'Private Winslow' does have a certain ring to it," he added, white teeth shining against dark skin.

Two Acres gave a smug smile, working without a shirt, showing muscles and a tan that was almost black. "No need to hurry now," he said. "Trouble won't get any bigger. He's probably cutting another piece, thinking about his story."

Word had spread quickly at daylight: The first sergeant had not returned last night from chasing tail. Better yet, he was in the major's jeep, leaving McCall afoot, guaranteeing some sort of explosion when he arrived. The men began moving chairs near the orderly room.

The main task of the morning involved rigging the litters and getting the two spare aircraft in top shape. Duke's shot-up wreck still sat at the edge of the ramp, looking pitiful with its cockpit all a mess, its blades sitting out on boxes. Everything was covered with a layer of rain-freckled dust.

All morning the men had been going back and forth to Dukemire's old bird. Despite regulations, it was now being openly scavenged, for the benefit not only of Dukemire's new aircraft, but of others as well. It was a sad sight, like a large insect being dissected by ants. The radios and battery, certain to be stolen, had been put in the orderly room for safekeeping, but other parts continued to be exchanged. Besides the seats, various instruments and uncracked lenses were switched, as well as any part that was newer or in better condition than that of another bird. When it was found that Dukemire's replacement aircraft had a high-frequency vibration, the tail rotor blades went as well. With each exchange, the inferior parts were not reinstalled, but were stuffed inside the cockpit or stacked among the wooden crates supporting the loose rotors of the damaged ship. It was a shameful thing to do to any bird, and the men began with hesitation. But once the process was underway—the aircraft slowly disintegrating—they just laughed and said the French could fix it when they were gone, knowing that it would never happen. With the help of everyone, the wounded helicopter slowly died.

"They're still there," Cowan said. The others followed his gaze. Across the field were rows of twin tails, the C-119s of Civil Air Transport lined up on the tarmac. Rankin had brought word that morning from Sarot: The civilian pilots were parking some of their birds, refusing to fly the Dien Bien Phu run until something was done about the ever-increasing flak. Actually, there was more to it than that. The men had not hired on for combat. Like everyone else, they were torn between helping the desperate troops and knowing that it would soon be for nothing. Adding to their frustration was the knowledge that their own country, the United States, was using them as mercenaries to assuage the official conscience about letting the soldiers at Dien Bien Phu be slaughtered. In that environment it was getting awfully hard for the pilots to justify dying for two thousand dollars a month.

The withdrawal of support by Civil Air Transport had the sudden effect of pointing out the absurdity of the French position at Dien Bien Phu. Besides a constant need for replacement personnel, the fortress now required a daily resupply of food, munitions, and medical supplies amounting to 120 tons, all to be delivered by air. The French Air Force, flying at full capacity, was not able to handle such a requirement, nor had it been *before* it was decided that there should be a battle called Dien Bien Phu. There were also operations going on in other parts of the country, primarily the Central Highlands— large, planned operations that also demanded air support. No amount of wishful thinking or later claims of miscalculation would ever be valid. Though the United States had a pair of aircraft carriers with two hundred fighters aboard cruising the South China Sea, there was still no word on whether or not they would come to the aid of the dying force, a force that by all appearances had been intentionally sent to slaughter by French High Command. Nobody in the 22d could say that he wanted the United States to get completely involved—knowing all the dead GIs it would mean—but it was getting harder every day to watch what was happening without being able to help.

"You ever hear from Brantley?" Dukemire asked. It had been two weeks since the CW2 had boarded the plane to Saigon.

"Not yet," Cowan said. Despite orders that there could be no outside communications, Cowan had sent a note south with an American pilot. "I got my letter back yesterday," he said.

Rankin frowned. "You got it back?"

"Yeah. Said he couldn't find the outfit."

"Well, where the hell did he look?"

"Probably about as far as the mirror behind the bar at the Tan Son Nhut O-club."

"Tell you what," Rankin said, surprising them all, "I'm going to be ready to head south whenever we get the word."

Cowan nodded. Not hearing from Brantley had done a lot to his attitude.

"I don't know," said Cody. "It's awfully hot down there."

"You just don't want to leave that girl."

"What girl?"

When the guys all laughed at his failed innocence, Cody could not help but blush. "She watched her old man shoot at me. What do you call that?"

"A damn strange relationship," said Rankin.

"Nothing but pure love," said Cowan.

"Where I come from, the *girls* shoot at you. You don't have to worry about their daddies."

"Where you come from they take scalps."

Two Acres dug for his knife. "Come here, Kinney. Let's see how I do."

"Look here," said Rankin. The men all turned and watched as a gray C-47 came down the taxiway toward the ramp. "The invisible colonel. Maybe he's bringing word that we're all being transferred to Dien Bien Phu." Beyond Depot Road, the door of the orderly room opened, and Major McCall emerged.

It was bad form to sit around with a colonel and a major watching, so the men got to their feet, snuffed the cigarettes, and went back to work. When the airplane came to a halt near the edge of the ramp, Major Legère arrived in a jeep, which he gave to the crew, then began directing men to unload some cargo. The commanding officer of the 22d climbed the steps and disappeared.

The discussion lasted fifteen minutes, and when Major McCall emerged he did not look happy.

"Here comes somebody," said Two Acres. A jeep was approaching on Depot Road in a hurry, veering around the big wallows. Major McCall had also noticed, and was staring expectantly toward the vehicle.

"Too skinny," said Kinney with disappointment.

The gunner was right. Rankin lifted his toolbox. "May as well get something to eat."

★

McCall approached the waiting airplane with apprehension. Now that training was halted, it seemed time for the 22d to move south to rejoin the mother unit, and for him to write his reports and move on to a task more suited to his capabilities. He was not aware of his anger until he mounted the steps, suddenly certain that this was not what Ezra Smith had come to say.

"Hello, Marsh," the colonel said from the shadows.

The sun was burning through a brief hole in the clouds, and it took a moment to see more than a silhouette against a window. Ezra was seated with two new drinks and a fresh fifth of Scotch on the table before him. He extended a hand. "Excuse my laziness," he said, motioning toward several spaced seats, "but I'm exhausted and have a backache to boot." He squinted and looked closely at McCall. "Where did you get the nicks?"

"Busted windshield," McCall said. He had only that morning removed the stitches. Smith frowned, but said nothing. McCall picked up a drink and turned to watch as a crate was forked from the aircraft to a waiting truck, a stencil on its side reading OU RIVER TRADERS, LUANG PRABANG. He took a seat, noting anew the plush furnishings. They had certainly not been paid for with Army funds.

"This aircraft is damned nice," Smith said, observing the appraisal, "but the total mode of travel is something less. I spent last night in Muong Sai, Laos, sleeping on a hard grass mattress, a foot-long lizard creeping around my room. I'm going to have to find other arrangements."

McCall watched the colonel a moment, detecting an untruthful tone, a deliberate effort at distraction. He decided to get straight to it. "I hope you've come today to tell me we're heading south, sir."

Smith's face fell as if his planned agenda had been disrupted. "I'm afraid not, Marsh." His eyes brightened. "But I assume that since you asked, it means you've made some progress. So what's the current situation?"

"Not all that different," McCall said with undisguised irritation. "Considering the limitations, I think I've personally been here long enough to make my reports. As far as the unit goes, we've done our job unless more aircraft are coming from Korea."

"No, no luck on that just yet. Everything is in limbo, it's not just you. But I agree. I'm working on getting something determined. Maybe in two weeks."

"Why can't the training all be done in Saigon, with the French pilots flying down for the course?"

"The French won't go for it. They want the option to pull their men if things get more desperate. The training—if there is to be any—has to be here."

"And in the meantime—however long that happens to be—we're supposed to cover convoys."

"Well, yes. Nothing heavy, mind you. Just keep some pilots in the air to look around so the Viets will lie low. They're good at waiting for things to pass."

"We're going to lose some men."

"That's always possible." The tone was reprimanding, an effort at control. To an extent it worked; McCall held his words. "Now, about the other things," the colonel continued. "You say you're ready to write your reports? That's good news. The one concerning your opinion of our prospects can wait. What I am especially interested in hearing is what you have learned about the market in military hardware."

McCall was now openly angry. Smith's mindless fixation on his pet interest to the exclusion of all else was another sign that it was time for him to hang up the uniform. He downed half his drink before he replied. "Ezra, I tried to explain this before. I know a lot about what is going on here—it is plain as day, and I'll put it all in a report—but I don't have the authority, the assets, or the freedom of movement to accomplish anything worthwhile. If this were a U.S. operation instead of French, then yes, I'd have enough to go on. I still wouldn't be ready to make a move, but at least I could pursue some things. You are letting your interest in the project exaggerate the potentials."

Now Smith was angry, which suited McCall entirely—whatever it took to communicate with the decaying mind. The old man searched his trunk for a suitable attitude, and came up looking hurt, remote, and condescending. Slowly the eyes evolved to the lidded arrogance of a camel.

"Have you accomplished nothing, Major?"

McCall was ready to leave. "Not quite, sir. As I said, I have some good leads. But because of the situation I am only able to make a half-assed attempt to solve a full-time problem. And I'm trying to do it from the outside."

"If I had known you couldn't handle it, I'd have chosen someone else," Smith said in his best colonel tone.

I wish to hell you had, McCall thought.

"What have you learned so far, Major? Precisely."

McCall sidestepped. "Enough to know where to look next."

"Which is?"

"I'll know more in a few days."

"Goddamn it, McCall!" Smith shouted, slamming a fist on the table, sending his drink skyward. "Tell me what you know!"

McCall stared at him calmly. Never would such a display have been permitted by the Ezra Smith he had known. "What's my chain of command, sir?"

The colonel blinked. "Beg your pardon?"

"My chain of command. Who would I report to if you were to drop dead?"

"Uh, well, General Sanfield, of course. I assumed you knew that. Why do you ask?"

"No reason, sir. Just making sure." He glanced at the spilled Scotch. "It is still too early to have anything conclusive," he added. "Everything will be in my report."

Smith seemed to lose all energy. He reached beneath the table for ice, then made another drink. He tried to pour more for McCall, but the major waved him away. "I'm sorry, Marsh," he said. "You're right about everything. I'd give you more help if I could. It's just that I've chased this thing so long. All I did in Korea was establish equilibrium, and I had to work like hell to do that. Now I'm about to retire, and I'm trying to fight my war through you."

McCall felt a mixture of sympathy and sickness. The Ezra Smith he had known was completely gone. "Maybe I'll have something soon," he said.

Smith looked up from his drink with sudden hope. "I tell you what, Marsh—something breaks, you let me know just as fast as you possibly can. I don't know how I'll do it, but I guarantee I'll get you some help up here to pull off whatever you decide. If it's slightly illegal or pisses off the French, we'll work around it. I know people who can help us get it done."

"You mean your friends in the CIA?"

"What do you mean, Marsh?"

"Come on, Ezra. I'm talking about this airplane. I'm talking about half the things that I see happening, about too many questions and no answers."

Smith was silent a long time. "Things are changing," he said. "I've only got a little longer, then I'm going to leave it up to you younger fellows to try and figure out what to do. Until then, I can't see that I have any choice but to do what I'm doing. That's all I can say, Marsh. I'm asking you to be patient, as a soldier and as a friend."

McCall nodded, quietly studying the man he had once known. "I'll do that, sir."

Off the hook, Smith seemed to perk up. "In the meantime, remember what I said. I'll send you some help if it's important. Any kind of help you need. Just let me know."

When McCall stepped down from the aircraft, the unloading of the cargo was complete. As he headed for the far side of the ramp, he was struck by the sight of the disintegrating OH-13. The fact that Colonel Smith had said nothing about it, the scattered parts within view outside his window, was further testament to just how much the man had changed.

Far off, a jeep was approaching on Depot Road. He narrowed his eyes, but could not make out the driver. That was his next unpleasant task—to report to the gendarmes that Sergeant Winslow was missing—but he wanted to give the man as much time as possible to show up on his own. He had almost reached his office when the jeep turned from the road. He got a sudden sick knot in his stomach. The vehicle was his, but Captain Sarot was driving.

"Something may have happened," Sarot said as a fog of dust engulfed them. From across the road came the sounds of running men. "They found it on Rue Yen Bay."

McCall gave the jeep a quick once-over, then saw the flattened box which Sarot held toward him. He frowned and glanced at the label before opening the flap. Inside was a crushed white orchid.

Chapter Seventeen

IT WAS NOT YET LIGHT when the others came in from the mess hall, but Burd Rankin was already behind the FM radio, sipping coffee and fiddling with the dial, intercepting conversations. Rankin shaved each evening, but his jaw was already dark with new beard. Dukemire took a seat and stared at the dirt floor, frowning and cocking his head at each call as if he might suddenly understand French. Cody straddled a bench and laced his fingers while Cowan stretched out on his back, picking his teeth with a splinter. Between the calls and surging engines along the runway came other sounds from beyond the wooden wall—low voices, banging ammo cans, smooth oiled steel. Winslow's absence made it all seem quiet.

"Heard anything?" Cowan asked.

Rankin shook his head. McCall had gone with Captain Sarot to check all the area units and make a few phone calls to town. Two Acres stuck his head through the open flap, and Rankin repeated the gesture without being asked. Acres disappeared, and a moment later they heard him tell the others in the cleaning shed, "Still nothing."

"Good morning," said Captain Sarot as he entered the tent on his cane. His voice was crisp, but with none of its normal happiness.

He stepped to the front holding a folded map. "No one has heard anything about your first sergeant," he said. He paused as if to make a hopeful joke, but it was too late for that. Winslow had been missing nearly thirty hours, and the gendarmes knew nothing. "Major McCall asked me to conduct the briefing while he checks with some men across the field." He looked at Rankin. "So, if you are ready . . ."

Rankin returned the radio to the proper frequency and joined the others on the front bench. Sarot pulled a chair from the table and sat close before them, the map vertical on his knees.

"Your birds are each equipped with one litter?" he asked. The men acknowledged in unison. "Good. Let us hope we will not need them." He looked at each man in turn. "Let me first thank you for what you and your men are doing. Those in the convoy will be grateful."

The men were mildly embarrassed, but not displeased that he had said it.

"As you know, Ho Chi Minh is receiving supplies from Red China, part carried in trucks through the jungle, but most delivered on the backs and bicycles of peasants. From the north through Kunming, from the east from Liuchou and Nanning, both regions served by railways. The northern route is too remote for us to do much about except by aerial attack. The eastern route—northeast of Hanoi—crosses the border between Cao Bang and Lang Son, then runs west through the mountainous region called the Viet Bac. Four hundred miles of jungle—six hundred by the route they have to take—completely across the widest part of Vietnam in order to reach Dien Bien Phu." He paused, perturbed by the admiring tone that had crept into his voice.

"More than three years ago, the French Expeditionary Force suffered a humiliating defeat, a panicked evacuation, at Lang Son. Since that time we have been unable to achieve authority in that area. A *bataillon de marche* has reopened Camp Chino on the road to Lang Son. From there they hope to intercept a portion of the enemy's supplies. Our nearest base is at Kep, slightly more than halfway between Hanoi and Camp Chino. It is there where you will refuel." He handed each man a sketch of the field.

"You will fly as before—two birds above the convoy, another at altitude nearby, and a spare will wait on the ground at the nearest base, either here or at Kep. You will join the convoy as it crosses the Canal des Rapides northeast of Hanoi at about ten hundred hours, and escort it to Kep. This is open country, paddies and hamlets. Trouble is less likely here, but do not be complacent. At Kep, you will refuel and have lunch, then the convoy will continue to Camp Chino. You can see by the map that this is where the route becomes more dangerous. More lives have been lost on this road than on any other in all Vietnam. The last six miles passes through an area called the Narrows, where the road is trapped between cliffs and the river. But you will not be escorting the convoy in this part. When you reach Hoa Lac, four Helldivers from the carrier *Arromanches* will take over your job, and they will see the convoy safely to Camp Chino. You will return to Kep for fuel, then back to the tropical paradise of Lam Du."

When he lowered the map, the men had not smiled at his joke. "You will be gone most of the day. On those papers I have included the radio frequencies for artillery clearance en route, for the airfield at Kep, and for the convoy leader. Major Legère assures me that there will be an operator with them who speaks excellent English. In the event of problems, Mr. Rankin, you do of course speak French."

"I can't be everywhere. Without good communications, we're almost worthless."

"I understand, and I have emphasized that with Major Legère. I have said this before, but in the event of an attack, please do not try to be fighters. You will be no help to us if you are shot down, and we don't want anyone hurt unnecessarily. There is an aid station at Kep, but the seriously wounded should be flown directly to Lanessan. You are all familiar with the landing pad on the levee?" When the men nodded, Sarot said, "Good. Are there questions?"

"What do you think happened to Winslow?" said Cowan.

Unprepared, the truth was on the captain's face. "I think he is probably with a woman," he said with an unnatural smile. "It is rumored that he regularly saw a girl near the place the jeep was found. Perhaps she has introduced him to opium and knotted silk." Only Cody and Dukemire smiled at the idea. Rankin and Cowan stared.

There was the sound of an arriving jeep, and when Major McCall entered and sat at the rear of the tent, everyone turned to check his face. He dug absently for a cigarette. "Any more questions?" Sarot said. "Then that concludes the briefing. Departure will not be until approximately oh nine forty, as you determine. Also, a small surprise. Today, I am going to be your operations officer while Major McCall conducts business in town. I will be on the radio if you need anything. If you are too far out to reach me directly on the FM, call Gia Lam Tower on UHF, and have them relay."

When Sarot and McCall had gone, Two Acres again stuck his head through the door. By then, reality had reached even the younger pilots. All four men shook their heads.

Operations was empty, the jeep driven by Captain Sarot no longer out front. McCall checked his watch: The flight had been gone less than an hour. There was no note on the table, and nothing but broken static on the radio. He began to roll and tie the sides of the tent, wrestling with the heavy tarp and with worries about Winslow and Sperek. He had spent the morning doing what he could for each man.

It was plain enough that Winslow was in trouble—if he was still alive. Sarot had alerted the gendarmes last night, but there was little else that could be done. After checking with every outfit at Lam Du and Gia Lam, then leaving Sarot at Operations, McCall had headed to town to check on Jack Sperek. Cody West had reported seeing Sperek, saying that the man appeared to be close to death. This seemed likely to be another exaggeration, but there was no question that Sperek was sick. He decided to drop in on him.

But West had not been wrong. McCall found Jack Sperek in wretched condition. Though there was food in the pantry, it looked very much like the man was simply starving. He forced Sperek to shower and change—ignoring protests that "the young punk" had made him do the same thing only two days ago—then packed him off to the doctor, François Sapeine. The examination took an hour, so McCall employed the time driving around Hanoi, checking faces while he searched without hope for some sign of Calvin Winslow. The effort was fruitless, but in his wanderings he did find Rue Yen Bay, the street where the jeep had been found. It was a narrow, treeless lane only three blocks long, straight and barren residential with dull plaster walls, flowerless balconies bleeding rust. A couple of old women on a worn stone step stared as he drove up and down, leaning toward one another to whisper. When he stopped and spoke to them in French, then fractured Vietnamese, they merely gazed beyond, flicking dark-veined eyes toward unexpected places. One got up and hobbled about, sweeping the walk with a stooping broom.

He searched the full hour. Apart from Winslow's predicament, driving through the city was depressing. Hanoi was like an old lady—painted, perfumed, and powdered, ruffles and old routines, unwilling to acknowledge defeat in a battle that had long ago been lost.

He passed the black market shop they had raided, and out of curiosity drove around to the alley. The back door stood open, and inside were empty shelves. He parked and walked through the abandoned place until he came out in front. The glass of the front door was broken, daggers arrayed on the floor. The courtyard was still draped with laundry.

Sperek was waiting on the doctor's steps with a paper sack full of potions and pills.

"What's the report?"

"He'll know in a couple of days."

McCall nodded, glancing at Sperek's arms, the empty legs of his khakis, and the pimpled throat, recalling the sturdy man he had last seen in England. The only thing of Sperek's that this ghostly apparition possessed was his name.

When they pulled into the drive, McCall decided to spring a question. "Where's the Ou River?" he asked.

Ready for anything, Sperek showed no surprise. "It drains northern Laos into the Mekong, the watershed just the other side of Dien Bien Phu. You planning a trip?"

"What is Ou River Traders?"

A weak smile slipped from Sperek's face. He hesitated, then said, "It's not commonly known, but it's the trading company that finances operations for the Viet Minh army. Ho Chi Minh started it six years ago to get control of the opium supply in the highlands. They use it to trade for cash and weapons."

McCall eyed Sperek, observing the lines of resignation. "How much of that opium ends up in Hanoi and Saigon?"

"Half, maybe more."

"But the opium dens in Vietnam are all operated by the French government." Sperek just looked at him. "Jesus."

"Like I said, Marsh, you need to leave the country."

"Never mind about me. You need to go back to the States and get healed."

"Can't just yet," Sperek said flatly. "Got a job to do."

"What job's that, Jack?"

He climbed carefully from the jeep. "Looking after you," he said. He gave the unhappiest grin that McCall had ever seen, then tottered away with his little sack, a decrepit old man of forty-two.

McCall paced the tent, frowning and checking his watch, wondering what had happened to Sarot. There was nothing on the radio but a soft crackling hiss, so he went to the orderly room to make coffee and check his desk for a note. But he found nothing there. He sat in his office, for once enjoying its smallness, the enclosed privacy, while he waited for the coffee to brew. He kept a bouquet of pencils in a tin can on his desk, and as he stood he knocked them everywhere. When he crawled beneath his desk, gathering the scattered items, he ran across a familiar stencil: OU RIVER TRADERS, LUANG PRABANG. He frowned, backed out of the hole, and looked around the far side of his desk. There it was again: OU RIVER TRADERS. Then he noticed the difference. Ducking underneath, he held his cigarette lighter and read TO: OU RIVER TRADERS. The one on the opposite side read FROM. He moved the lighter around, and soon found another label above his head: FROM: LAM DU DEPOT, NORTHERN VIETNAM MATERIEL COMMAND.

McCall sat on the floor, astounded. The crate had once been larger, disassembled, reconstructed, and used again. René Legère himself had suggested using the crate as a desk.

He knew the news the moment Sarot limped into the tent.

"A patrol boat found Sergeant Winslow last evening on the island beneath the bridge," the French captain said. "Between the pilings, out of view from above. He had been put there some time ago. Many people on the river must have seen him, but no one wanted to be the one to find a dead European." Sarot lit a cigarette and shook another from the pack for McCall. "He was naked, so it took until this morning for the gendarmes to realize that it might be your sergeant. I went in to identify the body."

McCall gave a weary sigh and sat on the edge of the table. There was an awfully big difference between thinking that someone was dead and *knowing* it. His stomach was gripped in a knot. "How was he killed?"

"Piano-wire garrote."

"Anything else?"

"He sometimes saw a girl on Rue Yen Bay, but it is believed that whoever left the jeep there knew that also. He was not with her that evening."

"Can you cover for me here?"

"Certainly. I had planned to be here all day. Has there been anything from the flight?"

"Not a word. I only got back about twenty minutes ago."

"That's good." Sarot checked his watch. "They should be beyond Bac Ninh by now," he said, almost to himself. "Go ahead, Major McCall. Do whatever you must. Everything will be under control here, and I will not leave again. Do you know where the morgue is?"

"I've seen it."

McCall drove away from Lam Du, barely seeing the road as he turned the wheel, mechanically following the path between the wallows. His stomach was still a breathless ache as if he had taken a strong punch. It seemed certain that wherever the sergeant had gone Saturday night, it was not to meet a whore. Winslow had quietly groomed himself all evening. Through the stacked crates that formed the wall between their rooms, McCall had heard the tocnail clippers, the brushes and files, the unlikely and tuneless humming. This woman was definitely special, French more than likely, probably somebody's wife. Winslow had then taken a nap, rousing himself at 2300 without an alarm. Half an hour later he appeared at McCall's door to see if there was anything at all that the major required before he went into town. "Have a good time," McCall said.

"Oh, I intend to, sir," Winslow replied with a happy grin. "Thanks for the use of the jeep." There was something strange about his appearance, then McCall realized that the bushy brows had been trimmed, swept up and back, forbidden to hang in their usual way like weathered piles of brush. It gave the man a startled look that did not fit at all.

Crossing the long bridge that spanned the Red River, McCall slowed and looked down to see what he could of the island. The water that flowed from faraway storms was higher than when he last looked, and the curved teardrop of sand was almost submerged, a thin spear projecting downstream.

He had no idea where he was headed—certainly not to the morgue—but almost as if the jeep were a horse with loose reins, it followed a familiar path and took him to the Café Ho Tay. He looked around as if he had just awakened, then stepped out and went inside.

"Miss Letei is not here," the headwaiter said.

"Where is she?"

"She is not well today."

It took several rings of the bell to rouse Su Letei from her house. McCall was not sure why he was there, but he wanted to talk to her. Finally a window shade moved. Across the street, two houses down, he saw a black automobile beneath the trees, a crooked elbow out the window. Then Su Letei opened the door.

"You must go from here," she said tersely.

He had seen the look before, and recalled at once that it had been in the presence of Chang Wu. "I'd like to talk a little while," he said.

"No, you cannot come in. You must go. They will see . . . "

He turned to the car down the street, back to the woman and back to the car. When he looked again at Su Letei he knew the entire story.

"I did nothing to encourage him," she said, completely devastated. "I had no idea . . . " She looked at McCall with sudden urgency. "You must speak to Mr. Pearbone at once. Do not put it off any longer. He is home today. Goodbye." She closed the door.

It was a day made strictly for the young, one of three or four in a lifetime, the kind wasted on the old because if any should notice it would only remind them of a time in the past. All the earth was a great wide room, spectacularly painted. Six thousand feet above the colorful land, an endless armada of purest white clouds sailed in from the sea, scattered in their shadows below, compressed and flat-bottomed from altitude. The air was a perfect clear blue that gave distance and depth to faraway peaks, made greens of the spread quilt even greener, and reds of the hills intense. Cody gazed all around, checking instruments with each swing of his head, but concentrating more on the view, trying to form a permanent image.

"Do you ever miss it?" said Mano.

"Miss what?" Cody replied, disturbed by the interruption. Today was the birthday of one of Mano's sisters. For the past hour everything he had said had been related to home. Cody had hoped that when they departed Lam Du the scenery and being in the air would make him change the subject. But Mano had managed to keep quiet only until the bits of thatch and white plaster of Bac Ninh were ahead.

"The valley," he said. "Life on the border."

Cody frowned and adjusted the volume of the VHF radio upward, though there was nothing to hear, only the brief calls between the three birds flying somewhere up ahead. The convoy was making predictable progress, and the pilots were going about their jobs with quiet efficiency. For this first leg—Hanoi to Kep—Cody was flying the standby bird and Cowan and Dukemire were escorting the convoy, while Rankin flew spare in the air. They had waited at Operations with Captain Sarot until Rankin relayed that the convoy was approaching Bac Ninh—the signal for the standby crew to crank and fly ahead to Kep, where they would refuel and wait again. It was the most boring of the four flight positions, but the panorama of the countryside made up for a lot. On such a day it was enough simply to be in the air.

"No, I don't miss it," he said.

"I sure do," said Mano quickly. He was relaxed with his weapon across his lap, brown hands resting easily on the grip and forestock, black hair whipping with the wind. "This is the time of year when the baby goats are ready to become *cabrito*—six weeks old, still tender with mama's milk, not yet on cactus and briars. It only happens once a year, and is a special time. My family always has a big fiesta on a ranch across the river, in a pasture beneath some mesquites. The men stack bricks and build a fire of dead mesquite, and they drink beer and tell stories while they wait for coals. The grill is only a wire shelf from an ice box, used for years and burned clean. Then fresh lime is sliced and the juice is squeezed onto the meat, then a little salt and a lot of powdered garlic and *chile*. I can hear the sizzle now, see the straight black lines each time the meat is turned, smell that wonderful aroma. I have an uncle who is always in charge. He sprinkles the meat with beer for flavor and to regulate the fire. No one can cook *cabrito* the way he does. Same meat, same fire, same everything—his is always better. He is very conceited about this one thing. It is all in life that he can do correctly."

Cody nodded. "I had an uncle who used to fix *cabrito* the same way," he said. Actually, because Cody had been very small when Ned was alive, he could only remember him doing it once, that last spring before Burma. Listening to Mano was stirring contradictory things. He wanted to hear about the big family gathering, and he didn't want to hear it at all. But his stomach was beginning to growl, and he could see blue-white smoke rising off a grill, men standing around, hear the sounds of their laughter.

"For two days the women prepare," Mano said. "They make mountains of flour tortillas, doing that special trick with the fingers that not everyone knows, like a spider making web. Corn tortillas require no skill, so these the men bring from the factory, a great mound of thick stacks in loose paper, piled in a battered old truck with cases of beer. And the women make *pico de gallo* and *salsa*, and *frijoles con chile y cebolla* that will make you cry even as you want more."

"Yeah, it's kinda that way where I come from," Cody said. That was a lie. He had heard of such meals, had even watched them with envy from a distance, but never had he tasted them himself. He wished that Mano would shut up.

"Have you eaten the head of a goat?"

"Uh, no. Never have."

"That is the very best part, even better than *cabrito*, though in a different way. When you eat the head of goat you always remember that time. The women do not eat it too much, but they like to fix it for the men." He grinned and clenched a fist. "*¡Duro!*" he said.

Cody knew about that. It was the same that was said about the dried, foul-smelling shrimp that the men ate like dead minnows and washed down with beer.

"They bake it in tins. Two or three heads are usually enough, depending on how many men, how much beer, and how ugly the women. When I was small my grandmother did the cooking, but now the heads always come from a shop. This is completely apart from the rest of the meal.

"There is a man named Topo, a *caballero* on the uncle's ranch across the river, who always brings his family, a very old man who carries a long folding knife. A place is worn in the pocket of his pants around the shape of that knife. It is Topo's job to clean the meat from the heads into a tub. All the men stand around, each with a beer, and watch while the women fix the tables and the little kids squeal and tug at the dogs. The head meat is tender, and only needs scraping from the bone. Nothing is left out—the lips, the nose, the tongue, even the eyeballs though they look different now— everything goes into the tub. When the skull is completely clean, Topo stabs his knife into the little line above the forehead, and with a slow twist, cracks open the bone. Then into the tub go the sinuses and brains.

"When everything is done, the meat is stringy and soupy and gray, with pieces of black and white. Topo stirs and chops with his knife so all the parts are mixed, and no one can say which piece went where. The men smile and drink their beer. Soon a teenage boy who is tired of being young steps forward and accepts the first tortilla from Topo while the women pretend not to watch. First a spoonful of meat from the tub, then a spoonful of beans, a little *salsa* and a lot of green *chile*, and when he has shown the men and the boys, and perhaps a *chica* near his own age, that to eat the eyeball or the nose slime of a goat is practically nothing, Topo hands him a beer. There are by then tears in the teenager's eyes, for the peppers are *muy caliente*. Somebody tells a small joke, and the men laugh and walk past the tail of the truck, and they cup the tortillas and bend down to Topo, who waits at the tub."

Cody was now starved. He was also angry at Mano for making him jealous. He wished that growing up had been as simple for him as eating the snot of a goat. He thought about the farm, or the fallow fields they called a farm, and instead of spring he saw summer. Summer, when the heat stood up and fell across the land like shimmering dust, and there was no escape. The cicadas sang like drunken violins, and lunatic birds gave laughing calls in the still mesquite. No, he didn't miss it. The only salvation, then and later, was flying. Just as it had saved him from those shoreless summers, lifting him up through that melting, glassy air to a cooler place, holding him there to gaze down upon it, it had later saved him entirely by taking him off to the Army. No, Mano could say what he might. The sense of a place was the sum of all that ever happened there, and nothing ever happened where he grew up that deserved to be missed. Grandpa West once said that being away and missing a place could make it seem better than being there ever had been. Maybe that was the case with Mano.

Bac Ninh was passing below on the left, and up ahead, strung out like a necklace, Cody could see the long convoy, slowing and bunching as it crossed the levees and bridge at the Song Cau. Far out in front, very low to the ground, blades flashing against the green paddies, were the two OH-13s. They moved back and forth across the road. It took longer to find Rankin, because he was not where the chase bird was supposed to be. Instead of holding at altitude where he could have a view of the other birds, the single helicopter was down low, off by itself, snooping among some low hills.

Mano was still talking, telling about each of the women in his family—his mother and grandmother, aunts and cousins—each in some context of food.

"Hey, Mano," Cody interrupted. He wanted to tell his crew chief to simply be quiet, but instead he said, "Talk about something besides food."

Mano thought a moment, and said, "I will tell you about a ranch I know in the Sierra del Carmen which has a bar long enough for forty men, and room to park this helicopter. It belongs to a man named Juan Luis Hinajosa Delgado, the richest man in all of Coahuila..."

Cody simply tuned him out. Mano was ordinarily quiet in the air, but today he refused to shut up.

They were quickly leaving the convoy and other aircraft behind, crossing the first band of important hills, approaching another river. A dozen miles to their right, straight out Cody's open door, lay the tip of a great mountain group north of Haiphong. Far off along their edge he could see the pale blue haze that had to be Ha Long Bay, but he only thought briefly of Moni'. Up ahead were more mountains, and beyond the flat place where he imagined Kep to be lay a green V, tapering down to a throat among mountains. Then he heard Mano again. He was back on the subject of food.

"...had made that dish for years, and it was always her job, everybody knew. But this time when it was already in the oven, another aunt slipped back to add something, perhaps to make it better, but I think to make it worse so next year she might have her chance. But Aunt Fila spotted her, and there was a terrible screeching and clawing—chunks of hair floating like when cats fight—and the dogs barked and the children cried and all the women became involved, and even some of the drunker men. It took several years to recover from that, and only when the problem aunt moved to Chicago. My grandfather eventually put it best with a saying which I have even heard the women whisper: Change your dress, change your hair, change the conversation, *pero no chingle la comida!*"

Cody laughed, glad that he had been listening. Kep was clearly visible now, and the canyon throat beyond. "Hey, Mano," he said, finally understanding. He cast a glance at his gunner. "It's going to be okay today."

Billy Mano did not reply. He sat silent for the remainder of the flight, moving his lips sometimes, looking down at his weapon and rubbing it with slow easy strokes.

Chapter Eighteen

"THINK THEY'LL SURVIVE?"

If Pearbone was startled, it did not show. He was working among his important iris, butt in the air, carefully lifting brown tubers from the earth with a trowel. He snipped the top of each plant before tossing it into a crate. The blossoming peak was barely past, a poor time for such work. A glance across the splayed spears showed many slender stalks still topped with shriveled membrane. Only a few blooms remained—purple, yellow, peach, and white—most on shorter stems where trees reached out with shade.

The older man straightened, dropped his trowel, and moved a gritty glove to the small of his back. "I think so," he said, surveying the yard. He was wearing his gardening clothes, the paint-marked khakis and white shirt. "They are very resilient. They will be sick for a while, but they will not die."

"You can't be taking them all," McCall said. There were hundreds, perhaps thousands in the several gardens.

"No, I can only take a few—enough to start a new garden." Pearbone backed carefully along his tracks, dropped the trowel and removed his gloves. "Glad you could come, Marsh," he said, extending a hand. His manner was relaxed, but serious. "If you had waited longer, I would have been forced to ambush you at the Café Ho Tay." He frowned suddenly and terribly. "A poor choice of words," he said. "I'm sorry about your sergeant."

He led McCall along a narrow walk between the plantings, then up the wooden steps to the veranda. "Have a seat. Be back in a minute." He jerked a cord on an overhead fan.

McCall settled into a big chair, the wicker groaning in protest. The chairs were deep, with tall armrests and tall curving backs, inclined just enough to take weight off the spine and make closing the eyes seem easy. The sun blinked between the clouds, a fresh cool breeze eddied around the corner, and Calvin Winslow was thrashing to death on Su Letei's porch. McCall's eyes sprang open.

Pearbone returned with a pitcher of limeade, iced glasses, a quart of gin, and a couple of chopsticks for stirring. McCall waved the alcohol aside, because it was the middle of the day, and because he wanted it. The limeade was fresh-squeezed, with just enough sugar to soften the tartness. Pearbone poured his own glass half full of gin before tilting the pitcher.

"Have you seen Su today?" he said.

"Just briefly."

"It was a terrible shock. She only found out this morning when the gendarmes came. She apparently barely knew the man, but it brought back so much." When McCall raised a questioning brow, Pearbone continued, "Her first husband was a French officer. He died in prison when the Japanese were here. She later married a planter who grew coffee up on the Chau River. He was killed by the Viet Minh for resisting payment of taxes. Then a few months ago, an American major took an interest in her. She was flattered, but nothing came of it. The major was soon killed by a Communist sniper. I believe that added considerable weight to what happened to your sergeant. How was she?"

"Pretty upset."

"Your being there probably did little to help. I went to her house this morning as soon as I heard, and stayed until the gendarmes were gone. You seem to have made an impression on Su."

"Do they know who killed Winslow?" McCall leaned forward from the comfort of the chair.

"This is not so simple as a raid on a mom-and-pop shop, Marsh. No, they do not know who killed your sergeant," Pearbone said, making no attempt to disguise the lie before changing the subject. "I have been to Saigon. As you have surmised, I have rented a small villa there. I am not supposed to discuss it, but I have been instructed to prepare to move south."

"Is it that close?"

"I'm afraid so. The prevailing thought is that once the fortress falls, and all the prisoners have been safely interred somewhere, Ho Chi Minh will move ahead with a massive assault in the delta. At the very least he will cut the highway from Haiphong, but the real prize, of course, is right here where we sit—Hanoi itself. The mere fact of my instructions tells everything about U.S. intentions. Nothing is left now for the French but to face the inevitable agony, and they know it. The one consolation is that then at least it can all be finished."

"For them."

"That's right. For them."

"We're deliberately letting them fall."

Pearbone downed his drink, ignoring the comment. He made another gin, poured more limeade for McCall, and sat absently stroking his eyebrows. "While I was in Saigon, I made cautious inquiry about you and your men," he said. "I was told essentially to mind my own business—more or less what I told you not long ago. At any rate, this tells me that, for whatever reason, Roach Harman is in control of your operation, complicating things considerably. Were you aware of this?"

"Not directly, but it had begun to look that way."

"I did some further snooping. I did not have time to get about much myself, but I have a friend who knows the right people to ask for almost any sort of information, and can do so without arousing suspicion. Through him I learned that your mother unit—the 22d Training Detachment at Tan Son Nhut—was disbanded two or three weeks ago, almost as quickly as it began operations. Minds were changed somewhere. They left their equipment behind, but the unit itself is gone. Your outfit no longer exists, Marsh. As before, you and your men are not officially here, the difference being that *then* you at least were legitimately based in Saigon. Now you are stationed nowhere."

Pearbone lit a cigarette, holding it gingerly between thumb and forefinger to take a puff. "I did not expect this to surprise you at this stage," he said, "but it confirms what I already wondered, that you are not here strictly on an Army assignment. That means Roach Harman. The only remaining question concerns why."

McCall rubbed his eyes, stalling. He was glad to have his suspicions confirmed, to know for sure that Ezra Smith had been lying, or at least skirting the truth, but he saw no profit in discussing it.

Pearbone frowned at his silence. "Does this mean nothing to you, Marsh?"

"Sure it means something. But our job obviously has nothing to do with gathering intelligence. Sounds to me like we simply fell beneath Harman's umbrella while somebody waits for a decision from Washington."

"There is no reason your unit could not have been held within MAAG."

"Unless they don't want to have to acknowledge we're here."

"But for what purpose?"

"I'm just guessing, but if it's decided to send more GIs over here—or even if they only go ahead and turn loose of the rest of the promised aircraft—things would be a lot simpler if we were already in place."

"I might believe that if I trusted Harman," Pearbone said. "You would think that being in the State Department I would know something of what he is up to, but I don't. Neither does anyone else, not completely. Sometimes he works directly for the White House, sometimes—I suspect—he works on his own. We never know which."

"Well, nothing is happening on this end."

"And what if that changes?"

"I'm still in the Army."

"Meaning that whatever Harman is up to, you just quietly go along?"

"Walter, I'm a soldier. I perform military jobs for my country. That necessarily requires that I 'go along' with things I may not understand. I have a chain of command which leads eventually to the president. If I don't do my job, then the chain is broken, and the mission—whatever it happens to be—will not be accomplished. In that case, I will be replaced by someone who *can* do the job. It is not my duty, my obligation, or my right to question the validity or necessity of a mission so long as it falls within reasonable parameters. Those parameters are damn difficult to define, and frankly, seem to change with my age. I expect that soon we will have troops here. Whether I happen to agree with that policy is irrelevant. Whether I agree with the reason I am here, or completely understand it, is by the same token irrelevant."

"But should you not have been told?"

"Yes, I should have been told," McCall replied with less force. "My commanding officer is not known for divulging a hell of a lot of information, and frankly, he's getting old."

"Colonel Smith?"

"Correct."

Pearbone nodded, frowned with his thoughts, then turned the conversation. "That little speech of yours sounds like one you have used before," he said, smiling wryly to soften the insult. "Over the years, I have carried about a few of those myself. Each sounded good at one time, but they inevitably became tattered. I have since dropped the habit. I found that forming new phrases forces me to think, to examine the possibilities. New patterns develop, making it less difficult to know when a position should be abandoned. Even so, I have to admit that the analysis almost always comes too late."

He paused to watch a hummingbird drive away another from the bougainvillea surrounding the veranda. "There is another aspect I am still working on," he said. "Just something I am curious about. One of those possibilities I mentioned." He looked directly at McCall. "It may be nothing, it may be of grave importance—I don't yet know—but it is imperative that you be in touch with me at least once each day until one of us leaves this area. But only at this house, never downtown, and do not worry about the hour. I will be here much this week, but if I am not when you come, there is a key to this door beneath the lip of the porch there beside the steps. Use the place as you would your own." He gazed sadly around the veranda and gardens. "Little enough time remains for it to be enjoyed."

McCall left the consul contemplating all that he had built within his walls of broken glass, departing by way of the side gate, then down the gloomy drive between neglected shrubs. He left with an image of Walter Pearbone slumped in a complaining chair, sipping iced gin, pondering a field of dead flowers.

He had not planned to stop again at the Café Ho Tay, but as he passed, wondering if Su Letei had recovered enough to face the noontime rush, he saw two things which stopped him cold. Beneath the trees beyond the porte cochere, its driver braced against one fender, was the black Mercedes that belonged to Chang Wu. And from her customary post within the open doors, Su Letei stepped toward him in a gesture of distress. He looked for a place to park.

She was no longer at the door. The café was busy. The din of the common babble could be heard from the street, but as McCall waited in the foyer it slowly hushed. Across the guests and tables, through the open doors beyond, he could see the slender form of Su Letei standing before the obscene shape of Chang Wu. He had the gardens to himself. At his feet lay a black pit bull, while covering the grounds in either direction were Chinese guards in dark suits. Chang Wu was speaking to Su Letei, his wide smile gashing his face like the slash of a razor, his eyes no more than swollen slits. His shapeless body filled the massive chair, flesh without bones. Su Letei nodded, then turned and crossed the restaurant with short, soundless steps, her face completely lifeless. She held his eyes as she walked up to McCall.

"I did nothing to encourage your sergeant," she repeated.

"I know that. No one blames you."

She glanced around the café. "I have loved this place," she said quietly. "I have talked much about leaving, but always I hoped it would be possible to stay. But there is but one future." She looked up at McCall. "I would like to see you if you ever come to Vung Tau."

She led him to Chang Wu while the restaurant watched. All the usual faces were there—de Matrin, Gereau, Solo Jacobé, plus Major Legère looking sheepishly hopeful. At the bar, talking to the reporter, Eber Walloon, old man Larkin was wrapped around a bottle. In the corner sat a large group of CAT pilots, they alone uninterested in what was taking place.

McCall did not know what he planned to say to Chang Wu, or why he was following Su Letei to his chair, or even why she was leading him there. It only seemed that they should face one another now, to acknowledge what had been done, and what might lie ahead. The fat face smiled with drunken power.

Su Letei stopped well short of the table, nodded to each of them, then immediately walked away. From one side of the garden, the skinny, snake-eyed guard approached, displaying scattered teeth in a wicked smile, sliding his right hand into his jacket. The pit bull opened its mouth and moved its eyes up McCall's legs.

"Please, sit down," Chang Wu husked. He held a tiny, inflated hand toward a chair, a gold-and-ruby ring cutting deeply into a finger.

McCall pulled the chair to one side, leaving his mean eye toward Chang Wu as he faced the restaurant. Snake Eyes immediately began working his way behind while the other guard moved forward.

"Tell your men to stay where I can see them or I'll kill them both."

"Do you believe you are that good, Major?"

"I'm prepared to find out."

The slits widened and flashed black, and the smile again was an ugly gash. Chang Wu flicked his fat fingers, and the men responded. "How do you like my new dog?" he said.

McCall gave the animal an appraising glance. "He looks dumb."

"Ah, he is, but he is very crafty when it counts. I brought him today to see how he behaves. He will replace the gray dog, who is about to retire."

"How do you retire a fighting dog?"

"In the pit, of course. That will be easy now. Interest in the fights has grown so great that the Blue Deep is now operating four nights each week." Chang Wu sipped his tea, his fingers delicately curled, the fragile cup absurdly small against his face. He touched his lips with a linen napkin. "It is important for us to use this time to reduce tension between us," he said. "You realize, of course, that you cannot win a contest against me, not even if you were to kill me, so let's proceed from that obvious point. I am glad you came here to see me. The truth is, I came here to see you. I wish to extend my condolences regarding your sergeant. I hope your anger can be tempered somewhat by the knowledge of good fortune—my men thought at first that it was you they had killed. Too bad that neither of us anticipated the interest of your sergeant. His death could have been prevented..." The face split again into a smile. "...or at least delayed. From what I have learned of the man, it was only a matter of time. Nonetheless, my men were careless. They have paid for their stupidity. That, of course, will not replace your sergeant, but I do apologize for whatever inconvenience his death might have caused."

It was time for McCall to go. He had killed a lot of men, and never once enjoyed it, but looking now at Chang Wu's creased throat, at the sunken pig ears, he knew that killing this man just might possibly be fun. The prospect was the edge of terrain seldom traveled, and felt like madness. He hoped that if the time came to kill Chang Wu, he could do it without passion, simply because it needed to be done. When he stood, the dog bobbed its head as if taking aim.

"I see that you still do not understand the puzzle of which you are part," said Chang Wu. "I do hope you are able to survive. That would be the greatest irony, and I would enjoy it immensely. It may even be good for my business. Good luck to you, Major. If we do not meet again, you can at least know that I will be keeping up with your progress."

McCall departed to the screeching, husking sound of the fat man's laugh, and to the sarcastic smiles of several in the room. He did not see Su Letei. As he walked outside he passed a bearded Legionnaire, but hardly noticed. He had almost reached his jeep when he heard Su Letei's voice.

"Oh, Major McCall," she said. "A telephone call for you!"

When she handed him the phone, he noticed that the Legionnaire was waiting in the alcove. He gave McCall a sullen look while Su Letei stood with silent poise.

"Yes?"

"Major McCall, you must come to Lam Du immediately," said Sarot, his tone distressed and hollow. "Something terrible has happened. Someone has set a trap for your men."

The convoy slowly gathered in a field beyond the road, an armored vehicle and a half-track first, then the flatbeds and six-bys with their loads of ammo, water, and rations, then two more armored cars. The jeep which led the way pulled to one side, waited as a tall man stepped out, then drove away toward mustard-green tents sprouting groups of antennas. A groaning of engines and gears, belches of black exhaust, and a gray-orange cloud settled over the camp.

Almost hidden in the deep grass beneath the aircraft, Mano pretended to awaken from a nap. Cody saw his eyes, but said nothing. He was sitting on the ground with his back against a strut, studying the movements of the helicopters as they prepared to land at Kep. During the past half hour he had seen many smaller types of airplanes come and go from the strip, but the sight of the helicopters made him smile. Airplanes only borrowed the sky, leaving no discernible impression as they coursed across and quickly disappeared, but helicopters *used* it, shaking and shaping it as they turned about, never in a hurry to leave. An airplane was only passing through, on its way to somewhere else, but a helicopter at any given moment was where it belonged.

Rankin landed last after holding at altitude to the south for a few minutes. When the three OH-13s completed refueling, they taxied across the strip, then landed and shut down in a line behind Cody's bird. Soon the men came up to join them. Mano and Whitney connected two ponchos and strung them between the engine supports and two carbines on fixed bayonets to produce a sizable piece of shade. The men flopped down like a bunch of hounds and had lunch and a short nap. Besides the regular rations, Cowan had brought a sackful of croissants from breakfast. They laid them on the hot exhaust of the nearest ship, then flicked away the bits of rust. When they were finished, Kinney carried the trash to the edge of the road, set it afire, and watched it burn before kicking sand across the ashes. While the others logged some Zs in the shade, Rankin crossed the road to talk with the drivers about what was ahead. He was smiling in his humorless way when he returned. Cowan pushed himself up on one elbow.

"What's the word?"

Rankin squatted and lit a cigarette. "The gooks have four favorite spots they like to hit," he said, "but after the first five or six miles, there's hardly anyplace where somebody hasn't paid the price." He paused while the others sat up to listen, all but Whitney, who was sound asleep and snoring. "It's about thirty-five road miles to Camp Chino, and on a good day it takes almost two hours for a convoy to cover. We'll have to watch the fuel. If they're running behind, we'll refuel by rotation. We'll give the trucks a fifteen-minute head start. West, you and I will do the initial cover. There are some low hills we've got to get through, then it should be easy all the way to the mountains. Cowan, you're spare in the air. Duke, you wait here, crank thirty minutes after we do, then head north-northeast. We should be somewhere beyond Khon Lau by the time you get there, not quite to the base of the mountains. Everybody watch your fuel, and keep in mind how long it takes to get back here. From this point on, the terrain starts to change—lots of low to medium hills, and some areas with no cultivation. In this country, that means jungle, even if it's only twenty feet deep. So stick close to the roads—we're out here by ourselves, and if you go down there will be no way to pull you out unless you're in the open. If you are forced to abandon a bird, set an incendiary grenade on the radios. If any of you think you need more ammunition, the guys in that front half-track say they've got plenty, just come and get it."

"Where are the places they hit most?" said Cowan.

"The first is only about six miles out, between some hills, but it's within artillery range, so anything that happens there will be small and quick. The favorites are in the Narrows at Hoa Lac and beyond, but the French-flown Helldivers will be taking over there. Before I landed I got a relay from Sarot confirming that. We'll probably hang around a few more minutes just in case we're needed to evacuate anyone. If the fighters happen to show up early, and anything happens, we just pop smoke and step aside."

Kinney and Two Acres exchanged grins. Even Mano, who had become as quiet as Dukemire now that they were on the ground, seemed to like the idea of some fireworks. It was why men joined the Army—not to kill people, but to blow things up.

There was the sound of trucks coming up the road, and when the men turned, Rankin immediately said, "Shit." It was four tankers filled with diesel, and six flatbed semis stacked with uncovered crates of artillery shells. They pulled up parallel with the main body of the convoy and parked beside the road, but left the motors running. Then another half-track came along, followed by two six-bys, each carrying four men in combat gear, manning twin pedestal-mounted machine guns. "Nobody mentioned this," said Rankin.

"That ordnance will make a nice plum," Two Acres said, smiling grimly.

"And the sloshing tankers will slow 'em down, and give the gooks something to block the road," said Cowan. He had a grass stem in his mouth, and paused to spit some pieces toward the sunlight. "They'd better make it six Helldivers, and two more on standby." He turned to Cody and Dukemire. "Just don't forget that our real job is to take men to the hospital. Don't get close to any of that stuff, especially the ammo. One of those blows, it'll knock you out of the air a thousand feet away. And when you do pick up

318

somebody, be sure he has more than a minor wound, but you also want someone who looks like he'll make it. Don't hesitate to tell the guys on the ground who you'll carry and who you won't."

Sergeant Whitney stopped snoring as if he had heard in his sleep. He sat up and blinked toward the loaded trucks. "Son of a bitch," he said, then lay back down. When the rest of the convoy began to crank, he stood and pulled his cap down tight, dusted himself, and said, "Let's get it, boys."

"Fifteen minutes," said Rankin.

Whitney's face went slack. He looked around, then lay back down in the flattened grass. In less than a minute he was snoring, and he didn't stop when the convoy took the road.

Finally it was time, and the men pulled down the ponchos and dispersed to their ships. Cody was strapped to his seat, the rotor blades rocking gently as he went through the start-up procedure, when Cowan suddenly appeared at his side. "Don't rely on Rankin's judgment," he said quietly. "I don't like the way he flies. Use your head, and pay close attention. If the convoy gets hit, there will be gooks everywhere, and they'll be trying to take you out. Don't let Rankin get you killed. These gunners we're carrying are just for the enemy to look at. Break off and take somebody to the hospital. Pretend your radios are out if you have to."

Cody was too surprised to say anything. He leaned out of the aircraft and watched Cowan walk back to his ship. He set the throttle and looked around. Mano was standing outside the opposite door, everything ready. "Clear!" he yelled, and Mano stepped away from the skid and repeated the shout. Then the starter engaged, the engine belched to life, and Cody sat watching the gauges, wondering about Cowan's remarks. The hissing blades moved faster, and the grass was pushed away, whipping in the breeze and changing colors. When a commo check was complete, Rankin called the tower, and the three birds hovered out to the taxiway, leaving Dukemire and Kinney to watch. They departed east in loose trail, circling northward on an angle that would intercept the convoy.

The low hills were no problem at all, but it was easy to see why the enemy considered them tempting. The incline was slight, but the convoy was bunched from crossing two narrow bridges. Less than a mile later the road was bracketed by commanding heights, both areas covered with low, dense jungle pierced by hidden trails.

Northwest lay an unpopulated tract six miles wide, warped by gullies and rolling crowns, all marked by oblong scars from old bombardments.

With the addition of ten trucks, the convoy was too long now for the helicopters to be completely effective. Rather than tagging the ten to the tail, a new order was made as they pulled out of Kep, spacing the explosive loads at intervals among the others. It made sense, in a way, but it was plain there were not nearly enough escorting gun trucks and armored vehicles. Either the French had undue confidence in the helicopters, somebody had miscalculated, or the needed equipment was simply not available. The line of vehicles stretched along the highway for more than two miles. All that the aircraft could do was check the roadway ahead and the nearby hills for signs of an ambush, then swing quickly down either side, looking for anything that might have been missed. Cowan held at fifteen hundred feet, high enough to keep an eye on both birds and the length of the convoy, but low enough to get down in a hurry.

Mano had settled down to a workmanlike silence now that the mission had begun and there was something to do besides think. He leaned far out of the aircraft, his weapon ready, watching the ground and glancing ahead toward the lead bird. Far in the distance the blue escarpment of mountains grew gradually greener. The foothills around it were marked with drifting cloud shadows.

Cody followed Rankin's lead without effort, maintaining a covering separation, back and to the right, while constantly checking the ground. He kept thinking about what Cowan had said. He began to focus on the lead pilot's technique, to observe with less awe, and to analyze what Rankin was doing. It was not long until he understood what Cowan meant. Rankin flew like a pure scout, one that had heavy covering guns lurking nearby, a visible threat to the enemy. But with no real cover besides the puny weapons of the two crew chiefs, it was suddenly clear that they were taking some hellacious chances—flying lower and slower than was really required, crossing the faces of ridges, sliding down throats of ravines much too far from the convoy. The more he watched, the more he saw in Rankin what he had never observed: The man who was so careful and adamant about safety in training and flight techniques seemed to abandon it all when it came to pursuit of an enemy. Despite his age and considerable experience, Rankin was still a scrapper—quiet and methodical, but misleading—still itching for a fight, still loving the contest between him and the man on the ground. This made Two Acres his perfect match. The Montanan was more blatant about it, physically stronger and rough, but down where it counted in the willingness to put his life on the line for nothing more than the enjoyment of pursuit and head-to-head combat, Two Acres had nothing on Burd Rankin.

As if on cue, Cowan came on the radio. "You're getting a long way from the convoy, Two-five," he said. With no response, Rankin brought the flight back to the highway, then moved quickly ahead. Soon the low hills were behind, and the long procession moved onto an undulating plain of chest-deep elephant grass and occasional green brushy ravines. A few miles ahead stood a strange and solitary chunk of gray limestone topped with tall trees. From that distance it resembled a frowning head with a bad toupee, an excuse to build a village there and to bend the highway past it for a view. But no one gave the place a second glance. The drivers pressed the throttles, scattering kids and skinny chickens, while the helicopters moved ahead. It was less than three miles now to the jumbled karst mountains, gray stone slabs with old green forests draping peaks and standing in cracked ravines. Long trails of vines hung from cliffside springs. The road curved right, following the base of the pocked escarpment eastward toward Hoa Lac. The pilots scanned the sky for fighters.

Cody watched the cliffs with growing excitement. He had to keep reminding himself of the danger. The land was just too spectacular, too colorful, to convey the black-and-white sense of war. Five-hundred-foot cliffs fell as steeply as if sliced with a knife, and almost everywhere were caves. Gigantic trees with long gray trunks clung exposed in improbable places. Where blades of stone projected from the mass, erosion had sometimes eaten through in tunnels. Rankin was sticking close to the road now, swapping sides well ahead of the lead vehicle, but Cody wished they could fly among the cliffs, slide up the narrow alleys, skim the trees and check all the caves. It was the kind of terrain to make a pilot forget that he was not a bird.

Dukemire's timing was perfect. The aircraft had begun to slide southward around the nose of mountains projecting toward the village of Hoa Lac when he called that he had them in sight.

"Roger, Two-one," Rankin replied. "Take up a holding pattern at two thousand. Watch for big boys inbound—we're a little ahead of schedule, but they should be here about now. Two-four, how's your fuel?"

"I'm still good."

"Okay, Two-four, come on down and take my place. I'll move ahead as rover."

"Negative, Two-five," Cowan said. "You won't have any protection at all out there by yourself. We should all be turning back in a few minutes anyway."

"Negative on your negative!" Rankin snapped. "Get your butt down here!" With that he peeled sharply away, leaving Cody alone above the roadway. "Stay put until he gets here, Two-three," he said more calmly to Cody. "Take up his wing and just keep doing what you've been doing." He dropped very low to the highway, pulling away toward Hoa Lac.

"Coming left," Cody said to Mano.

"Clear left," came the reply. "I've got him in sight, nine o'clock, real high."

A moment later, Cody had Cowan in view. As he completed the orbit, Cowan called coming up on his left, then moved ahead to the position of flight lead. He began working the convoy with skill, using only the slightest commands.

As they approached the village of Hoa Lac, two things happened at once: The hills to the south and east, which had been low and unthreatening, suddenly closed in, bringing with them the blue Song Thuong and the railway which followed another course from Kep; at the same time, the land—even more beautiful—now suddenly looked deadly. The blue throat they had seen from long distance fell open like the maw of a shark—steep cliffs on one side, a great ridge of mountains on the other, seeming to close ahead where the canyon made a bend. Cody looked up at cliffs that were essentially the same as those of a few moments ago, at the clear and swift river coursing out of the canyon—green paddies and bamboo, jungle and boulders and cloudy blue sky—and it suddenly felt like war. Old burned-out hulks of trucks and tanks nosed into the paddies, attesting to the dangers of the canyon.

Something else was different. Cowan was the first to notice. "Where'd all the people go?" he said. All the way up from Kep, there had been civilians walking with loads or riding bikes along the highway, and always in the fields there were peasants working—women gathering greens, old men chopping at paddies with heavy hoes, red oxen harnessed to wagons filled with wood or thick bamboo, gray buffalo and small flocks of ducks tended by children. All were now missing, leaving only the road and the river, and fresh green strips of wet paddies on either side. The drivers had noticed as well. Even from the air they could be seen through the windows, craning their necks toward the cliffs.

"Something is definitely about to come down," said Rankin. From high on the eastern face, he followed the steep slope downward, turned briefly south along the river, then cut directly across the valley floor ahead of the lead armored car. "I just talked to Kep Tower," he called to the rest of the flight. "The Helldivers have been diverted. They're not coming. We are going to have to stay on station for the last six miles." His bird turned sharply right near the base of the cliffs, climbed parallel with the face, and flew directly up the canyon. A mile ahead, a huge chunk of limestone some three hundred feet tall stood away from the body of the cliff like a calf of a glacier, causing the road to swerve around it. Rankin shot the slender gap between the gray walls of stone, then his helicopter disappeared.

"Two-one," Cowan called to Dukemire, "drop on down to one thousand. Try to keep Two-five in view if you can."

"Two-one, roger." Dukemire had let his orbits slip far back on the convoy, but now he turned directly up the center of the canyon. He searched ahead, but Rankin's bird was still lost beyond the cliffs. The two scouting birds below swerved left across a jungled slope studded with house-sized boulders beneath the cliffs, then swept across the open elbow at the narrow part of the canyon.

Suddenly everyone heard the hammering sound of a machine gun as Rankin came on the radio, his voice softly urgent. "Okay, we got 'em," he said. Two Acres' machine gun in the background was firing without interruption. The drivers in the convoy heard the gunfire ahead, and at once drew themselves tight and stomped the throttles. Black smoke belched from the exhausts.

"Where are you, Two-five?" Cowan called, circling back from the river with Cody close behind. Whitney and Mano both checked their weapons and leaned out of the aircraft.

"Around the bend," Rankin said. The machine gun was still pounding away, but his voice had changed. Then he began to cough, and he released the key of his mike.

"There he is," said Dukemire. "At the bend." Then everyone saw the 13 coming around the stone calf, a hundred feet off the ground. The nose dipped, then drew back. Two Acres was no longer firing.

"Two-five, can you hear me?" Cowan called. There was no response. He led his wingman across Rankin's path, timing a turn back to the left to slide in close to the wounded bird. "Drop back, Two-three," he said to Cody. "Keep your angle, don't fly my path." Cody affirmed with two clicks of the mike.

Rankin's bird was slowly descending, flying straight down the narrow field between the road and river. By then Cowan was around on his right, and could see that the pilot was wounded. Two Acres seemed to be holding him up with one hand as they slipped toward the paddies. "Duke, come on down to five hundred. Lower than that if it looks like we need help. Two-three, I'm following him in. Drop back and set up a covering orbit."

"Two-three, roger."

Rankin's bird was no more than thirty feet off the ground, coming in too fast in a shallow approach, when a full attack commenced all over the convoy. Mortars pounded all along the highway, and rounds from recoilless rifles sailed overhead. Almost immediately a tanker was hit, and went up with a tremendous explosion, sending a slender red-and-black fireball into the sky. The truck careened to the right through a narrow canal, sending up water and steam, then a huge burst of flame and black smoke as it overturned and ruptured. The convoy moved faster, the armored cars and guntrucks returning fire into the jungle, the enemy still unseen. Red-orange flashes moved up and down the roadway, just missing the desperate vehicles.

"Slow it down," Cowan was saying. "Pull the stick back, pull her back, pull her back, *pull her back!*"

Rankin was barely conscious now, but Two Acres, trying to help with the controls, could hear Cowan's calls. Still holding Rankin with one hand, he grasped the cyclic with the other just as the bird slammed into the wet paddy, sending up a wide slanting spray. The aircraft bounced, still moving forward too fast. It tilted earthward, came back and struck its heels and tail stinger, then pitched forward again. It was only saved from going completely over, crashing down upon the shattered plastic bubble, when the advancing main rotor blade struck the mud, jerking the aircraft completely around. The tail boom folded and the helicopter flopped over on its right side.

The convoy had come to a dead stop. Another tanker had been hit, and this one jackknifed, completely blocking the roadway. The other vehicles stacked up behind, no room to turn around. When the truckloads of troops dispersed into the ditches and the adjacent canal, four machine guns emplaced in caves in the cliffs above began a methodical slaughter. Mortars continued to thunder down, carefully placed to avoid the prize—the six truckloads of artillery shells.

The moment that all the flying debris was down, Cowan's bird was immediately hovering inches above the mud. Whitney clipped his weapon to the doorjamb, then jumped out and slogged knee-deep in wet rice toward the wreckage. Two Acres was already pushing Rankin up through the door. The pilot was pale and terribly wounded, all jellied blood in front. Whitney took him over his shoulder and had made it halfway to the waiting litter when a wide rank of enemy burst from thick cover at the edge of the river, firing as they advanced. Whitney was immediately struck low in the back and hips, and fell face-first into the water with Rankin on top. Two Acres had just gotten his machine gun in order, and came up firing, mowing down men, but taking heavy fire in return.

Circling overhead, Mano immediately began firing on the advancing rank while Cody moved the ship to an enfilade. Two Acres had climbed backward out of the wreckage, trailing an armful of ammo, and was using the engine and transmission for cover. Cowan was still only a few paces away. Then one of the machine guns high on the cliff switched targets, and the water erupted all around in geysers.

"Dukemire!" Cody yelled. He looked around, but could not see the spare. Cody had continued to move the bird around, Mano firing steadily, but they were taking lots of rounds. The bubble was pierced in several places, and Cody could feel the thumps and sometimes hear the sharp cries of bullets bouncing off the engine. Through it all, Cowan refused to leave the men on the ground, but kept shifting around, using the wreck for screening cover. All the enemy from the river were finally gunned down, the watery field littered with bodies, but sporadic fire was still coming from the riverbank. Then the machine gun on the cliffs got their range, and there was no defense at all. The two birds couldn't leave, and they couldn't stay and expect to survive.

Cody glanced up then, looking past the geysers and up the trail of tracers to the gun on the cliffs, and he saw something unbelievable. Dukemire and Kinney were there, sliding along the stone face toward the gun. There was a sudden exchange of fire, tracers careening everywhere from the rocks, and the machine gun position was knocked out. When he dropped his eyes to the base of the cliffs, Cody saw that the convoy was now being swarmed by enemy, fighting hand-to-hand.

Mano shouted, and the sky was suddenly filled with bullets. When Cody's head came around, he saw another group of twenty men advancing from the river. With complete discipline, half the rank held on Cody's bird while the remainder raised their weapons and in a single stroke annihilated both Cowan and Two Acres. Cowan slumped forward; his aircraft nosed into the paddy, flipped upside down, and exploded.

"Rankin's still alive!" Mano yelled, still firing at men in the open.

"Cover me, Duke!" Cody yelled. There was no response. He dropped the ship down until the skids were skimming the water, moving sideways toward Rankin while Mano blasted away, glancing all around for Dukemire. Then Cody saw him, circling low, coming almost straight toward them. They had been shot to pieces on the cliffs. Kinney was hanging by his belt out of the aircraft, blood streaming from his neck. Dukemire was doing the only thing left— using the helicopter as a weapon.

Mano was still firing, but had unbuckled and stepped out on the skid. Rankin was just below them now. As Dukemire zoomed past, taking down several gooks coming across the paddy, Mano stepped down, grabbed the pilot beneath his arms, then backed up into the aircraft. "Let's go!" he yelled.

They were taking fire again, lots of fire, straight through the cockpit, when Cody pulled in power. He heard Mano scream. Dukemire was back for another pass in a head-on duel with a man on the ground. The gook got off a short burst before his body was shattered.

326

"You okay?" Cody yelled.

Mano grimaced with pain. "Hit in the leg," he said. He braced his good leg and looked back at the wreckage, the bodies, and the column of smoke from Cowan's ship. "Dukemire's behind us," he said. He turned back and stared at the pilot he held in his lap with locked and bloody hands. Burd Rankin was limp.

Two French chopper pilots and a half-dozen parachutists from the 1st Colonials stood or straddled the benches in Operations, listening with Captain Sarot for incoming radio calls. Every face turned as McCall stormed into the tent. Sarot waved a hand, and the men immediately filed out.

McCall had raced all the way, holding the horn, dodging the stupid peasants that jumped across like mindless chickens at his speeding approach. He traveled Depot Road more airborne than not, jumping vales and swales. A shower of dust and tumbling pebbles was thrown by his skidding halt.

"How bad is it?" he said.

"Very bad," Sarot replied, his face pale. He paused as the last man left the tent. "It is difficult to say, but it appears that all of your men have been killed but three. They are on their way to Lanessan now. And for us, the entire convoy was lost, to the last man, as well as six trailer loads of howitzer shells captured intact by the enemy. A reaction force led by five tanks tried to reach them from Camp Chino, but a separate ambush had been arranged for them. They were driven back with heavy casualties and the loss of two tanks."

"Who did it?"

Sarot was staring across the tent with eyes lowered, every trace of energy gone, and his pride with it. "The Viet Minh, of course," he said quietly.

"You said it was a trap, and that someone here set it!" McCall hissed, trying to hold his voice down.

Sarot would not meet the bad eye. "That was an indiscreet remark," he said hollowly.

"Goddamn right it was, you foul-breathed son of a bitch!" He grabbed Sarot by the front of his shirt and jerked him toward his face. The cane fell to the floor. "Now who fucking did it?"

Sarot gave him a curious look, then shame overtook him. Tears welled in his eyes. "It was someone outside," he said.

"Horseshit! Nobody outside could do such a thing!"

Sarot looked directly at him, his eyes full of pain as he spoke. "Such things do not include captains."

Chapter Nineteen

HE AWAKENED EARLY, but lay a long time watching the pallet wall beside his cot, listening before turning to look. Finally he stepped out to the edge of his space to see what he had already heard, that yesterday was not an imagined moment. The tent had never seemed so immense. Morning light gave the barest tones to surfaces of wood. He touched his chin, and dimly heard sounds in the distance.

Lieutenant Atherton, whom he had only glimpsed, was gone as quickly as he arrived. Brantley made his decision, and no one had heard from him since. Then Cowan. He refused to leave the paddy just as he refused to go south, and now was upside down and crushed and drowned and burned. Rankin shuddered and bled himself out in Mano's arms, giving up the total of all his experience in one final lesson to the man who held him and to the pilot an arm's length away who was doing everything he could, which was nothing. And Dukemire, whose dumb courage always seemed like stupidity, was in the hospital with Mano, bullets through both legs, shrapnel in his throat, an earlobe shot neatly away.

He sat in his shorts, contemplating the morning, the difference of all the mornings to come. Across his chin was a horizontal slash held with catgut and covered with gauze—an extra, bleeding mouth he had known nothing about until the medics at Kep gave him a mirror. He watched the empty tent, knowing now about war, the secrets of soldiers—young men learning what old men knew and wouldn't or couldn't tell, crossing to enduring uncertainty. It was the same lesson from long ago, the time he was too young to understand.

Three days before his eighth birthday, Mr. Zia delivered the box with the mail. It was addressed to Grandma and Grandpa West, but the postman sat on the porch and lent Cody his knife and helped with the reinforced tape. Cody's father had already told him about Uncle Ned, how he died at a place called Salween Gorge, halting the Japanese drive into southern China along the Burma Road. Uncle Ned would never be coming home, he said. Cody had listened, chin out, shoulders square like a little soldier, solemnly accepting the news: Uncle Ned was dead. Dead Uncle Ned, he said to himself, testing the sound. School was out, but a few days later a girl in town told him something which gave him hope. She suggested he pray, saying that it had worked for her: A male dog had given birth to puppies because she prayed. Ever after, each night before he went to sleep, again before he got up, then later as he played alone far down by the arroyo, he prayed to God who had power to change such things. Soon, he was sure, word would come that a mistake had been made, and that it would be some other kid's uncle who had lost his life in that mile-deep hole on the opposite side of the globe defending the Chinese. He prayed and prayed, then one day Mr. Zia arrived with a box.

The sticky black tape made streaks on the knife, but Zia said it was okay, cleaning the blade on the heel of his shoe, watching as Cody unfolded the flaps. Down by the road, Grandma West stood at the side of her house and waved for Zia to bring the mail, but he pretended not to see. The man whose face was crinkled brown, and who limped from his own piece of war, knew all about Uncle Ned. He always brought his letters to Cody's house, and sat and helped him read them if it happened to be a Saturday—and it often was— or forced them beneath the door so Grandma West would not get them first. The box was stiff, and Zia used his big hands to hold the ears while Cody pulled aside the waxy paper.

Red-white-and-blue, and forty-eight stars, quality material, carefully stitched. Cody sat on the porch with his legs crossed, the flag in his lap folded square and heavy and thick, and looked up in confusion at Mr. Zia. "It's for your Uncle Ned," the man whispered, looking away.

When Zia limped off with his old leather bag, Cody took the flag inside and locked the door. He sat on the floor and had it almost unfolded when the tears gushed out and all he could see was an underwater blur of red-white-and-blue. When his father came home in the evening, he found him asleep on the unfurled flag.

He did not leave the tent until noon except to go to the latrine, but got half dressed and opened the doors and lay sweating on his cot, going over the scenes, letting them go over him. Burd Rankin was dead. So were Kinney and Cowan and Two Acres and Joe Whitney. He kept watching them die. Then Pepe the Paratroop came and made him put on a shirt and go to the mess hall.

Pepe spoke quickly and softly in French, concluding carefully in English. "I am sorry," he said. As they left the tent, he added, "Tonight we go to Dien Bien Phu."

Cody glanced at him, saying nothing. Pepe had spoken simply, without inflection, but everything was there in the self-conscious flutter of his lids, the way he held his mouth, the quick, uncertain movements of his head. A barrier of language could sometimes help. For the first time Cody noticed how young Pepe was.

The mess hall was crowded and loud. Most of First Company was there, excited about being called up, the doubt and fear forgotten in the pure relief of *knowing*, believing that whatever lay ahead could be no worse than sitting and waiting for it to come. There was a mood to the room that was nothing if not manly, preparing to face things together. It affected them both, Cody accepting his shock and sorrow, Pepe shedding all signs of uncertainty, assuming instead a grinning cockiness that could take him anywhere. A number of men who had heard what happened nodded at Cody in greeting. When the two were seated with their meals, several passed by the table to speak briefly in French or English, giving a brotherly pat to his shoulder before walking away.

After lunch, Cody accompanied Pepe to the long rigging sheds to watch the men prepare. Pepe suited up completely—from parachute to rucksack, steel pot to rifle, canteens and grenades, everything secured—going slowly through the routine. When he was done he looked like a military junk pile in the shape of a man. Cody followed as Pepe clattered toward his tent, then derigged and arranged his gear beside his cot. Pepe sat drenched in sweat, panting softly, but he seemed to be ready.

Cody held out his hand. "Good luck, Pepe," he said. "I'll come out tonight and watch you go. Maybe I'll still be here when you get back."

Pepe stood and took his hand, nodding in only partial understanding. "*Bonne chance, stupide Américain,*" he said.

"Same to you, whatever you said."

He found Major McCall in the orderly room with Captain Sarot. Both were sitting on plywood desks, sipping coffee and looking grim. Standing before the two officers, Cody became aware of how groggy he still was, as if despite the hour he was not yet completely awake. "Excuse me, sir, but have you heard anything from the hospital?" Sarot stood and took a chair against the wall.

"Yes, I just came from there an hour ago. They are both doing okay. The doctor said that Mr. Dukemire should be on his feet in about two weeks. Private Mano will be down a little longer. He lost some bone, and he's going to have a pretty good limp."

"Are they going back to the States?"

"As soon as arrangements can be made. They'll go south first, then to Manila or Tokyo. How's the chin?"

"It's okay, sir. Just a little sore." He wanted to ask what was going to happen now that the unit was out of commission, but was not sure it should be discussed in front of Sarot. "What about the others, sir?"

"The bodies were recovered this morning by a patrol from Camp Chino. They are on their way to Hanoi now."

Cody nodded and glanced at the floor. "Okay if I go to town to see the guys, sir?"

"Sure." McCall checked his watch. "You'll need to wait an hour or so, then I think they'll let you in. In the meantime, go to the aid station and get that bandage changed. Be back here before dark."

The aid station was a small shack at the edge of the road between the tents of First and Second Companies. Cody went directly there, but it was impossible not to stare across the road toward the flight line, what he had avoided all day. There were only two helicopters now—the one he had flown back from the Narrows, and the disassembled bird that they all had scavenged to death. Dukemire's had been left at Kep, and would likely remain there. He had been bleeding too badly to fly any farther, and had completed the trip to Hanoi aboard a French helicopter with Mano and the bodies of Kinney and Rankin. Cody had gotten stitched up at Kep. He had waited two hours for the morphine to wear off, then, against the protests of the medics, had refueled his aircraft and flown with drunken determination to Gia Lam. Somebody at Kep—he didn't know who—had carefully sponged up most of the blood in his ship, then stolen Mano's machine gun and all the ammunition. Cody did not care, but bad as he felt when he landed at Lam Du, he had to smile sadly at what he found: While they were away another thief had propped the loose main rotor of the scavenged ship across the top of the engine, dumped all the spare parts in a pile underneath, and made off with the wooden crates. His own helicopter did not look much better. There were holes through the floor and console and throughout the plastic bubble, shining spots of damage on the engine and the transmission housing, holes in the rotor blades, and even a pair in the skids. But the major components still worked; the blades still turned and the tanks still held fuel. It was still a bird that flew. Parked side by side, the two helicopters were a sight—a derelict, desperate little air force. He had shut the engine down, numbly checked everything over, and was tying the blades when Pepe the Paratroop came out to see what had happened.

"Gonna limp for the rest of my life," said Billy Mano, grinning weakly from his hospital bed. The smile went slowly away. "My daddy should be alive."

His left leg was bound and splinted its entire length, thick gauze pads beneath and on either side of the wounded thigh. He was very pale, eyes glazed with medicine and pain. Cody felt helpless, completely at a loss what to say. The bed behind him was empty, but directly beyond Mano lay a man encased in gauze from the chest up. All that showed was a black island of hair at the top, and two sparks of eyes. Cody looked away, feeling the accusation, very conscious of the tiny piece of gauze on his chin.

"I have done terrible damage to our reputation," Mano said in a whisper, the glint in his eyes more than just drugs and pain. When Cody leaned close, Mano's breath was putrid. "They had me in this recovery ward with three nurses when I woke up. The guy next to me was yelling, trying to get out of his straps, and I needed to piss really bad. So a nurse comes to make the man quiet, but he won't be quiet, so she comes with a needle and knocks the bastard out. I am about to burst, so finally I raise my hand, and the nurse comes and I tell her. She brings a little bottle, and the other nurses come for no reason but to look at a Texican's dick. So the nurse holds the bottle, and the others lean over and look, and I am just out of surgery and my little *taco* is only a blue button, and their eyes are bigger than that, and I'm straining and hurting so bad, trying to piss with a lady's fingers one inch from *los huevos*, and I think of all the dicks they have gathered around in the name of nursing, and that of all the times when I needed to be big, this was the most important. I have a huge hole in my leg and will limp for the rest of my life, and my pecker shrinks up, and the girls don't understand. All of female France will be talking about what runts we are in Texas."

Cody laughed quietly with Mano, then saw the staring eyes again. This time he returned their gaze, beginning to be angry. "I stopped in to see Duke," he said.

"How is he?"

"They say he's okay, but it's hard to tell right now. They won't let him talk because of his throat, and they're feeding him through tubes. His legs are not near as bad as yours."

Mano looked at the splinted leg, and became very serious. "The doctor said that if it had been only a little worse, he would have cut it off. I told him that it was good luck for both of us, because I would have tracked him down someday and cut his throat."

Cody heard a young woman's voice behind him a few beds away, and when he turned he saw Moni' in her white uniform, leaning over a man who was strapped to the bed, and who had no legs. He was French, and was asking her questions with low urgency, and she was reassuring him, soothing him, stroking his face with a damp cloth. She gave him her prettiest smile, touched his lips with her fingers, and with her eyes lowered, turned and walked out of the ward with complete poise.

"I gotta go, Mano," Cody said.

"I don't blame you, man. She's good-looking."

"You think so?"

Mano just smiled. "You're crazy. Go talk to her before she gets

334

away. Who knows? Maybe someday you can save our reputation."

"I'll see you tomorrow, Mano."

When he reached the sidewalk, Moni' was nowhere in sight. The wards were divided into separate buildings, and she could have been anywhere, but he had only taken a couple of steps when he saw her, huddled and kneeling a few paces away alongside the ward she had left. He could hear her breathless, whimpering cry as he approached. "Moni'," he said, and reached down and lifted her toward him. She leaned against his chest, and he held her as she shuddered with sobs. Suddenly she pushed back and stared up at his face.

"Cody!" she cried, her face covered with tears, lips contorted with relief and fury. "I thought you were dead!" she said. She beat both fists against his chest, then threw her arms around him and cried even more. "I thought you were dead."

He held her and stroked her head while he fought a happy mist from his eyes, knowing now that she cared. Soon her crying ceased, and she wiped her tears and tried to compose her face. "I am very glad that you are alive," she said solemnly. "I have not been anywhere but here for three days. Everyone is staying around the clock, sleeping on cots in case something happens and some wounded are gotten out of Dien Bien Phu. But the chances do not look good. The wounded there may all die. They are trying here now to decide what to do."

Cody was thinking that he understood everything about her now, and that the contradictions were not hers so much as those of the world around her.

"I must go back inside," she said, still upset. "It is very good to see you, but now you must go."

"In a minute," he said. He bent and kissed her, then held her close, her head beneath his tender chin as words unexpectedly came. "I flew over Bai Chay today," he said, his voice low. "The boats were out on the water, and the sky was turquoise blue. The fishermen were coming in with their nets, and women were wading ashore with baskets, sea birds following all around. A tide had come in the night, and the beaches were flat and clean as if no one had walked there before, and out in the bay the mountains wore halos of clouds. I thought about how it would be if you and I could be there together, and all the things that we could do..."

He kept talking like that until she was calm and it seemed to be true and they had been there together as lovers. And as he spoke, he promised himself that someday, someday the two of them would go to Bai Chay.

The night was dense with city odors, the flavor of hundreds of sidewalk grills, thousands of supper fires in homes and hovels, stale flowers wilting in beds, motor traffic still moving downtown. McCall took an intentionally long detour past the far side of Little Lake, continuing all the way to Rue Nguyen Cong Tru before turning left toward Lanessan Hospital. He wanted to miss the confusion downtown. Something was happening there: A fan of light stood up from the city like a sun about to rise, or one that had set, causing him to envision what was happening on Rue Paris and in the square and upon the wide steps of the magnificent opera house. The city—all of French Vietnam, for that matter—seemed to display a delirious futility, as if by singing and dancing it could hold back the inexorable march of what was to come.

Jack Sperek was right. Somewhere it had all changed while no one was watching. The French had been the users and were now the used. They had trapped themselves, so busy with manipulating that they had failed to see who really held the strings. Now there was no way out but to lose the war, and they had unconsciously gone so far in that direction that they could do it willingly now without being aware.

When the jeep was parked, he went directly to Dukemire's ward. He was worried about the pilot, and wanted to speak to his doctor. Dukemire had been asleep that morning when McCall arrived, but an orderly soon came and awakened him to dress his wounds. McCall was allowed to watch, but the young orderly warned him that Dukemire was not permitted to speak, nod, or do anything that would cause his throat to flex. Metal braces with thick cotton pads were on either side of his head. McCall leaned close to observe the proceedings, and to give the pilot an after-action report, commending him on his courageous performance while he examined the wounds. The legs looked just fine; both bullets had missed bones, and the flesh would quickly heal. But he was not sure about the throat. The jagged piece of shrapnel had barely missed the jugular, slipping alongside the larynx, cutting a small groove in the white cartilage, threatening the connecting nerves before bouncing off the spine. Other than exposing the hidden parts, the wound itself did not look bad. But what worried McCall was the fear in Dukemire's eyes, as if the kid might have tried to speak and discovered that it was impossible. The major did not want to chance upsetting him, but he did want to talk to his doctor.

He passed a man in pajamas and robe on a bench near a kerosene lamp. Beside him were battered crutches. He was smoking and pondering a bandaged stub where a foot had recently been. McCall glanced at the stub and braced himself to receive the eyes, but they rose only as far as his feet, watching his boots walk past.

He turned into Dukemire's ward, and had walked halfway to his bed when he suddenly stopped and looked around to be sure he had the right place. The man who had no jaws was there, as well as the one with no legs. Across the aisle was the unconcerned kid with half a head of blond hair, missing a small piece of skull, but nowhere was anyone who looked like John Dukemire.

"Can I help you, sir?" said a black orderly. He was very tall, slightly bent, and spoke thickly in French as if his tongue were numb.

"Yes, I am looking for my men. One was in this ward this morning."

"The two Americans are gone, sir. They came for them half an hour ago."

"*Who* came for them?"

"American medics in an ambulance. They said they were evacuating them to Saigon."

"That's impossible! Who were they?"

"I do not know, sir. They were Americans in civilian clothes, and wore white smocks like mine. They arrived in an ambulance from the airfield."

"Did they show you any papers?"

"No, sir, and I did not ask. They were Americans, and seemed to know what they were doing. They knew the men were here, and clearly had authority. Perhaps you should speak to my superior, sir."

"Perhaps so," McCall said, trying to understand what had happened. He had made no report to Saigon, but it seemed that the French must have passed the word, maybe hospital management wanting to lighten the load.

A telephone beside the orderly's station began to groan. "Excuse me, sir." He walked away on long legs. After a moment he motioned to McCall. "For you, sir."

He reached for the phone. "Major McCall."

"Pearbone here," came the curt reply. "Glad I found you, Marsh. I just heard from Saigon. My source couldn't check on other men in your outfit, but you and Sergeant Winslow are both listed as missing in action. In Korea."

He drove as fast as he dared, his mind racing as he tried to deny the obvious, that he and Winslow—perhaps the entire outfit—had been sent on a one-way mission. Each time the gray image of Ezra Smith came forth, he shoved it back. The man had used up all his excuses. There were possible explanations, but none good enough when it came to the lives of his men. He focused on his driving, the resistance of the clutch, the precise feel of each gear, the roadway ahead, and the sound of the motor. When he turned off the highway, then again toward Lam Du, he began to check for aircraft. There was nothing on the runway or the adjacent taxiways or even the ramp beyond. He weaved down Depot Road, feeling sick enough to vomit.

He found Cody West beneath a bulb on the steps of the orderly room, looking confused and worried and angry. He walked out when the jeep left the road, then jumped back to avoid the skid. "Are they gone?" McCall said.

West threw a vacant salute. "Yes, sir," he said. "About twenty minutes ago. I was over at First Company, and a French guy named Christian who speaks English saw it and came and told me. He said Duke and Mano were in a lot of pain, but the medics didn't seem to care. They were in a hurry, and wanted to know where I was. Asked for me by name. Christian said he was pissed because of the way they were acting, and wouldn't tell them anything. Then he came to find me, but when I got over here the C-47 was taxiing away."

"Then they've already taken off?" McCall said, hopelessly scanning the field.

"Yes, sir. They're gone."

McCall slammed the wheel. "Damn, damn, *damn!*"

"What's happening, sir?"

McCall stepped from the jeep. "Pack your gear, West. Two sets of clothes, two days' rations, web gear, rifle, bayonet, and ammo. Here are the keys to the container. Get a half-dozen grenades. Be back here in ten minutes, and don't talk to anybody."

"Yes, sir!" West charged toward his tent. When he returned, McCall was feeding a small batch of papers into a flaming drum. West threw his duffel into the jeep, then hurried over to McCall with his rifle. "Ready, sir," he said. He tossed the keys, a glimmer in the firelight. McCall snagged them by reflex.

From where he stood, McCall could see the shapes of the two battered aircraft framed against some hangar lights. Even the helicopter that was still whole looked deficient in flat silhouette, its blades tied and cocked at a steep angle. Strangely, for the rush of the moment, it brought to mind the childhood rhyme:

> *Birds with broken wings*
> *Can yet do many things*
> *Like peck and claw and cry*
> *And pierce the wicked eye.*

"Can your bird fly?" he said.

"Yes, sir," West replied.

"Do you think you can land at the farm?"

West was shocked. "Without getting shot? I don't know, sir."

"You need to try. Is there a place to land?"

Cody thought a moment. The area near the house was covered with trees, but the clearing in front of the porch was probably large enough. "I think so," he said.

"Okay. You're going to need to land blacked-out. In fact, leave here the same way, and don't call the tower for clearance."

"The radios are shot out, sir."

"Good. When you land, try to do something to hide the ship from the air. Stay there until I come or send word. It might be a few days."

"What if something happens to you, sir?"

McCall gave a twisted smile. He liked this straightforward kid. "Don't trust anybody but Captain Sarot or a U.S. diplomat named Walter Pearbone. Nobody else."

"What about Mr. Sperek, sir?"

"No. Not Sperek. Sarot or Pearbone, that's it." He paused and took a breath. "Now listen close, West. You're going to be on your own for a while. Whatever happens, use your head, think it through, then do what you've got to do."

"Can you tell me what's going on, sir?"

"Somebody's trying to kill us, that's all I know."

"Who is it, sir? And why?"

"I don't know. Now get going. If you can't land where you won't be seen, don't come back here. Set down by the road. I'll be along directly, and we'll think of something. If I don't see you, I'll know everything's okay. Now move."

Cody stood stock still. "Are Duke and Mano dead, sir?"

McCall set his mouth. "I'm afraid they probably are."

Cody West stared in the direction the airplane had gone, then back at the major. His lips moved without words while McCall remembered earlier thoughts about pilots and soldiers, and about commitment. "Go on, son," he said. "We've got to get moving."

West retrieved and shouldered his gear, then hurried toward the flight line while McCall fetched some items of his own. When he returned, the blades of the chopper were untied, and he could just see the red glow of a flashlight in the cockpit. Then the engine coughed and came to life, the blades soon beating along in an urgent swish. McCall turned toward the lighted window of Major Legère's shack, considering what he now had to do. He watched West make his departure, checked that his .45 had a round in the chamber, then drove the short distance through the gates of Lam Du.

A radio was playing inside. When he knocked, the volume was lowered, then turned completely off. "*Oui, qui est là?*"

"Marsh McCall."

There was silence, then Legère said, "One moment."

McCall waited impatiently. It was almost 2200, and Legère was probably ready for bed. He listened for sounds of escape. But whatever else he might have become, Legère was no coward. He opened the door, his face a mask of false righteousness and real shame. "Yes?" he said stiffly. He was dressed, but wore no visible weapon.

"We need to talk," said McCall.

"I'm sorry, Major, but it is late. I will be happy to see you tomorrow." He started to close the door, but stopped when McCall moved his hand toward his .45. He backed away and motioned him inside, then toward a chair.

Legère's room was neat and unpretentious, a soldier's domain much smaller than it appeared outside, the rest of the building occupied by administrative offices beyond a solid wall. There was a simple cot with a thin mattress, two straight wooden chairs, a small table, shelves and lockers and books. On a cabinet at one end sat a hot plate, a coffeepot, and the radio. McCall was surprised. In his position at Lam Du, Legère could have arranged every convenience.

They sat on opposite sides of the table, Legère staring blandly, more ashamed than frightened. McCall went straight to it. "I'm not going to kill you for murdering my men," he said.

"I do not have to take that kind of talk! Leave here at once!"

McCall drew his .45. "Shut your mouth, Legère. I'd just as soon pull the trigger. But I need your help, and you need mine. Somebody has been planning your death for a long time. What I have to say might save you—I don't know—but you're dead otherwise, and me with you. If that's all I'm facing, we can finish this right now. Keep both hands on the table."

Legère stiffened and looked straight at McCall. "Say what you have to say, then get out of my quarters," he said.

"I was sent here to find you," McCall said, "to discover you as a black market supplier and a collaborator. You were assigned to watch over me to make it easy for me to watch you. I didn't know this when I got here—I'm part of the same plan. As soon as I arrived, little events like the staged incident at Haiphong began to occur so I'd be led in the right direction."

Legère had settled into a lidded slump like a lectured child, waiting only for time to pass, but now his eyes flickered. McCall continued, "I suspect there is a big organization involved, of which you are only a small, unconscious part."

"This is absurd," Legère said.

"I wish it were. The most obvious place to look is among your superiors. How high up, I don't know, but they knew that Ezra Smith was sending me up here to snoop around, and they knew it would be a good time to clean house and pin everything on you."

Legère smiled and shook his head. "This is an incredible fantasy," he said.

341

"Not quite. Everything will be proved within the next couple of days. If I am correct in my assumptions, Colonel de Matrin should be sending word tonight or tomorrow for you to come see him." When Legère looked startled, McCall said, "He's already done it?"

"Yes," he answered with hesitation. "But it's merely—"

"It's merely to present you with all the evidence before you disappear. You get the blame for everything, and he retires with complete impunity."

"But I don't see..."

"Neither do I. There's still a lot I don't know. But it would certainly explain the way you got your job."

Legère was shocked, but his thoughts were moving quickly in the right direction. "You think something was planned that long ago?"

"Looks like it."

Legère shook his head and laughed, going now the other way. "No, I'm sorry, Major McCall. You have an amazing story, but I cannot accept it. Now, if you don't mind..."

"I don't know if I can get out of here alive or not, Legère, but I do know that I can kill you without being punished. You're the sole known contact with Ou River Traders. Once you're gone, there's nothing left to discover. Whether I kill you or they do, the results are the same. The pressure will then be off me. Your life depends on me, Legère, and mine may depend on you."

An earlier image returned to McCall, and he saw a way that it might be used. "Have you ever discovered the nest of a bird that roosts on the ground?" he said.

"What? No, I cannot say that I have."

"If there are eggs or chicks, the parent bird will flutter across the ground pretending to have a broken wing in hopes of leading a predator away. *You*, Legère, are the bird with the broken wing. The difference is that the wing really *is* broken, but you don't seem to know it. The only thing left to figure out is who is still sitting in the nest."

"I fail to see—"

"As I said, I was sent to find you. Apparently, it is now considered that I've done that. It's time to wrap things up. I'm sure you'll know more after your meeting with Colonel de Matrin. When is it?"

342

"Tomorrow, at my convenience. I had planned to go in the afternoon."

McCall thought a moment. "Make it as late as possible."

Legère's face was now pale, fatigued with knowledge. "You said that we needed to help each other," he said. "Just what do you propose?"

"For me, I don't yet know. I'll get word to you—"

"Where are you going?"

"I'll be in touch. For you, I'll help you get to Dien Bien Phu, if you're willing to go. If you can survive there, things might work out here by the time you get back. That may not sound too good, but if you stay here, I think you'll be dead before the week is out."

"Dien Bien Phu does not frighten me, Major McCall. It is the kind of thing I came to Indochina to do. If I had been allowed to be a soldier, I might have been dead by now, but never would I have ended up in such disgrace. If what you say is true, my only concern is that I might be prevented from going." He paused to stare at the table. "Nothing could possibly happen there that could be as bad... as bad as being revealed for what I am."

"I'm sure that Colonel de Matrin will agree."

"What kind of agreement can we have?"

"Only to help each other. You tell the colonel you want to go to Dien Bien Phu. I'll do everything to ensure that you make it onto a plane headed west."

Legère hesitated, then surged ahead. "I was forced to arrange the ambush," he said. "I guess you can only watch the dogs for so long..."

McCall's finger tightened on the trigger. Trusting himself no longer, he stood and went out the door.

The aircraft was worse than he remembered. When he later wondered how he could forget so much in just one day, he would understand why war stories are never true. He knew the certain bits that he had seen—Two Acres and Whitney in the mud, Cowan flipping upside down and burning, Kinney hanging limp, Dukemire knocking heads, bloody cottage cheese from Rankin sliding slowly over Mano's arms—but these were photographs surrounded by va-

343

por. Only faintly had he known the disintegration of the cockpit, the rattle and whir of flying pieces. His aircraft had taken some rounds....

Now he sat and fanned the red flashlight around, staring as if he had taken a seat in someone else's war. There were bullet holes and jagged rips all over. The only instrument that worked was the needle-and-ball, and even it was useless without panel lights. There was no need to worry about departing or landing blacked-out, or not calling the tower; nothing would work. Nonetheless, the fluids were still up, the blades still went around, and the engine sounded strong. Surely the bird could make the short hop to the farm.

Beyond the ramp and the drainage ditch stood several men in a dim arrangement of jeep lights in the assembly area along Depot Road. The plans for First Company had apparently changed, probably because of weather at Dien Bien Phu. Three of the six C-47s scheduled to take them on their one-way trip were now parked to one side in the darkness. Men were working around them, but it was clear they would not be departing soon. From the time he had just spent with them, Cody knew the frustration of Pepe and his friends, going crazy all over again as they waited to learn their fate.

Just after sunset Pepe had come with some others to invite him to their tent to share their last night at Lam Du. The evening was warm and humid, and called for sitting outside, but the tent drew them into its closeness where a dim bulb set faces aglow, igniting the smoke in churning illumination. The walls closed in like night around a campfire, and the sagging roof compelled them to sit on the floor. They opened the flaps and formed a loose ring, and talked and told stories. When the generator failed they made a lantern of kerosene and sand in a can pierced by bayonets, and the dancing slots of light lent action to their words. Cody listened to the language he could not understand, and he laughed when they laughed. He saw the light on the faces and thought of Rankin and the others, then Dukemire and Mano, and knew that these men were no different. Then an officer came and made a stern little speech, and drew from behind him a bottle of wine. They poured to tin cans while Cody sat back, but when it was seen that he had been missed they found another can and every man tipped his cup until Cody had a share. Then each made a short toast. Cody was last, and he was unprepared because they would not understand, and because by then his vision was blurred. He studied the faces, the wine in his cup, the faces again. "I wish I were going with you," he said. They all touched cups and the ring of doomed men tossed down the dark wine.

The scene would stay a long while. He rolled the throttle until the tachometer in his head said thirty-one hundred, and waited until a B-26 at the end of the active runway began its roaring run. Then he brought the durable little craft to a hover before departing directly across the tents of First Company.

He immediately knew he had made a mistake, forgetting how black a night could be with thin clouds, no moon, and no electricity. Back home, it was not uncommon to cross twenty-mile tracts without seeing a single light, but that was in a vacant land, and flying with functioning instruments far from the ground. Below him now were thousands of people, but the land between Gia Lam and Hanoi was as black as if totally empty. He watched the lights of Hanoi rise from a single line until they were a tilted plane as viewed from three hundred feet. He aimed the aircraft toward Moni's house, then realized something else: The farm was equipped with electric bulbs, but they almost certainly did not work. That was the reason for the oil lamp on the porch, and why he could never spot Moni's house at night from Lam Du. He fervently hoped that Handsome Dan would be awake and sober, and that he would try to comprehend before he opened fire.

He missed the farm on the first pass, but when he reached the lights at the approach to Doumer Bridge, he turned and mentally measured the distance, then began a gradual descent, watching the lights of Gia Lam for perspective. He leveled off at what seemed like two hundred feet, but still could see nothing. He turned and retraced his route again and again, adjusting on each pass. There was still no sign of Handsome Dan Blackweed or his rundown farm.

Finally, a jeep emerged from Lam Du, weaving down Depot Road before turning toward town upon the highway. Now Cody could better judge his speed and height above the ground, and he passed the jeep, turned, and overtook it, descending to less than a hundred feet. When he heard two short bleats of the vehicle's horn, and the headlights blinked, he knew he had done all that he could. He established an orbit overhead, hoping that it was McCall.

When the jeep came to the drive, it turned in and stopped at the chain so that the path was illuminated where it disappeared into the trees. Now Cody had his fix, and he moved directly across the house, very low and at little more than a hover above the invisible trees. Almost immediately, a dim light appeared, and he could see the shape of the veranda. Then Moni's father walked out from beneath the roof, a lantern in one hand and his rifle in the other. He lowered the lantern, then stared up at the sound of the helicopter, squinting at the dust and wind. He gripped his rifle with both hands and shook it in warning.

"Don't shoot!" Cody yelled down, hoping that his voice could be heard above the engine's roar. He guided the aircraft in a small orbit around the tiny clearing, still unable to see the boughs of the trees directly, but beginning to establish a perimeter of silhouetted leaves. Blackweed glanced down the drive toward the jeep, then back at the aircraft, and it suddenly seemed he understood. He hurried into the house and quickly returned with a flashlight. Still holding his rifle, he walked all around the opening, displaying trees and limbs with the beam of light. Then he positioned himself out of the way, and motioned that it was okay to land. He swept the light around, displaying the various limits, then turned his back at the last moment against the blast of dust and debris as the bird touched down.

Safely down, Cody took a deep breath and rolled the throttle off, maintaining a close eye on Moni's father. Something was strange about the man. Then he realized that the mustache was gone. When Blackweed cautiously gripped his rifle, Cody yelled, "Don't shoot, you old coot!" He had to smile at his little rhyme, particularly because he knew that he was not understood. When he shut the throttle off, and there was just the sound of blades swishing overhead and a soft grind from the tail rotor, he added, "Hello, Weed. Great to see you. How come you're not completely shit-faced staggering drunk?" He raised the collective to slow the blades.

When the rotor stopped, Weed stepped slowly up to his door, studied Cody carefully, then solemnly proclaimed, "I will get drunk tomorrow. Moni' is completely correct. You are a very foolish young man. What are you doing here?"

Cody stared, his mouth wide and suddenly dry. Blackweed's accent was strong, but his knowledge of the language seemed at least as good as Cody's. "You speak English," he said.

"Of course. Who did you think taught Moni'?" He looked

around at the riddled cockpit. "Why are you here? And why you don't repair your aircraft? It looks like rubbish."

"I ran into some old friends of yours," Cody said as he unbuckled and stepped out. Then he remembered McCall. "I'm sorry about what I said, but I was getting even for you shooting at me. I need to ask a really big favor—can I stay here a few days? I need a place to hide."

The man was still staring at the wreckage of the cockpit. "Yes," he said. "You can stay as long as you wish."

"Great. I'll be right back." He ran down the dark drive to the last of the trees, and waved to McCall that all was okay. When the jeep was gone, he returned to the house more carefully, unable to see the ground at all in the tunnel of trees. He found Moni's father in his chair, the lantern on its hook overhead.

"Next time you do that," the man said, "carry a flashlight. There are banded kraits here, vipers that kill in only a few seconds. They like the driveway at night because of the rats that come to eat in the paddies."

Cody sat down, still embarrassed, not knowing what to say. In the lantern's light the lip was small and pale and strangely naked. Cody expected many questions, but the old man—who did not look so old anymore, and no longer resembled his father—merely studied him with interest. "Why didn't you say that you spoke English?" Cody asked.

"Because I was once like you and did foolish things. It was my turn for the silent laugh. Do not feel too bad. Without foolish young men, life would be dull, but without foolish old men, things would only be better."

"Have you heard anything from Moni'?"

"Yes. I have a note." He felt his shirt pockets, then leaned and drew it from his hip. "My daughter is two miles away, and she writes me a letter." He unfolded and scanned the single sheet. "She is staying at Lanessan now."

"I know. I saw her yesterday."

"Ah. When you went for your chin? How did she look?"

"She looked just fine. She looked tired, but she looked just fine."

"She is a good nurse," said her father. "It is hard for me to believe she is old enough for that . . . or old enough for someone like you to come and pester." He scanned the note, and his face grew tired.

"Things are worse at Dien Bien Phu," he said. "The helicopter unit that they moved across to Laos has been all but wiped out. The Viet Minh allow them to land and pick up the wounded, then as they leave they fire in unison and shoot them out of the sky." He lowered the letter. "She says she will be home tomorrow by sunset, but does not know how long she can stay. That means she will be leaving again immediately." He sighed. His head shook faintly, and a quick shudder went through him. "If this goes on, I am much afraid of what might happen."

Cody heard only the words of a worried parent. "She'll be okay," he said.

Her father nodded absently. "This Dan Blackweed that you call me..."

Cody cringed.

"He was a cowboy, was he not?"

"I guess so."

"Then why do you give me that name?"

"I got confused. He was a little before my time. I thought he was a bad guy in the silent movies."

"Oh, no. It was later than that. He was a hero. He always won the fight and always got the lady. Did you think I look like him?"

"Yeah. With the mustache. Actually, you looked like my dad, and he looked like Handsome Dan. It was something I called him when I was mad."

He thought a moment. "Then that explains a few things," he said.

"It does?"

"Yes. Moni' told me about your father's crash."

"How did she know?"

"Her aunt told her, then she told me."

"How come everybody is suddenly so interested in my personal life?"

"Maybe people are interested in *you*. But that is what happens when you let go of old secrets. Now I understand some things. Did you think I was a ghost?"

"Maybe. I don't know. You did look a lot alike."

"That unfortunate man," he mumbled, thinking again. "Do not be too concerned about your father."

"Are you kidding? I was responsible for his death."

"So is he now to be responsible for yours? You are here because of him, him and the dead uncle you admire. They prepared the way, but left you little choice. It is every man's job to bury his father. Most do it twice—once in the ground, once in the head. My father had a stroke. He was alive and useless for many years, so by the time he died the burial for me was complete. Yours happened the other way. I think it is time that you buried your father. Whatever regrets he may have had in life, I do not think that you were one."

Cody blinked and kept his eyes turned away. "I really am sorry about the name," he said. "So what's your real one?"

"My name?" He thought a moment. "I think my name is Handsome Dan Blackweed," he said with a smile. "I always win the fight, and I always get the lady." He held the smile as long as he could, and when it finally slipped away he looked miserable.

"How long have you been here?"

"I came to Indochina a young man like you in 1920. For years I drove trucks and heavy equipment, building dams and roads and the endless canals . . ."

Blackweed seemed to welcome the chance to use his English, and to talk to someone at last who had not heard all his stories. He spoke without interruption for almost two hours. The young pilot listened and watched the path that the C-47s would take if First Company made its flight into sudden battle. He thought about Dukemirc and Mano, bandaged and helpless, flailing uselessly at the sky. Then the breeze stopped and the mosquitoes came and drove them inside.

"You can sleep in Moni's bed," her father said as he reached for the lantern. But a sudden flash from the city stopped his hand, and as both men turned with eyes wide, a red-orange blossom of fire churned into the sky above Hanoi. A few seconds after it disappeared, there came a low crack and a thundering boom that rattled the glass in the windows. It was much too far to say for sure what had blown, but the blast seemed to rise in the direction of the Café Ho Tay. Soon they heard the moving wail of sirens.

Chapter Twenty

"SHE'S OKAY, but the Café Ho Tay is completely destroyed."

"You're sure she's all right?"

"I just came from there. She's fine. Her house was a bit jumbled by the blast. Everything glass is broken, and the roof and rooms on that side are damaged, but by extraordinary fortune she was in her study on the opposite side. She had only been home a few minutes."

"Any official ideas who did it?"

"Nothing they'll discuss," said Pearbone. "The gendarmes believe someone was inside when she locked up. They say it could have been anyone. I think the field is much smaller than that, but Su is a person who makes enemies by simply minding her business. Women hate her, men love her jealously, the police suspect her success, and other businesses complain because every important soul who comes to Hanoi wants to meet Su Letei and be served at her restaurant. Her only rightful enemies are the Legionnaires, but they earned their place with her. They seem the most likely, but it does not matter. The responsible party will never be found. As with all matters Indochinese, the truth is not convenient."

McCall sat back and closed his eyes. It had been an endless night, and still another was ahead. Walter Pearbone had been at the house when McCall arrived with his gear, but once the major's jeep was ensconced where the Buick was normally housed, the diplomat had returned to the embassy residence for the night. McCall left a light on in the kitchen, then sat in the dim study with coffee, going over every detail of his time in Hanoi, writing it down and burning the notes. Taking the puzzle apart piece by piece, he found that it could be reassembled more than one way, each presenting a different view. All would depend upon which he chose to believe.

All at once the unlighted room was ablaze, filled with the brightest sun, the house shuddering with thudding concussion. He rushed to the window with his carbine, then quickly upstairs from room to room until he had a view of the ruins and flames of the Café Ho Tay. The trees all around were burned bare. He went downstairs, quietly out the back and along the shadowy drive. Most of the neighborhood was awake, and lights were on next door. A man, his wife and daughter, and a very old man with a cane were on the porch in their gowns. Soon an automobile came down the street, its windows lowered, the self-appointed messenger shouting, *"Le Café Ho Tay! Le Café Ho Tay!"*

"What a shame," McCall heard the woman say with unmistakable acid, but her husband was silent. The family watched a little longer before going inside.

McCall was in turmoil, wanting to check on Su Letei, knowing that it would only expose him to his enemies, and that the blast may have been staged for that purpose. His face was a bitter scowl as he went inside.

For the remainder of the night he worried about Su Letei and searched for a reasonable plan that could get him and Cody West out of Hanoi alive. When the coffee could no longer hold him awake, he sat with his rifle in his lap and took brief, fitful naps that left him exhausted. Just before dawn he slept forty minutes. When he awoke, mossy-mouthed and tired, the problem had grown to unexpected dimensions, but he thought he perceived a solution. He made fresh coffee, and sat grimly examining what could only emerge through sleep, the voice he could no longer deny. By the time Walter Pearbone arrived, the course before him was set.

"I have to return to the compound in a little while," Pearbone said. "Would you care for some toast and juice?"

McCall opened his eyes. "You bet," he said. He stretched and looked out at the gardens while Pearbone went to the kitchen, reminded again how sad it must be to be giving it up. He got a flash of what the house would look like in a few years—packed to the rafters with communized paupers—and knew the depth of Pearbone's grief.

"They're putting on three more birds tonight to accommodate volunteers to Dien Bien Phu," Pearbone said across the hall. "They are arriving from everywhere now, a few at a time. Nothing made it out last night—the valley was buried in fog—so I suppose they will all be going together."

McCall was about to join him when the door chimes rang. Pearbone glanced across, motioned him back, wiped his hand through a towel and went to the door. The voices were muffled, then Pearbone's voice grew loud. "I'm sorry, Lieutenant Jacobé, Major McCall is not here."

"Excuse me, sir, but I believe he is. It is imperative that I speak to him immediately."

McCall reached for the carbine, then stood listening against the wall.

"...mistaken. Now, if you don't mind, I am in the middle of preparing breakfast."

"Mr. Pearbone, with respect, I refuse to be sent away. I know he is here, I watched the place much of the night. It will be better if it is I who speaks to him rather than whoever comes after me."

There was a pause, then Pearbone abruptly said, "Very well, come in, Lieutenant. You can see for yourself that he is not here, then I can finish my breakfast. But I assure you your insolence will be reported." McCall could hear footsteps in the hall. "Please wait here in the study a moment," Pearbone said, "then I will show you around the house."

The instant that Solo Jacobé stepped into the room, McCall caught him with a choppy butt stroke to the head, making a sound like a mishandled melon. The lieutenant was down with a loud grunt and cry, his glasses hurled across the room and shattered. "Monsieur Marsh!" he groaned.

"Spread 'em!"

Jacobé complied and McCall relieved him of his sidearm. The vice-consul stood in the hall, his anger at the lieutenant replaced with distaste for the violence. When McCall gave him a nod he returned to the kitchen.

"Monsieur Marsh," Solo Jacobé said as McCall grabbed him by the collar. Blood was oozing from one ear.

"On your feet, you little prick." McCall shoved him toward a chair.

"I had forgotten how rough you play," Solo Jacobé said, holding his head and moaning. He looked up with pained amusement. When he saw that he was bleeding, he withdrew a handkerchief and held it against his ear. "But I suppose I deserved that. I knew you would have it figured out by now. I am truly sorry about the glass. I got a little too close."

"The glass? Well, I'll be..."

"You did not know?" Jacobé briefly closed his eyes. "I have made another mistake." He dabbed at his ear, wincing with pain. "I only wanted you to think that someone was trying to kill you," he said. "Someone was, and someone still is, but *they* did not want you to know. I also knew that if you believed that someone wanted you dead, you would begin to use your skills to learn why."

"Did you ever consider just walking up and telling me?"

"That was impossible. You were being watched too closely. It was important to both of us that we have nothing to do with each other. But I had to make you aware. Also, you were not yet ready to believe."

"You waited long enough to get involved."

"Not at all, Monsieur Marsh. I was here from the beginning, *before* the beginning. I did not know it would be you that they sent, and I underestimated other things as well, but I am the reason you came to Hanoi."

"Keep talking," McCall said. When Solo Jacobé glanced toward the hallway, he added, "He's one of the few I trust."

"It is not a matter of trust," the lieutenant said. "I am sure that Mr. Pearbone knows a great deal more than he ever admits, but I see no need for him to know how much *I* know, and how much I tell you. It can benefit no one."

Walter Pearbone sensed the hush in the conversation. He went out through the kitchen door that let onto the veranda, then moved through the gardens, snapping wilted heads from flowers with quick mercy.

"It was I who went to Colonel Smith to get this whole thing started," said Solo Jacobé.

McCall blinked and raised a brow, then sat on a sofa where he could watch the lieutenant and see Walter Pearbone through the windows. He relaxed his grip on the carbine, but held it across his lap. "Then you arranged the incident in Haiphong?"

"No. That was Colonel de Matrin, to get you started on the discovery of Major Legère. That's why they let your pilot escape with the jeep even though he had killed one of de Matrin's men."

"He killed a man? *Dukemire?*" McCall frowned into space.

"This thing is very large," said Solo Jacobé. "I once thought I could destroy it all. Then it came to me that what was being planned was the exposure of Major Legère so that the others could escape."

"The others?"

Jacobé paused. "Colonel de Matrin...and his partner, Roach Harman."

"The Korean King."

"What is that?"

"Nothing. So no real surprises, in other words."

"No," Jacobé said quietly, his eyes briefly on the floor. "No real surprises. Colonel de Matrin started the system, then Roach Harman forced a partnership. The arrangement was good for them both because of overlapping security and Harman's access to aircraft traveling to Laos, Hong Kong, Taiwan, and the Philippines. They've made millions together."

"Why did you go to Colonel Smith?"

Jacobé seemed to wrestle with a decision. "I was running out of time," he said, "and I was afraid that I might have misjudged de Matrin's intentions. I thought that if Colonel Smith sent someone, that person might be the one to identify Major Legère's part."

"And that's all? From what you've said, that would have happened anyway."

"I hoped for more, and I still do. When I saw that it was you he sent, I was excited and scared—scared that you might be assassinated like Major Tunnell. I think that he may have been sent here for a similar purpose, but without my involvement. In any case, his death gave me the idea to go to Colonel Smith."

"Why couldn't you have done this job yourself?"

"Too many important people involved. My unit has long been

ordered to discover nothing. We issue empty reports. So I have been working alone. I have had good luck and bad. I now have a trail that leads directly to Roach Harman. But he and de Matrin and others between are protected. Too much damage would result from their discovery, too much embarrassment. The careers of other men would fall right along with them, perhaps even to include the current government of France. So all protect the criminals because all are at the same time protecting themselves. The war is about to be over, and everything will be forgotten. Major Legère is a token, but he is the only one with direct exposure. The others will be more difficult, and could escape entirely."

McCall eyed the lieutenant, certain he was leaving things out. The Solo Jacobé he had known, the determined kid they called Lapeste, would have *never* given up, no matter what obstacles lay in his path, and McCall did not believe he was giving up now. But could he trust him completely?

"So you put the wheels in motion, but since that time you've just been sitting back watching?"

"Not exactly sitting, but my part has been unimportant. To answer your real question, Monsieur Marsh, I had no other choice."

"At the price of my men being killed?"

"I did not expect that part. But if it had come to that, yes, I would have done the same. At the price of the lives of your men. Even at the possible price of you being killed, my friend. Thousands of my countrymen have uselessly died. If I could do something to reduce that figure, and if it included watching you die, then yes, I would probably do that thing. But I would give my own life more easily."

McCall said nothing, acknowledging Solo's honesty, aware that had their positions been reversed he would have willingly sent Solo Jacobé to his death. There was nothing else to consider.

"Okay. De Matrin got careless, and you found his tracks. But how were you able to get evidence on Harman? He seems awfully well protected."

Jacobé diverted his eyes, then looked over his shoulder to check on the position of Pearbone. Finally he looked at McCall. "I made a deal with Chang Wu," he said. When McCall simply stared, he continued. "That was the only way. He knew all the answers, and it was to his advantage to cooperate. He knew that Harman was about to retire, but he also knew that he would never let go completely. It was a way for him to thin the ranks, to be in complete control of the new market when France has lost and the United States sends troops. For my part, Chang Wu was the only one with real power that I could use. And if it later worked out that Chang Wu should fall as well, then all the better."

McCall knew now that he had been right about Solo Jacobé's not giving up. And he knew that he could trust him. Something was still missing from his story, but once again he agreed with the lieutenant's method; had their roles been reversed, he would have left that part out himself.

"I believe there is a way that Harman can be had," he said. When Jacobé's eyes widened, he knew that the lieutenant's plan was not complete. "We can talk about that later," he said. "Meanwhile, I have made an agreement with Major Legère." Jacobé's eyes bulged. "I spoke with him last night, explained his position. I think he believed me. We are meeting again tonight, then he is going to join the volunteers to Dien Bien Phu. I promised nothing beyond helping him get that far."

"But why would you do such a thing?"

"Because I needed an ally, and because Legère is not worth it. Once his part is exposed, everything will be heaped on him. The more this happens, the cleaner everyone else becomes, making further prosecution just that much more difficult. The perfect scenario for those at the top would be for Legère to die."

"Which may happen at Dien Bien Phu."

"It may, but it's guaranteed if he stays here. They would probably make it look like suicide, then go public with enough evidence to link everything to him."

"But why are you meeting tonight?"

"I think there will be others there."

Jacobé pondered a moment. "You are not telling me everything," he said. But when his eyes met McCall's, there was too much guilt in his own for him to pursue it. "You are taking a terrible chance."

"I'm dead if I don't."

"That is not enough. You need a backup. What if Legère arranged a trap with Colonel de Matrin? They don't yet know about me, so they probably assume that if they kill you the entire case would be dropped. Then all that de Matrin would have to do is kill Major

Legère at the same time. It would be easy for him to make up a story to explain it, and he would be believed. You've got to let me be there. Does Legère know the time and place?"

"Not yet."

"Then let me speak to Legère. I will tell him only that you and I are old friends, and that you asked me to deliver a message. I will give him incorrect information—an address nearby, a time slightly later. That will dilute the potential a bit. In any case, I will be there with my rifle."

"What about your glasses?" McCall said, glancing toward the shattered fragments.

"They were only plain glass. It is time I stopped wearing them anyway."

McCall studied Solo Jacobé. No need to acknowledge that his life would again be in Lapeste's hands, just as on the day with the Germans. And if things worked out another way—the way he believed that they might—Lapeste could save him once more. "Okay," he said, "here's what we'll do . . ."

"I'm sorry," said Walter Pearbone when the lieutenant was gone. "There seemed no other way. Has your position been compromised?"

"I don't think so. I knew that boy when he was just a kid in the Resistance."

"Can you trust him now?"

"I'm going to have to," McCall said. Jacobé's story made sense, and it meshed completely with the facts.

Pearbone returned to the kitchen, threw out the cold toast, and began anew. Then they carried everything out back. They ate and drank the coffee in silence, watching the morning move through the gardens. A brief shower had crossed over the city in the hour before dawn, washing the air and stirring the sweet rotting fragrance of soil. As the sun made its climb and a morning breeze moved, the damp tops of bamboo sprinkled sparklets of gold.

"Have you come up with a way to escape your predicament?" Pearbone said.

"I don't know." McCall lit a smoke. "I need you to do two things for me," he said. He studied the diplomat's face, knowing he would find nothing there. Pearbone gave him a bland look. "I need you to try to find Eber Walloon. I have no idea where he might be right now. Simply tell him that I've got what he's been looking for."

Pearbone sipped his coffee and seemed to consider. "There is no need to speak in code," he said. "It will not be difficult to locate Eber. He is in Saigon today. He can probably be here by tonight." When McCall simply stared with unstated questions, Pearbone continued. "Eber Walloon has become my access to the world—the one that in recent months has been deliberately kept from me."

McCall was stunned, certain that information flowed both ways.

"Eber Walloon is the one who learned that you were listed as missing in action in Korea. With that alone he may have saved your life. He also knows a great deal about your particular area of interest. Ever since the experience at *Time* he has made the study of Roach Harman a secret obsession. He is a man you can trust, and he will not betray your confidence."

"There's one more thing," McCall said. "I need you to get word to Ezra Smith right away. It'll involve some details—and I'll write it all down—but basically I need you to tell him that I'm meeting tonight with the man I came here to find, and to send me some help that he can absolutely trust."

"I can have no connection with this," Pearbone said.

"Of course. Just relay the message. Say that I came to you because I needed to get it there fast, and I wanted to avoid the possibility of French interception. I'll be out of here tonight."

The old turtle eyes moved over McCall, then out to examine the gardens. After a minute the vice-consul stood and began taking things to the kitchen.

Jack Sperek sat at his table, contemplating the basket of bread while his boots tapped below, mashing imaginary spiders. At a time when they should have been outside earning an honest living, the spiders in his house were more numerous than ever. He had developed a reflex for killing them, patting his boots about in random search so that they might not set up camp in his baggy pantlegs. The effort was not completely wasted; Dr. Sapeine had been gone only a few minutes when he felt the familiar pop and squish beneath one toe. But it might have been a roach.

A stab of pain interrupted his thoughts, and he braced himself, but what came instead was a moment of sliding vision as when he had been long without sleep. Soon he was able to relax. At least twice a day there was a much larger pain that he knew now to be his liver, a deep important pain that for hours after left a memory he could feel. Sometimes he dreamed about the pain and could not awake.

He was thinking about the bread and the disgusting descent his life had been and the hopeless void of what was ahead. Somehow it all seemed connected. He thought about luck and the way it attached itself like an odor. Good luck was as inexplicable as bad—though not always so easy to observe—but either type seemed to come the same way, in groups linked together for years. But he had no serious complaints; even in the worst of times when he had no idea how he would deal with the current catastrophe, he had never felt singled out for purpose.

He was convinced that what was happening to him now was his own fault. Dr. Sapeine had stood in his door, as pink and tired and disillusioned as God, and made the solemn proclamation. "What's the point, Doc?" Sperek asked, and the doctor said that he did not know. He left a sackful of pills, and with one small loaf of that morning's bread, went drearily on his way.

"What's the point?" Sperek muttered, thinking that what had happened was like the bite of a spider, unobserved until some part turned black and began to rot, and then it was too late. The news changed nothing except the end of the story. He still had a job to do—and it would have made no difference if the doctor had said he would die tomorrow. Sperek retrieved the note from beneath the cloth in the basket and reread his orders. It was good to have an assignment. This was especially true in view of the doctor's report. He was determined to take his time, pay careful attention to everything, and if he could not enjoy the experience itself he could at least examine its smallest detail. He made a slow, hideous grin as he considered the double deceit. What a pity that it would be unknown. The timing could not have been better, a positive sign of good luck.

He had been up and about all day, ever since the old woman arrived with the first basket of bread, amazed by the energy the note had released, feeling better than he had in weeks. The notes were not always there, or had not been for a very long time, but for the past two days they had come in the old way, alerting him to be ready for something soon. After reading this morning's note, he had showered and dressed in fresh clothes, then spent the day puttering around the house. Then the woman came with another basket and another note—all the details. Excited, he began to clean house. Twice he grew weak, and was forced to take naps, but was quickly up again, thinking about the necessities of the night ahead as he worked. He opened windows and swept and killed spiders, then carried accumulated trash to a burn pile in back. Cleaning the place made him feel so good that he stopped to eat and rest, then began again. He threw magazines and stacks of newspapers and worn-out clothes on the pile, then some old boots that had grown blue hair, and a bathrobe he never used. He moved slowly, and could not carry much, but he made trip after trip. Soon he was groping about for things to discard, and it made him laugh. He rested again, carefully set aside the dark clothes he would wear tonight, then took everything else from his closet and locker and heaped it upon the pile.

It required gasoline to get it going. He sat on the edge of the stoop and cleaned his rifle, considering the yellow words down the side of the jeep while black smoke boiled into the dusky air. He wondered how much McCall had guessed. Probably quite a bit, though that alone could not save him. He wished he could find the kid first, but it would turn out the same either way. He listened while the flames made a sound like a windblown flag or the speedy passage of something huge. He forced the patch down the spiraled hole until the riflings gleamed blue.

Handsome Dan Blackweed had been drinking since six. The sun was down and there was no sign of Moni'. The two of them sat on the porch and watched the borders of paddy water change. The frogs began their evening call.

Cody had spent the cool of the morning in her room upstairs, as much for the breeze and the leafy view of Gia Lam as for the sense of Moni'. He could not see the ramps past the clutter of tents, but little was happening at the airfield. Moni's room was large and simple and clean with windows on two sides and drapes of cheap linen. A painted curved-iron bed stood tall, thickly freckled with rust. A dresser, a washstand with pitcher and bowl, a worn-out rug, and a damaged armoire did not nearly fill the room. When Cody peeked inside the armoire, he was surprised to find nothing but a single white blouse and the flowered skirt. He quickly closed the door, ashamed.

In the afternoon he dozed on the porch or wandered around the yard, scuffing dirt and wishing McCall would come. He walked down the drive, but never so far that he might be seen. The snakes were all sleeping somewhere. He stuffed his hands in his pockets and studied the riddled bird as if it were in a museum. It did not scare him anymore, but it made him wonder why the others were dead and he was alive. The wound on his chin no longer bled, and he removed the gauze and clipped the gut like errant whiskers.

"I think I will never see her again."

When Cody looked, her father's eyes were welled with tears. There was only an inch left in the bottle. "Sure you will," he said. "She'll be along directly."

"I don't think so. I think she is already gone."

"Gone where?"

"To Dien Bien Phu."

Cody was shocked by the pronouncement. "That's crazy," he said, but recognized at once the potential. "The flights didn't go out last night," he added. "Not even the paratroops."

Blackweed turned his pitiful eyes. "Do you believe that is true?"

"I know it's true. I listened and watched all night. Nobody went out, not the flights going west. There must have been weather." Despite his confident tone, he was suddenly worried. He remembered Moni's words at the hospital, and knew that he could have misunderstood. Her father might be right, even if his timing was wrong. If the wounded could not be gotten out of Dien Bien Phu, then volunteer medics and nurses might parachute into the camp instead. It was a chilling possibility because Cody was sure it was the kind of thing that Moni' would be willing to do. He took care to hide his concern; it was hard enough to think without having to deal with a blubbering old drunk.

When the sun had been down a half hour, and the paddies were violet and black and pink, the old man broke his bottle and announced, "I am going to go find her."

362

Cody was sprawled on the steps, scratching mosquito bites. "How do you plan to do that?" he said.

"In my truck, of course." He reached for the lantern, descended the steps more steadily than Cody expected, and walked into the gloomy darkness around the house.

Cody hurried to catch up with the light. In all his wanderings he had avoided the rear of the house. The yard there was shaded like the front, but completely overgrown, a lair for mosquitoes and snakes. He had seen a barn far back, but from the look of it, had assumed that it housed only junk. He walked close to the lantern, watching the ground.

Blackweed bent and tossed aside a limb, then raised a long board from the double doors. When they swung them open Cody stared at the front of a dusty, cobwebbed truck. It was a '37 Chevrolet with sweeping fenders, heavy wire wheels, protruding headlights, and no doors. "Wow!" he said softly as he stepped inside. "What happened to the doors?"

"One day it was hot, and I was driving backward with them open."

Cody gave him a look and thought, Probably drunk, you dumb shit, but all he said was, "My grandpa had a '36. Does it run?"

"How else would I drive it to town?" He handed Cody the lantern, then removed a rag from the seat and slapped at the dust. He wiped the left windshield, then climbed inside. "Do you want to go?"

"I'd better stay here."

"Very well." He engaged the starter. It made a few sluggish cranks, suddenly picked up speed, and the engine came to life. The tappets rattled, then quietened as smoke and swirling dust filled the light. Blackweed switched on the headlights. He glanced at Cody again for the satisfaction, then put the truck into gear and pulled away.

Even in the lantern's yellow glow Cody could see the tires were cracked with age. He stood a moment watching the single taillight move through the trees, then he looked around. The ancient dry dirt floor was covered with thousands of tracks—rats and birds and snakes. He heard the rattle of chain at the gate, then the sound of the truck moving off. It was only crickets and frogs after that, and the beating of wings on the lantern. He went to sit on the porch, alone and suddenly lonely. Before long he went up to lie on the bed where Moni' occasionally slept.

He was not sure what awoke him, but when he reached for the carbine it was not there. He sat up and listened, eyes wide in the darkness. Someone was downstairs at the door. He slid off the bed and tested the wooden floor, and when he took his first step his rifle went crashing across the boards. Quickly he scrambled on hands and knees to find it, no longer sure where he had left the lantern. He jumped to the door, then to the landing, his heart pounding wildly. A flashlight sprayed the stairs.

"What are you doing?" Blackweed said. "Where is the lantern?"

"Just a minute," Cody replied, remembering his matches. He struck one with a thumbnail, then crossed the room and lit the lantern. "Did you find her?" he said, his heart still thumping as he came down the stairs.

"No, I could not, but I spoke to my sister-in-law. It was her restaurant we saw last night."

"The Café Ho Tay?"

"Yes." He paused, overcome with despair. "We've got to move quickly. I was right. A group is going to Dien Bien Phu, and Moni' plans to be with them. They were to have gone last night, but for the weather. I went to Lanessan, but they said she was somewhere in the city, not yet gone to the airfield. We've got to try to stop her!"

As they rushed down the steps, Cody suddenly stopped. "Wait!" he said. "Help me pull the chopper out!"

"That will be useless to us!"

"Not if we miss her, and she takes off for Gia Lam. I can get back a lot faster in this. I'll land at the Ho Tay. Meet me there, then we'll go to the hospital."

Blackweed hurried to help with the bird. It was still on the dollies, the boards they had used as runners still in place. Carefully they moved it into the open. Cody untied the blades, and in less than a minute he had the bird running. He gave a thumbs-up, and Blackweed went to his truck. Cody brought the bird up to RPM, checked overhead for traffic, then brought the helicopter slowly up through the trees. When he was clear, he dipped the nose and headed directly for the Café Ho Tay.

He arrived in slightly more than a minute, and landed on the lawn within the curved sweep of the drive. While the blades coasted to a halt, he surveyed the damage. The Café Ho Tay was nothing but low burned walls and a couple of corners with charred frames for windows. The nearest trees stood bare, a few stubborn leaves still clinging, the rest fallen to earth as if in a sudden winter.

He tied the rotor blades, then jogged around the corner, where he found Su Letei on the sidewalk in front of her house, adding luggage to a stack at the curb and watching in his direction. She smiled with great sadness. "Where are you going?" he said.

"To Vung Tau. There are extra flights south tonight because of the volunteers."

"What about Chang Wu?"

"I expect he will bother me no more. His perfect picture has been crumpled."

"Have you seen Moni'?"

"You are too late for her," she said. "She is already gone."

"Where?"

"To Gia Lam for the trip to Dien Bien Phu. She hid from her father at Lanessan, but stopped by here a few minutes ago. She said—" Su Letei paused, and it seemed that she would cry, but she only lowered her eyes, filled her chest with new air, and continued, "She said to tell you that she wished things had been different, and that you could have gone together to Bai Chay."

"I can still catch her!"

"Perhaps, but I am not sure it will make a difference."

A set of slow headlights rounded the corner. Cody stepped into the street, expecting to see Moni's father, but the vehicle was a jeep. It moved awkwardly through the turn, failed to make it, and stopped with a front tire against the curb while the driver groped for reverse. Finally, with grinding gears, the vehicle straightened and came toward them, flashing its yellow message beneath a street lamp: *Help me, Maria. Please help me.* It stopped beside Cody, Jack Sperek at the wheel, dressed all in black.

"What luck," Sperek said with a grin, panting from the effort of driving. "Get in, kid."

"What for?"

"Got a little job."

"I can't right now. I gotta go somewhere."

"I wasn't asking, kid. Get in the jeep."

Su Letei walked up. "What is the matter?" she said.

"You're leaving town, lady. None of your concern." Sperek turned to Cody. "Your major's in deep trouble. Let's go."

"I can't, I told you! What kind of trouble?"

"Somebody's gonna kill him. I need help."

"No," said Su Letei. Then she seemed to understand. She backed away in horror. "No!" she yelled. "Don't believe him, Cody! It's a trap!"

Cody looked from her to Sperek. "Who's trying to kill him?"

"I'll explain on the way. Now get in. You drive. There's not much time." He put the jeep in neutral and struggled across.

"Don't do it, Cody! He is an assassin! Please, *please* don't!"

"Stow it, bitch. He's dead if you don't, kid. Same as if you did it yourself." He reached between the seats for his rifle. "Get in, goddamn it! Now!"

"No, no, no!" Letei screamed. She grabbed at Cody's arm.

A taxi had pulled up a few feet away. The driver got out, the same old man with the mustard scar. He stood dumbly watching the spectacle.

Cody looked around, trying to decide what to do. There was no way to know if Sperek was lying; some called the man an assassin, but the major still called him a friend. He checked the sky toward Gia Lam. Nothing was airborne yet, maybe weather again out west. He looked at the terrible man in the jeep. If Sperek was lying, surely he would be no match, but if he was telling the truth, McCall might be dead. He checked the empty sky. Maybe he could do both things. He didn't know what he would do if he lost Moni', but he couldn't just walk away and let Marsh McCall die. The decision made, he climbed behind the wheel and slipped the jeep in gear. To his surprise, the war-burned Su Letei was suddenly silent, her mute acceptance more jarring than hysterics. She looked blankly at the luggage, then flicked a finger at the man with the mustard scar.

Chapter Twenty-One

HE APPROACHED THE ABANDONED shop on foot. Though Solo Jacobé had said that he or his friend Antoine would keep watch on the place all day, McCall was filled with deep misgiving, prompted as much by an odd mental dullness as by the prospect of danger. Everything was supposed to be set: Jacobé had successfully met with Legère, and had even arranged for a driver to meet the French major near Colonel de Matrin's, to deliver him at the appointed time—slightly late, across and down the street—reducing the possibility of ambush. All that remained to be worked out was the details of McCall's own meeting.

He had tried to do precisely that all day, but some essential part of his brain refused to participate, as if by denial the problem might cease to exist. He had never been this way, but he felt removed and apathetic, wishing at times that he might simply go to bed and forget the whole thing. But as darkness swallowed the city, and the hours to prepare were gone, he was forced from the house. He roughly slapped himself before backing from the garage, driving unready toward something unknown, purely on habit and instinct. He thought of Jack Sperek, and was suddenly sure what part he played in the total scheme. It made him realize that despite the daylong torpor his mind had been steadily at work, some part of his brain apparently convinced that his conscious participation could only interfere.

Everything depended on who showed up. The message that Pearbone had passed to Ezra Smith's office had been designed as a sieve. Certainly its content, like every aspect of McCall's assignment, would be learned by somebody else. Someone would land in the net, and if this affair was the cleansing that it appeared, it would be someone important: The time for flankers was past. McCall approached the shop with anticipation and dread, like the moments before combat—fear of what had to be faced combined with an eagerness for it to come and be done.

The energetic moon that rose with dusk was fading above the city, settling down to a night's routine, painting the alley with unwelcome light and panels of pure darkness. He moved quietly, hanging close to the bamboo edge as he cursed his own ineptitude. In ordinary times he would have arrived hours early, by daylight, and would not have blindly relied on another's assurance that no trap had been set. Maybe this was the way a man died, a short but critical lapse of sustaining force. He heard the dead crunch of leaves and the efforts of small creatures. A dog growled and hurried away.

The back door stood open, just as he had left it. But everything was wrong. McCall's worry grew suddenly stronger when he realized that he had no idea where Solo Jacobé was waiting. This was all such utter insanity. He checked his carbine and pistol by touch, then rushed across the alley. A big gulp of air, then he was through the door and left, crouching in cavernous darkness. Nothing moved. With the rifle ready, he drew a penlight. Still in darkness, he envisioned the layout of the shop and back room, the rows of racks and the position of the stairs. He felt like an idiot all over again. Nothing to do but check everything, do it quickly, and get it finished. Flicking the light in photographic flashes, he jumped between aisles with each moment of darkness, then doubled back, bolted the outside door, and checked the other rows. From across the room came the scurrying sound of something small.

He paused beneath the stairs, steeled himself, then flicked the flashlight again and rushed up to the room which had once held a killer dog. When he found it empty as well, he began to believe that Solo Jacobé had done his work. Without waiting to consider, he went quickly downstairs, then through to the front in a crouch, no longer using the light.

Sweat was streaming from his face as he moved to a side wall where he could watch the courtyard. The sky was screened by an overhanging roof, but all was still darkness, the moon not yet clearing the rooftops. He knelt to catch his breath, continuing to feel better about Solo Jacobé, but wondering where he was hiding. He leaned and scanned the second level, laundry still all around. Probably up there somewhere, he decided. The people would be no problem; they would go inside, seal themselves off, and wait for the white men to settle their business.

Slowly the courtyard began to brighten, spurring a decision to move. He unbuckled his web belt, then slipped the .45 from its holster and tucked it in at the small of his back. He went silently to the door, flinched to the crunch of glass, then moved left to put the moon to his advantage. When he came to some slatted crates of garbage smelling of long-dead fish and feces and rotten vegetables, he crouched to wait. He heard high Asian voices overhead, and glanced up toward shapes of narrow doorways, ceilings flickering beyond to sooty lamps. The open doors were reassuring and troubling; no trap had been set, but where was Solo Jacobé? The sky continued to brighten, then slowly a platinum moon cleared the rooftops, claiming a growing strip of the courtyard.

Then he smelled it, the odor of blood and bowels beyond the stench of fish. He backed slowly away from the slatted crates, still squatting, feeling slime and stickiness beneath his boots. When the coolness of the wall touched his back he took out the penlight again. He might give his position away, but he had to know. He flicked on the light.

The face was young, but not that of Solo Jacobé. It was pressed against the wire and slats, staring out with scaly eyes. The body was folded, dumped upside down with garbage and filth poured over. Covering the ground all around was a pool of drying blood, red only in places where McCall's boots had broken the film. He snapped off the light, leaned against the wall, and waited, wondering about Solo Jacobé.

An hour passed in which the courtyard was flooded with moonlight and his presence was somehow detected. There began a curious silence; the children upstairs were called inside, and though the night was warm, the doors began to close. A breeze swirled along the tunnel and around the enclosure, rattling leaves and bits of paper. Transparent clouds hurried across the sky. He heard two vehicles pass on the street a minute apart, then came the deep rumble of aircraft firing up at Gia Lam. When the sound diminished on the wind, he heard footsteps moving firmly and openly in from the street.

When the man stepped into the moonlight and halted, McCall waited a minute for anyone who might follow, and for the overwhelming sickness to subside. He had already known who would come—what Solo Jacobé had been unwilling to discuss—but now that the proof was before him McCall found that he was not prepared. With his carbine loose at his side he stood and stepped forward to meet the man whom Ezra Smith had called the Prince of Tonkin.

"Hello, Marsh. Where's the other party?"

"It's just you and me, Ezra."

"I see."

"I thought maybe I could talk you into something different, help me bring down Harman." He saw the white head shake, and knew that it was just as well.

"You're a few years too late for that," Smith said. A hand at his side came level, holding a .45. "Go ahead and put it down, Marsh. Kick it away." He waited for McCall to comply. "How long have you known?"

"Not long enough."

"You're slipping, Marsh. Just like you thought I was. But I suppose I did take advantage. I have just come from a conversation with my old friend Maurice de Matrin." Smith looked around the courtyard. "He had one of his men stop by to be sure we didn't have any unnecessary interruptions," he said. "Colonel de Matrin tells me that Major Legère has decided to volunteer for Dien Bien Phu. An excellent choice. I also know he was to meet you tonight. That, too, will work to our advantage. You've been a lot of help, Marsh. I suppose you heard the aircraft starting up a few minutes ago. They say the weather is clearing over Dien Bien Phu."

The sickness McCall had felt was replaced with cold fury. What he had interpreted in Ezra Smith as encroaching age was nothing more than simple treachery and deceit, the kind that only someone disguised as a friend could have achieved. Less than ten feet lay between him and the colonel. While he calculated his chances, he wondered dimly about Solo Jacobé. There was no longer any question that the lieutenant was not here. "How long did you have this planned, Ezra?"

"Forever, it seems. Since before Major Legère wandered into Lam Du. I'm sorry I don't have time to explain everything. I'm really quite proud of what went into this. Suffice to say that we had a man in place, but Major Legère discovered him. So we gave *him* the job. That was a stroke of luck, because it allowed us to continue to operate through Chang Wu, yet become invisible. All we had to do then was to make Legère aware of the profit potential, create some problems and let his gambling debts grow, then wait for him to turn. His part had to be discovered, of course. Then I remembered my capable old friend Marsh McCall. Harman agreed. He said that what we needed was the same naive fool who fought World War II."

"Did it have to involve the other men?"

"A matter of convenience. I just needed somebody I could count on, and I could always count on you. Your men were spare parts. Just like that French lieutenant who started all this, and his friend. I couldn't have them talking about it later."

"Or Jack Sperek?"

"You figured that out? That was also unavoidable. Old hands like you two are just too good." The colonel paused. "By the way, I have not forgotten about that last young pilot, the one named West. In fact, in a truly special bit of irony, Jack Sperek is taking care of him for me right now." The colonel's teeth shone as brightly in the moonlight as his hair. "Did you happen to write that report for General Sanfield?" he asked. "No matter. I spoke to the general just yesterday. He said that Washington has canceled the project. Suddenly nobody wants to learn anything about Vietnam, to be faced with proof that they're wrong. All the decisions for years to come have already been made."

He shook his head and smiled. "Games of the mind," he said. "I'd really like to talk longer, but I have to be sure Major Legère does not miss his plane. I'm sorry it had to be you, Marsh, I really am. But it had to be somebody. We're both old soldiers, and like I said, old soldiers always die."

★

By the time Jack Sperek told him to stop, Cody had begun to believe he had made a terrible mistake. They were in a section of town that looked vaguely familiar, sinister by night. Cody tried hard to keep track of the turns, asking questions that went unanswered, and thinking about how quickly Su Letei had written him off as dead. There had been nothing she could do, but the woman had been around death too long. He began to watch Sperek. All the feeble man could do was grip the dash with both hands and mumble directions through the streets. When they finally stopped, Sperek was heaving for air. Cody heard the sounds of aircraft across the river at Gia Lam.

"Can you shoot?" Sperek finally said.

Cody's fear became anger. Though he kept trying to believe that somewhere in Jack Sperek was a decent man, something kept telling him different. "Better than you ever could," he said.

Sperek managed a deadly smile. "That's good, you smart fuck. Carry the rifle." He began the struggle to get out of the jeep, leaving Cody to stare. "Shag ass," Sperek mumbled, and shuffled away in the dark, his belt and pistol slapping loosely against his side. Cody watched until he was almost gone, then lifted the rifle, slid the bolt back and felt for a live round, then ran down the empty street after Sperek.

"You're gonna kill a man," Sperek said.

"Who?"

"The one who's gonna kill Marsh if you don't. So get all your deciding done now. Don't talk anymore after this."

They came to a space between two buildings, barely wide enough for a man to squeeze through. Sperek turned immediately into the pure darkness. "Hold on to my shirt," he whispered. Cody did as he was told, sliding along sideways, holding the rifle clear of the walls. A stench of raw feces overwhelmed him, and he soon felt ankle-deep muck at his boots. High overhead, beyond ledges and pipes, he could see a thin crack of sky. Sperek kept moving, slowly but without hesitation. When it seemed they were in the very heart of the buildings, he turned left into a larger passage where they saw the faintest silhouette of open stairs. Sperek stopped, moved behind Cody, and tapped his side. "Carry me up," he whispered.

To his surprise, Cody bent and let Sperek cling to his back. He held the rifle tightly in one hand, and used the other to hook beneath a skinny thigh. The weight was almost nothing. He found a rail, and moved quietly and slowly upward. "Keep going," Sperek said at the landing, and Cody climbed the next flight. It was much brighter now, and at the next level he could see a patch of moonlight on a wall across a space. Sperek tapped to be let down. "*Very* quiet now," he said, his lips touching Cody's ear. They inched slowly toward the light, and in a moment could hear voices of men. Sperek pulled him down to hands and knees. "Not a sound," he said as they eased ahead.

Cody's heart was pounding with anticipation and fear. He was going to kill a man, he told himself, but one who had killed Duke and Mano, and who was still trying to kill him and McCall. He did not understand, but there was no question what he had to do. He remembered the major's words: "Think it through, then do what you've got to do." He must have known it might come to something like this. Cody tightened himself with resolve when they came to the edge of the walk and could look down into the courtyard.

There were two of them there, and though it was impossible to make out the faces beneath the caps, one thing was instantly recognizable in the moonlight: The man whose back was partially toward them, and who held a pistol on the other, had a head of the purest, glowing white hair—exactly like Cody's grandpa.

He felt a finger against the bone behind his ear. "Right there," said Sperek. "A half inch low."

"What if he squeezes the trigger?"

"He won't."

Cody brought the rifle up, and aligned the sights on the hair behind the ear. When he saw his grandpa's head he couldn't move.

"Do it now," Sperek whispered.

"He's got white hair."

"Shoot the motherfucker!" Sperek's voice was a deadly hiss. "Now, goddamn you, *now!*"

Cody got a glimpse of the rotting melons he had relentlessly murdered in the fields of his youth, the red way they exploded, and how he had imagined them as the heads of Japanese, the ones who had killed Uncle Ned.

"I'm sorry it had to be you, Marsh, I really am," he heard the man say. "But it had to be somebody. We're both old soldiers, and like I said, old soldiers always die."

The night disappeared in a roar of yellow-blue fire. He dropped the rifle and rolled away, stunned and unbelieving. "Okay, kid," he heard Sperek say. "Okay. You did real good. Now take my jeep and go catch that girl."

McCall had his pistol drawn and cocked before Ezra hit the ground. He swung in a crouch and was headed for cover when he heard the tumble of boots down the stairs. All he saw was a glimpse of a running man, then a departing silhouette in the tunnel. There were a few muffled sounds in the tenements above, but no one came out. Slowly McCall relaxed and stood, his weapon loose at his side, and turned to contemplate the body. Ezra had fallen limply, shoved by the bullet, and lay sprawled on the moonlit stone. The sick-sweet scent of blood and ruined flesh was in the air. McCall stared down at a clump of white hair surrounded by a field of spreading black.

He had returned his weapon to his belt when he heard a metal banging from above, and he crouched and reached. The sound continued. A flashlight clicked on. McCall glanced again at the body, then moved quickly toward the stairs.

He found Jack Sperek slumped against a wall, legs outstretched, a .45 on the floor beneath one hand. A flashlight stood on end at his side, and the sharp-edged light made a cadaverous mask of Sperek's skull. McCall stared in dumb surprise, prompting a weak smile from Jack Sperek.

"Last thing you thought you'd see?"

"Where's Solo Jacobé?"

"Was he invited?"

"Then who did the shooting?"

"Your boy West. Not a bad kid. He's gone to tend other business."

"You've been poisoned, Jack."

"I know. It was Harman. Had the bread dusted, even added a little heroin. Addicted to what was killing me."

"Why, Jack?"

"Like I said, I knew what they were up to. And they knew I had nothing to lose. But they miscalculated a bit. Had me lined up to kill you before I died."

When McCall started forward, Sperek lifted the .45 in both hands and held it on him.

"We can still take him out, Jack."

"He's untouchable."

"No, he's not. I know the way."

"Then that's enough for me. I kept you alive. That'll be my contribution. I've got a few things to account for myself." He paused, then added, "But just for the record, since nobody knows, one thing I didn't do is kill George Tunnell. Maybe I would have eventually, I don't know, but he died the same way as your sergeant, messing with the Chinaman's bitch. She started the story about the Viet Minh sniper. She was using Tunnell, just like she's been using you, ol' buddy. You're her ticket to Vung Tau."

"Come on, Jack."

"You're dumber than I thought, pal. Who do you think blew up the Café Ho Tay?"

Sperek was breathing hard from so much talk. His eyelids drooped, then sprang wide as McCall started to move. He tightened his grip on the gun. "You're the best there ever was, Marsh," he said. "Time to bring in the bodies. Adieu, old friend."

"No, Jack..."

With a pivot of wrist and forearms, Sperek turned the pistol to his mouth. McCall felt the blast as if it had hit him in the stomach. He turned and gripped the rail.

"Major McCall." Legère's voice was trembling. "Major McCall, I've been looking all over. I was given the wrong address. We have to go now."

McCall looked up and nodded. Legère was carrying his rifle, parachute, and full combat gear. He stooped for Sperek's weapons, leaving the flashlight burning. He took a final look, whispered, "Adieu, old friend," then went numbly down the stairs.

As they sped away in the jeep, another vehicle overtook them, Solo Jacobé madly sounding his horn. McCall ignored him, driving like a lunatic while Legère strapped into his gear. At last the lieutenant gave up the chase.

Solo Jacobé stopped in the street, relieved that not all had been lost. But that knowledge did nothing to mend his deep sickness at what had to be true. He turned the jeep and drove toward the Chinese shop.

Less than half an hour ago he had awakened in his bunk, overwhelmed by tragic sensation. It engulfed him at once. Outside it was fully dark, and through the window he could see that the moon was up. He had overslept his nap. But worse, Antoine had not awakened him. Without turning on a light, he quickly and silently dressed, remembering the early misjudgment, wondering again about the honesty of his own motives. He heard the fateful phrase as he had a dozen times or more, always discounting the import, steadfastly denying that he had put Antoine in danger for no other purpose than self-preservation and the attainment of goals. "I have confided in a friend who I would trust with my life," he had said in Saigon. The words were not really true, but they had allowed him to walk away from the jaws of the beast, assuring his safe return to Hanoi. But the phrase was not forgotten, and now the words had returned in manifestations of death. Jacobé checked his weapons, then slipped out the back to his jeep.

He had known all along that he would be too late. He only chased McCall to let him know that he was there, and to say that he was glad he had not been harmed. Then he stopped and went back to do what now was his to do. He stopped at the tunnel, then proceeded on foot with his rifle.

The courtyard was empty except for the body of Ezra Smith. He walked up to it and stood over it before looking around. On the next level, behind some hanging clothing, he heard whispers and a closing door. Then he saw the light above. Full of dread and pain and sickness, he found the stairs and went on up. He was relieved and vaguely disappointed when it was only Jack Sperek, the moment still to be faced. He took the flashlight and hurried downstairs to have it over with.

He missed him at first, rushing instead into the empty Chinese shop, checking the back room, upstairs, even outside in the alley. Then he went back through as if he had just arrived, switched off the light, and moved left from the door beneath the black shadow. When he came to the crates where McCall must have waited, he could smell the odors of death. He flicked on the light and saw the face of his friend staring back through the slats.

I will not fail, he heard himself say. But it might involve a sacrifice. *Not even at the cost of my life.* But the life of your best friend?

He ran from the courtyard, down through the tunnel, and out to the middle of the street, then stared up at the moon and the faded night sky, gasping for breath, moaning in grief and guilt and self-condemnation.

I will not give up, the voice said. *Whatever momentary torture or agony of years, whatever death I might have to endure, I will send those responsible to a just and burning hell.*

A sudden silence and calmness came over him, and he lowered his eyes from the heavens. Above the square shapes of the city, contesting the power of the moon, stood a high dome of light that blazed all around the thatch roof of the Blue Deep. He looked toward his jeep, again toward the lights, then hurried to the vehicle. The hand flares which Antoine had left were still there.

They raced through the city without stop signs, slowing only slightly at the guarded approach to the bridge. Far to their left up the river, a glow of lights bleached the northern sky down low.

"They are fighting at the Blue Deep," Legère said. "Chang Wu's famous gray dog will be in the pit. Half of Hanoi is awaiting the outcome."

McCall said nothing. He was thinking about Cody West, wondering where he had gone.

"Colonel de Matrin said I will receive the Croix de Guerre for my efforts at Dien Bien Phu—posthumous, of course—and that three days from now he will be in the sun at Cannes, beginning his retirement—all just as you said. I owe you much, Major McCall. I set out to slay a dragon, and merely chopped off a toe. I wish you better luck."

McCall did not respond. What Legère owed could never be repaid, but it was not easy to accept thanks from a man for being allowed to kill himself.

When they bounced across the railroad tracks, then swerved to Depot Road, scattering gravel, they could see the last three C-47s lined up on the tarmac. They slid to a halt, and Legère jumped out without a word, running clumsily to join the tail of a line. He turned at the last moment and threw a salute, then disappeared through the hatch.

A flash of light caught McCall's attention, and as he looked toward the Blue Deep he saw the white starburst of a flare arcing down from the sky. Then came another, some fool celebrating something with military fireworks.

He watched from the jeep until the airplane bearing the traitor had cleared the field. He rested his arms and head on the steering wheel, then straightened and lit a cigarette. In the morning he and Solo Jacobé would meet with Eber Walloon. No one would ever know how the story came to be unearthed, but in France's anger at the United States—still trying to find someone to blame for her own mistakes—and with *Le Monde*'s increasing hostility toward the layers of government lies about all aspects of the war, the news would be unstoppable. Soon after, Eber Walloon would get his story in *Time.* No wall of power could save Harman now. The president and secretary of state would maintain distance, professing astonishment. Harman would fall while half of official Washington pissed its pants with joy.

He flipped his cigarette across the tarmac and put the jeep in gear. It was time to locate his last surviving man—in the words of Jack Sperek, time to bring in the bodies. He could see a light in Operations, and he drove in that direction. The moon was bright now overhead, dusting all the camp with a layer of light that looked like snow, making even the wrecked helicopters look good, his birds with broken wings.

His gut was suddenly all bullets at what he saw, and he slammed the brakes and beat the wheel and cursed out loud. Before him were two parked choppers—the one they had taken apart so that others might fly, and the one that had flown to the last—the one belonging to Cody West. Its blades had not been tied, and they rocked and bumped in the breeze moving down off the field.

As he blankly stared, the sky beyond the choppers began to change, the white smear above the river reddening as with the dawn of a misplaced sun. Soon a flaming great shaft like Satan's red tongue rose wickedly into the sky.

★

The gray dog stepped into the pit. He quickly checked the opposite door before lifting his head to the crowd. He could not know the diplomats from the civilians, the politicians from the generals, but he understood that they were there to watch and to urge the two of them on. He was even aware that it did not matter who won, so long as there was a good fight. He was not new to this.

He surveyed the crowd and observed their frenzy, then turned as the door came open and his opponent stepped into the ring. The screech of the crowd rose wildly. He was a small but hard creature, lean and yellow and not young, not new to this either. While the handlers fidgeted with the chains, the two eyed each other across the space. It would be a good fight, and it would not matter who won, perhaps not even to the one who lost. The gray dog knew that now, and it seemed that his opponent knew. It did not matter who died.

The handlers began to move closer, but immediately stopped. Something was different. The raging sound had changed. When his handler jerked at the chain and shouted, the gray dog looked up and saw an amazing sight. The crowd had gone completely berserk, beyond anything he had witnessed. Far above, through billowing smoke, was a ceiling of solid flame, squirming and racing across the dome. Out of the flames came rats and snakes, some ablaze as they dropped writhing down onto the crowd. Then the burning ceiling began to collapse, falling like volcanic chunks down over the ones who had come only to watch. The handlers dropped the chains and ran, but the dogs just stared. Then the men with ringside seats, smashed by the panicked mass all around, came over the wall and into the pit where it did not matter who died.

He could feel the buzz beneath his boots and butt, vibrations coursing through his bones until his body was attuned and he felt a thing he did not expect. He glanced along the dim hold, wondering if Pepe the Paratroop was among this group. The air smelled of men and smoke and gun oil and preservative. Completely apart from the reason he was going, there was a definite reassuring grandness in being involved in the tragedy waiting so long for those with sufficient courage, and for those with too little. Along the somber line of faces, one glowed red and disappeared, then another as men sucked cigarettes and listened to powerful engines, miles of darkness rushing past. He tugged at the unfamiliar straps and thought about Moni' somewhere up ahead doing the same. Maybe she was thinking about him; he was suddenly sure of it.

A man beside him lit a smoke, and Cody closed his eyes to the sudden flare. When he opened them again, the French major who ran Lam Du was kneeling before him.

"What are you doing here?" Legère said. He looked at Cody's rigging, and began to make adjustments. "Stand up."

Cody reluctantly did as he was told, but he would not look directly at Legère, thinking that it was none of the bastard's business. "No reason," he said.

"The same as the rest of us then."

"I am trying to find a girl."

Legère's surprise was brief. "One of the nurses?"

"Yes. I was too late to stop her."

"You were the one with Jack Sperek?" When Cody did not reply, Legère said, "Perhaps you will make history as the only American at the fall of Dien Bien Phu. Come, sit next to me. I will show you what you need to know." When Legère moved back to his jump seat, a man beside him nodded, then switched places with Cody. While the engines droned endlessly on, Legère alternately gave him instructions, lapsed into long periods of silence, then suddenly blurted short phrases in French that men around him ignored.

Beyond the basics of what he should do when the red light came on, Cody paid no attention. It seemed that every man aboard shared his seat with private gods and demons. He wondered about the man he had killed, and was surprised to realize that he felt nothing at all. The colonel had killed Dukemire and Mano, and may have killed them all. He was sorry it had fallen to him to do, but he was glad he had saved the major's life. He felt his carbine and thought about what was ahead.

He believed he understood old man Larkin now, willing to do anything to get control of his life, to shape it to his own design. If that meant living on the dark side of the earth, or dying in somebody's war, then that was what it must be. But even then it was impossible to escape the sense of a blind projectile on a predetermined course, spiraling through darkness like a bullet. It seemed that he had never made a decision in his life; things just happened.

380

"Do you know where the hospital is?" he yelled to Legère.

"It is in many places now. Everything is underground. Much of the original site collapsed beneath the bombardment, burying the patients. Your nurse could be anywhere, and it is very difficult to move around."

Cody had already stopped listening. He was thinking of how it would be, the black earth all craters, blinding flashes sandwiched in total darkness, bodies and flying walls of dirt, the ground jerking in utter madness. Among the craters could be enemy, and somewhere among the blood and bombs and slashing steel would be Moni'.

Finally the order was passed to extinguish all smokes. Then a buzzer rudely sounded, and the men jerked and got to their feet, facing forward. The one-minute light began its red warning. Cody followed the lead of the man ahead, clipping his static line to the cable. Then a rumble began like distant thunder, quickly becoming rapid, distinct explosions. Flashes of flak filled the windows, and the aircraft buffeted about as if crossing a bumpy field. Then the light turned green, and the lines moved forward. He checked that his steel pot and carbine were secure, shuffling in short, tight steps. He thought about Moni' and how brave she was, how she might this moment be floating down to the same unknown hell, even less prepared than he.

Then the jumpmaster met his eyes and touched his shoulder, and he turned and took the long step. A sudden jerk popped his head downward, then he was swinging, careening from side to side before settling beneath the parachute. All he could do at first was stare. The entire world—the ground and sky and exploding hills around— was a popping, grinding roar, an unceasing stutter of beautiful flashes. On all sides were other descending chutes. He looked beyond his boots, but saw only jerking glimpses of earth. Somebody screamed below. He thought about steeples and parachutes, and put his heels together. Bullets sang past, and he heard the soft thumps that they made overhead. He wondered how he would ever find Moni'.

NOTE

French forces at Dien Bien Phu surrendered to Viet Minh troops on the evening of May 7, 1954. Numbers pertaining to casualties and prisoners are difficult to pin down, simply because both sides made deliberate distortions for political purposes. Perhaps ten thousand French Union prisoners were marched to distant camps, where a large percentage subsequently died.

Regardless of the numbers, both forces were sent to the valley at Dien Bien Phu to bring a quick end to the war, and to die by the thousands. This was achieved.

It took fifty-six days for the warriors to fight the battle. Seventy-three more days were required for diplomats to place a line on the map between North and South Vietnam, to conclude that the war was indeed over, and to begin to release the survivors.

NORTHERN VIETNAM